FROM THE
POTATO FAMINE
TO THE SAVAGE FRONTIER
OF AMERICA . . .

RORY—He would make a place for himself and win honor in America, but he would forever hear the call to return to Ireland, to finish the bold battle he had begun . . .

RACHEL—She gave herself to Rory mind, body and soul, but could she give him the one thing he wanted most—a son to inherit his name, his place, his dream . . .

DEIRDRE—Rory's sister. In the midst of famine and misfortune, she found happiness in the arms of a young English officer. They pledged eternal love and parted. When next they met, she would be another man's wife in a strange land . . .

SEAN—Rory would search America to find his youngest brother and then be plagued by doubts. The young stranger who so resembled the Manions remembered almost nothing of his past . . .

THEY FOUGHT FOR FREEDOM
AND DIGNITY. . . . THEY LIVED
THEIR SOARING PASSIONS
AND BOLD, DEFIANT DREAMS!

THE MANIONS OF AMERICA

AGNES NIXON'S

THE MANIONS OF AMERICA

ROSEMARY ANNE SISSON

A DELL BOOK

Published by
Dell Publishing Co., Inc.
1 Dag Hammarskjold Plaza
New York, New York 10017

Dell ® TM 681510, Dell Publishing Co., Inc.

ISBN: 0-440-15393-X

Printed in the United States of America
First printing—October 1981

*In memory of the unsung souls
whose suffering inspired this work*

During the Dark Ages, proud Ireland kept the lamp of learning aflame for all of Europe. Then the Conquerors came, horde after horde, and for nine hundred years these ravaged but valiant people fought history's longest battle for freedom. . . . But it was finally Fate that dealt this small country a blow far worse than any the Invader could invent. In a single decade it caused a third of the population to die and a million more to flee to America. . . . It was called The Great Famine and it began in 1845.

—AGNES NIXON

PART I:

A SACRED WRATH

CHAPTER 1

The huntsmen made a fine sight as they followed the hounds across the green Galway hillside. It had been raining, and their horses' hooves kicked the black mud up in their faces, but the riders had seen the fox streaking across the marshy ground and cared for nothing else as they went yelping and halooing after him.

Rory O'Manion, coming out of the thatched hut to see what all the row was about, tossed his thick black hair back from his forehead and eyed them with contempt. He was very thin and his cheeks were hollow, but in the pallor of his face his blue eyes burned with a dangerous fire, like sunlight glinting on ice. Inside his shabby, clumsy clothes, his body was like a wild animal's, lithe and alert. He watched the fox run and the Ballyclam Hunt follow, and then he saw another procession traveling up the road. It consisted of parish priest Father O'Dowd, two men and a woman. One of the men was carrying a tiny wooden box, and Rory knew at once that Peter O'Keefe's youngest child had died, and that this was his funeral.

The fox crossed the road in a streak of red and slithered through the hole in the stone wall that bounded the O'Manion land. The hounds were baying after him, and the horsemen followed. Suddenly Rory realized that they were galloping straight toward the little funeral party. He started forward, but all was over in a moment. Mary O'Keefe screamed, and Father O'Dowd turned, shocked, his surplice fluttering in the wind. The little group scattered out of the way of the flying hooves, and Peter O'Keefe stumbled aside, trying in vain to save the homemade wooden coffin as it fell to the road.

"My baby!" cried Mary O'Keefe. "Mother of God, would you be throwing him on the hard ground and the sweet breath scarcely left his body?"

But the horsemen thundered heedlessly across the road and leaped the stone wall into the O'Manion potato patch.

Rory's rage increased as he saw the leading rider, Lord Fitzmorris, a huge man with grizzled hair, and after him Cyrus Clement, slumped heavily in his saddle like a red-faced sack of meal.

"You sacrilegious pigs!" shouted Rory. "Have you no decency in you, that you would ride through a child's funeral?"

He was in such a blind rage that he was ready to fling himself under the horses' hooves, but he found his arm seized and held.

"For God's sake, Rory!" cried Padraic.

"What has God to do with this?" Rory yelled back. He wrenched himself free, flinging his brother violently against the clay wall of the house.

The breath was nearly knocked out of Padraic's body, but he managed to gasp, "Don't make trouble, Rory. Especially now."

"*Now?*" Rory repeated furiously, turning on him. "Do you think I'll have an O'Manion born with *them* on our land?"

"Look!" said Padraic suddenly.

Cyrus Clement's horse, jumping the stone wall on the far side, had slipped in the mud. It fell heavily and rolled on its rider. Struggling to get up, it fell again.

At last the horse managed to scramble to its feet and trotted away, reins loose and stirrups swinging, but Cyrus Clement lay still on the muddy ground.

"There's some justice, anyway!" said Rory.

Padraic, still trying to get his breath back and rubbing a bruised elbow, came to Rory's side, and they watched together as Lord Fitzmorris reined in his horse, turned and rode back. John Houlihan, the Ballyclam agent trotting at the tail of the hunt in his sober black coat and breeches like a dog at his master's heels, dismounted and ran to kneel beside Cyrus Clement. He tried to lift the inert body in its red coat and then looked up alarmed, at Lord Fitzmorris, who sat looking down from his big bay hunter.

"I think he's badly hurt, My Lord."

"Get him to Ballyclam House," said Lord Fitzmorris. "You—Montgomery—ride on to Dr. Fleming's. Houlihan, tear that fence down—make a stretcher."

Rory watched, infuriated, as Houlihan and other men tore down the boundary fence. He glanced at Padraic and saw resentment in his face, too.

"If they want our help, why can't they ask for it," said Padraic, "instead of destroying our property? Do they think we can buy the wood for a new fence any day of the week?"

"Damn them! I'm going to stop them!" said Rory, but Padraic caught his arm again.

"No, Rory. The man's hurt—dying for all we know . . ."

"Then let him die, and welcome," said Rory, "but not on our fence!"

He tried to free himself, but this time Padraic held him fast. "He's our landlord," he said.

"And our rent's paid!" said Rory.

"Yes," replied Padraic, "unless Houlihan puts it up again and turns us all out of house and home. Even if you have no thought for yourself, at least have some for Mother."

Rory hesitated, glancing back at the house, and as though echoing Padraic's words, a high scream of pain came quickly from the broken window. They both set off quickly toward the doorway, but Deirdre met them before they reached it.

"Fetch Mrs. O'Hara," she said.

"I'll go," said Rory and was already running toward the road, but he was stopped by Deirdre's voice speaking again.

"Padraic, you'd best go and try to find Father," she said. "Tell him to come at once."

Rory turned and saw the anguish in his sister's green eyes and heard the terror in her voice.

"It isn't like last time," she said. "There's something wrong. I know it!"

Darkness fell early that evening. The rain returned, driven by the west wind, and beat against the O'Manion cabin until it felt like a ship in a storm, with Moira O'Manion's cries of pain bringing a nightmare feeling of helplessness—a woman overboard, crying for help, and no one to save her.

Shane O'Manion moved restlessly about the room, glancing with desperate anxiety toward the flimsy door beside the fireplace that divided the bedroom from the family living room and kitchen. Hunger and hardship made him look more than his fifty-five years, and yet he somehow managed to maintain that characteristic Irish look of pride and dignity, even in a house so small that he could hardly stand upright and so poor that it was lit only by a turf fire and a tallow rushlight set on the scrubbed wooden table.

Rory stood by the windows, trying to stuff rags into the broken glass they could not afford to replace. Padraic sat by the table with little Maeve on his knee, her curly red head on his shoulder. Turning away, Rory caught Shane glancing at both of them, as though he was aware that his two elder sons were each characteristically employed. They were twins, but not identical. Where Rory's hair was black, Padraic's was brown, and while Rory's blue eyes glinted like steel, Padraic's held in them all the gray-green tenderness of the Galway hills. It was as though Padraic was Rory's shadow, or rather, his lighter other self, that self he could be and yet would never consent to be—gentle, loving and reasonable.

Shane turned quickly as the door opened and his youngest son, Brian, came in, carrying a basket of peat, his hair dark and sleeked from the pouring rain. Only he and Maeve had hair of the authentic dark red of western Ireland, the color of Moira's hair before sorrow and hunger drained its life and richness. As Brian struggled to close the door, Shane moved quickly to take the basket from him.

"Sit down, my boy," he said. "I will put the turf on the fire."

A sharp cry of pain came from the bedroom, and Brian looked up quickly at his father and took an involuntary step toward the room.

"Mammy!" he said, but Shane's hand was on his shoulder.

"Sit down and learn your lessons," he said, "for that is what your mother would wish."

"Yes, Da," said Brian, and he went to fetch his slate and sit in the chimney corner.

Shane could not always feed his children, but he could always command their obedience and respect, and even Rory at his wildest could be silenced by a stern glance from his father or a quiet word in the Irish language, which they always spoke among themselves.

As Shane came to kneel by the hearth and build up the peat fire that burned there day and night, he felt a touch on his shoulder and, looking around, found that Maeve had slipped off Padraic's knee and come to help him. Solemnly she took a piece of turf out of the basket and held it out to him. Shane smiled with tears in his eyes and put his arm around the thin little body in its ragged dress.

"Ah, Maeve, *alanna!*" he said. "Haven't you the loving heart in you that knows how to bring comfort in the darkest hour!"

The cries of pain from the bedroom were sharper now and more continuous, like an animal caught in a trap. Brian put his slate on his knees and his hands over his ears to shut out the awful noise, but there was no escaping it. Shane's face, as he put the last piece of turf on the fire and swung the great iron pot of water back over it, revealed each cry as a knife wound in his own body.

Rory's eyes met Padraic's. "It's never been as long as this before," he said, and took a step toward the bedroom. "I don't trust that drunken old—"

The door opened, and Mrs. O'Hara stood there. "You'd best fetch Father O'Dowd," she said.

They all stared at her for a moment, and then Padraic got up. "I'll go," he said.

He moved swiftly to drag his rough frieze coat down

from its hook and went out into the wind and rain, slamming the door behind him. Mrs. O'Hara was about to withdraw, but Rory stopped her.

"What's wrong?" he demanded.

Annie O'Hara had been the midwife in Ballyclam for as long as he could remember. She had brought many babies into the world, some alive and some dead. She was dirty and slovenly, but she would go anywhere for a glass or two of poteen. Not a member of the gentry would allow her inside his house, but then the gentry could afford a doctor and the O'Manions could not.

"What's wrong?" Rory repeated fiercely, and saw instantly in her face that she herself did not know.

He heard his mother's voice calling faintly from the bedroom.

"Rory? Is that you?"

Rory pushed Mrs. O'Hara aside and went in. His mother clasped in one hand the holy medal on its chain around her neck. Deirdre, kneeling beside the bed, clutched the other. Rory, meeting his mother's eyes, saw how desperate the situation was. Moira O'Manion spoke to him from that far world of pain so hopelessly removed from ordinary life.

"Rory, do something! The baby—it isn't right."

Seized by another spasm of pain, she broke the chain of the holy medal.

"Help me, Rory!" she cried. "Help me!"

"Ah, sure," said Annie O'Hara comfortably, "sorrow has long legs, and there's no turning the will of God."

Rory could smell the whiskey on her breath from three feet away.

"It's all right, Mother," he said. "I'll fetch the doctor."

It was nearly a mile to Dr. Fleming's house, and even as he rang the bell, Rory knew what the answer would be from the neat little maid who opened the door.

"Sure, Rory, isn't the doctor at Ballyclam House, and Mr. Eamon gone with him? Mr. Clement had his horse fall with him out hunting, and the doctor drove there as if the devil was after him and never came back, and his dinner in the oven burned to a cinder!"

It was two miles to Ballyclam House, back in the direction he came from, and as Rory stumbled up the drive, blinded by rain—laurels and rhododendrons lashing his face—he was sobbing for breath. He turned the last bend and saw the lights of the house, and the pony and trap standing outside. It gave him new strength to run up the steps and hammer on the door. As soon as the butler opened it, Rory thrust past him and was inside. He saw Lord Fitzmorris still in his red coat and mud-splattered breeches, drinking port in the drawing room with two other men, and saw the agent, Houlihan, lurking uneasily in the hall. But, more important, he saw Dr. Fleming halfway up the graceful staircase, black bag in his hand.

"Dr. Fleming!" called Rory. "My mother! She needs you!"

Dr. Fleming was a small, tidy Anglo-Irish Protestant living a life delicately balanced between two worlds, happy with neither, faithful to none. He smiled at Rory, but his eyes wandered anxiously toward Lord Fitzmorris in the drawing room.

"I will come as soon as possible, my lad," he said,

"but I cannot leave Mr. Clement just now. I'm afraid he cannot last long."

"Then if he cannot last long, leave him and come and save my mother and her child!" said Rory.

Lord Fitzmorris had come to the doorway of the drawing room, and they were both aware of it, but Rory kept his eyes fixed on Dr. Fleming's.

"I need you," Rory said, "and I need you now!"

There was a sharp crack, like the firing of a gun, as Lord Fitzmorris picked up his long hunting whip and cracked it almost in Rory's face.

"Damn you!" he said. "Get out! Haven't you the decency to allow a gentleman to die in peace in his own house?"

Rory flinched, and was angry with himself for flinching.

"Gentleman?" he said. "Gentleman, who would ride through a child's funeral?"

Lord Fitzmorris glared at him. "Houlihan," he demanded, "are you in the habit of allowing ruffians like this into your master's house?"

"No, My Lord," said Houlihan, and he advanced hastily upon Rory. "O'Manion, if you're not out of this house in ten seconds, you can tell your father to get off his land."

It was a fearful threat, and Rory knew that there were ways in which Houlihan could carry it out and that they could all be homeless. But in that instant Rory could think of nothing but his mother's need.

"I'll have the doctor first!" he said.

Lord Fitzmorris cracked the whip again. "Come on, you fellows!" he shouted. "Let's see this beggar off— teach him a lesson he won't forget!"

And suddenly Rory was the fox and knew what it

was to be hunted down. But as they advanced upon him, there was an unexpected intervention. Eamon Fleming stepped out of the dining room, which opened off the hall on the other side, placing himself between Rory and the upraised whips.

"No, My Lord," he said. "I won't allow it."

Lord Fitzmorris glared at him. "What the devil? You're the doctor's son, aren't you?"

"Yes, My Lord. This man came here for my father's help. I think he should have it."

Eamon looked up the stairs toward his father, and even Rory, obsessed as he was, felt embarrassed for him as he saw Dr. Fleming glance toward Lord Fitzmorris and then away.

"I'll come as soon as I can. I can't leave Mr. Clement."

"But you can leave my mother to die!" said Rory.

He moved toward the staircase again, but Houlihan was there, and Lord Fitzmorris, whip in hand. Eamon put his arm around Rory's shoulders and urged him toward the door.

"For God's sake," he said, "get out of here while you can!"

The old butler, Tobin, had the door open, and Eamon pushed Rory outside into the wind and the rain.

As the front door slammed behind them, Rory angrily freed himself from Eamon's grasp.

"She's ill! She may be dying! Doesn't your father understand?"

He saw the pain in Eamon's face, but what did he care for that? Eamon Fleming was a Protestant, born in England. What had he to do with the true Irish, like the O'Manions?

"If there's anything I can do," said Eamon. "I'm in my third year in medical school—"

Rory turned on him. "I need a doctor!" he shouted, "not an *apprentice!*"

They stared at each other helplessly.

"All right," said Rory. "Come on."

They began to run together down the drive.

The first cold light of dawn was at the window before the cry of the newborn baby was heard.

"Thanks be to God!" said Shane and crossed himself.

But Eamon appeared in the doorway of the bedroom, and one look at his face was enough.

"I'm sorry, Mr. O'Manion," he said. "I did what I could, but it was too late. I managed to save the child, but your wife—I'm afraid she may not have the strength."

Less than an hour later Rory felt a sense of unreality as he stood in the bedroom with his arms around Brian, watching his mother's life slipping quietly away. Father O'Dowd had given her the last rites, and the children had been roused from their sleep to kiss their mother good-bye. Now she lay with her eyes closed beneath the picture of the Sacred Heart. Her face was like alabaster amid the faded red hair spread out over the pillow, and she looked so calm after the long agony that it seemed unthinkable she should die. Did a ship sink after it had come safe to harbor?

The baby began to cry again, and Moira O'Manion opened her eyes. She saw Shane kneeling beside her, holding her hand, and behind him Deirdre, hushing the baby in her arms. Her eyes moved on as though searching for something in a light that was fading fast. They rested for a moment on Padraic as he stood holding Maeve, and Moira gave a moan.

"Mother!" Rory burst out. "Mother, what is it?"

"Rory?" she said faintly.

"I'm here."

Rory left Brian and went to kneel beside her, taking her other hand in his. It felt cold and lifeless already, but her green eyes were fixed on his face with a burning intensity, as though her very spirit spoke to him.

"The baby—"

"He's a fine boy, Mother. We named him Sean, as you wished."

"Yes, but—"

Her strength was failing fast now, and it was terrible to see her struggling to hold death at bay until she could say what she was determined to.

"You're the strong one, Rory," she said. "Look after him. Look after—my Sean."

"I will," said Rory.

No oath sworn on a hundred sacred relics could have meant more to him than those two words, but he felt his mother's hand stir in his, and she endeavored to move it toward the edge of the pillow. Realizing what she wanted, Rory felt underneath it and found the holy medal. He was going to put it in his mother's hand, but instead she closed his hand upon it. "Save it for Sean," she whispered. Rory looked down at the silver medal on its broken chain. When he looked up again, his mother's eyes were still fixed upon his face, but she was dead.

Shane put his gray head down on the bed, still clasping his wife's hand in his. "Moira!" he cried. "Oh, my Moira!"

Father O'Dowd began to pray, and the others knelt, weeping, but Rory could not pray with them. Prayers spoke of love and forgiveness, and there was nothing in his heart but hatred and bitterness. He rose from his knees and strode out of the room. Eamon Fleming came to meet him, but seeing the expression on Rory's face, he stood aside. Rory stooped beneath the low doorway and went outside.

It was barely light, but through the trees he could see the distant white pillars of Ballyclam House. When he thought that his mother's life might have been saved, his tears began to flow, but they only seemed to increase his anger.

"You'll pay for this," he said. "I swear on my mother's holy medal, someday Ireland will be free."

The elegant Georgian house danced through his tears. "The curse of God upon you and yours!" said Rory.

CHAPTER 2

"Papa, you must come," called Rachel Clement.

She descended the companionway in a swirl of skirts and opened the door of the cabin, where her father sat holding his head in the hopeful but mistaken belief that even if the ship wallowed, he could keep his head still. Harry Clement had no sea legs, and the voyage from England had been rough.

Rachel eyed him reproachfully. She loved the sea. and, like all good sailors, she secretly felt that sufferers from seasickness would do a great deal better if they did not give in to it.

"Papa, dear!" she exclaimed. "You would feel much more benefit from some fresh air than being shut up in this horrid cabin. Besides, you must come now. We can see Ireland!"

Harry knew that when his daughter made up her mind, she usually got what she wanted, and besides, he was in no condition to argue. So ruefully he allowed her to help him into his new caped tweed traveling coat, picked up his hat and followed her unsteadily up to the deck. The white horses riding playfully up and down on the waves made him feel queasy again.

"Well," he said grumpily, "where's this Ireland of yours?"

"There, Papa," said Rachel, hurrying to the rail. "See? That beautiful blue-green coast. And it is not *my* Ireland. It is ours. It is our new home."

As he joined her, she clasped his arm in both her hands, leaning fondly against him. "Oh, we are going to be so happy here! I know it!"

Harry looked down at the fresh young face turned so lovingly and trustingly up at him beneath the charming bonnet, and he smiled. "I'm sure we shall, my dear," he said.

As though to reward him, the wind and waves were suddenly and miraculously calm. The ship had sailed into the great welcoming haven of Galway Bay. The sails flapped, commands were shouted, and the sailors ran about to prepare for the arrival in port.

"Thank God!" said Harry devoutly. "I hope you *do* like Ballyclam, Rachel, for I can assure you that it will be a very long time before you persuade me aboard a ship again."

Rachel laughed and turned her gaze once more across the translucent water toward the shore.

"I love Ireland already," she said, "and I know that I shall never want to leave."

With every moment the rapidly approaching land looked more beautiful, but even if it had not, Rachel thought, she would have loved it. Anything was better than that grimy house in Bayswater, with its worn carpet and threadbare covers and general air of genteel poverty. Rachel's mother had died when she was a child, so for as long as she could remember, she had been the mistress of her father's house. They had never known real hardship, or rather they had never quite gone hungry, but Rachel knew all too well what it was like to puzzle over the account books and find that they had overspent by fourpence. She was too familiar with that moment when she must ask the cook to buy the cheapest cut of meat because she knew that she would not otherwise be able to pay the butcher's bill at the end of the week. And with every month came the renewed anxiety as to whether they would be able to pay the rent.

What had made it all particularly exasperating was the knowledge that if her father had been the elder son, then *he* would have inherited the property in Ireland instead of Uncle Cyrus. Once, when things were really desperate, Harry had written to his brother, asking for a small loan to tide them over. He had received in reply a curt note advising him to live within his means.

"My dear," said Harry now, "I think I will just see to the luggage. We shall be landing shortly, and Mr. Houlihan said that he would send a coach to meet us."

Rachel watched her father fondly as he bustled about counting trunks and hatboxes. No more grubbing in the city for him. No more trying to be an insurance broker —a task for which he was totally unsuited since he believed the best of everyone and, if someone owed him money, was too much of a gentleman ever to ask for payment.

"Now he can *be* a gentleman," thought Rachel happily, "and live in a beautiful house, and just sit back and watch the rents roll in. And I—"

She did not know precisely what she would do because she was not sure what she would find when she arrived. But it was just that sense of the unknown that was so deliciously exciting and made it all such an adventure.

"I shall have my own horse, of course," thought Rachel, "and do lots of riding and hunting."

Fortunately her Uncle James in Philadelphia, who had married her mother's sister, had paid for her schooling at an exclusive academy for young ladies just outside London. Her best friend, Emmeline, lived in a big house in the country, and Rachel, visiting her, had first learned to ride there and quickly discovered that she adored it. Emmeline, who was rather a timid rider, was horrified when Rachel insisted that the groom should teach her to jump, but as she went flying over the hedge, hat askew and clutching the pommel, Rachel loved the feeling of danger and the sense of physical release, of letting her body run free with the horse. Oddly enough, it was the same sensation she discovered she enjoyed when dancing a waltz with a young man whose hand, at first placed decorously around her waist, slipped incautiously during the dance, lifting and whirling her, his fingers on her breast. Danger! And excitement! And then, when the music stopped, it was all decorum again, and, "May I fetch you a glass of lemonade, Miss Clement?" Only the two of them knew that they had shared that mysterious sensation she did not fully understand, yet which she knew instinctively was forbidden.

Her school friends who had mothers to tell them of such things had confided in her, whispering in dark corners that there was something quite horrid that happened after one was married. It happened on one's wedding night, apparently, and was something to do with having children, but one must never mention it to anyone, not even to one's husband. Their faces were awed and horrified as they spoke of it, and yet Rachel could not help wondering if it had not something to do with that daringly improper experience she had shared in the excitement of the dance. If so—but perhaps, she thought, that was the nice part, and the nasty part came afterward.

Her father spoke behind her, and Rachel hastily banished the subject from her mind.

"Shall I have your dressing case brought up with the other luggage, or do you mean to go down to the cabin again?" inquired Harry.

"Oh no, thank you, Papa, please have it brought up on deck. I do not care how windblown I am; I have no intention of going below again. I cannot miss a moment of this."

She leaned on the rail once more. Other passengers were beginning to gather on deck, but she was hardly aware of the bustle and confusion about her.

"I shall get married, of course," thought Rachel. "It will be so romantic to be married in Ireland."

Probably, she thought, she would marry one of her brother's fellow officers. She was glad that David was in an Irish regiment and that, by a great piece of good fortune, they had just been posted to Galway. Dreamily Rachel remembered the regimental balls to which David had escorted her, the candlelit chandeliers, the music, the officers so trim and elegant in their uniforms, the trousers so tight, the jackets brilliantly trimmed with silver.

Rachel gazed at the beautiful land of Ireland, the tall ships in the harbor and the picturesque ruined cottage on the shore.

"I shall marry a soldier," she thought, "and live happily ever after."

Rachel was almost sorry when it was time to go ashore. The anticipation had been so delightful. But as she began to move down the gangway, excitement rose in her again. Everything was new and amusing: the old stone archways, the fishing boats and the crowded quayside. She paused and looked about her, smiling, but in the next instant she heard a fearful scream.

"Pat! Ah, no, Pat! Don't go! Don't go!"

Rachel looked, startled, toward the sound and saw a woman, barefoot and wearing a dress and shawl so ragged that they showed her flesh through them. The woman ran and stumbled toward the man who was about to step aboard the ship moored alongside. He, too, was ragged and painfully thin. He turned and caught her in his arms, and Rachel was so near that she heard their words. It was like being at a play, but it was the kind of play that she had never seen before.

"Now, Eileen!" cried the Irishman, his voice torn with anguish, "haven't I said I'll send the money for you and the little ones to follow?"

The woman clung to him with fingers that were skeleton thin. "If you leave now, I'll never see you again. I know it!"

"Ah, don't, Eileen! Eileen, *acushla,* you're breaking the heart in my body!"

He tore himself free and stumbled up the gangway while the woman fell to her knees on the quayside, sobbing aloud in an abandonment of grief that Rachel found shocking. In England even the poor suffered in silence.

"Well, my dear," came her father's cheerful voice from behind her, "I believe we have all our luggage, though I would not absolutely guarantee that a hatbox or two has not been left behind!"

Rachel laughed. As soon as she heard of their inheritance, she had gone straight out and bought ten new bonnets. Oh, bliss! After all those years of trimming and retrimming the same old hat until she could hardly bear the sight of it! She prepared to continue down the gangway but saw again the Irishwoman crouched, sobbing, on the dock.

"Papa," she said, "that poor woman—she seems to be in such distress."

"My dear," said Harry, "I have always heard that Ireland is full of beggars. Take no notice of her or we shall have them all around us."

"Yes, Papa," said Rachel, relieved.

She, too, had heard of the Irish beggars, and it was so much more comfortable to think that this was one of them instead of allowing herself to get involved in the feelings of Pat and Eileen, who seemed to be parting from each other with such anguish. But before she stepped ashore she glanced at the ship moored alongside and read the name *Sylvania, Philadelphia.* So the man was going to America. But why, if his wife did not want him to?

"Mr. Clement! Mr. Clement!" cried a voice from the throng of carriages on the quayside.

"Ah, that must be our coachman," said Harry, and then, "Good gracious!"

The driver who was endeavoring to catch their attention by waving a broken whip had a round, red face, beaming with good nature, and wore a threadbare black coat, velveteen breeches that seemed to have developed mange and a battered top hat. The broken-winded old horse he was urging toward the foot of the gangway was harnessed to an extraordinary-looking vehicle with seats on each side and a space for luggage in the middle.

"He doesn't *look* like a coachman," remarked Rachel, "and that certainly is not a coach."

"String!" said Harry, as they approached it. "Those straps are tied together with string."

"Bootlaces, Papa, I believe," said Rachel, immensely diverted.

Her father did not think it quite so funny. He felt that his new dignity as a man of property was being assailed.

"Really," he said, "I should have thought Houlihan could have managed something better than that."

But the driver climbed down from his perch with an air of ineffable courtesy and good nature.

"Your Honor, my young lady!" he cried, and took off his hat and swept them a tremendous bow. "Welcome to Ireland!"

"Er—thank you," said Harry, taken aback. "Do I understand that you have been sent from Ballyclam?"

"Michael O'Connor, Your Honor, at your service. Now, if you and my young lady get your bits and pieces aboard, me and Lightning will have you there in the twinkling of an eye."

"Lightning?" repeated Rachel with an amused glance at her father.

Michael looked quickly between them.

"Ah, my lady, don't be deceived by the look of him. Didn't I raise him meself from a foal? And if you put the pope on his back, wouldn't he outrun the devil himself?"

"I'm sure he would," said Harry. "The question is, will he reach Ballyclam House with us and our luggage."

"He will," said Michael and threw an anxious glance at the mountain of luggage. "Or if he does not, sure there's many a good man with a donkey and cart who would bring the rest of it after us."

Harry looked exasperated at Rachel, but she laughed and clutched his arm, delighted to have met so soon after their arrival one of those Irish "characters" who were even more famous than the Irish beggars.

"Dear Papa," she said, "let us travel to Ballyclam with Mr. O'Connor, on his . . . his . . ."

"Me jaunty-car," Michael supplied helpfully.

"On his . . . er . . . jaunty-car, and let us hire a donkey and cart to bring our luggage after us."

"I suppose we have no choice," said Harry with a touch of grimness.

Rachel put her hand in his and prepared to climb up to the perilous sideways seat, but paused, examining the harness more closely.

"Papa," she said, awed, "It really *is* a bootlace!"

* * *

"Allow me to offer me condolences on the death of your brother," said Michael over his shoulder as they rattled along the quayside. "He was a fine gentleman, a fine gentleman."

"Er—yes," said Harry. "Thank you."

"Too bad he had that argument with the horse!" said Michael, and he took a sharp turn under the archway.

Rachel looked at the back of his head quickly. Had she or had she not caught a fine note of irony in his voice?

By the time they had traveled a very short distance out of Galway, Rachel found that the novelty of their conveyance had worn off and that she was heartily sick of it. The road was rough, the vehicle had no springs and the old horse stumbled over every loose stone. In the event, it had emerged that Michael had a cousin, Tom Flaherty, who just chanced to be on the quay and just happened to own a donkey and cart. He took the heavy boxes, while the smaller luggage, including Rachel's hatboxes, were piled on the jaunting-car. Unfortunately it also emerged that Michael "just chanced to have no straps about him whatever," so that every jolt and jerk sent the bags and hatboxes tumbling down upon his passengers.

"Why on earth couldn't Uncle Cyrus have a proper carriage?" gasped Rachel, narrowly saving her fragile dressing case from crashing to the road during a particularly ferocious lurch.

"As I understand the matter," said Michael, casually inserting himself into the conversation, "your uncle had a wee falling out with the coachman, Patrick O'Fee, he having taken a drop too much and the coach having driven itself into the ditch."

"How dreadful!" Rachel exclaimed.

"Ah, sure, there was no harm done," responded Michael, "and it was a thing that might happen to anyone, but Mr. Clement chanced to take exception to it, the wheel of the coach being broken and himself having to trudge five miles back to Ballyclam."

"So I should imagine!" said Harry. "I hope he dismissed the fellow instantly and packed him off without a reference!"

"Ah well," said Michael obscurely, "Paddy O'Fee chanced to be Mrs. Docherty's first cousin on her mother's side—and, sure, he'll have the wheel mended in a week or so, now he knows Your Honor is coming."

Harry goggled at the back of Michael's head in its battered old hat. "But you can't mean that the man is still employed at Ballyclam?" he demanded. "And that the carriage still isn't mended?"

Michael did not appear to hear him, and a moment later the near hind wheel of the jaunting-car went over a boulder, and Harry's foot slipped off the narrow step.

"Papa!" cried Rachel, clutching him in alarm.

Michael looked solicitously over his shoulder. "Is Your Honor quite comfortable?" he inquired solicitously.

Harry, struggling back into his perilous seat, gazed at him, speechless.

Michael turned contentedly back to his driving. "I always consider," he remarked, " 'tis the great advantage of jaunting-cars that they give you a fine view of the countryside. Now who would want to travel in a nasty closed carriage when he can enjoy the fresh air and journey like a king?"

Rachel was suddenly convulsed with laughter, and even more so when Harry's eyes met hers in silent outrage. She began once more to look about her with interest. She had a great capacity for enjoyment and, having always been very active, physical discomfort did not dismay her as much as it did Harry, who for many years had done nothing more energetic than travel in a hackney carriage through the streets of London.

"Look, Papa!" she cried. "See that quaint little thatched cottage! How pretty it is! And all those dear little children!"

But as they drew closer, she frowned. The children were almost naked, sitting in the mud outside the cabin, which consisted of one windowless room built of clay. A slatternly-looking woman in a tattered shawl came to the doorway, staring at them with wild eyes.

"What a pity it is all so dirty!" exclaimed Rachel. "It would look so much prettier if they whitewashed the walls . . . and why do they not mend the thatch?"

She glanced at Michael O'Connor, but he seemed to be concentrating on his driving, staring straight ahead. Rachel found it slightly irritating tthat he should have been so ready to enter the conversation before and now did not answer her question.

"Mr. O'Connor," she said, raising her voice and speaking very clearly, "why do these people not mend their thatch and whitewash their walls as an English laborer would do?"

Michael O'Connor answered with none of his customary quaint loquaciousness. "They cannot afford to," he replied briefly, "and Peter O'Keefe is not a laborer. He is a tenant farmer."

Rachel was puzzled. Surely a farmer would have more money than a laborer, not less. And, anyway, who ever heard of someone too poor to buy a coat of whitewash?

They were level with the house now.

"Ugh!" said Rachel. "What a dreadful smell! It appears to come from those plants in their front garden. What are they?"

Michael glanced at her over his shoulder and seemed to be doubtful whether or not her question was a serious one.

"The leaves are so black and ugly," continued Rachel. "What are they?"

"Those are praties, my young lady," replied Michael, still with that odd look on his face.

"Praties?"

"Potatoes, and they have the blight on them."

"Hmm," said Harry. "I understand that a lot of the trouble here comes from bad husbandry. I can tell you this: If any of *my* tenants are like that, I shall very soon get rid of them!"

They were approaching a crossroad, and the old horse seemed inclined to go straight on, but Michael hauled on the reins so that Lightning stumbled around onto the narrower road.

"Here, just a minute!" Harry called out, craning his neck to look back over his shoulder. "It's straight on to Ballyclam!"

"I'm taking Your Honor by the shortcut," said Michael, with all his former amiability. " 'Tis no more than five miles."

"Yes, but that signpost said three miles to Ballyclam."

"Ah," responded Michael darkly, "I dare say it might. Them fellows that paint the signposts, the truth is not in them."

Rachel began to laugh again, but her father was gazing ahead, and his eyes widened in horror.

"Good God!" he exclaimed. "The fellow is driving us straight into the river!"

CHAPTER 3

"I said no violence!" exclaimed Padraic.

"Violence?" repeated Jim O'Brien. "What else is it but violence when they raise the rent till we've no way of paying it?"

O'Brien was a sturdy, bull-necked man with short, curly hair. Padraic, staring at him, was aware that Jim was years older than himself, with a wife and child to support. He was aware, too, of Rory, leaning brooding and silent beneath the archway of the ruined abbey.

"It's very hard, I know, but—"

"*Hard?*" Jim repeated again. "It's murder, and we've a right to resist murder."

"But it is the system we must change," said Patraic. "We have our own Irish member of Parliament now, and—"

Rory suddenly launched himself into the argument. "Ah, Padraic, you've no more sense than would go in a pig's ear! Do you think we'd trust the Irish lickspittles who'd sit in an English Parliament? I'd rather kill the enemies of Irish freedom wherever we find them!"

"Whisht, Rory, will you keep your voice down?" begged Tom Noonan. "If the peelers knew there was a meeting of the Young Irelanders here, we'd all be hanged as high as the steeple within the week!"

Rory grinned, and the others grinned, too, even Padraic. Tom Noonan was a little fellow with ginger hair and a mother of whom he was frightened to death. He had the instincts of a daredevil and the courage of a mouse.

"Tom Noonan," said Rory, "if you can't run faster than a bunch of Irish policemen who've grown fat on English money, you've no right to be a member of the Young Irelanders in the first place!"

They all laughed, even Tom Noonan.

Oh, God! thought Padraic. Didn't Rory always know the way to make them laugh, and to lose the truth of the argument while they were laughing?

"If Jim's right," said Rory, "and the potatoes are failing again this year—"

"I tell you," Jim broke in with a note of ferocity, "I dug the first of mine today and they are rotten!"

They looked at each other, and when Rory spoke again, all laughter had vanished from his voice. "Shall we wait," he said, "until all those who would have the courage to fight are corpses?"

"*I'll* not wait," said Jim O'Brien, "until Houlihan comes to turn me off my land, and I must see my Molly and my little Maureen starving in a ditch. The pig went for rent last year and not a bite of it did we eat, and the cow the year before, so there was no buttermilk for the little one, and since Houlihan put it about that I was a troublemaker, no one will give me work. Now he's raised the rent again, and he knows I can't pay it. If I lose the land I'm finished entirely. There's nothing I can do but fight."

"And we'll fight with you!" cried Rory. "Won't we, lads?"

They were fired by his courage, as they always were. "We will! We will so!"

"But we can't fight with our bare hands," said Rory. "We must have guns."

Padraic had sat down on a broken pillar but got quickly to his feet at this, confronting Rory. "No, Rory," he said. "Resist evictions, I agree. Take our case to the courts. Use the law of the land—"

"What good is the law to us?" demanded Rory. "The law is on the side of the landlord."

"Then we must get it changed."

"Will you get it changed in time for me?" asked Jim O'Brien, but this time he spoke very quietly. "Or for Peter O'Keefe or Liam Brady?"

Padraic looked at him in despair. How could you tell a man to be patient while his wife and children starved to death?

"I just know," he said, "that our only hope is to put our case in Parliament—"

"An English Parliament!" Rory broke in.

"The Parliament where Daniel O'Connor won the right for our voice to be heard!" replied Padraic, and he knew from the glances among the other men that he had won that point at least. "If we ever give up the rule of law, we're lost," he said, gaining confidence. "They'll have every excuse to hunt us down like animals—and we can't fight the whole British army."

"Ah, that's true," said Tom Noonan.

"I've two sons in the army," said Tim O'Farrell, an older man with grizzled hair. "Do you think I want to find myself looking at my own boys down the barrel of a gun?"

"Maybe not," said Rory, "but how about the agents, and the landlords, and the gombeen men and the informers? Would you think it a crime to defend your-selves against them?"

His voice rose at the end of the sentence, like a true orator's, and Padraic felt the men's anger rise with it. Ah, Rory, Rory! he thought. Can you only preach hatred and never love?

But Rory glanced around in triumph. "We can pick them off like crows on a fence," he said. "But for that we need guns."

"Please, Rory," said Padraic, "no guns. If we go down that road, there's no turning back."

It was as though they were alone together, and the whole world they had shared since they were born hung in the balance between them. But Rory's single-minded fierceness never faltered. Padraic thought that if it had been St. Patrick himself who pleaded with Rory, his answer would have been the same.

"I say we need guns," said Rory, "and we need them now."

"We should take a vote on it," said Padraic.

Rory hesitated for a moment, and then nodded. "Right," he said.

He turned his eyes toward Eamon Fleming, who had stood silent all this time, newly joined and only half-accepted by the other Young Irelanders.

"Eamon?"

Eamon spoke firmly. "Yes. Guns."

God defend us, thought Padraic, from the Protestant Irishman converted to the cause of Irish freedom!

"Your vote, Tim?" asked Rory.

Tim O'Farrell shook his head. "I've heard my father talk of the days before Catholic Emancipation, when we had nothing. Let's build on the rights that Daniel O'Connell has won for us. No guns."

"Jim?"

"Guns!" said Jim O'Brien, uncompromising as always.

"Joe?"

"Guns," said Joe Kerrigan, after a brief pause, "if that's the way the others feel."

He was a man who kept quiet and went with the tide, not against it, and Padraic saw a slight curl of Rory's lip before he turned to Tom Noonan.

"Well, Tom?"

The daredevil in Tom Noonan rose above his mother, whom, truth to tell, he hated more than the devil. "Guns," he said.

Rory looked at Padraic.

"You know my vote," said Padraic. "No guns. No violence."

"And you know mine," said Rory. He looked around the group. "That's five to two," he said. "Guns it is, and I know where we can find some."

"Where's that?" inquired Jim O'Brien.

His voice was firm enough, but Padraic was aware of a nervousness among the others, as though they were half-inclined, now that it was settled, to regret their decision.

"Carralough Castle," said Rory.

Tom Noonan gave a squeak of terror, and Rory chuckled.

"I'm sure Lord Fitzmorris would be delighted to give us some of those fine sporting guns of his—and we'll try to give him the benefit of them afterward."

"Jasus, Rory!" exclaimed Tom Noonan, "who but you would think of breaking into a castle?"

But the daredevil notion had suddenly united them all again.

"You're a crazy man," said Tim O'Farrell, "but if it's Lord Fitzmorris you're after, devil take it if I don't come with you myself!"

"Rory, those walls are ten feet thick!" said Jim.

"Well, I wasn't thinking of tunneling our way in," replied Rory. "We'll just slip in by the window—and I'm thinking there might just be a friend inside the place who'd leave one unlatched."

"When will it be?" inquired Joe Kerrigan.

"As soon as I can get in touch with the fellow inside," replied Rory. "I'm not going in without a good, sound plan."

"How many guns can we get?" asked Jim.

"As many as he's got," answered Rory, and he grinned. "We'd better have Michael O'Connor's car."

"Where is Michael, anyway?" demanded Jim O'Brien.

"Houlihan told him to go and meet the new English landlord from Galway," answered Kerrigan, who always knew what was going on.

"From Galway?" cried Rory. "Good luck to them! Michael gets lost doing the Stations of the Cross!"

Rory went out, and the others followed, laughing, but Padraic remained behind. Somewhere he saw the vision of a free Ireland, free by her own right and her own inspiration, without cruelty or violence. But always that vision was like the horizon. As they sailed toward it, so it sank out of sight. He looked up at the delicate tracery of the stonework against the blue sky, and sorrow filled his heart.

He heard the voices of his friends as they began to disperse in different directions and heard Rory call after them. "I'll send you word by Brian."

Brian, thought Padraic. Was that loving, eager

young brother of theirs to be drawn inextricably into violence and death? He leaned his forehead against the cold, holy stone of the abbey.

The voices faded into the countryside, but Padraic saw Rory waiting for him by the lane. It was always the same. Rory's temper created their quarrels, but his heart allowed them to make up. For all their differences, the bond of love and brotherhood was greater.

As he climbed the hill, Padraic heard Rory calling after him, but he ignored him and walked faster.

"Padraic! No fighting, is it? No violence?"

Rory pushed Padraic and he stumbled but recovered and walked angrily on.

"I'll make you fight, see if I don't!" said Rory, and punched him.

Padraic's temper snapped and he turned to hit back, but Rory snatched Padraic's cap off his head and ran away with it.

"Give that back!" yelled Padraic, infuriated.

He chased Rory and caught him, still angry, and tripped him up. But as they rolled on the ground together, Padraic saw that Rory was grinning, and suddenly they were tumbling down the hill, laughing and pummeling each other like a pair of schoolboys.

"Hey!" said Rory suddenly, sitting up. "What the devil is Michael O'Connor up to?"

He and Padraic watched, fascinated, at the sight of Michael driving the jaunting-car with its handsomely dressed English passengers straight down into the fast-flowing river.

"Are you sure this is safe?" demanded Harry, hanging on for dear life.

"Now, don't let Your Honor be troubling yourself in the very slightest," replied Michael. "Lightning and me has been through this little stream a hundred times and never the least mishap."

"Stream?" Rachel repeated as the water lapped above the step on which their feet rested. "I would call this a—a raging torrent!"

"If my young lady will just lift the hem of her gown a trifle," Michael suggested helpfully, "sure she'll get no more of a wetting than the drops of dew on a rose."

Rachel grasped her gown and petticoat and lifted them above the rising water. The jaunting-car lurched down into the riverbed.

"We shall be drowned, Papa!" cried Rachel. "I know we shall!"

"Up, Lightning! Up, my young beauty!" adjured Michael, addressing the animal he remembered from twenty years before.

The old horse strained and staggered, and one wheel of the car sank into a soft patch.

"Up, Lightning, up!" cried Michael.

The car tilted perilously and came to rest.

"Oh no!" cried Rachel. "What do we do now?"

Michael eyed Harry. "I suppose," he insinuated hopefully, "Your Honor would not be feeling inclined to get down and dip your feet in the stream—just to lighten the load?"

Harry, speechless with indignation, prepared to descend, but his movement threatened to upset the delicate balance of the car.

"No, Papa, no!" cried Rachel. "Don't move or the cart will go over!"

* * *

"That idiot, Michael O'Connor!" exclaimed Padraic. "He'll drown himself and everyone with him. We'd better give him a hand."

"If it's the English landlord," said Rory, "he can drown him and welcome! But I agree we might as well save the horse."

Padraic laughed at him and began to run down the hill. He plunged into the water and waded alongside the carriage.

"Michael," he said, "what do you think you're doing?"

"Is it yourself, Padraic?" Michael called back cheerily.

Rachel, clinging to her seat on the tilting car, saw beside her in the water a slim young man with curly brown hair, gray-blue eyes and a humorous face. In spite of his rough clothes and his Irish brogue, there was something very charming about him, and she was glad that she was wearing the bonnet with the pink velvet ribbon bows.

"Ah, sure now, wasn't I just driving the new English landlord to Ballyclam," said Michael, "and the lovely young lady, his daughter, with him, so I thought I'd take the shortcut."

Rachel caught the look of amusement in Padraic's face.

"Your own particular shortcut, is it, Michael? Don't you think maybe you cut it a bit too short this time?"

He touched his cap to Rachel and went to put his shoulder to the wheel. "Come on, Rory!" he yelled. "Give a hand, can't you?"

Rachel was aware of another young man standing on the hillside above the stream, but she was more concerned lest the car should overturn in the water with themselves and all their luggage. Padraic tried to heave the wheel out of the soft riverbed, and Michael stood up again and shook the reins.

"Hey up, Lightning! Hey up!" he called.

The bootlace broke, and the old horse floundered and sank to his knees.

"Oh no!" cried Rachel. "Oh no, the poor horse will be drowned!"

The other young man leaped down into the water, and she became aware of his black hair tossed back and his blue eyes gazing impudently into hers.

"We mustn't let the poor horse drown now, must we?" said Rory.

He splashed through the water and grasped the horse's bit and struggled to get him to his feet. The jaunting-car tipped still further.

"Oh, do be careful!" cried Rachel, alarm and exasperation mixed.

Rory paused in his exertions and looked at her.

"Would my lady prefer to get out and walk?"

Rachel opened her mouth, looked at the rushing waters and closed it again. She saw Rory's grin before he took hold of the horse's bit. For a moment Rachel was afraid that he might go down under the plunging hooves, as poor old Lightning struggled to get up. Then the jaunting-car moved forward, lurched onto firmer ground and, with Padraic putting his shoulder to the wheel, surged up onto the bank.

Rachel, still grasping her gown and petticoat, became aware of Rory's eyes on her ankles and neat little boots. She hastily lowered her dress and lifted her chin. "Thank you," she said. "What is your name?"

"Rory O'Manion," he replied. "What is yours?"

Rachel stiffened. He was wearing the clothes of a

farm laborer, but his tone was quite wrong, much too familiar.

"I am Miss Clement," she said.

"Welcome to Ireland, Miss Clement," said Padraic. She turned to see his kind, gentle face and smiled. "Thank you. And thank you for helping us."

Harry, feeling that he had lost some dignity, endeavored to assert himself. "Is this the road to Ballyclam?" he inquired.

Michael had descended and, unbelievably, was knotting the broken bootlace yet again. Rachel saw a glance pass between him and Padraic.

"It is," said Padraic.

Rachel noticed that he spoke much more coldly to her father than to her.

"And when do we reach the Clement property?" inquired Rachel.

It was Rory who replied from the other side of the jaunting-car, close beside her.

"Never!" he said. "This is O'Manion land."

Harry's attention was caught. "What?" he said. "What's that?"

Once more Padraic and Michael exchanged a quick glance, and Rachel was aware of it. Michael began to climb up onto his perch and beamed at Harry with the old, easy charm and amiable smile.

"Ah, sure, Your Honor, Rory is a great one for the jokes. Hey, up, Lightning! Come up, there!"

The old horse pecked and stumbled and set off at a jolting trot. Rachel, glancing back, saw Padraic, courteous, friendly and kind, smiling after her. But before they turned the corner, it was Rory who caught her eye and held it—Rory with his black hair and blue eyes, taut and challenging, like an animal ready to spring.

"Ah, well," said Michael with an ingratiating smile at Harry, "all's well that ends well, and we'll be at Ballyclam in ten minutes—or it could be fifteen."

As long as she lived, Rachel would never forget that first sight of Ballyclam House. It was hard to say how it differed from an English country house. It had the same Georgian pillars, the wide windows, the gracious steps, the terrace, the lawns and flower beds, and yet—there was something easy and pleasant about it. It reminded her of Michael O'Connor and his jaunting-car. The car was ancient and rusty, the harness was tied up with string and a frayed bootlace, the horse was old and sad. And yet—it was with such grace and courtesy that he had said, "Welcome, my young lady. Welcome to Ireland."

So it was with Ballyclam. There was grass growing in the stones of the terrace, and the drive was overgrown with laurels, and the flower-beds needed weeding, and yet the house seemed to say, Welcome, my young lady. Welcome to Ireland.

The only discordant note was struck by the man who awaited them at the foot of the steps. He was dressed in black—black coat, black breeches, black boots, and he took off a hard black hat as Harry descended from the jaunting-car and turned to assist Rachel.

"Good evening, Mr. Clement," he said. "My name is John Houlihan."

It was Houlihan who introduced them to the servants, all lined up in the hall with an uneasy look, as though they were unaccustomed to such formality.

"This is Tobin, the butler," said Houlihan.

Tobin's boots were down-at-the-heel and his hands trembled a little from age, but there was a gentle smile on his old face.

"I hope you'll be very happy, my young lady," he said, "here at Ballyclam."

"Thank you, Tobin," replied Rachel, touched.

"And this is Mrs. Docherty, the cook."

"Good day to you, Your Honor," Mrs. Docherty said, "and good day to you, my young lady. Not knowing what you'd be wishful to be eating after your journey, sure I thought it best to throw together a pair of stuffed pork tenderloin steaks and a touch of me honey mousse."

"That sounds—delicious," said Rachel.

It really did. She tried to imagine Mrs. Carter idly tossing together such a meal in Bayswater and failed.

"This is O'Fee, the coachman," said Houlihan.

Harry turned his indignant gaze toward Rachel. She suppressed her amusement. Even to her untutored gaze, Patrick O'Fee's watery eyes betokened the habitual drunkard. Rachel looked sternly at Mrs. Docherty's first cousin on her mother's side.

"When will Mr. Clement be able to use the carriage?" she inquired.

"Sure, I'll have the wheel mended for him by next week at the latest," said Paddy O'Fee.

"And the earliest?" Rachel demanded.

She saw the twinkle in his eye and, inexcusably, found herself twinkling in reply.

"Sure," he said, "if His Honor should chance to have a use for the carriage by tomorrow, I don't doubt it will be ready for him."

Rachel smiled, gratified, but before she could express her approval, Paddy O'Fee spoke again.

"Or it could be the day after that," he said.

Mrs. Docherty took over the introductions of the female staff.

"This is Lily, the parlormaid," she said, "me sister's cousin's daughter, and this is me niece Bridget, the housemaid, but she won't be here long, on account of she's getting married."

"Oh," said Rachel.

It appeared to her that, alone among Mrs. Docherty's relatives, Bridget looked neat, trim and pretty, a credit to the household.

"We were going to have the wedding party here at Ballyclam," said Mrs. Docherty, "but with the master and your young ladyship here, sure, we'd never dream of taking the liberty."

It took a moment for Rachel to realize that her good nature was being subtly tested. She smiled at Mrs. Docherty.

"But of course you must have the wedding here," she said, "and Mr. Clement and I hope that Bridget will be very happy."

Bridget curtsied, and Mrs. Docherty beamed.

"God bless you, my young lady, for the kind heart of you!" she said.

Rachel inclined her head graciously, but as she followed Houlihan and her father toward the drawing room, she heard Mrs. Docherty's sotto-voce addition. "The old master," said Mrs. Docherty, "would have seen us in our graves before he'd have allowed such a thing, and him as hard as the devil's forehead!"

The drawing room was a graceful, beautifully proportioned room. Houlihan, leading the way, glanced up at the portrait of a lumpish, red-faced man in a pink hunting coat which hung over the fireplace.

"Mr. Cyrus Clement's death was a great tragedy," he said.

"Yes," replied Harry. "Very sad."

He met Rachel's eye with the wicked look in it and knew that she was thinking that Uncle Cyrus's portrait should be moved as soon as possible out of sight into the attic.

"I hope you'll continue to act as my agent, Mr. Houlihan," said Harry, "collect my rents and so on."

Rachel caught the quick flash of relief in Houlihan's face.

"Certainly, Mr. Clement," he said. "I'll be only too happy to take care of all that side of things."

"Good," said Harry, equally relieved.

"And if there is anything else I can do?" inquired Houlihan.

Harry glanced at Rachel. She drifted back toward the door. "We shall be needing some more servants," she said casually.

"We shall?" repeated Harry, startled.

Rachel knew that he was thinking of the cook and the little maid-of-all-work whom they had left behind them in Bayswater. She turned and saw Houlihan glancing between herself and Harry, trying to assess the situation.

"Any of your tenants," said Houlihan tentatively, "would be glad to come and work here."

Rachel paused and turned in the doorway. "Are the O'Manions our tenants?" she asked.

Houlihan's face hardened. "Indeed they are."

"I mean to ride," said Rachel, "so we shall need a groom. And from the look of the grounds, a gardener, too."

She strolled out into the hall. "Those two young

men," she said, "who helped us in the river—one of them was called O'Manion—Rory?"

"Rory O'Manion?" said Houlihan, quickly.

"He made some joke about this being O'Manion land," said Harry. "I thought he was rather impudent."

Houlihan gave a short laugh. "I'm surprised he didn't claim the whole of Galway!" he said. "He has been brought up by his father to believe that the O'Manions are descended from the kings of Ireland."

"Really?" said Rachel. The idea rather appealed to her. It had a fairy-story element in it—two young princes in shabby clothes rescuing her from the river.

"You will soon discover, Miss Clement," said Houlihan with a sneer, "that everyone in this country is descended from the kings of Ireland."

"Really?" said Rachel again, and then added innocently, "Except for you, Mr. Houlihan?"

Houlihan gave a quick frown before replying, "Oh, I don't bother with any of that nonsense."

Rachel looked at him thoughtfully for a moment and then moved toward the staircase. "Anyway, that young man—Rory, was it?—seemed to be very good with horses. I think we should employ him as a groom."

"My dear Miss Clement," said Houlihan as though he were kindly instructing an ignorant child, "I assure you, he would be quite unsuitable."

"Indeed?" responded Rachel, beginning to mount the staircase.

Houlihan came out into the hall. "There is no great harm in his brother, Pat," he said, "except for some bee in his bonnet about Irish self-government, but Rory is an out-and-out troublemaker. I certainly would not advise you to employ him, even if he would consent to come, which is very unlikely."

Rachel turned on the staircase, her voice suddenly sharp. "At least," she said tartly, "you might do as I say and *ask* him!"

Houlihan jumped as though he had sniffed a rose and been stung by a wasp. He glanced toward Harry, who had come to the doorway of the drawing room.

"Don't you agree, Papa?" said Rachel sweetly.

Harry glanced between them and smiled uneasily. "Perhaps, Mr. Houlihan," he said, "we might give the young man a chance."

CHAPTER 4

"Work at Ballyclam House? Never!" said Rory. "Whose fine notion was that?"

"Houlihan rode by an hour ago," said Deirdre. "He said you were to work as groom and Padraic in the garden. And the young lady has a lot of pretty clothes about her. They want me to do her washing."

"They can want!" said Rory. "We'll not go near the place."

"I should look at the potatoes first," said Padraic.

"There's nothing wrong with *our* potatoes," said Rory.

"Is there not?" asked Shane.

Rory looked at his father quickly. He himself had been away since early that morning at Carralough Castle, lounging about in the back kitchen until the Young Irelander who worked as footman there could slip out for a quick word and a promise to leave the third tall window from the corner unlatched. Rory had returned, elated, running down the hillside with great leaps and bounds. His spirits were all the higher because he and Padraic and their father had dug their potatoes the night before and found them perfectly sound. They were the lucky ones. They were the lucky ones, and one day he would set Ireland free!

Shane was hoeing the garden while Padraic mended the fence and Maeve, as usual, came along behind her father helping pick up the weeds. Now Shane straightened up, and Rory saw his face and read disaster in it.

"You'd best go and see," he said.

Rory walked toward the potato patch, and even before he got there, the stench hit him. He looked aghast at the neat trenches. The healthy golden potatoes they had dug the night before and laid out to dry were now a mass of stinking corruption.

The others followed him, and Deirdre put her apron over her nose and mouth. Those potatoes represented the whole family's food for the coming year, and yet so awful was the reek of corruption that it made them choke even to come near them.

"We shall be glad of the Ballyclam wages to buy food," said Padraic, and Rory turned on him angrily.

"*You* work there if you like!" he shouted. "Grovel about in the earth and try to please *my young lady* with your pretty flowers! I'd rather starve!"

He began to walk away, but Shane's voice stopped him in his tracks. "Is that the promise you made your mother?" he said sternly. "To starve, and let the little ones starve, too?"

Rory looked at him, stricken. Maeve, always uneasy when there was anger in the air, slipped her hand into her father's. As Rory looked back toward the potato patch, she followed his gaze.

"Da," she said, "if the praties are bad again, what will we eat?"

"I do not know, *alanna*," replied Shane, his eyes on Rory's face.

"Did we do something wrong," asked Maeve, "that God has taken the praties from us?"

"Oh, my Maeve, I do not know!" cried Shane and caught her up in his arms and held her close.

Rory heard the baby crying from the house. Deirdre made a move, but he stopped her and went inside. He knelt down beside the woven cradle in the hearth, and his hand touched the silver medal around his neck before he lifted the crying child and hushed him in his arms. The baby stopped crying and looked back at him with a quirky, toothless smile.

"Ah, Sean," said Rory, "isn't it love that makes slaves of us all?"

A week later Rory was leaning against a gate at the Horse Fair. All around him were Irishmen happily telling each other lies about horses, and in the midst of them was the biggest liar of the lot, Mickeen O'Rourke, busy selling a showy-looking gray to Mr. Clement.

"Sure, Your Honor could not find a better horse, not if you searched the length and breadth of the land for twenty years!" said Mickeen.

He led the horse up and down, holding him very firmly by the halter and never letting him raise his head.

"He—er—he certainly does look quite strong," said Harry Clement.

Mickeen eyed him lovingly. English, and knew nothing whatever about horses! What more could the heart of an Irish horse trader desire?

"I can see," said Mickeen, "that Your Honor has a

rare gift for spotting the qualities of a horse. Sure, hasn't he the true Irish hindquarters on him, which will take him over any stone wall in the country?"

Harry knew enough to turn his eyes toward the rear of the horse, but at Mickeen's final words, he looked back at him, alarmed. "But this horse is for my daughter. I don't want *her* to be jumping stone walls."

"No more you do," responded the trader, neatly changing tack, "and quite right, sir, quite right, indeed, to have a care for the beautiful young lady. But aren't I saying that, though she may never *put* him at a wall, still, he's such a high stepper that she can walk him over one and never know it's there."

"Ah," said Harry doubtfully.

"And hasn't he the fine raking shoulders," Mickeen continued hastily, "which speak thoroughbred in every line of them?"

The horse strained at the halter, and the trader seemed to be having some trouble keeping his feet on the ground, but he managed to smile at Harry, his black eyes twinkling with good nature and honesty as he brought the horse to a stop.

Harry looked around at Rachel, who stood watching critically nearby. "What do you think, my dear?" he said.

"He's certainly very showy," said Rachel dubiously.

"Ah, my young lady has the right of it!" cried Mickeen heartily. "Showy he is, and will show himself and the young lady off to the very best advantage. Buy this horse and you'll ride as light and easy as the Fairy Queen. Sure, don't I always say, a beautiful horse should have a beautiful lady on his back, and there'd be no doubt of it in the present case, no doubt whatever."

Harry was amused but gratified by the compliment

to his daughter, but Rachel, eyeing the horse more critically, remarked, "He does seem to jerk his head rather a lot."

"You are quite sure he is a lady's horse?" asked Harry.

"Indeed he is," said Mickeen. "He's nodding his head to say he's as gentle as a lamb—and Your Honor can have every last particle of him for no more than thirty pounds."

"Thirty pounds!" exclaimed Harry. "That is far too much."

The trader sighed and shook his head at Harry as though he had just suffered a great disappointment. "Ah," he said sadly, "I can see Your Honor is a man who knows too much about horses for me who's been buying and selling them since I was a gossoon."

"Twenty pounds," said Harry, gratified.

Rory straightened up, and Mickeen O'Rourke threw a hasty glance toward him and then looked back at Harry.

" 'Tis like stealing money from me own pocket, but I'll let you have the horse for twenty-five pounds."

Harry hesitated.

"Don't ask me to make it less," Mickeen begged, "for I'll be the laughingstock of Galway now."

Harry smiled, pleased with himself for his sharp trading, and turned to Rachel. "Well, my dear," he said, "I suppose the horse is yours if you fancy him."

"What's his name?" asked Rachel.

"The Nailer."

Mickeen caught Rachel's quick frown and hastily added, "But you could always change his name to something more pretty if you'd a mind to."

Rory spoke unexpectedly at Rachel's elbow. "I

wouldn't change it," he said. "The Nailer is a grand name for him, for unless you nail his front hooves to the ground, he'll always prefer to walk on his hind legs."

He neatly twitched the halter out of the trader's hands, and the Nailer reared terrifyingly up. Rachel and Harry started back, alarmed, and there was a general laugh and a few ribald comments from the men around.

"There goes the Nailer dancing a jig as usual!"

"You might as well cut his two front legs off, Mickeen, for there's a beast with no use for them at all!"

The trader managed to grasp the halter and brought the Nailer down to earth again, and Harry spluttered at him indignantly. "You—you were prepared to sell that horse to me for my daughter!"

"Ah, sure," said Mickeen, "wouldn't any horse rear up if you startle him?"

"Especially," said Rory, "if he's been doing the same thing for fifteen years to my certain knowledge."

"Fifteen?" demanded Harry. "You told me he was a five-year-old."

"A five-year-old!" said Rory with a grin. "Ah, Mickeen, you went a bit far that time."

The trader opened his mouth and shut it again. Rory glanced across the field. "How about that little chestnut over there?"

The trader hastily tied the Nailer to the fence and tried to put himself between Harry and the trim little horse.

"Ah, sure," he said, "the gentleman would never want to be thinking of that little bag of bones."

"You mean because you're selling him for your

cousin and you have to share the price with him?" inquired Rory politely.

"Rory O'Manion!" cried the indignant trader. "Why do you have to put your two penn'orth of meal in the broth?"

Rachel's eyes met Rory's in an involuntary moment of shared amusement before she turned and walked toward the pretty little chestnut.

"This is the one I like, Papa," she said. "May I have him?"

Harry glanced at Rory, received no warning and so took it that the sale was acceptable. He decided to assert himself. "Very well," he said. "I'll buy him for—for fifteen pounds."

Mickeen opened his mouth, but Rory was quicker. "No, no," said Rory, looking Harry firmly in the eye. "That horse is worth twenty-five pounds—which is more than I can say for the Nailer."

While Harry settled up with Mickeen O'Rourke, Rory strolled over to Rachel and the chestnut.

"Will I ride him back to Ballyclam for you?" he asked.

"Thank you," said Rachel. She smiled at him. "And thank you for not allowing my father to be cheated."

"Ah, well," said Rory, cheerfully, "I'd not have minded *him* being cheated, but if I'm to be his groom, I'd no wish to be thought as big a fool as him!"

Rachel's smile vanished and she gasped. "Really— Rory, is it?—that is no way to speak to your employer."

"Your father is not my employer," said Rory. "He is our landlord, and that is why I'm working for him."

"Against your will?" asked Rachel.

It was a more direct question than he had expected

from her, and he glanced at her and then away. "Ah well," he said, "there are compensations."

"Oh?" said Rachel, and there was invitation in her voice.

In the short time that she had been in Ireland, she had received many charming, easy compliments spoken in the soft West-of-Ireland brogue, but she had a feeling that a compliment from this young man would be something quite special. He was silent for a few moments and then looked up at her.

"It's always a pleasure," he said, "to work with a beautiful horse."

His face was quite solemn, but Rachel saw a flash of devilment in his eyes and knew that he had deliberately led her to expect a compliment and then made a fool of her. She managed to conceal her annoyance.

"I'm glad you approve of my choice," she said. "I forgot to ask his name."

Rory began to stroke the horse lovingly. "He's never really had a name," he said. "His mother was called Tara, so he's known as Tara's Colt."

He glanced up at Rachel. "So you can have the satisfaction of naming him yourself."

"Oh, dear!" cried Rachel. "That's like naming a child!"

She saw a startled look in Rory's eyes, as though he had not expected her to understand that.

"So it is," said Rory and caressed the horse again.

Rachel watched his hand—a remarkably slender hand, for all the dirty fingernails—as it stroked and smoothed the gleaming chestnut body.

"I shall call him Flame," she said.

"Flame it is," said Rory, and he seemed pleased.

A cart clattered by, and Flame's eyes rolled wildly.

"He's broken to the sidesaddle," said Rory, "but he's a spirited little creature. Are you sure you can manage him?"

Rachel looked him directly in the eye. "I like a challenge!" she said and turned away toward Patrick O'Fee and the waiting carriage.

Rory, riding the chestnut horse bareback up the road, heard Rachel's imperious English voice.

"Rory!"

He pulled on the halter, and Flame turned, dancing a little.

She spoke carelessly and impersonally, as to a servant. "I would like to ride my little horse tomorrow. Have him saddled for me early, if you please."

Rory nodded and spoke very formally. "Very good, Miss Clement."

She sat back in the carriage, satisfied. That will teach him, she thought, to pretend he is going to pay me a compliment and then not do so.

But she had caught the flash of anger in his eyes and knew that she was playing with fire.

The air was fresh from the overnight rain when Rachel came downstairs next morning to a solitary but enjoyable breakfast of Mrs. Docherty's potato cakes and kidneys baked in their overcoats of fat. She had already learned that Mrs. Docherty's coffee had a fearful brackish taste to it, as though it were made of bog water, and had accustomed herself instead to tea for breakfast. It occurred to her that Ireland had a way of luring strangers to accommodate themselves to its own customs in the very moment when it appeared to be most willing to oblige.

"Will I be wetting you a fresh pot of tay, Miss Rachel?" inquired Lily with the eager air of hospitality that was so much more engaging than the cool correctness of an English parlormaid.

"No, thank you, Lily," said Rachel. "I told Rory to have my horse ready early this morning."

"Ah, sure," said Lily, "him and Padraic is just having their breakfast in the kitchen. He'll be ready as soon as you get there—or it could be half an hour later."

It seemed to Rachel that Padraic and Rory ought to have had their breakfast at home, and that her horse should be ready the moment she wanted him and not half an hour later. But Ireland was too strong for her.

"Thank you, Lily," she said and poured herself another cup of tea.

Before she left the dining room and went out by the side door into the stable yard, Rachel saw through the long windows that Padraic was working in the herbacious borders. She saw Rory putting the bridle on Flame and heard his voice addressing the horse.

"Whoa, whoa! my beauty. Whoa, Flame! Now isn't that the fine name you have on you now? 'Tis just the name for Tara's Colt, since the freedom of Ireland burns like a flame—and didn't the young lady name you herself?"

Rachel walked to the door, and he looked up and must have known that she had heard him, but he didn't seem disconcerted. "Good morning," he said.

She knew that she was looking very pretty in her blue velvet riding habit and the hat with the white curled ostrich feather, and he eyed her appreciatively—rather too appreciatively, since he was only a groom and she was his mistress. But somehow she could not quite think of him as a servant.

"Why did you say that this was O'Manion land?" she asked suddenly.

"Because it was, three hundred years ago."

Rachel began to laugh. "Three hundred years?" she said. "I don't think you can claim it back after so long!"

Rory looked at her challengingly above the chestnut mane. "We have long memories in Ireland."

"Really?" said Rachel. She answered the challenge, giving him look for look. "Well," she said, "my father has now inherited this property, and I can assure you that we have no intention of leaving, so I'm afraid you will have to make the best of it."

She turned on her heel and walked out of the stable yard, speaking coolly over her shoulder. "Bring the horse out when he is ready, will you?" she said.

Padraic, on his knees weeding the border, saw Rachel approaching.

"Good morning," she said. "Pat—that is your name, is it not?"

Padraic rose to greet her. "In fact, my name is Padraic." He pronounced it "Parrick."

"Porrick?" repeated Rachel, amused.

"That is Patrick in the Irish language."

"Good gracious!" said Rachel. "I did not know there *was* an Irish language!"

"There was a time," said Padraic, "when a man could be jailed for speaking the Irish language."

"Oh," said Rachel. She thought it over. "That's dreadful!" She thought it over again. "But, of course, it would be more useful for people in Ireland to be able to speak English."

"More useful for the English!" said Rory just quietly enough for Rachel to be able to pretend she had not heard him. He led the chestnut horse out and tethered him to a hook in the stable yard, then went into the stable again.

Rachel looked at Padraic. "Are you older than your brother, or younger?" she asked Padraic.

"We are twins," he replied.

Rachel looked at him in astonishment. "Twins? But you are not in the least alike!"

Padraic smiled. "Aye, too bad he doesn't have my saintly nature. We want the same things, only in different ways."

Rachel laughed but kept to the point. "Why is your brother always so—so angry?"

"My father says that Rory feels too much and thinks too little," he responded.

"And you?" asked Rachel.

She suddenly saw the anguish in those gray-blue eyes, the strain and pain of trying to bridge two inter-locked, divided cultures.

"I am sure," she said, "that you don't feel too little!"

He spoke very gently, very sadly.

"If Ireland ever shall be free,
Her head and heart must come together.
As, if a rainbow is to be,
It springs from rain and sunny weather."

The words struck home to Rachel, lodging in her heart forever. She looked quickly at Padraic, with his dirty hands and shabby clothes. "Who wrote that?"

She saw the answer in his face.

"I believe it was you!" She laughed. "I've never had a gardener who wrote poetry before!"

She saw the grave expression in Padraic's face, and

the laughter fell from her face. In that instant class, as she had always understood it in England, ceased to exist for her. In Ireland every man was a king.

"Do you mind having a gardener who writes poetry?" asked Padraic gently.

She answered with equal gentleness. "No. No, I think I rather like it."

She turned toward the stable yard, but then paused and looked back. "But it would never happen in England!"

And suddenly she was laughing again, but this time Padraic was laughing with her.

Rory brought a sturdy cob, Sunset, out into the stable yard, and Rachel walked toward him.

"Miss Rachel!"

She paused and turned. Padraic came toward her, smiling, a late rosebud in his hand.

"That's a charming riding habit," said Padraic, "but it needs something to bring out the roses in your cheeks."

"Thank you," said Rachel and took it, answering his smile. She tucked the rose in the pin of her stock and then looked gravely up at him. "Thank you, Padraic," she said.

He nodded gravely back at her, and she was glad to see that, in using his Irish name, she had been able to give him gift for gift.

Rory had tied up the cob and stood waiting to help Rachel onto her horse. She felt in him an impatience that matched the restlessness of the chestnut, jerking its head and clattering on the cobbles. Rachel got up onto the mounting block as Rory got the horse under control again and brought him alongside.

"He's quite fresh," he said. "Are you sure he's not too much for you?"

Rachel settled herself in the saddle, took the reins and gave Flame a sharp tap with the whip to show him who was in charge. "Just watch me!" she said and went off at a spanking trot that broke into a gallop.

Padraic and Rory stood watching her go.

"She'll kill herself!" said Padraic.

Rory grinned. "Not that one! She'll kill the horse first!"

A window was flung up and a furious voice shouted from behind them.

"You, there! O'Manion! What do you mean by letting my daughter ride out alone?"

"Aren't I just going after her?" replied Rory, adding under his breath, "Though it's more than she deserves."

He fetched the cob and jumped on his back, setting off at the same instant down the drive. Harry's voice thundered after him.

"You're her groom, and it's your duty to accompany her."

"I will, when I can catch her!" said Rory.

He snatched a switch from the hedge and gave Sunset a blow that made him jump and go from walk to canter in one stride.

Rachel allowed Rory to catch up with her at the end of the drive.

"You're right," she said as Flame tittupped about in the lane, "he *is* fresh. Where can we have a good gallop?"

"This way," said Rory, turning Sunset's head. "We'll ride by the old abbey. But take it easy, will you? If you break your neck, I'll get the blame for it."

Rachel laughed at him, and Rory reluctantly found himself grinning in reply.

In all her life, Rachel had never ridden a horse like Flame, and she learned from him just as any sensitive rider learns from a good horse. Like every good horse, Flame had neatness, generosity and courage, and he leaped those Irish stone walls as though they were bales of hay. But Rory, being a better rider, he kept that staid horse Sunset close at Flame's heels, and soon the wild, passionate ride became more competitive and daring. They jumped the low wall into the abbey grounds.

"Whoa!" said Rory. "Whoa back!"

But Rachel still urged Flame toward the higher wall that bounded the ruins.

"No!" he yelled. "Rein back! He'll never make it!"

Rachel, thinking that he was challenging her courage, still urged the little horse toward the high wall. It was only as she approached that she saw the jagged stones on the far side of the double wall.

"How stupid!" she thought. "I'm going to die, and it is all his fault!"

In that moment Rory managed to urge his horse alongside, grab Flame's reins and, as he turned, he got an arm around Rachel's waist and they both tumbled to the ground.

Rory, rolling in the grass with Rachel, thought that she would be angry. Instead, he saw that she was smiling.

"Thank you!" she said gently. "I didn't know those rocks were there."

As they rolled over, he lay on top of her, and he sensed her startled sexual awareness at this contact. Unthinkingly, instinctively, he kissed her. Rachel was instantly outraged. She raised her crop to strike him, but Rory grasped it.

"Ah no, *agra!*" he said.

He kissed her again, but this time it was deliberate. It was quite different from any kiss that Rachel had known before, timidly and apologetically taken behind the potted palms, with the orchestra politely playing, and yet it immediately summoned those suppressed memories, those hints of dark, exciting possibilities. A polka, a waltz, a wild ride on a horse—and then, as his body pressed on hers, something much more dangerous, something much more frightening and desirable!

Passion flared between them and in another moment would have been consummated, but the sound of a horse's hooves clip-clopped along the lane, and a voice called, "Who's that?"

Rachel gasped and tried to free herself.

"Ah, take no notice," said Rory. "It's only a soldier."

"Dear God, it's my brother!" said Rachel, and tried to hide her face in Rory's chest.

David reined in his big black charger, looking puzzled at the two figures rolling in the grass and the riderless horses running free.

"Rachel? Is that you?"

Rachel scrambled up, trying to tidy her hair and smooth her skirt. "David!" she exclaimed. "My—my horse ran away. He was going to jump that wall, and—our new groom, O'Manion—he saved me."

Rory was on his feet, looking from under his dark brows at the tall, slim man with fair hair and mustache and the smart red uniform. Lieutenant Clement looked at him with a slight frown.

"In that case, I'm obliged to you," he said. "O'Manion, is it?"

"I'll get the horses," said Rory.

"When did you arrive?" she asked.

"I landed this morning," he replied, "and called in at the house on my way to report to the colonel."

He picked a piece of grass off her riding habit and glanced after Rory. "Father said you were trying out a new horse. He was worried about you. You're not hurt?"

"No!" said Rachel quickly. "No, I'm—quite all right."

Rory returned with the horses. Flame was frisky after his free run and was giving him some trouble. David's eyes rested on the groom and the chestnut.

"Ireland is different from England, Rachel," he said. "You should be careful with these spirited animals."

Rachel looked at him quickly. "Yes," she said. "Yes, I know."

David's eyes rested on Rory again for a moment before he mounted and turned his horse back onto the road. Then he suddenly reined back, and Rachel flinched, startled.

"I forgot to mention to Father that I'll be dining at Ballyclam tomorrow."

"I'll tell him," said Rachel.

David saluted and rode on. Rachel let her breath go and walked toward Rory.

"You're a good liar, me darlin'," he said and grinned.

"How dare you!" said Rachel furiously. "You have no right to call me that!"

"Then I'll just have to think it, won't I?" said Rory.

Rachel turned away to mount but suddenly found

that the shock of the fall and what had happened after, and the strain of the unexpected encounter with her brother, had been too much for her and tears were running down her cheeks. She leaned against the saddle, trying to recover, and wiped the tears away with the back of her hand in an absurd, childish gesture. She became aware of Rory close beside her and looked up at him, half-afraid, and saw a look on his face that surprised her—a sort of reluctant tenderness. He held his hands together to help her to her saddle.

"Come on, now," he said, "off home with you. There's no harm done."

Rachel mounted, and they rode home in silence, with Rory a sedate half-length behind her. But she knew in her heart that it was not true.

CHAPTER 5

David was frowning as he rode on. He remembered the look of fear in Rachel's eyes when he had turned back, as though she had expected some kind of challenge. He remembered, too, that his first thought as he approached the abbey had been that there was a village boy and girl enjoying a tumble in the grass—and good luck to them! Then he had seen the white ostrich feather in the hat and the velvet riding habit, and had thought, Good God! that is a lady! And then he had recognized Rachel.

Her explanation that she had fallen off her horse must be the true one. Anything else was unthinkable. She had always been daring and willful, and Father

had spoiled her abominably. And it was true that at
dances men gathered around her like flies around a
honey pot, and that if she had been someone else's
sister instead of his own, he might have said she was
a bit of a flirt. But, good heavens, she was barely
eighteen, and anyway she was incapable of the kind
of behavior that—that—And with a *groom*! But still
the picture he had seen was distinct in his mind—the
man lying on top of her, his hand pulling at her skirt,
and she with her arms around his neck—

No! thought David. No, it was impossible!

He was enough of his father's son to shake the
thought of it away and to put his horse to the canter,
resolving to forget it. She had fallen off her horse, and
that was an end of it.

Riding fast through the wild countryside, David was
glad that he had been posted to Ireland. It was true
that there was not too much chance of advancement
here, but the racing was good, and Dublin was famous
for beautiful women. He meant to go there as often
as he could and take full advantage of all the amuse-
ments Dublin had to offer, second only to London in
that respect. It was true that he did not much relish
the task of keeping order among a civilian population,
especially with these poor devils of Irish peasants, who,
if the newspapers could be believed, were half-starving.
One would much prefer a decent war somewhere, fighting French or Afghans, or on the Indian frontier. But
there it was; the job had to be done, and David intended to do his duty to the best of his ability and try
to earn his colonel's good opinion and, if possible, a
promotion. And mostly to get what pleasure he could
out of it.

The road led toward a stream shaded with bushes and overhanging trees. As David approached he saw that the fast-flowing water became shallow and formed a stony ford. He urged his horse forward, splashing and clattering and churning up the steep bank on the far side. As he rode on David became aware of a figure straightening up from beside the water.

"Me washing! All me washing ruined!"

David reined his horse back and turned. He saw a small, slim girl, barefoot, her dress caught up to show her ragged petticoat. Laid out on the grass were various lacy items of female attire. She had dark-blond hair and green eyes, and was, David thought, amused, the prettiest washerwoman he had ever seen. He looked at the washing again. The hooves of his charger certainly had splattered the garments with black mud.

"I say," he said. "Awfully sorry. I didn't see you there."

He felt with two fingers in his pocket and brought out half a sovereign and tossed it to her. "Here," he said.

She made no effort to catch the coin. "And I suppose you think that makes everything all right?"

David was even more amused at her indignation. She stood there, hands on hips, a barefoot Irish girl, an open invitation—and it was an invitation he had no inclination to refuse. He dismounted and caught her in his arms and attempted to kiss her. She resisted, and when he persisted, she let fly with a furious tirade in a foreign language he took to be Irish. He laughed and still held her.

"I wonder what that meant?" he said. "I suspect that it wasn't entirely complimentary."

"If you don't understand the Irish language," she said, "perhaps you will have no trouble in understanding this!"

And she fetched him a clout across the side of the head which sent him staggering back, clasping his face, but still amused.

"Good God!" he exclaimed. "What a right hook! Have you been taking boxing lessons?"

"Maybe I would have," she said, "if I'd known that I would need to defend myself against an English *gentleman!*"

The word did strike home just a trifle, but David, recovering, smiled again. "My dear girl, I didn't mean to insult you—"

"Did you not?" she broke in. "I suppose it is the custom in England to kiss any young lady you chance to see, whether she will or no?"

David did not know quite what to reply. He had kissed plenty of English housemaids, certainly, but never against their will, and he had taken it for granted that a barefoot Irish peasant girl would hardly be more particular.

"I've heard," she said, "that the English ladies and gentlemen laugh at the ragged Irish with their bare feet. Well, I tell you this—a girl in Ireland needs no *chaperon*—"

She pronounced the *ch* as in *church*, with a strong note of contempt.

"—needs no chaperon," she repeated, "unless some fine English *gentleman* comes in his big boots to insult her!"

She looked so pretty with her green eyes and rosy cheeks, and yet so innocent, that David felt his heart jump like a creature imprisoned and struggling to be free.

"I really do apologize," he said.

She frowned disbelievingly. David glanced about him in the grass, saw the gold coin, stooped and picked it up.

"Please accept this," he said, "as a token of regret for my ungentlemanly behavior."

She looked at him, unmoving, still frowning. But she made no resistance as David took her hand and put the gold coin into it.

"I hope that next time we meet—" he said.

"That time will never come!" she cried.

He closed her hand upon the half-sovereign and bent his head and kissed her hand.

"I hope you're wrong," he said.

He still held her hand. "My name is David," he said.

She drew her hand away. "And mine's me own business!" she said.

But she didn't throw the coin down, and, as David mounted and rode away, he glanced back and saw her staring after him, frowning.

David was smiling as he turned a corner, still thinking of the little green-eyed, barefoot Irish girl. He became aware of a fracas on the road ahead, where a small troop of mounted soldiers were riding among a group of Irish peasants. He recognized men of his own regiment, including a sergeant and several troopers.

"There's O'Brien!" yelled the sergeant, suddenly pointing to a sturdy man with short, curly hair. "Trooper Craig, get him!"

The trooper, a big, red-faced man, spurred his horse

among the terrified women and children. The man he was pursuing saw a woman in the horse's path, a red-headed child in her arms. He had begun to run but now turned back to defend the woman.

"Get out of it, you bloody Irish beggars!" shouted Trooper Craig in a strong Scottish accent.

The woman with the child screamed and staggered aside, and the man he was pursuing seized the reins of the trooper's horse, which reared up and threw its rider to the ground. The sergeant leveled his gun, and the woman screamed again.

"No, Jim! No! Don't shoot him!"

David spurred his horse in between. "What's going on here?" he demanded.

The sergeant did not lower his weapon in order to salute, though he did go so far as to nod his acknowledgment of David's rank as the trooper got heavily to his feet, grasping his horse's reins and scowling.

"Sir," said the sergeant, "we have orders to arrest this man, O'Brien, as a rebel."

"Arrest him, perhaps," said David, "but I'm sure you have no orders to harass women and children or to shoot an unarmed man."

The sergeant reluctantly lowered his gun and nodded to Trooper Craig, who seized O'Brien. Another trooper dismounted and began to bind the man's hands behind his back. They were very rough with him, and when his wife tried to intervene, they flung her roughly off as well, even though she had a little girl in her arms. O'Brien looked up at David, and David was shaken by the naked hatred in his eyes.

"You would have done better to have let them shoot me," he said.

David had to exercise some self-control to reply coldly and calmly, in a professional manner. "You are only being arrested. You will get a fair trial."

O'Brien's great contemptuous laugh was even more shocking than his look of hatred.

"You think I'll live to see a trial?" he said. "You must be new to this country!"

Because it was true, David was angry, and puzzled, too. This was Ireland, perhaps, but it was still part of the Queen's Dominions, the British Isles. The rule of the law still ran here, as it did in England. The troopers had found a halter and now put it around O'Brien's neck. It seemed that they meant him to run in the road behind the troop, and already he had a bruised cheek and his nose was bleeding. The dark-haired woman crouched on the roadside, sobbing, rocking the little redheaded child in her arms. David wasn't sure whether he would have been so angry if he had not encountered that other wild-eyed Irish girl by the stream, but he was very angry indeed.

"Sergeant," he said, "I expect this man to arrive safely at Galway Barracks, and if there is one more mark upon him, I shall put you on a charge!"

The sergeant glared at him resentfully. "Yes, sir," he said.

David prepared to ride on but heard the sergeant's voice behind him with a sharp edge to his Ulster voice.

"Perhaps you don't know, sir, that this man was turned off his land for failing to pay his rent, and that since then he's been going around making threats against his landlord."

"Oh?" said David. "Who is the landlord?"

The sergeant looked toward O'Brien, and Trooper

Craig grinned, and in that moment David knew that he had stupidly fallen into a trap.

"Mr. Clement, of Ballyclam!" said O'Brien fiercely.

The moon was very bright that night. It shone into the window of Rachel's bedroom at Ballyclam, but it did not wake her. She had not been able to get to sleep. She tossed and turned, hot and restless, and did not know what was wrong with her. Or if she did, she would not admit it even to herself. She got out of bed and went to the window and leaned out. The entrance to the stable yard was bright in the moonlight.

Rachel fetched her cloak and put it around her shoulders over her nightgown. She tiptoed barefoot down the stairs. The kitchen was dimly lit by the red glow of the kitchen range. Crossing the huge, stone-flagged room, she was startled by a sleeping figure in front of the fire and realized that it was the boot boy, Christie, who just chanced to be Mrs. Docherty's brother's wife's nephew. He was snoring heavily, and Rachel went silently past him, slipped back the bolt and went out into the stable yard.

The little chestnut, Flame, whinnied as Rachel opened the half-door. She went inside and put her arms around him and her face down on the mane, slowly and sensuously stroking that smooth, shining body.

"Flame," she said, and then—"Rory," and was afraid to hear herself speaking his name. As she leaned against the horse's sleek neck, she saw something glinting on the stone floor. She bent down and found it was the holy medal that she had seen around Rory's neck just before he kissed her. She remembered the scent of the clover, the fierce softness of his lips.

CHAPTER 6

"Glad to see you, my boy!" cried Lord Fitzmorris. "Glad to see you!"

David was slightly surprised by the warmth of his welcome, but responded cordially enough. "Thank you, My Lord."

He was perfectly well aware of his father's gratification at the presence in Ballyclam House of the greatest landowner in the district. He was conscious, too, of his father's agent, Houlihan, lurking just inside the room.

"Would you care for a glass of Madeira, My Lord?" inquired Harry.

"Splendid! Splendid!" said Lord Fitzmorris. "Can't stay long, though."

David was aware of an intimate glance that passed between Lord Fitzmorris and John Houlihan—Irish landlord and Irish agent, with his father subtly excluded. Houlihan moved to pour the wine from the decanter, and Fitzmorris turned to David.

"Very glad," he said, "that the government is sending us some more troops at last. Not a moment too soon, if you ask me!"

"I suppose," said David, "that with the famine there is bound to be some unrest."

"Famine!" cried Lord Fitzmorris. "You don't know the people around here. At the first sign of a spoiled potato, they yell *famine* and use it as an excuse for insurrection."

Houlihan offered him a glass of Madeira, and Lord Fitzmorris paused to accept it before continuing.

"Take that fellow, O'Brien—"

"O'Brien?" said David quickly.

"Believed to be a member of the Young Irelanders, sir," said Houlihan.

He reminded David of one of those rather oily adjutants who muttered in the commanding officer's ear to ensure that he got everyone's name right.

"He actually tried to murder a soldier in broad daylight," said Lord Fitzmorris, and looked toward Harry to invite his comment.

"Shocking!" responded Harry hastily. "Quite shocking!"

David smiled. "So it would be, Father, if it were true," he said, "but it is not. I was there myself and saw the whole thing. It's true that O'Brien pulled the trooper off his horse, but he was greatly provoked—"

Lord Fitzmorris almost choked over a gulp of Madeira. "Provoked?"

Harry looked dismayed, and David found Houlihan at his elbow, offering him a glass of wine. David waved the wine and Houlihan away, but by that time Lord Fitzmorris had gotten his breath back.

"There are houses being burned and agents attacked all over the country," he said. "That's *true*, isn't it, Houlihan?"

"Quite true, My Lord."

Lord Fitzmorris looked back at David. "And yet you say that a man who was being arrested as a suspected rebel was *provoked*? That's a curious attitude for a soldier, I must say!"

Harry hastily intervened. "Lord Fitzmorris," he said,

"I'm sure my son will do his duty as energetically and as impartially as—"

He might as well have waved a red flag at a bull, as Lord Fitzmorris turned infuriated little blue eyes upon him. "Impartial?" he roared. "How can he be impartial between landowners and rebels?"

"My Lord," said David, "I only mean—I only mean to say—"

He paused, thinking of the hatred in O'Brien's eyes. Certainly a man like that was capable of acts of violence. On the other hand—he remembered the wife and child threatened by the troopers' horses. Surely it was no part of a soldier's duty to attack women and children, or to indulge in acts of violence himself? As he endeavored to find the words to express his views, Lord Fitzmorris gave an indignant snort.

"If you ask me, you have no idea *what* you mean! Hardly been in the country for ten minutes, and you think you can tell us all how to run it. That's none of your business. You have sworn to protect the Crown—"

David stiffened angrily. "Certainly, My Lord. But I've been here long enough to know that there *is* a famine—"

"David," Harry interposed nervously, "the people around here normally eat potatoes, and I'm told that they are perfectly adequate and very nourishing."

"But, Father, the potatoes are blighted! The crop has failed!"

"Quite right, my boy," said Lord Fitzmorris, suddenly calm and cheerful. "That is precisely why you are here. The potatoes have failed for the second consecutive year. It is very sad, but it is not our fault. And if the proper steps are not taken to control the troublemakers, they will turn this beautiful country of ours into a blood-soaked battlefield."

David remembered again the hatred in O'Brien's eyes.

Lord Fitzmorris stood up. "You can be as impartial as you please," he said, "in India or anywhere else, but here in Ireland your duty is to look after the interests of the landlords. We're the ones who pay the taxes—and it's not just to keep you riding around the country in a fine uniform saying that rebels like O'Brien are provoked."

He tossed off the last of his Madeira and handed the glass to Houlihan before directing his eyes toward David again—sharp little gimlet eyes in that large face.

"You do your duty, my lad!" he said, and strode to the door.

Harry took a nervous step after him and was nearly bowled over when Lord Fitzmorris turned back.

"Good-bye, Clement," he said cheerily. "You must come and shoot some partridges one day."

"Yes," said Harry, relieved. "I should like to."

David had an uneasy feeling that if his father had been a dog, he would have given an ingratiating wag of his tail.

"Houlihan," said Lord Fitzmorris, "I want a word with you. You'd better consult with my man, Sinclair, about getting the wheat shipped out."

He went out, and Houlihan followed him with a slight, deprecating glance at Harry.

"Damned impudence!" said David. "Discussing your affairs with your agent without so much as a by your leave!"

He strolled to the window and saw Lord Fitzmorris

preparing to get into his coach and speaking to Houlihan, both glancing back toward the house.

"None of my business!" David said indignantly.
"What does he think I am—a fool?"

He turned away from the window and saw his father's
expression.

"He thinks you are the son of a landlord," said
Harry, "and so you are."

"Father—" David protested.

"I am a landlord now, David," said Harry. "I have
a—a position to maintain, and if we are to live in this
country, I have to accept that. And so do you."

David looked at him in dismay. Was it possible that
the inheritance of Ballyclam could turn his kind,
thoughtful father into an unfeeling brute like Lord
Fitzmorris? Could he really ignore the signs that had
already impressed themselves upon David's reluctant
eyes—the ragged, starving people, the broken, ruined
cabins, the land laid waste by tragedy?

"I shall do my duty by my tenants, naturally," said
Harry, "but Lord Fitzmorris is right: these are difficult times, and we have to know which side we are on."

He saw David's troubled look and suddenly smiled.
Harry never could be stern or angry for long. "We
shall soon get used to it all," he said. "Don't forget,
David, Ballyclam will belong to *you* one day."

He put his arm around David's shoulder. "How
about having that glass of Madeira now, eh?"

David laughed and tried to put behind him the
thought of the rotting potatoes and of the woman
sobbing in the ditch with her child.

"Good idea, Father," he said. "I'm sure you're right."

* * *

But it was easy that evening to forget the harsher side of Irish life. The three Clements were delighted to be together again, enjoying each other's company in their new home. The candles in the chandelier of Waterford glass shone down upon the gracious dining room, the polished wood and fine silver, and Mrs. Docherty had produced one of her most remarkable dinners in honor of David's first night at Ballyclam.

"I can't imagine how she did it," said Rachel, "when they are holding the wedding in the kitchen tonight." She chuckled. "But I expect that most of this was prepared for the party, and that *we* are getting the leftovers."

"There you are, David," said Harry resignedly. "Now you see the penalties of being a landowner—you not only have to feed your servants but most of their relatives as well!"

David's eyes met Rachel's in shared, affectionate amusement. It really was delightful to see their father playing the part of the man of property and enjoying it so much!

After dinner David and Rachel strolled out onto the terrace. She drew her shawl about her bare shoulders, and they stood in silence for a few minutes, gazing out into the moonlit garden.

"I think Irish nights smell sweeter than English ones," she said.

David found himself remembering the little Irish girl by the stream, with her burnished hair and green eyes.

"I believe they do," he said.

They became conscious of music coming from the direction of the kitchen quarters, a curious combination of violin and penny whistle from the sound of it.

"What on earth is that?" exclaimed David.

"It must be Bridget's wedding party."

They listened to the music.

"How can it sound so cheerful and yet so sad?" said Rachel. She suddenly clutched David's arm. "Come on, let's go and pay them a visit."

"No, better not. They would think it an imposition," replied David.

"Of course they wouldn't. Mrs. Docherty would be delighted. And after all, it *is* our kitchen."

"All the more reason not to force our company upon them."

"But I have a present for Bridget, and I haven't given it to her yet."

"Very well," said David, "*you* go. I'll stay here and smoke my pipe."

"Oh no," cried Rachel, "I wouldn't like to go alone. And anyway, I expect you are right. I don't want to embarrass them."

But as she prepared to go inside, she cast a longing glance toward the sorrowful gaiety of the foot-tapping music.

David laughed. "All right," he said. "I know you want to go. If I must, I must."

Rachel and David paused in the doorway of the kitchen. The huge, crowded stone-flagged room was lit only by the turf fire in the hearth and by tallow candles that threw a mellow glow on the smiling faces and the dark or russet heads of the dancers who moved, lively and yet graceful, to the music. In the far corner a man with the face of a saint and the noble gray head of a king made his violin sing, and beside him Michael O'Connor, his round red face shining with heat, drink and enthusiasm, played an instrument that appeared to be something between a penny whistle and a fife.

Almost immediately Rachel caught sight of Rory dancing with a girl with black eyes and an impudent smile, and David, glancing toward the fireplace, saw the priest talking to a slender girl with shining hair and green eyes. He knew her at once for the girl he had met by the stream. In that instant the assembled company became aware of David and Rachel in the doorway. The music stopped. The gaiety vanished as though an evil spell had fallen on the room, and dancers and spectators alike stared motionless toward the door. David, in his scarlet uniform, saw hostility in the faces of the men, and Rachel saw the eyes of the women upon her low-cut evening gown.

Oh, God! she thought, we shouldn't have come! Oh, why did we come?

The gray-haired musician rose and spoke with old-fashioned courtesy. "Welcome, my young lady. Welcome, sir. Won't you join the company?"

"Thank you," said David. "Thank you, Mr.—?"

"O'Manion. Shane O'Manion."

Rachel was reminded of Houlihan's words and thought that it was not difficult to believe that Rory's father was descended from the kings of Ireland. The evil spell was broken. There was a stir and murmur and a few smiles, and Mrs. Docherty hastened to greet them and to introduce Father O'Dowd. Rachel gave her gift to Bridget, who stood blushing in her plain white dress, with flowers in her hair, beside her young bridegroom in his ill-fitting black suit, clearly borrowed or inherited. Then Shane O'Manion, with a smile and a nod and a tap of the foot, put his fiddle under his chin and set the dancing going again.

The room was very warm, and Rachel was glad to accept from Mrs. Docherty a glass of lemonade. David, on the other hand, had been presented with a glass of honey-colored liquid poured from a large stone jug, which was freely circulating among the men and the older women. He took a sip of it and nearly choked.

"Do you know," he said quietly to Rachel when he could speak again, "I believe this is poteen."

"It's what?"

"Whiskey, brewed in an illicit still."

"Is it good?" inquired Rachel.

David cautiously tasted it again. "Excellent!" he said. "We'd better ask Tobin if he can buy some for Father."

Rachel laughed, but saw David's eyes go past her and glanced around to see a baby in its woven basket lying by the hearth, and Deirdre bending over him.

"The music doesn't seem to trouble your little brother, Deirdre," she said, seeing Sean sleeping peacefully.

Deirdre smiled. "Ah, sure, Miss Rachel," she replied, "my father has been the fiddler of Ballyclam for as long as I can remember, and the house is always full of music. 'Tis when the music stops that Sean will cry."

She turned away and found that David had stepped past Rachel so that she came face to face with him.

"Good evening," he said. "You didn't let me finish my sentence the other day. I was going to say, I hope when we meet again, you will be good enough to teach me some Irish dancing."

She eyed him severely. "Irish dancing needs no teaching," she said. "You just let your feet follow the music."

But David had seen the dimple in her cheek, and when he took her hand to draw her out into the dance, she did not resist.

Rachel watched them, smiling, her own foot tapping

in time to the irresistible gaiety of the jig, but she saw Rory nearby drop out of the dance scowling, as David and Deirdre entered it, as though he would not share even this innocent pleasure with an English officer. Rachel hesitated and then called out to him.

"Rory!"

He turned with a fierce glance under his dark brows that made her catch her breath. She felt in the netted purse she wore at her waist and brought out the silver medal. She had mended the chain and had been carrying it about with her, waiting for the right opportunity to return it to him—or so, at least, she told herself.

"I think I have something that belongs to you," she said. "I found it—"

She stopped short, and the color came into her cheeks as she realized the awkwardness of telling him that she had found it when she went looking for him in the tack room. But he was too glad to see it to notice her hesitation.

"Thank you," he replied. "I thought I'd lost it forever."

As he took it from her, she thought that he had never before shown her so undefended a face. He stood looking down at the medal in his hand and then, glancing up, met Rachel's eyes.

"It was my mother's," he said. "She died when Sean was born."

"I'm so sorry," said Rachel.

Just then Shane OManion spoke over his fiddle's music. "Won't you join in the dancing, my lady?"

Rachel looked up at Rory. Though she couldn't tell whether it was in anger or pleasure, he took her hand. As they began the jig, Rachel saw that Padraic had approached with the intention of asking her to dance. His face still reflected his disappointment.

But, for as much as Rachel liked and admired the gentle Padraic, she was glad it was with his tempestuous brother that she was dancing.

David and Deirdre danced together, hands clasping hands in the firelight.

"It's fortunate that we are not now beside the stream," said David.

"Why is that?" asked Deirdre, but an unexpectedly wicked sparkle in her eyes showed that she knew quite well.

"I'm afraid I should get another box on the ears."

"Indeed, you asked for it!" said Deirdre with spirit.

"So I did, Deirdre," said David humbly.

Deirdre's eyes stopped sparkling and flashed angrily. "My name is Miss O'Manion," she said.

"Yes. Of course. I beg your pardon," said David.

But his hands were in hers, and their feet moved together in time to that Irish music with its unique blend of sweetness, gaiety and sorrow.

"You can call me Deirdre," she said.

Rachel, dancing lightly and easily with Rory, saw the young bride and groom standing together and smiled, but then saw the tears streaming down their faces. She looked quickly at Rory, frowning. He answered her unspoken question.

"For them this is not only a wedding party. It is farewell."

"Farewell?"

"Tomorrow they sail for America."

"America? Why?"

Rory's face hardened. "To have children who'll know the taste of milk and meat and eggs. They must go to America and leave behind all that they love, or stay here and starve."

He saw the stricken look in Rachel's face and spoke more gently. "Our hearts will be with them, and theirs with ours. But never in this life will they see Ireland again."

In the glow from the flickering flames, Rachel saw tears glistening in Rory's eyes and felt that though he still held her hand, he had left her alone again.

CHAPTER 7

Carralough Castle, built by the Normans five hundred years before, stood above the smooth lawns and well-kept flower gardens, as incongruous as a granite grave-stone in a drawing room.

"Jasus!" said Tom Noonan as they crouched behind the sunken fence. " 'Tis like putting your head in the lion's mouth and asking him to oblige you by shutting his jaws!"

"Lions have teeth to be pulled, like anyone else," said Rory, "and we're here to pull 'em. Third window from the left. Come on!"

He led the way, and the others ran after him, dark figures loping across the shadowed lawn.

"Give me a boost up," said Rory.

It was an anxious moment until he could reach high enough up the tall window to find that little gap in the apparently fastened latch, slip his fingers in and push it up. There was a nerve-wrenching moment as the window creaked when he pulled it on its ratchet, but the next minute he had it open wide enough to scramble inside.

"Come on!" he said.

Eamon Fleming was the second to leap down onto the polished oak floor, with Tim O'Farrell after him and Tom Noonan, nervously, last. The hall was as big as a barn, with a huge, curved staircase winding up out of sight at the far end. But opposite the windows the light of the waning moon glimmered onto a glass-fronted cupboard, full of sporting guns.

"Where's Joe Kerrigan?" said Rory.

Tom Noonan jerked his head toward the window. "He said he'd wait to take the guns from us."

"Right," said Rory. "Let's get 'em!"

Eamon was already at the cupboard. "Mistrustful old devil!" he exclaimed under his breath. "He's put a new lock on it!"

Rory looked in dismay at the shiny new lock and then at Eamon, and in the moonlight saw Eamon grin as he produced from his pocket one of his father's medical instruments and began to force the lock.

"Keep it quiet, Eamon!" Tom Noonan begged.

Rory and Tim exchanged an amused look, but it was agonizing all the same to hear that metallic scraping noise echoing in the huge, silent castle.

"Murder-in-Irish, Eamon!" muttered Rory. "If this is how long you take to operate, the patient will be dead and buried and you still trying to get inside him!"

There was a clatter and the cupboard swung open, and in the very instant a voice shouted, "Who's that? Who's there?"

"It's himself!" said Tim O'Farrell. "Run for it!"

Tom Noonan needed no second bidding, and the two of them arrived at the window at the same instant and, panic-stricken, tried to struggled through it together. The blast of a shotgun shattering the glass beside them somehow overcame the laws of natural dynamics and they tumbled through. Eamon, following them, glanced up the staircase and saw, aghast, the huge figure of Lord Fitzmorris, wearing riding boots and a pink hunting coat aver his nightgown, standing at the top of the stairs, shotgun in hand. Heading for the window and feeling horribly exposed on the bare expanse of the polished moonlit floor, Eamon was even more aghast when, glancing back, he saw that Rory was still by the cupboard.

Eamon turned back. "Rory!" he gasped, "for God's, sake, get out of here!"

The shotgun blasted again, and Eamon realized that in turning back he had saved his own life. Frightened out of his wits, he grabbed Rory and hustled him toward the window, bundled him out and fell headlong after him. He felt a fearful pain and saw Rory set off running, but could not follow.

"My ankle!" he gasped.

Rory turned back, swearing, and hauled Eamon up over his shoulder like a sack of wheat and staggered away with him across the moonlit grass. They had no doubt that His Lordship would be clattering down the staircase, reloading as he came.

"Come on, Rory! Come on!" cried Tom Noonan, and Rory fell after him just as the shotgun thundered out again.

They all crouched, groaning for breath, in the hollow, their faces pressed to the damp grass.

"Let's find Michael and get clear before he has the keepers and the dogs after us," said Tim O'Farrell, adding bitterly, "All that, and not a single gun did we get!"

"What makes you think that?" inquired Rory, and they saw him grin.

Rory had not come away from the raid empty-handed. The moonlight glimmered on the barrel of a gun.

Joe Kerrigan had already run to warn Michael O'Connor of trouble, and Michael was waiting to whip up old Lightning and be off. When the others had been dropped off at the crossroad, Michael drove on to the doctor's house, and Rory helped Eamon in by the back door, hopping and groaning with the pain of his injured ankle.

"Is it broken?" said Rory.

Eamon shook his head. "Sprained, I think, but it hurts like hell. I'll have to fall downstairs tomorrow. My father will want to know how it happened."

"It's easier to explain than a load of buckshot in the seat of your breeches," said Rory with an unfeeling grin. He helped Eamon to the foot of the stairs.

"I can manage now," said Eamon, but he still kept hold of Rory's arm. "Rory, was there an informer?"

Rory looked at him quickly, puzzled.

"Was he waiting for us?" said Eamon.

"No! If he'd known we were coming, he'd've had every man in the castle waiting to capture us."

"But if he didn't know which day, but only that a raid was planned? Did you tell Joe Kerrigan to wait outside?"

Rory understood the question he was really asking. "Ah, get away with you! He's one of us. He took an oath, like the rest of us. It was *you* woke His Lordship, making enough row with that damned scalpel of yours to wake the dead!"

"Maybe," said Eamon.

They started at a noise from upstairs and realized with relief that it was Dr. Fleming snoring. Rory grinned again.

"Just you get on two feet again," he said. "The sooner we rescue Jim O'Brien from Galway Barracks, the better—and we can do it now we have a gun."

Eamon, beginning to hop up the stairs, turned, open-mouthed, hanging onto the banisters.

"One gun?" he demanded in a hoarse whisper. "One gun against Galway Barracks?"

Rory was still grinning. "I'll think of something," he said.

"Come on, Flame!" cried Rachel, clapping her hands with excitement. "Come on, Rory! Oh, he's winning! He's winning! Come on, Flame!"

The Crossmalin races were in full swing, and although the racecourse consisted of no more than a field, with the course marked out with sticks, it could not have generated more enthusiasm if it had been the Derby with a royal horse running. There was a makeshift wooden stand at one end for the gentry, and the general population moved cheerfully about it, making bets and drinking frequently from suspicious-looking stone bottles that circulated under the noses of the two policemen. Their lack of curiosity as to the origin of the contents of the bottles could possibly have derived from the fact that every so often they strolled behind the stand themselves and, as they said, had a wee nip.

Rory, bending low over Flame's neck, flashed past

the winning post, beating Lord Fitzmorris's horse into second place.

Rachel watched them go and then descended from the stand, still smiling, and made her way toward Rory, who had dismounted and was loosening Flame's girth.

"Oh, well done, Rory!" she called, hurrying to put her arms around the horse's neck. "My dear little Flame! I knew he could do it!"

"Look out!" said Rory. "He's sweating. You'll get your pretty dress dirty."

"Oh, what do I care for that!" cried Rachel. "It was a famous victory, and everyone was so pleased."

Rory glanced at her sideways, and then gave the reins to his young brother standing near.

"Here, Brian, walk him up and down for a bit, and then I'll ride him back to Ballyclam."

"He never waits for orders!" thought Rachel, half-amused and half-annoyed, and said aloud, "Perhaps *I* would like to ride him home."

"You're not dressed for it," said Rory, "and, besides, you'd ride him too fast. He's won the race for you. Isn't that enough?"

"Yes, quite enough!" said Rachel, smiling. "Look after him, Brian."

She was shocked by the look she received from the redheaded boy in return, a cold, silent look of hostility, before he led the horse away. But no, she thought, she must have been mistaken. Why should young Brian hate her? She refused to let it spoil her enjoyment.

"I am so glad we came," she said. "Papà did not want to. He never went to the races in England, and I am sure I would never have either. But it is so different in Ireland. Everyone is so happy."

"*Happy?*" said Rory.

She looked at him, startled.

"How can they be happy," demanded Rory, "when they are starving?"

Rachel stared at him, stunned by the suddenness and sharpness of the attack.

"He won!" cried Rachel. "Oh, Father, I knew he would!"

She turned and hugged Harry, delighted, and all the crowd below laughed and clapped, delighted at her pleasure.

"God bless you, my young lady!" cried one large man just below her. "It's glad I am your little horse won, though every penny I possess was on Black Carraig!"

Lord Fitzmorris, bluff and good-humored, called out from his place next to Harry. "Tom O'Halloran," he said, "aren't you ashamed to be getting drunk and betting on horses instead of feeding your family?"

"I am that, Your Lordship!" Tom O'Halloran called back, staggering slightly. "Indeed I am!"

Everyone laughed, and Rachel laughed, too. There was something irresistible in the happy-go-lucky way in which the Irish took their pleasure in the moment, obeying with unforced enthusiasm the biblical command to take no thought for the morrow.

"You see, my dear Clement?" remarked Lord Fitzmorris, turning carelessly to Harry. "Give these people money to relieve their distress, and what do they spend it on? Drink!"

"Yes, My Lord," agreed Harry, amused. "I see what you mean."

He turned, still smiling, to David, and was surprised to see him frowning.

"Come on, my lad," he said, cheerfully, "let's go and

collect our winnings. Rachel, this will buy you a new bonnet!"

"Look!" he said. "Look around you! Do you think the Irish people are ragged and barefoot by choice? Do you think they *choose* to look like skeletons and send their children begging?"

It was as though the happy, drunken, cheerful Irish crowd had vanished, and in its place she saw individual faces and figures, vivid and horrible, as in a nightmare. Hollow-cheeked, with sticklike arms and legs and wild eyes sunk in their sockets, they had that awful quality of the pitiful and the repulsive.

"No," she said, again, but this time it was in protest against what she was forced to see.

"They live all the year round on potatoes," said Rory, "and grow wheat that they sell to keep the roof over their heads. But the rent goes up and up until they cannot pay it, and now the potatoes have failed for the second year, and they have nothing to eat—nothing at all!"

"Don't!" cried Rachel. "Don't! I am very sorry if the people are hungry, I am sorry. But—"

"*Are* you?" Rory broke in contemptuously. "What do you care? Let them starve! They are only Irish!"

He turned away. "Brian!" he called.

Rachel found herself trembling as she watched him tighten the girth and mount Flame and ride away. And as her eyes met Brian's, she saw again, this time unmistakably, that terrifying look of hatred. She went to find her father, still beaming and triumphant, with his winnings in his hand.

"Papa," she said, "do you mind if I go home?"

He was instantly solicitous. "My dear, are you unwell? I'll come with you."

"No, I am just a little tired. I don't want to spoil your pleasure. I will send the coach back for you and David."

Leaning back in the corner of the coach, Rachel thought that she might have said to her father, "I am just suddenly very old." Children only feel their own sorrows. The first step out of childhood is to feel the sorrows of another. Rory, in forcing her to feel the sorrows of Ireland, had robbed her of her childhood, and she suffered the loss of that innocent, unfeeling creature who had stepped ashore at Galway as though it were an untroubled Eden.

Rory did not, in fact, ride Flame straight back to Ballyclam. Instead he rode him at an easy pace to Galway, reining back above the barracks. The great granite edifice made his heart sink. From the top of the hill, he could look straight down into the courtyard, and looking at its barred windows and closely guarded doorway, he was pretty sure that he knew where the prisoners would be kept. But the whole place was swarming with soldiers, and the huge castellated gateway was guarded, like the gates of heaven, with St. Peter taking a day off and handing them over to Oliver Cromwell for the occasion. It wasn't often that Rory's courage abandoned him, but this was one of those times.

He had dismounted to give Flame some breathing time before the return journey and was about to mount again when he became aware of some activity at the main gateway. A coach had arrived at the gate, a coach with a crest on its side and a coachman and footman in a familiar livery. The gates were opened. It seemed to Rory that there was a great deal of saluting and very little close examination.

"Well, well," said Rory. "Lord Fitzmorris, coming to dine with the colonel, no doubt."

A beatific smile spread over his face. "Flame, me little Irish beauty," he said, "I think you and me will go and fetch that gun and put it in a safer place. I believe I might just have a use for it."

When the last race was over, David, about to get into the carriage, paused. He had just caught sight of a group of girls talking and laughing, and one particular girl parting from them.

"Father," said David, "I think I'll walk back to Ballyclam—get up an appetite for Mrs. Docherty's dinner."

He was strengthened in his resolve to walk home by the sight of Houlihan in the carriage, whom Harry, in the exuberance of two more wins, had invited to dinner that night.

"Miss Deirdre!" called David.

She turned, startled.

"Are you alone?"

"Oh—yes. Maeve and Sean were tired, so Father took them home early."

"Then—may I escort you?"

She glanced at him but did not say no, so he fell into step beside her.

They walked in silence, except for a word or two about the races and the wedding, but they both knew that the moment would come when they paused beside the stream and turned to each other.

"You had better not come any further," said Deirdre. "My father would not like to see us together."

"Very well," said David.

But he did not move, and neither did she. They

stood staring at each other until he bent and kissed her.

"No box on the ears?" he said gently.

He kissed her again. Suddenly she broke free, pushing him away.

"No!" she cried. "No!"

"Deirdre!"

"No. 'Tis myself is to blame," she said. "I should never have walked home with you."

"Ah, Deirdre," said David. "My beautiful Deirdre!" and drew her close again.

"How can you be so cruel?" she said.

He looked at her, aghast. "Cruel?" he said. "What harm can there be in a kiss or two?"

"And then what?" she demanded.

He could not answer. He had not thought beyond that moment. She turned away.

"Do you think I'd allow just anyone to kiss me?" she said. "Supposing I should come to care for you—what could it lead to but grief and sorrow? You an English officer, and me an O'Manion! Would you think what that means? Would you think what Rory would do if he knew?"

She turned back, and their eyes met.

"I can't think of anything," said David, "except what I feel for you."

He kissed her again, and this time she put her arms around his neck and kissed him back.

At that instant Rory stepped out from behind the bushes on the far side of the stream.

"Stand aside, Deirdre," he said.

David turned quickly and saw Rory pointing a gun at his heart.

CHAPTER 8

On his way back from Galway, Rory had stopped at the Fleming house, and Eamon limped out of the back door to join him.

"You'd better hurry up and lose that limp," said Rory. "It'll be a sight too conspicuous."

"Heaven defend us!" said Eamon. "I know that look in your eye. You've got some mad scheme for rescuing Jim O'Brien."

"Not mad at all," said Rory, with a wicked look. "Very sane and practical, and it'll only need the four of us—you, me, Michael O'Connor and Tom Noonan."

"Tom Noonan?" said Eamon, surprised. "Are you sure he won't cut and run at the last minute?"

"I'm not sure at all," replied Rory wtih a grin, "and I wish he was a foot taller for this particular job, but Tim O'Farrell has a wife and children and I don't want to ask him to risk it."

"How about Joe Kerrigan?" inquired Eamon with a shrewd glance.

Rory was silent for a moment while Flame nibbled the grass on the verge.

"Ah well," he said, avoiding Eamon's eyes, "no sense in taking more chances than we have to." He looked up and pulled a slight face, then held out his hand. "Did you get that ammunition?"

Eamon felt in his pocket and brought out a small canvas bag. One great advantage of having in the organization a highly respectable Protestant medical student was that he could walk into a gunsmith's in Galway and buy ammunition without the least question or suspicion.

"Thanks," said Rory, taking it. "Too bad I didn't have time to pick up some of His Lordship's, but you seemed to be in such a hurry to be off."

He shortened the reins and prepared to ride on, but he paused, and the cheerful glint came back into his eye.

"You'd better have your father's scalpel ready," he said, "for Galway Barracks. If anything goes wrong we'll all need to cut our throats!"

"Oh, God!" exclaimed Eamon, "it *is* a mad scheme. I knew it!"

Rory rode on, laughing.

On the hillside above the O'Manion cabin was a broken-down cow byre, and it was here that Rory had hidden the gun after the raid on Carralough Castle. He was far from sure that he had not been recognized, and he was certainly likely to be suspected. He had no desire whatever for the police or soldiers to find the gun in his bed if they came to search the house. Now he drew it out from beneath the ruined thatch and took it from the piece of sacking in which he had wrapped it, rubbing the polished barrel lovingly. Flame blew through his nostrils and jerked away from the unfamiliar object.

"Whisht, now, Flame!" said Rory. "You'll oblige me by taking care of this for a while at Ballyclam. I'm sure the young lady would not have the least objection. I won her race for her, and she can do me a favor in return."

He prepared to wrap the gun up again but at that moment caught sight of two figures by the stream below. He knew Deirdre at once, and the other a second later. As he identified David Clement, he saw them embrace. A cold rage took hold of him. His sister with an English officer—and the landlord's son at that! He tethered Flame behind the shed, took out the ammunition, loaded the gun and came quietly down the hill.

"No, Rory!" cried Deirdre as she saw the gun. "Rory, no!"

Rory ignored her, keeping his eyes on David.

"Isn't it enough for you," he said, "that you take our land, but you must take our women as well?"

"It isn't like that," said David.

"Is it not?" said Rory. "Because you danced with her in the kitchen at Ballyclam House, you thought that she was there for your pleasure—and that you could toss her a few coins in payment, no doubt!"

David looked at Deirdre, stricken, and then back at Rory.

"She—I—"

"Don't die with a lie on your lips," said Rory contemptuously.

He leveled the gun again, his finger on the trigger.

"Very well," said David. "The truth is that I love your sister."

He did not know it until he said it, but the moment he said it he knew that it was true.

"No, David!" cried Deirdre, horrified. "Don't say that!"

David kept his eyes on Rory. "I love her, and I want to be a friend to Ireland."

"The best thing you can do for Ireland," said Rory, "is to leave here and never come back."

"My father owns Ballyclam," said David. "Ireland is my country now, as much as yours."

Rory could not escape the sincerity in his words, though he refused to accept them.

"Then I'll have your promise," he said, "here and now, that you'll never see my sister again."

"It would be best, David," cried Deirdre, her eyes fixed fearfully on the gun. "Indeed, it would."

David glanced at her and smiled and moved a strand of hair out of her eyes, and then looked back at Rory.

"I'm sorry," he said. "I'm afraid that is a promise I cannot give."

He turned and began to walk back toward the crossroad. Deirdre saw Rory level the gun and take aim.

"No, Rory, no!" she screamed.

David paused for a moment and then walked on. Rory's finger closed on the trigger, and the gun exploded. David stopped, his face rigid with shock. The bullet had hit the tree beside him, and a piece of bark grazed his cheek. He felt the blood and turned, and saw Rory's eyes, cold and fierce.

"That was just to show you I meant it," he said.

"So did I," said David. And then, with a change of tone, "By the way, your possession of that gun is quite illegal. I advise you to get rid of it as soon as possible."

He turned and walked on toward Ballyclam, and Rory glared after him, angry and frustrated but reluctantly admiring his courage.

"Deirdre," he began, but was stopped in his tracks by the look she turned upon him.

"I am your sister, Rory," she said. "I am not your slave!"

She ran lightly across the stones in her bare feet and was walking toward the O'Manion house with that new, proud swing to her step before he could find an answer.

* * *

"My dear Miss Clement," said Houlihan at dinner that evening, "if the tenants don't pay their rent, then of course they have to be evicted. Otherwise"—he threw a quick, ingratiating smile at Harry and at David—"otherwise, what would happen to the landlord?"

"I admit it isn't pleasant," said Harry.

"Pleasant!" cried Rachel.

Tobin offered her a dish of Mrs. Docherty's wild duck, cooked with juniper berries and red wine, and she helped herself.

"It's horrible!" she said.

Harry glanced uneasily at Houlihan as Tobin trod on in his down-at-heel, squeaking shoes to offer the dish to David.

"The expenses of this house have to be kept up," said Houlihan, "and the servants' wages paid, and the estates maintained. The money has to come from somewhere—unless you want your father to be ruined?"

"No, no, of course not!" said Rachel.

She was aware of Houlihan helping himself to a double portion of duck. Horrible man, with his big nose and small eyes, like a vulture! What right had he to eat so much and stay so thin?

"We . . . we have to collect the rents, Rachel," said Harry. "What would we live on if we didn't? Who would pay for your clothes, for David's allowance?"

Rachel looked across the table at David and saw dismay in his face.

"But they're hungry!" said Rachel. "The people are hungry. They're *starving!*"

David cleared his throat. "Surely, Father," he said, "there must be some way of feeding the people here."

"I assure you, Lieutenant Clement," said Houlihan, "that if we gave them food without them working for it, they would never work again."

"So we just sit here, and eat," cried Rachel, "and let them starve!"

She pushed her chair back and ran out of the room. David got up and would have followed her, but Harry stopped him.

"My dear David," he said irritably, "sit down and eat your dinner. You, too, Houlihan. There's no point in letting good food go to waste."

But he himself got up and followed Rachel out while David and Houlihan continued their meal under the subtly critical eye of Tobin.

Harry found Rachel on the terrace and came toward her, still irritable and unsettled.

"My dear Rachel," he said, "you are taking all this much too much to heart."

She turned to him. "Papa, it's murder!"

"There, now!" exclaimed Harry, exasperated. "That's just what I mean. It's very distressing, but it isn't murder. It's not *our* fault that the potatoes have failed, and the government is doing what it can—soup kitchens, work schemes—"

"But it isn't enough!" cried Rachel desperately.

"My dear girl, there's nothing *we* can do!" said Harry angrily. "We can't come here and change this country overnight!"

Rachel turned on him with equal anger, but then she saw the troubled look in his face.

"I know, Papa," she said.

He put his arm around her and they looked together out into the sweet-scented garden.

"Remember all those years," said Harry, "when

things were hard for us? If your uncle hadn't sent us money from Philadelphia, there were times when we might have gone hungry ourselves. Now that we have our bit of peace and good fortune, don't you think we might enjoy it?"

She leaned her head against his shoulder. "Yes, Papa. Oh, yes."

It was a prayer rather than a promise. She reached up and kissed his cheek.

"Go and finish your dinner," she said. "Mrs. Docherty told me her wild duck was fit for St. Patrick himself, so I'm sure it's not too good for you, my dearest, kindest Father!"

"Won't you come, too, Rachel?"

But she had seen over his shoulder the glimmer of a light from the stable yard.

"No, thank you. I will have some broth later if I want it. Don't worry, I shan't starve."

She said the words, smiling, without thinking, but they touched a tender nerve in his conscience, and he stiffened and took his hand away.

"Of course you won't, my dear," he said. "Why should you?"

He turned and went inside.

Rachel leaned on the balcony, smelling that fatally sweet, damp Irish night air and seeing the mellow golden glow of light from the stable. She knew that it was foolish—dangerous, even—to go there, but as she drew her shawl about her and walked down the steps, it seemed that she went like a sleepwalker, her eyes wide open but unseeing, moved by some unseen power outside herself.

Rory stood up quickly as she came to the doorway of the stable.

"I saw the light," she said.

He put something quickly out of sight and turned to face her. "You should be at dinner," he said roughly, "with that fine soldier brother of yours."

"Don't," she said. "Don't be angry." She moved about the stable, touching saddles, bridles, his coat where it hung from a peg. She knew that his eyes followed her.

"I couldn't forget what you said to me at the races," she said.

"At least you listened," he said. "Ireland has spoken to deaf ears for too long."

"Ireland!" she said. "Is that all you ever think about?"

He didn't move, but his voice changed. "I can think of other things," he said, "in their time and place."

"What kind of things?" She knew it was a dangerous question, but she asked it just the same, and she knew that he would take a step toward her, as he did.

"I think of a wild ride with a wild, foolish girl. I think of grass so sweet it makes my body ache."

He came closer. "I think of a land that comes in the night, like a woman with dark hair, whispering of love. She is very jealous. But if a man is true to her in his heart, she understands—that he is a man."

He was very close now, and now, too late, she fully understood the danger.

"I must go!" she said, but his hands were upon her.

"Rachel."

She remained very still, but he twitched the shawl from her bare shoulders, and she felt his hands stroking and searching, soothing and arousing. Flame whinnied in his stall.

"Rachel, look at me."

Slowly she turned in his embrace, and their bodies melted together like one body.

"Say my name."

"Rory."

He kissed her, gently at first, and then with increasing passion.

"Yes, Rory, oh yes! Yes!"

CHAPTER 9

Next morning it had been arranged that Rachel and Harry should pay calls on some neighbors. Patrick O'Fee brought the coach around to the front door, quite sober at such an early hour, and Rory went to the horses' heads as Rachel and her father descended the steps. Padraic, painting the fence nearby, noticed that Rachel did not speak to Rory or even smile at him, and yet he was conscious of some new awareness that flashed between them like summer lightning, so swift and invisible that he thought he might have imagined it—and yet he knew that he had not. Then the carriage bowled away down the drive, and Rory stood watching it go. Padraic put down his paintbrush— Harry Clement, in his innocence, had chosen the color green!—and came to join him.

"They say Jim O'Brien is to be put on trial soon," he said.

"So they say," Rory agreed briefly.

He began to turn away, but Padraic stopped him. "Don't do it, Rory. Let him come to trial."

Rory turned on him. "He's accused of assaulting a soldier. What trial would he have?"

Padraic hesitated. "But every time you defeat the law by violence, there's less chance that we can use the law to protect our people."

"Tell that to Jim O'Brien," said Rory, "when they're hanging him."

Padraic couldn't find an answer.

"Do you still say I should leave him there?" demanded Rory.

"You've no chance of succeeding!"

"I can try," said Rory.

"Oh, damn you, Rory!" said Padraic with sudden rage. "If you're bound and determined to do it—"

"I am," Rory broke in, "and there's an end of it."

"All right," said Padraic, "then what can I do to help?"

Rory, turning away again, stopped short, turned back to stare at him and began to laugh.

"Well, well, my little brother, there's a bit of the devil in you, after all. You're not quite the angel you'd have us believe."

"And not so much of the *little*!" said Padraic. "Just because you insisted on coming into the world first—"

"Ah well," said Rory, "I always was an impatient man. Did you mean it?"

"Yes."

"Then you'll be glad to know there'll be no violence; not if I can help it. Will you cover for me tomorrow afternoon? Don't say I'm not here—just that I'm up at the barn getting some hay or something like that. Oh, devil take it, you can think of some lie for once!"

"I'll try," said Padraic solemnly, "though it'll stick in my gullet. Anything else?"

"No," said Rory. "Oh—yes."

His eye had fallen upon Padraic's occupation. "I see that Mr. Clement has a fancy to have his fence painted green. Maybe you'd just put a pot of that green paint under your coat when you come home tonight!"

Lord Fitzmorris's coachman sat on the box waiting for his master. Lord Fitzmorris was attending a meeting of landlords in the big room above the office of the Board of Works in Crossmalin. The road immediately outside was too narrow for the coach to remain there, so the coachman had drawn up a short distance away in the square, but he had chosen a position from which he could keep his eyes on the doorway. His Lordship did not like to be kept waiting, and the moment he emerged, the coachman must wheel his team around, pull up outside the entrance, one footman must jump down and run to the horses' heads and the other must open the door of the coach so that His Lordship could step straight inside. The meeting was likely to last for some considerable time and, in fact, the coachman could hear the angry voices through the window and even distinguish his master's furious bellow above the rest. But he was a careful man and was taking no chances. Lord Fitzmorris had once emerged unexpectedly and very nearly caught him leaning against the wheel smoking his pipe, and he only escaped instant dismissal by pretending to examine the traces with the hot pipe in his pocket burning his leg to the bone. So now he sat with his eyes fixed intently upon the doorway.

A voice spoke behind him. "Don't turn your head.

There's a gun at your back. If you move so much as a whisker, you're a dead man."

Lord Fitzmorris's coachman was a careful man, and he had not the least desire to be dead. He did not move so much as a whisker.

Some time later a coach approached the huge gates of Galway Barracks. The sentry, seeing the familiar livery of the footman on the box and recognizing the coachman's cockaded hat, merely glanced inside to salute the top-hatted figure sitting at his ease in the far corner, and waved the coach through. He might, perhaps, if he had looked attentively after it, have noticed that the second footman, standing up behind seemed rather small for the livery he was wearing, and extremely small, in fact, to be a footman at all. Fortunately the sentry had no curiosity about the coach whatever. Lord Fitzmorris was a frequent visitor to the barracks and was often entertained to dinner at the mess. Moreover, it was a gray evening, and the light was not very good.

The coach bowled briskly around the courtyard and came to rest, rather uncertainly, outside the guard room. Every straining button on the coachman's coat was more than doing its duty, as though it had been made for a less portly man, and one might have wondered, too, whether he was accustomed to driving quite such mettlesome horses. The footman on the box climbed down and went to open the door. The footman standing up behind remained where he was. It could be that if he had attempted to descend he would have fallen over the tail of his coat. The occupant of the coach prepared to descend just as the regimental sergeant-major emerged from the guard room.

"Wait, Rory!" said Eamon, standing to attention beside the door.

But it was too late. Rory had already begun to step down.

The sergeant-major glanced at the coach. He saw the crest and the footman in his livery. He also saw the top hat of the occupant who was descending, and saluted. The visitor touched his hat in response, but since he was still stooped forward, the sergeant-major could not see his face. The sergeant-major walked on, twirling his mustache.

"We can't do it with him there," said Eamon between his teeth.

"He's got to take himself off sooner or later," replied Rory, bending his head down to brush imaginary dust off the coat Eamon had borrowed from his father for the occasion, together with the top hat. The waistcoat and the shoes were Eamon's, and both were uncomfortably tight.

"I can't stand here like this forever," muttered Rory. "I'll have to chance it."

"There he goes!" said Eamon.

Rory looked up to see the sergeant-major vanishing through a doorway and instantly turned to snatch the gun out of the coach.

"Good luck," said Eamon.

Rory glanced at him. "I hope Seamus is right," he said, "about where Jim is being kept and how many soldiers there are."

"Jasus!" said Michael O'Connor, who, with the best will in the world, could not keep his eyes straight ahead as a coachman should. "There's an officer just inside the door."

"Is there?" said Rory. "Good!"

He hastened inside, flung a friendly arm around the shoulders of the officer and poked the gun firmly in his back.

The colonel, whose office overlooked the courtyard, strolled to the window and glanced casually down. About to turn away again, he paused. Lord Fitzmorris's coach was in the courtyard, but they had no dinner engagement and, in addition, what was it doing outside the guard room?

A man in a top hat emerged, his arm around the shoulder of an officer. But the civilian was much too slim to be Lord Fitzmorris, and the officer was improperly dressed, his coat unbuttoned and his hat askew. The colonel endeavored to open the window, but it was stuck. The western winds blowing off the Atlantic did not encourage enthusiasm for fresh air, and it had not been opened for months, if not years. He saw the officer get into the coach, followed by the civilian.

"Take it easy to the gate, Michael," said Rory, "and then drive like hell!"

The coach moved off, and the colonel saw, emerging from the guard room, the officer of the guard. He was wearing only long johns and was holding the side of his head. The regimental sergeant-major, emerging from a nearby doorway, saw the officer and hastened toward him. The officer ran to meet him and seemed to be attempting to explain, but the sergeant-major gripped him firmly by the elbows and rushed him into the guard room. Clearly he thought that the officer had gone mad and should be got out of sight as quickly as possible.

The colonel finally managed to fling the window up

and leaned out. "Stop that coach!" he yelled, but he was too late.

The sentry, observing the familiar coach and horses, glanced inside and saw the top-hatted occupant accompanied by an officer. He waved it through, and the great gates were closed behind.

As Michael O'Connor whipped up the horses, Rory and O'Brien were suddenly grinning at each other.

"If Your Lordship had been a day or two later," said O'Brien, "you would have had to climb up and untie the rope from my neck to set me free."

"I like to save myself trouble," said Rory.

O'Brien stopped smiling. "Rory—" He couldn't find the words.

"Ah, come on now, Jim," said Rory, and he unbuttoned the waistcoat and loosened the boots with a sigh of relief. "I'll miss you, so I will."

He reached down and picked up a bundle of clothes from the floor.

"You'd better put these on. Your wife and little Maureen are on the quayside, and Eamon has booked passage for you all to Philadelphia. The ship sails with the tide, and with any luck that'll be before that officer manages to explain what happened!"

O'Brien tried to smile back, but there were tears in his eyes.

"I'll never forget this, Rory," he said. "As God is my witness, I never will!"

"It's an outrage!" said Lord Fitzmorris. "It's a damned outrage!"

David, having scarcely arrived back at the barracks before being summoned to accompany the colonel to Carralough Castle, endeavored to conceal the amusement he felt. The horses were unhurt. The coachman and footmen had been found blindfolded but unharmed in a hay barn, and their liveries had been neatly folded and placed inside the coach. But the coach had been painted an extraordinarily vivid green all over itself.

"And by now, I suppose," said Lord Fitzmorris, "that ruffian O'Brien is out of the country, and everyone deaf and blind. Sinclair!"

His agent, a sturdy, sensible Northern Irelander, stepped forward. "Yes, my Lord?"

"What have you found out?"

"My informant is certain that it was the Young Irelanders, My Lord."

"Yes, yes, I dare say!" exclaimed Lord Fitzmorris, exasperated. "But exactly *who*?"

He turned his sharp blue eyes on David. "Perhaps you can tell us, young man."

"My Lord?" said David, startled.

"You seem to be on very good terms with the people around here. Perhaps there is something you haven't told us."

For a fearful moment David wondered if he knew about that walk home from the races with Deirdre. But that was impossible. He drew himself up.

"My Lord, if you are suggesting that I would withhold information—"

"Lieutenant Clement!"

It was the colonel's voice, but David glanced only briefly toward him.

"Excuse me, sir, but as an officer in the service of the Queen, I won't allow any man to question my loyalty."

"Good," said Lord Fitzmorris. "I'm glad to hear it." He drew a sheaf of papers out of his pocket. "Then perhaps you will *do your duty* and carry out these orders."

David glanced through the papers and then looked at his colonel. "Eviction of tenants," he said. "Are these your orders, sir?"

"Naturally," replied the colonel. "If Lord Fitzmorris —that is to say, if the magistrate has made the judgment, then it is your duty to see that it is carried out."

David saluted him very formally, and very deliberately ignored Lord Fitzmorris.

"Very good, sir," he said. "Sergeant!"

"Ugh, what a stink!" remarked the sergeant as he and David rode at the head of the troop along the road that bordered the Fitzmorris and Clement properties.

"Them bloody Irish! They're so lazy, they leave the potatoes into the ground till they rot."

"Sergeant, those potatoes have the blight," said David. "If anyone eats them, men or animals, they die."

"You may be right, sir," said the sergeant peaceably, "but if you ask me, they're a shiftless lot, these Irish. I don't believe they could eat anything but potatoes, not if their lives depended on it!"

David did not reply. His eyes were fixed on the sight ahead of him.

The poor-looking mud cabin hardly seemed worth defending, but the door and single window were barricaded with uneven planks of wood. The police inspector and constable stood outside, and a ragged group of men and women and children watched, some of the men with cudgels.

"Come on, now, O'Keefe!" shouted Inspector Burke. "I have a warrant here from the magistrate. It'll be the worse for you if you don't!"

A wild face appeared at the barred doorway.

"How can I come out? Where would we go?"

The inspector glanced at his constable and prepared to move toward the door but became aware of the men grasping their blackthorn shellelaghs and closing in upon him. He paused and then saw with relief David riding up with his troop.

"I'm glad you're here, sir," he said.

David glanced around at the threatening men with their cudgels. Their lawlessness was a challenge to the Queen's authority, which he had sworn to maintain, and it was a challenge he could not ignore.

"Sergeant," he said, "get those people out of the way and break down the door."

But still David felt dismay at the unequal contest as the sergeant and the troop went into action, scattering the crowd and using a sort of three-pronged battering ram to break down the door. As Peter O'Keefe, his wife and children were dragged, screaming, out of the house, David saw with horror Rachel riding into the clearing, accompanied by Rory.

"What are they doing?" cried Rachel, dismayed.

"It's just another of Lord Fitzmorris's tenants," replied Rory, "who can't pay his rents."

"But it's horrible—horrible! Who would do such a thing?"

David spurred his horse toward them.

"For God's sake," he said to Rory, "get my sister out of here!"

"No," Rory answered, and he took hold of Rachel's rein. "No, let her see how the 'friends of Ireland' behave!"

Inspector Burke approached, throwing an uneasy glance at Rachel but then concentrating upon David.

"I'm sorry, sir," he said, "but we shall have to pull the place down or they'll be back inside by tomorrow."

David hesitated, met Rachel's eyes and then looked back at the inspector.

"Do what you have to do," he said.

Rachel watched, aghast, as the soldiers went into the cabin and threw the pathetic remnants of furniture and possessions out into the mud and then set a ladder up against the roof. As Trooper Craig thrust an iron hook into the thatch and tore it off, Mary O'Keefe screamed as though the hook went into her own body, and all the women began to keen as though someone had died.

"Oh no!" cried Rachel. "Where will they go? Where will they live?"

"In a ditch," replied Rory, never moving his eyes from the scene before them. "But don't worry, it won't be for long. They'll soon be dead."

The thatch was tossed aside and fire from the hearth tossed on it to consume it while the soldiers began to knock down the crumbling walls.

"I can't bear it!" said Rachel and tried to turn her horse's head away, but Rory kept his grip on the rein.

"It's known as tumbling," he said in a voice full of hatred. "It's done all over Ireland—on your father's land as well!"

"Don't!" cried Rachel. "I don't want to know!"

She struck at his hand with her whip and, startled, he released the rein, and she urged Flame away. Rory looked down angrily at the red mark on his wrist and then kicked his horse into furious pursuit.

Rachel, riding blindly along the wooded path, heard the thundering hooves behind and felt an unreasoning panic. It seemed that all the rage and injustice of Ireland was at her heels, and she must escape from it or die.

She came upon a bend in the path, and Flame shied and skidded in the mud so that she nearly fell. Rachel reined him back and then brought him to a halt. Rory, coming around the corner, jostled up behind.

"If you ever strike me again—!" he began furiously.

But Rachel was staring at the ditch, terror in her eyes.

"Look!" she said. "Look, there's something there!"

Like a corpse rising from a grave, a skeleton hand clawed its way up from the ditch, and after it a woman in rags. Her huge dark eyes in their hollow sockets fixed themselves on Rachel's face, and she muttered the same words in Irish over and over again.

"What is she saying?" Rachel demanded, and she began to dismount.

"She says her baby is starving," said Rory. "She asks you to get it into the workhouse."

Rachel saw that the woman was supporting herself on one elbow and that in the other arm she was trying to hold out a little creature, almost naked. Rory was quicker off his horse and went toward the woman and bent down and took the baby from her.

"Of course we will look after your baby!" cried Rachel, "and you, too!"

The moment she had given the child into Rory's hands, the woman sank back into the ditch.

"Come," said Rachel, "let me help you."

She knelt beside the woman, putting her hand on the arm, so thin that it was like touching a bare bone, and then she started back with a cry of horror. The eyes that were still fixed upon her had no life in them. The woman had died in the very instant of relinquishing her child. Rachel looked wildly up at Rory and began to unbutton her jacket and take it off.

"The baby!" she cried. "At least we can save the baby. Quick, wrap him in this!"

She scrambled to her feet, holding out the jacket, but Rory was looking tenderly down at the little creature he held.

"The baby is dead," he said. "She didn't know it was already dead."

He laid it gently down in the woman's arms and covered them both with her shawl.

"Oh no!" said Rachel. "Oh no!"

She turned and put her arms down on the saddle and her face in her arms and burst into tears. Sobbing bitterly, she felt Rory put her jacket around her shoulders.

"I'll take you home," he said.

She looked up at him with tears streaming down her face and then looked toward the woman in the ditch. "We can't just—leave them!"

"I'll see they have a decent burial. Come on."

He put his hands together. She put her booted foot in them and he lifted her to her saddle. He did not grudge the mud on his hands, and she knew it.

When Rory helped her down in the yard at Ballyclam, he kept her hand in his.

"Will you come to the stable tonight?"

"Oh yes!" she cried. "Yes!"

But there were still tears in her eyes, and she leaned her head against his shoulder for a moment before she went inside. He stood looking after her, angry and fearful. He had stepped into a pleasure ground and found it to be a trap. Like a wild animal, he fought for his freedom but only became more entangled in emotions he had never thought to feel. She was willful, spoiled, ignorant and, above all, English. Why could she not also be heartless, stupid and frivolous? Why did she have to arouse in him such tenderness as well as desire?

CHAPTER 10

"I'll never see you again, Lieutenant Clement!" cried Deirdre. "Never!"

"Deirdre, it had to be done," he said. "I did my best to ensure that it was done without violence."

She flung down the washing she was gathering up from the bushes where she had spread it to dry.

"Without violence?" she repeated. "Was it not violent to drag a family from the only home they have on earth? How would you feel, Lieutenant Clement, if you saw your sister thrown down in the mud and all her bedclothes and sticks of furniture thrown after her? Oh yes, Rachel has lace, indeed, on her sheets and pillowcases, and they had only rags, but it was all they had!"

"Believe me," he said desperately, "I feel as you do. It was the most dreadful duty I have ever had to perform, and I hope to God I'll never have to do it again!"

He stooped to pick up the linen, and she stooped beside him.

"Will you leave the army?" she said, softly.

He looked at her, aghast. "How can I? It's my career. It's my life."

"And it's the death of our love, so it is, for if you

are in the army, you will be turning our friends and neighbors out of doors until at last you come to turn us out."

"Deirdre—"

"No," she said, and she took the linen from him. "You know that what I say is true. Do not come this way again, for I have no wish to see you."

She was about to rise, but he put his hand gently on her arm.

"Can you say that?" he asked. "Can you say you never want to see me again and mean it?"

She stared at him as they knelt facing each other by the stream, and they were lost in each other's eyes. He drew her close and kissed her.

"Ah, David!" she whispered. "Ah, we're destroyed entirely!"

She kissed him and then drew herself gently out of his embrace, gathered the washing and ran away up the path toward the O'Manion house without a backward glance. David stood up and watched her go.

As she hurried up the muddy path, Deirdre saw Brian walking along the road on his way back from school, and she stopped short. He looked at her with that scowl that was so like Rory's, under his thatch of red hair, and she knew that he had seen her with David.

In the patch behind the house, Shane O'Manion was shoveling the winnowed wheat onto the cart while Maeve held the donkey's halter, moving him on at intervals. At the sight of Brian, Shane straightened his back gratefully.

"Come, my boy," he said. "We have to get this wheat to Houlihan today, and my back is older than my heart."

He held out the wooden shovel, but Brian did not move.

"Father," he said, "Rory says there should be no selling of wheat while a single person starves in Ireland."

Shane threw down the shovel with a violence more horrifying because it seemed so much out of character, and Deirdre, following Brian in, paused, startled.

"Does Rory know no better than that?" their father demanded fiercely. "We need the wheat to pay our rent, and while we do that, no man can take our land."

"Rory and Padraic are earning money at Ballyclam," said Brian, "and my sister, washing the young lady's pretty things." The russet-brown eyes Brian turned upon Deirdre were almost black with rage.

"And why would they not?" asked Shane. "The money they earn will buy us food for the year to come —yes, and for those less fortunate, like Peter O'Keefe, who from their desperate need come begging to our door."

"Are you angry, Da?" said Maeve.

Shane looked at her, and his stern face softened. "No, my Maeve. I am not angry."

He looked back at Brian. "You bear the name of Brian Boru, the last king of Ireland. Remember this: While we pay our rent, this land is ours, and no one can turn us from it. No, not the queen of England herself! Even if we starve, we must never lose the land."

Shane pointed to the shovel. "Pick it up, my gossoon," he said. "That wheat goes to Houlihan. He may roast in hell, but our rent is paid, and the land is ours."

Harry looked, puzzled, at the piece of paper Houlihan put in front of him.

"What does it mean?" he asked.

Houlihan took the sheet of paper back again and began to translate the angular Celtic writing, scrawled in black ink with a sharp hole in the middle of the paper where a thatching hook had driven it into a door. Rachel, writing a letter to her aunt in Philadelphia, listened but did not turn her head.

" 'Pay no rent,' " read Houlihan. " 'Thrash no wheat, while food is being sent out of the country. Kill those responsible.' "

He looked up. "And it is signed, 'The Young Irelanders.' "

Harry took the paper back, as though those Irish hieroglyphics meant something to him. Houlihan looked toward Rachel. Her head was bent over her letter, unnaturally engrossed.

"I hope you will now realize, Miss Clement," he said, "that your sympathies are somewhat misplaced."

"Oh?" said Rachel without turning around.

"Especially," continued Houlihan doggedly, "since your groom, Rory O'Manion, is strongly suspected of being the leader of the Young Irelanders around here."

Rachel put down her pen and turned to look at him. "That is a serious accusation, Mr. Houlihan," she said. "Unless, of course, you have proof?"

"We have—informers," replied Houlihan.

"Oh, I see," said Rachel, contemptuously. Informers!" And she bent again over her letter.

Harry looked at Houlihan. "The wheat," he said uncertainly, "will you be sending it—?"

"I will take it to Galway myself," said Houlihan. "These people," he added, and glanced at the paper but spoke to Rachel, "these people do not seem to realize that the Irish economy depends upon her exports. If we stopped all export of wheat, it would not prevent the famine, but there are merchants who would be bankrupted. One has to be practical."

"Oh . . . yes . . . certainly," replied Harry, knowing nothing whatever about the Irish economy and even less about Irish wheat merchants. "Well—er—you will see that the wheat is safely transported?"

"I will make it my personal responsibility," said Houlihan, and he glanced at Rachel and went out.

Rachel was aware of Harry moving quietly toward the desk to stand beside her.

"Is he?" said Harry.

Rachel was engrossed in writing her letter. "Is . . . who . . . what, Papa?"

He reached over and took the pen from her hand. "Is Rory O'Manion a member of the Young Irelanders?"

"I don't know," she replied.

It was the exact truth, but not the whole truth, and she could not meet his eyes. She and her father had been too close for too long for her to hope to lie to him now. She did not *know,* but in her heart she was sure of it.

"Now, Rachel," said Harry, "this has got to stop. If Rory O'Manion *is* a rebel, there is nothing we can do to protect him, but he can do great harm to us."

"Yes," she said. "I know.'

Harry put the pen down on the desk. "If I get absolute proof that he is guilty," he said, "I shan't hesitate to act."

He turned and walked out. Rachel picked up her pen and read through what she had written.

"My dear Aunt Charlotte. We are settled into Bally-

clam House now, and find ourselves very comfortable.
Please tell Uncle James—"

About to dip the pen in the ink, she paused. She
could not remember what she had been going to write.
What could she say? How could she tell her American
uncle and her mother's sister what it meant to live in
a land where misgovernment meant that a woman and
child could die of starvation in a ditch. And what it
was to love a man who was determined to resist it to
the death?

"Keep down, boys!" said Rory.

"Ah," said Tom Noonan, "I don't believe Houlihan's coming this way at all."

"Quiet!" said Rory.

They all listened and heard the rumble of wheels
and the sound of horses' hooves echoing back from
the hillside.

"Now listen, lads," said Rory. "We don't want to
hurt our own people. Con Murphy will be driving the
wagon. I'll hold the gun on Houlihan, and Con will
stop, don't you worry. Cover your faces."

The little group of Young Irelanders crouched down
behind the wall, pulling handkerchiefs up to their eyes.
They saw the wagon approaching and Houlihan driving beside on his black horse.

"Right, lads!" cried Rory and leapt over the wall.
Houlihan's horse shied. The other Young Irelanders
followed Rory but paused, dismayed, as the tarpaulin
was raised and big, rough men jumped down, cudgels
in their hands. Houlihan had set a trap for them.

In the wild scrimmage that ensued, the Young Irelanders had much less strength, but they had the advantage of desperation.

"Never mind the fellows!" Rory yelled. "Get the wagon!"

He saw Tom Noonan struggle up into the driving seat of the wagon, shoving Con Murphy down onto the road, and Eamon catching up a stone to hurl at one of the hired ruffians. Suddenly he saw his chance, with Houlihan isolated on the roadside. He pointed the gun at him.

"Tell your men to stand aside or I'll fire!" he yelled. "I mean it!"

Houlihan saw that he did.

"Stand aside, men!" he shouted, his eyes mesmerized by the gun barrel.

They obeyed him. Tom Noonan's hat had been knocked off in the struggle, but he had reached the driver's seat and managed to gather the reins. Eamon and the other Young Irelanders clambered aboard, and Rory, keeping the gun pointed toward Houlihan, backed toward the wagon. Eamon hauled him aboard as Tom Noonan whipped up the horses.

Houlihan suddenly shouted after them, spurring his horse on. "I'll see that every last one of you is hanged! Don't think I don't know you! Tom Noonan! Don't you think I don't know your red hair?"

Horrified, Tom Noonan hauled on the reins. "Shoot him!" he shouted. "He knows me!"

"Drive on!" shouted Rory.

"Shoot him!" yelled the others.

Rory leveled the gun but hesitated. And Eamon grasped the gun.

Tom Noonan suddenly whipped the horses on, and the gun exploded. Houlihan fell back in the saddle and the horse bolted up the hillside, dragging Houlihan after him, his boot caught in the stirrup.

Rory and Eamon looked at each other, shocked.

"Which of us—"

"I don't know!"

The wagon rocketed on down the road, and Eamon and Rory, looking back, saw Houlihan's foot come clear of the stirrup. The horse galloped on up the hillside, but Houlihan lay still.

Rory, hiding the gun beneath the thatch at the rear of the O'Manion house, felt a shadow fall between him and the setting sun. He whirled and saw Padraic.

"You did it, didn't you?" said Padraic.

"Stay out of this," said Rory. "He chose to be the servant of the landlord."

"Yes," said Padraic, "he was an Irishman, and he chose to do it. But by all that's holy, what gave you the right to kill him for it?"

Rory could not find an answer, but at that moment Brian came around the corner of the house and stopped short, his face glowing with excitement.

"Rory!" he cried. "The ambush—Houlihan—did you kill him?"

Rory was aware of a thunderous gleam in Padraic's blue-gray eyes but ignored it.

"Shut up!" he said to Brian. "Go to Tom Noonan. Tell him—"

"No!" Padraic shouted with unexpected ferocity. "I won't let you, Rory! Keep the boy out of this. Isn't it enough that you're a murderer? Do you have to make Brian one, too?"

"I'm not a boy!" Brian flashed back at him with all the anguish of adolescence. "I'm more of a man than *you* are!"

He said it with the cruelty of adolescence, too, and

the words struck home instantly. In a rare moment of blinding rage, Padraic swung the back of his hand across Brian's head, knocking him to the ground. He was immediately contrite.

"I'm sorry, Brian. I didn't mean to—But you shouldn't have—"

He tried to help Brian up, but the boy scrambled free and gave him a look of hatred before turning his gaze toward Rory.

"What shall I do, Rory?"

"Go to Tom Noonan," said Rory. "Tell him to go to his cousin in Limerick and lie low until we're sure that no one else heard his name."

"I will," said Brian and was gone.

Rory finished hiding the gun beneath the thatch and turned away, and saw Padraic steadfastly regarding him.

"So you have won Brian to your violence," he said. "In that case you have murdered him as surely as you have murdered Houlihan."

"It's horrible!" said Rachel. "Horrible! Poor Mr. Houlihan!"

She had never liked him, but to be murdered. She had not wished that for him, indeed she had not.

"Yes," agreed Lord Fitzmorris. "Very unfortunate."

His tone showed that he felt that Houlihan as a man was dispensable, but as an agent. . . .

"If we don't make an example here and now," he said briskly, "not an agent will be safe in the whole of Ireland. We have to hang every Young Irelander in the county, starting with their leader."

Rachel saw that Harry was about to speak and hastily

forestalled him. "Lord Fitzmorris, won't you have some breakfast? Let me ring for some fresh coffee."

"No, thank you, Miss Rachel," replied Lord Fitzmorris. "I'm on my way to see the colonel in Galway. There's only one way to deal with a venomous snake, and that is to cut off its head."

Rachel flinched, and Harry glanced at her, but Lord Fitzmorris was already on his way to the door.

"When you get your new agent," he said, "get a good, sensible man from the North, like my man Sinclair. The trouble with Houlihan was that he came from these parts and knew all the people around here. He was too soft with them!"

Lord Fitzmorris went out.

Rachel looked after him, *"Soft* with them?"

"Wasn't he?" said Harry.

Rachel looked at him quickly and was dismayed by the sternness of his expression.

"Houlihan knew that Rory O'Manion was a member of the Young Irelanders, and yet he did nothing about it."

"He had no proof—" began Rachel, but her father continued firmly.

"We should never have employed that young man, and Houlihan told us so. Well, I'm not taking any more chances. I shall dismiss him."

"No, Father!"

Harry's face now was very stern indeed. "Rachel, if you have allowed your personal feelings to become involved—"

"No!" she replied. "No."

Oddly enough, it wasn't difficult to lie to her father on this. Her feelings for Rory, and those passionate encounters in the stable, lit only by the stars, belonged to a different world from this Georgian dining room and the fine china and family silver.

"I like Rory and Padraic, of course," she said, "and Deirdre, and the dear little children——"

Harry was slightly reassured. His sternness relaxed a little. "It's natural, my dear," he said, "that you should feel sympathy for these people, especially our own servants. But when it comes to condoning rebellion and violence——"

"But, Father, it's because they feel that nobody *cares* that they turn to violence."

She got up and came around the table to put her arms around his neck and her cheek against his. "We want to make a life here—a *real* life, not just ignoring everything that's going on around us, like—like summer *visitors*."

"We can't save the whole of Ireland," muttered Harry irritably. "All I can do is ensure that my tenants are looked after as well as—as well as possible. I shall advertise for a new agent immediately in the Belfast papers."

In a blinding moment Rachel saw how her two lives could come together into one.

"No, Father, don't do that," she said.

She released him, but as he looked up, surprised, she possessed herself of his hand and sat down beside him. "Father," she said eagerly, "Lord Fitzmorris was wrong. Houlihan was a bad agent, hard and unfeeling, like Uncle Cyrus. The people around here looked upon him as a traitor. But if, instead of getting some-one from the North who had no sympathy with them, we put one of *their own* in charge——"

She saw his eyes widen in stunned astonishment as

he read her mind, but she held his hand tightly in both of hers. "Why not, Father?" she said. "Why not Rory O'Manion?"

"It's unthinkable!" Harry exclaimed. "I'm perfectly certain that he is a member of this group of malcontents—"

"So much the better if he is!" Rachel broke in. "So much the better if he is their leader. Then he can prove to the people that not all landlords are bad. They will know that they can trust him."

"Yes, I dare say," said Harry. "*They* might be able to trust him, but could *I*? Good heavens, Rachel! Do you realize what a chance you're asking me to take?"

She released his hand and stood up, looking down at him, inspired by the thought that she was fighting for her life, hers and Rory's together.

"Father," she said, "nothing is safe in Ireland now. If you're poor you starve, and if you're an agent you can be shot, and if you're a landlord you can have your house burned down. But the famine won't last forever, and we want to build a life for ourselves here afterward—a happy, happy life for us and for all the people who depend on us. Isn't it worth taking a chance for that?"

Harry was silent for a moment. His daughter was always stronger than he was, quicker and more clever. Once she had really made up her mind, he never could resist her. He looked up at her.

"Surely," he said, "if we were going to have one of the O'Manions for our agent, Pat seems the likely candidate."

It was a rearguard action, but a dangerous one for Rachel. She had to win her point without giving away her motive.

"Ye-es . . ." she said, and her look of impartial consideration would have done credit to an actress. "Pat would be very good, but Rory would be better. He's very determined, and that's what you need in an agent who has to do unpopular things and make people accept them because they respect him."

She hesitated, then took a calculated risk. "But it's your decision, Father."

"Hmm," he said, and she saw that the sop to his self-esteem had turned the day. "Very well. I'll offer the job to Rory O'Manion."

Determined to keep well out of the way, Rachel went up to her bedroom when Harry summoned Rory to the library. But she could not stay away. It meant too much to her. Like a child during her parents' dinner party, she crept out to the staircase and sat on the stairs, listening intently. The door was ajar, and Rory's first words came dismayingly up to her.

"*Agent*? *Your* agent? You are asking *me* to be a traitor to my own people?"

Rachel heard Harry's voice, offended. "If that is how you look at it—"

"How else can I look at it? Working with the police and the army, turning people out of their homes to live in ditches!"

"I should have thought there was a good deal more to the post of agent than that. I should have thought there were ways to—to do a great service to your country."

"Were you thinking of England or Ireland?"

"Both, of course," replied Harry. "One cannot prosper without the other."

"No," said Rory, "but one can starve while the other grows fat!"

Rachel, clasping the banisters, flinched at the hatred in his voice. She heard her father push his chair back.

"Very well," he said. "It was my daughter's idea to offer you the post, but—"

"Your *daughter*?" repeated Rory. "I think Miss Clement does not know me very well."

Rachel shrank back as Rory came to the door. Harry's voice followed him.

"Obviously not," said Harry. "I am offering you an excellent opportunity, but if you are unable to—"

Rory turned on him, furious. "Damn your opportunities!" he shouted, "and damn you! I am an O'Manion. Do you really think I'd stoop to become the agent of a jumped-up musharoon English landlord?"

Rachel knew how this insult would strike home to her father's insecure self-esteem, but she was unprepared for the fierceness of his anger as his intended kindness was thrown back in his face.

"Why, you—you Irish bog trotter!" he roared. "If you are too proud to be my agent, you are too proud to be my groom! You will take a week's wages in lieu of notice, and if I find you on my land one hour from now, I will shoot you as a trespasser!"

Rachel caught up with Rory as he set out along the lane that led from Ballyclam toward the O'Manion house.

"How could you, Rory!" she cried. "Oh, how could you!"

He turned on her. "How could *you* think I'd accept?"

"Rory, it's the perfect answer. If they don't suspect you now, they soon will."

"Suspect me?"

"About Houlihan. Oh, Rory, don't let's lie to each other. Let's never lie. I knew you were involved."

"That his face readily acknowledged his involvement was, in its own way, a tribute of love.

"No one would suspect an agent of fighting for the freedom of Ireland," she pursued eagerly.

"No," replied Rory. "Because no man working for the freedom of Ireland could ever be an agent."

She moved closer. "Ah, Rory, don't you see? If you were my father's agent, you'd be—you'd be living—"

"I'd be living in the agent's house," said Rory.

"Yes," breathed Rachel, "right by the gates of Ballyclam House. And every night I'd come—"

Her arms were around his neck and she was kissing him. He responded passionately and then fought free, as from a trap.

"Yes, I want you!" he cried. "Yes! Night after night after night! And while we take our pleasure with each other, my Ireland dies, day after day after day!"

She clung to him more fiercely. "But if we were married, it would be my Ireland, too! Oh, Rory, I love you, and I know that you love me!"

It almost seemed that he might yield, but in the next minute he had torn her arms from around his neck.

"No! I can't live as an agent of the enemy!"

He turned and strode away up the lane. Rachel ran after him.

"Am I your enemy?"

He stopped and stood motionless for a moment and then strode on, and Rachel watched him go.

"Oh, damn your Ireland!" she cried. "And damn you! You're a nation of madmen!"

He began to run.

Rory did not go straight home. He could not face the questions he knew would be asked if he arrived home so early in the day. He had too many questions to ask himself. He walked and walked until the green hills spun about him and his knees trembled beneath him, and physical exhaustion wiped his mind clean like Brian's slate. But at last he had to turn and trudge back, stumbling like an old man, and he looked down from the hill at the small thatched cabin with the blue peat smoke emerging from the single chimney. It was as though he had been away for many years, and he stood there as an exile, afraid to enter. But how absurd that was! This was his home, and he would fight for it to the death. Nothing and no one would ever make him leave it.

Deirdre was at the fire, stirring yellow meal in the pot. It was the stuff called maize which the government for some mysterious reason had brought from America and carried all the way across the sea to sell in Ireland. The Irish people had no way of grinding it down, though somehow they contrived to pound it down and boil it into a sort of yellow mush, more suitable for pigs than human beings. But at least, thanks to their wages from Ballyclam House, the O'Manions could afford to buy it, unlike many others, and even to give some to those less fortunate who came begging to the door.

Deirdre glanced around as Rory came in. "You're early this evening," she said and then called out, "Maeve! Set the dishes on the table!"

Maeve came reluctantly from nursing her wooden doll and climbed up on a stool to get the bowls down from beside the fireplace. "Is it the yellow mealie stuff again, Deirdre?" she inquired.

"It is," replied Deirdre, "and if there were no wages coming into the house, it's glad you would be to have it."

"I am glad," said Maeve, scrambling down with her father's earthenware bowl, "but I do not like it."

Deirdre glanced at Rory to share her amusement with him, but he avoided her eye and lifted Sean from his cradle and sat down with him by the hearth. The baby laughed and clutched at the silver medal around Rory's neck.

"Padraic is late tonight," said Shane.

Maeve had finished laying the table, and the meal was ready. Rory still sat with Sean on his knee, and Shane, aware of his silence, glanced at Deirdre, who silently responded, puzzled and troubled. They all heard footsteps, and Brian looked out the window.

"Here he is," he said. "With a horse. Where did you get the horse, Padraic?"

Padraic came in, paused and looked around, his eyes wary. As Rory looked at him across the room, some instinctive knowledge flew between them. Rory put Sean down in his basket and rose to his feet. Padraic deliberately advanced to the table, felt in his pocket and put down some coins.

"Here are your wages," he said, "in lieu of notice."

"*Notice?*" repeated Deirdre. "Rory, have you—?"

Rory did not look at her. He kept his eyes fixed on Padraic's face. "Who asked *you* to bring me my wages?" he said.

Padraic took a deep breath and glanced around at all of them before he spoke.

"As agent at Ballyclam," he said, "it is my business to pay the wages."

Deirdre crossed herself.

Padraic looked from her to Shane, and then directly at Rory. "Someone has to make some sense out of this mess," he said. "Someone has to care more about Ireland and her people than about his own pride, and it seems I'm the only one who'll do it."

Rory strode to the table. "You damned traitor!" he said. He picked up the money and threw it at Padraic. "You've sold your soul for money. You may as well take mine as well!"

Shane suddenly intervened. "Rory," he said, "you earned that money, and we need it to buy seed potatoes for next year. Pick it up."

"*You* may grovel for it, Father," said Rory, "for I will not!"

He was himself shocked by the words as he spoke them, but there was a kind of madness upon him. He saw Brian's face, glancing quickly between himself and his father, and Deirdre moved to pick up the money but was stopped.

"No, Deirdre," said Shane. He spoke to Rory very quietly. "Pick up the money."

Rory still hesitated for an instant, but the natural authority of his father was too strong for him. He stooped and picked up the money and put it on the table. Then he turned to look at Padraic again.

"You had better go and live in the agent's house," he said. "There is no room for you here."

"That is for the head of the house to say," replied Padraic.

He looked at Shane, and they all followed his gaze. There was a long silence before Shane spoke.

"Padraic, you have chosen to be agent. It is in the agent's house that you must live."

Padraic's face showed the pain that he felt at these words, and Rory felt it with him. Without another word Padraic turned, stooped under the low doorway and was gone.

Shane turned his eyes toward Rory. "I sent him away for the sake of peace in this house," he said, "but it is half of yourself that went out that door."

"No!" said Rory, violently.

Shane looked at him sadly. "Deny it if you will," he said, "but suffer it you must."

CHAPTER 11

In the library of Ballyclam House, Padraic and Harry pored over the account books while Rachel sat on the window seat working on a piece of embroidery. Padraic was very much aware of her presence. It was the only alleviation of a wearisome and dismaying task, and now and then she would glance up and smile at him as though she understood his feelings.

"The Morans," said Harry. "Their rent is overdue."

"Their potatoes have failed entirely," said Padraic, "and they have seven children to feed."

"So you think I should remit their rent."

"Unless you want them to starve," replied Padraic. Harry glanced uneasily at Rachel, but her head was bent diligently over her embroidery. He returned his gaze to Padraic.

"No," he said. "No, of course not! But—"

But Padraic had already dipped the pen in the ink and written "remitted" in his neat, elegant hand. Harry made a desperate effort to assert himself.

"But there must be *some* of my tenants who have some money put aside"—he caught Padraic's eye and hastily went on—"or have some other work than just sitting outside their houses, smoking. Now look here, Pat, the money has got to come from somewhere or I shall be bankrupt!"

"Yes, Mr. Clement," said Padraic wearily.

He went out to the stables and saddled Houlihan's horse. He missed Rory desperately, his teasing and laughter, even the quarrels that had always been so much a part of their life together. He hated the solitary meals that Mary Kate, another of Mrs. Docherty's nieces, came to prepare for him, and that he ate all alone in the small dining room in the agent's house, which smelled of damp. He missed the warmth and music of home and, above all, he missed that moment in the evening when they all knelt down together to say the Rosary. It was then, kneeling together in the familiar room, with the firelight illuminating each beloved face like a benediction, that they forgot all the bickering and troubles of the day and knew that they were a family and that nothing could ever part them. To kneel and say the Rosary alone in the agent's house was each evening like Gethsemane, and to ride out every day into the country that had once been full of friends and now was full of enemies was a kind of Calvary.

Padraic led behind him a donkey with panniers hung on each side. If he could not get the money, he would accept produce instead. He knew who could afford to pay and who could not. Keeping his eyes and ears open, he knew which men had managed to get a few days' work on the roads from the government's work scheme or which family had received a letter from America containing the begged-for money. He used his knowledge shamefacedly, but he used it, even though he knew that he was taking food from their mouths, because he knew as well that if he didn't, Mr. Clement would indeed go bankrupt, leaving them to the mercies of an absentee landlord, or that a worse agent would be employed, who would not accept a few eggs or a handful of moldy wheat but would turn them off their land, and then they would be homeless as well as starving.

But as he rode toward Moran's cabin today, what happened was all too familiar.

"Inside with you!" cried Moran to his wife, "inside with you, and bar the door. 'Tis the agent."

"Wait!" Padraic called out, struggling with the halter of the recalcitrant donkey. "Mick! Mick! It's all right. I haven't come for the rent."

Moran paused, scowling. In the old days he and Rory and Padraic had often gone hurling together.

"Mr. Clement says you need not pay this week," said Padraic.

"Well, fine for him!" replied Mick Moran, "for I could not pay it, anyway. As for you, Padraic O'Manion, don't think to come here currying favors in the job your brother refused. Will 'no rent' feed my family? Go back and ask your English master that!"

He followed his wife inside and slammed the door,

and Padraic saw the wild face of the oldest child staring at him through the window and then being snatched away, as though he were the devil.

It was a relief as Padraic approached Con Murphy's house to see that Con remained sitting outside the door smoking his pipe. He still wore the bandage around his head from the blow he had received from the fight at the wheat wagon. Padraic knew that Con could afford to pay and smiled at him as Con stood up and silently put a couple of coins in his hand.

"Thanks, Con," he said.

Mrs. Murphy spoke nervously from the doorway. "Would you step in for a cup of tea, Padraic?"

Padraic was about to accept gratefully when Con turned on his wife.

"Are you crazy, woman?" he said. "Isn't it enough that I'm known to have driven Houlihan's wagon? Would you invite this man inside our house and destroy me entirely?"

He pushed her inside and went in after her and shut the door.

Annie O'Hara lived in a tumbledown house up the road. Widow as she had been for many years, she was not destitute. Padraic knew that whenever she delivered a baby, she received something either in money or produce. The door was barred, but Padraic thought he saw a movement at the window. He knocked on the door.

"Annie! Mrs. O'Hara! It's me, Padraic O'Manion. I've come for your rent."

The coins hit him in the face.

"Take it, and bad cess to you!" said Annie O'Hara.

One of the pennies had cut Padraic's forehead, and he had to wipe the blood from his eye as he climbed onto his horse again. She'd not have chanced that with

Houlihan, he thought. Houlihan would have raised her rent and had her out of there in a week. His spirits rose slightly, however, as he rode on toward Michael O'Connor's place. Michael was an easygoing man who knew how to trim his sails for the good of Ireland. And Padraic happened to know that he could pay his rent this week, so there was no problem there.

Michael was up a crooked ladder, mending the thatch on his roof.

"Ah, Michael!" called Padraic. "How are you today?"

Michael turned on the ladder, not exactly smiling, but amiable enough.

"Is it yourself, Padraic?" And then, "Sure, it's no use coming for the rent, for I've not a penny in the house. This famine's terrible bad for business. There's me poor old jaunty-car rusting away and Lightning glad of a bite of a nettle to keep the skin from his ribs."

"Ah, come on, now, Michael," remonstrated Padraic, smiling, "you've five pounds from that donkey you sold to the lawyer."

"Does the landlord know that?" asked Michael.

Padraic's smile faded under his steady gaze.

"Sure," said Michael, "we were better with John Houlihan, for he was no friend we told our secrets to, to carry back to his master."

He took a small bag from his breeches pocket, took out the money for the rent and handed it down. As Padraic came close and reached up to take it, Michael's eyes met his.

"Here's my rent, Padraic O'Manion," said Michael, "and may the curse of God go with it!"

Padraic took the money, stunned, as though he had received a blow in the face. Michael turned back to his

work on the thatch as though Padraic had ceased to
exist.

It was still quite early in the afternoon, but it was
beginning to grow dark and a drizzle of rain was falling, or rather, Padraic was enfolded by that fine mist of
Galway rain which is hardly visible but drenches to the
skin. He had one more call to make and flinched from
it as a dog flinches from a boot which has kicked him
too often before. As the weary horse plodded on along
the wet paved road, his hoofbeats seemed to say, "May
the curse of God go with you! May the curse of God
go with you!"

Padraic reined in outside Joe Kerrigan's unkempt bit
of a house, and this time he did not dismount but
shouted from the saddle.

"Joe! Joe Kerrigan!"

Kerrigan opened the door. "Good day to you, Padraic," he said.

He spoke in a normal, friendly voice. It was the first
friendly voice Padraic had heard that day.

"I've come for the rent," said Padraic and waited for
the customary change.

"Ah well," said Joe Kerrigan, "I've managed to
scrape a few pennies together, and you may as well
have them before I forget and put them to a better
use!"

He grinned at Padraic and jerked his head toward
the drinking house down the road.

"You look as if you've ridden far today," he said.

"The journey seems longer," Padraic answered,
"when you're an unwelcome visitor upon the way."

Kerrigan reached up for the money. "The way I
look at it," he said, "the job has to be done, and better
it's done by one of our own."

"Thanks, Joe," replied Padraic, and meant the thanks both for the money and the words. "There are not many who think as you do."

He began to turn the horse's head. "Well, I'm off home, or rather," he said bitterly, "to the agent's house. At least Houlihan had a liking for poteen, and since he's no use for it now, I might as well drink it."

Kerrigan took a step after him. "Ah, wait a bit, Padraic," he said. "A man shouldn't drink alone, especially in low spirits."

Padraic looked back and was grateful for the expression of kind concern on his face.

"Come in, lad," said Kerrigan. "Come in and have a jar with me."

He smiled at Padraic, and Padraic was glad to smile back and know his smile would not be thrown in his face.

"Thanks," he said. "Thanks, I will."

He dismounted, tethered the horse and donkey and followed Kerrigan inside the house.

Rory, too, had had a miserable day. At first his rage had made him able to pretend to himself that he did not miss Padraic, but as time went by, although he still felt a deep, cold anger, it was increasingly as though he was living only half a life. The other half of him was plodding with Padraic on that deadly and heartbreaking round of the Ballyclam tenants on Houlihan's horse.

Moreover, he could no longer go to Ballyclam, and he refused to admit to himself how much he missed Rachel. She rode by the O'Manion house once or twice, stopping to speak to Deirdre or his father while her eyes spoke to him, but what good was that? His body ached for those stolen nights in the stable, and he knew that hers did, too.

That afternoon he went out to dig out the peat, glad to deaden his misery by fierce physical exertion. He hid the gun beneath a piece of sacking on the bottom of the donkey cart. The death of Houlihan was still heavy on his conscience. It was one thing to talk of killing for Ireland but quite another to see a man die at his hands. He knew that the police and army were still being urged by the landowners to find the murderer, and if they came for him, he had no intention of being taken without a fight.

The gray afternoon wore away, and a fine mist of rain turned his frieze coat into a damp prison within which he struggled to dig the black turf, turn it and dig again. It was almost too dark to see what he was doing, but he could not bring himself to go home. He did not want to kneel and say the Rosary with Padraic not there to say it beside him.

Rory heard the sound of horse's hooves and straightened his back, and saw Padraic riding toward him along the paved road which one of the government's work schemes had built through the peat bog. At the same moment Padraic saw him and reined in the horse. Rory threw the long, sharp spade down beside the trench.

"What the devil do you want?" he said, and spoke more ferociously because he had so much longed to see his twin. "Get on your horse and ride to hell where you belong, with all the other agents!"

Padraic slipped off the horse and stood supporting himself with his arm on the saddle. Rory realized that although Padraic was not quite drunk, he had definitely had a few jars. They stood and stared at each other, all alone there in the wild Galway countryside. Rory drew a deep breath.

"Why?" he said. "Why did you do it?"

Padraic shrugged helplessly.

"Was it to be near *her*?" asked Rory with an unconscious note of jealousy.

"No!" answered Padraic, and then, "Well, partly."

He saw Rory's scowl.

"And partly that I thought I could do some good for Ireland. And then—"

Through the poteen came that sweet, irresistible smile. "You don't know what it's like, Rory, always to be the shadow."

Rory stared at him, astonished. "*Shadow?*" he exclaimed. "Can I write poetry like you? Can I sing the Irish songs and tell the Irish stories? Did Father ever love me as he loves you?"

Padraic frowned, puzzled, and Rory realized that this had never occurred to him. "You damned fool!" Rory cried in a mixture of affection and exasperation. "Didn't you *know*? If you're the shadow, what the devil do you think *I* am?"

"Maybe," said Padraic, "apart we are both shadows, but together we make one man."

They looked at each other in silence and really saw each other for the first time.

"Rory," said Padraic, "let's work together to save our people and our poor godforsaken country!"

"Not while one of us is an agent!" said Rory fiercely, resisting to the end.

"Then I'll resign the job. Rory, if we stand together, no one can beat us."

Padraic released his hold on the saddle and staggered uncertainly toward Rory.

"Will you stand away from the tail of the horse!" said Rory and ran to clasp him, laughing, in his arms.

They hugged each other, still laughing, and in that moment when they were at last one, they heard the voice of Brian as he ran, breathless, up the road.

"Rory!" he cried. "Rory, he betrayed you!"

Rory drew away from Padraic, looking, startled, up the road as Brian ran gasping up to them.

"What? Who did?"

Brian turned his eyes on Padraic with all that cold judgment of right and wrong that belongs to adolescence. "He did. Padraic."

"No!" said Padraic.

"I was working in Regan's bar," said Brian, "and Sinclair was there—Lord Fitzmorris's agent. Kerrigan came in. He said you killed Houlihan. He said Padraic told him."

Rory turned his eyes toward Padraic. "Did you tell Kerrigan?"

"I—he's one of us!" said Padraic.

"*Did* you?" Rory demanded.

"I—I don't remember," said Padraic.

"The hell you don't!" said Rory.

The old enmity began to boil up between them.

"Rory, the soldiers will be after you," said Brian. "You'll have to run for it."

Rory's eyes were still fixed on Padraic. "Did you tell him?"

"What if I did?" said Padraic, anger rising up in him with the drink. "You *did* kill Houlihan, didn't you? I suppose you'll kill *me* if you get the chance!"

"Yes, you damned traitor!" shouted Rory, "so I will!"

He grappled with him, and they wrestled together, as so often before.

"You've always been a millstone around my neck," cried Rory. "One day I'll be quit of you for good!"

He thrust Padraic violently away from him and saw him fall and heard him give a gasping cry. He rushed to kneel beside him, horrified, and knew instantly that the sharp edge of the spade had penetrated his back.

"Padraic?" he cried desperately.

Padraic, in his agony, turned his eyes upon Rory. "The—curse—of God—" he said.

Rory heard his words with intense horror.

"Padraic!" he cried. "Forgive me!"

Padraic fixed his eyes on Rory's face and tried to speak, but Rory was never to know what he meant to say. Padraic was dead. Rory put his head down, sobbing, on Padraic's body.

"Come away, Rory, come away!" cried Brian. He saw soldiers approaching along the road and pulled at Rory's sleeve.

"We have to leave him!" he cried. "If the soldiers find you with him, they'll kill you, too!"

Rory looked up and saw Trooper Craig and another soldier riding toward them up the road. It was the last element in his guilt that the dreadful, essential instinct of self-preservation took over. He stood up, snatched the gun from the cart and began to run with Brian up the hillside. They heard the troopers' voices behind them and, glancing back, saw one trooper dismount beside Padraic's body. But the other, Trooper Craig, rode on after them, raised his musket and fired, and Rory fell.

"Got him!" yelled Trooper Craig, and he spurred on up the hill.

Brian seized the gun from Rory, took wild aim and shot the trooper. Stunned as he saw the soldier fall from his horse, he flung the rifle away from him.

"Come on, Rory! Come on!" he sobbed, and half-dragged, half-supported his wounded brother away.

On the dark turf Padraic lay dead, his white face turned up to the brooding gray sky.

CHAPTER 12

Rachel sat at the piano after dinner that evening, playing and singing while her father dozed in his chair. She wore her father's favorite dress but had chosen the song to suit her own mood.

> The minstrel boy to the war is gone.
> In the ranks of death you'll find him.
> His father's sword he has girded on,
> And his wild harp slung behind him.

David came in, and she smiled at him. He came to stand behind her, turning the pages. Harry woke up when the song finished.

"Charming, my dear," he said, "charming."

Rachel was about to rise from the piano, but David's hand was on her shoulder.

"No! Go on playing!"

She glanced up at him, startled. He turned the page, and she began to play again. David leaned close.

"Your groom is in the stables," he said. "He's been shot."

Rachel's hands faltered. David glanced at Harry, dozing over his newspaper.

"Go on playing!"

"How—badly is he—"

"I don't know," said David. "I've sent the boy for Dr. Fleming's son. Can't risk the doctor. He's a wanted man."

Harry snored slightly and woke himself up, and David paused. Rachel played on but could not trust herself to sing the words on the page before her.

Believe me if all those endearing young charms,
Which I gaze on so fondly today,
Were to change by tomorrow and fleet in my arms,
Like fairy gifts fading away.

David leaned close again, turning a page.

"The servants mustn't know," he said. "Keep Father out of the stables and stay with him until he goes to bed."

"Yes," replied Rachel. "Oh, David, thank you!"

He could not miss the heartfelt emotion in her voice. He looked at her, astonished.

"I'm not doing it for you—or for him. I'm doing it for his sister."

"Dierdre?"

She looked up at him and saw the truth in his face as he saw it in hers.

"Oh, David! Not you, too!"

"Rachel—" he began, but if he intended some brotherly admonition, she had no time for it.

"Please, David," she said, "please save him!"

Harry coughed, woke up and began to read his paper

again. Rachel played on and felt David's hand gently pressing her shoulder.

"I'll do what I can," he said under his breath, and then aloud, "I think I'll just take a turn around the garden, Father. Good night."

Brian held the lantern as Eamon, his father's black bag behind him, tried to get his courage together for the task of extracting the musket ball from Rory's shoulder. David stood watching, reluctantly involved. He could see that Rory was in great pain and knew how much worse it would be once Eamon started probing the wound. He had taken the precaution of fetching a jar of poteen from the cellar and now offered it to Eamon.

"Here," he said. "Better give him a swig of this."

Eamon held the jar to Rory's lips, and he drank, choked and was in more pain than ever, but managed a grin.

"Eamon," he said, "either that poteen will get me or you will! Get on with it, can't you?"

Looking back afterward, Rachel would always remember that evening with astonishment, wondering how she could possibly have played the piano, smiled at her father, lit their candles with a steady hand and walked upstairs, knowing every instant that Rory's life was in the balance. She waited until she knew her father was safely in his bedroom and then, a cloak over her evening dress, ran down the stairs, through the kitchen and out to the stable yard. David stopped her.

"No, Rachel!"

She thought that Rory was dead. No blow would ever strike her to the heart like that again.

"Is he—"

"No. Eamon's got the musket ball out, but it's a bloody mess in there. He's bandaging him now."

She would have waded to Rory through a sea of blood, but at that moment Eamon emerged, white and shaken, rolling his shirtsleeves down.

"I must get home now," he said, "or my father will miss me."

He turned to Brian, who followed him out, marked forever by an experience no thirteen-year-old should have to endure.

"Go to your family now, Brian," said Eamon, "and tell them he is safe."

The slight, redheaded boy nodded and was gone.

"Is he?" said Rachel. "Is he safe?"

Eamon turned to look at her. "I don't know. I got the ball out, but he has lost a lot of blood and has a fever. I don't know."

"I must go," said David. "I'm on duty at the barracks tonight."

Eamon stopped him. "Will you give him up?" he said.

David turned on him angrily. "I would, if I thought he'd get a fair trial!"

He found himself looking at Rachel as well as at Eamon, who spoke in a matter-of-fact manner.

"There's no chance of that."

David did not express agreement, but his next words acknowledged the truth of Eamon's words.

"You must get him out of the country."

"No!" cried Rachel. "Oh, no!"

David turned on her and was suddenly the stern elder brother.

"Do you want him to hang?" he demanded. "Rachel, we've done all we can—perhaps too much already. I'll

help get him out of the country for Deirdre's sake and—
for yours. But there it ends."

He turned and walked out. Rachel turned to Eamon.

"What does he mean—'out of the country'?"

"To America," answered Eamon. "It's his only hope
—that is, if he lives."

They both looked back at Rory, pale and unconscious, each breath so fragile that it could be his last.

"I must go," said Eamon.

Rachel looked at him, aghast. She had never nursed
so much as a sick dog, and now—"

"What shall I do?" she cried.

Eamon shrugged. "Pray," he said. "There's nothing
else."

The long night wore away. It seemed to Rachel,
kneeling beside Rory, that life was surely flowing out
of him. She saw from the window the first gray light of
dawn and heard a blackbird sound his warning note.
She remembered hearing that people died with the first
light of dawn, life flowing out with the ebb tide. She
got up and went to the stable door and pushed it open,
smelling the fresh, green scent of morning. She did not
pray. Her whole being was a prayer. She heard from
behind her a deep sigh and knew it was Rory's dying
breath. She turned and ran to kneel beside him. He
groaned and turned on his side, and slept. Rachel put
her head down beside him in the straw.

"Oh, God!" she said. "Oh, thank you, God! Whatever you want of me, whatever you ask—Oh, God,
thank you!"

Rory, weak but recovering, found Rachel beside him
with an earthenware bowl and a silver spoon.

"Broth," she said. "Eamon said you should take some nourishment."

Rory looked up at her, amused, and then was struck by anguished recollection.

"Padraic!" he said.

"I know," said Rachel tenderly. "I know."

"I killed him."

"No. It was an accident. Brian told me."

"The last thing he said was—'The curse of God!'"

"He didn't mean it," said Rachel. "He loved you." She managed to feed him a spoonful of broth.

"The trooper I shot," said Rory, "did he die?"

"Not you!" cried Rachel. "David said that it was Brian who shot him."

"No!" said Rory as fiercely as he could through his weakness. "Brian had nothing to do with it."

She knew he was lying and was afraid, knowing that the shooting of a trooper would arouse more animosity against him than the shooting of an Irish agent, but she knew, too, that the protection of his young brother would always come first with him. She fed him another spoonful of broth.

"The trooper didn't die," she said. "The soldiers have been to your house—it's all right! They didn't hurt your family. But they're searching everywhere they think you might be hidden—"

And with the words they heard the beat of horses' hooves in the drive. Rory struggled to get up.

"No!" cried Rachel. "You'll start the bleeding again. No!"

She held him close, and he was so weak that her strength overpowered his. He sank back, sweating with exhaustion.

"Take your cloak," he said. "Take everything that could show you've been here. If they find me—"

"I don't *care!*" she cried.

"But I do," he said.

She kissed him and gathered up her things and went out. He tried once more to rise but found himself incapable even of raising himself onto his elbow and sank back again, helpless.

Rachel put on her cloak and composed herself before she turned the corner from the stable yard. The first thing she saw was David, mounted, among the troop of soldiers, with the colonel in command. So, she thought, David's duty had been too strong for him and he had betrayed Rory to the army. But she was determined to fight it out to the end in her own way.

"Why, David!" she exclaimed, and then with a charming smile, "Colonel Maitland! What a delightful surprise!"

Colonel Maitland saluted stiffly. "Good morning, Miss Clement," he said. "I'm sorry to trouble you. Very awkward in the circumstances. But we have to search the house."

"Search *our* house?" cried Rachel, laughing merrily. "Whatever for?"

Harry Clement emerged, astonished, on the steps of the house. "What on earth is going on?" he demanded.

The colonel saluted him and spoke very formally. "Mr. Clement. We are searching for a fugitive who is suspected of murder. His name is O'Manion. We have reason to believe that he may be here."

Rachel's eyes met David's accusingly.

"Here?" said Harry. "In *my* house? Do you think I

am the sort of man who would give refuge to a murderer?"

"There is no personal imputation, I assure you," said the colonel. "We are searching every house where—"

"Have you searched Carralough Castle?"

The colonel was brought up short. He coughed, embarrassed. "As—as a matter of fact, it was Lord Fitzmorris who said that O'Manion might be here."

Rachel's eyes met David's again in relief. Harry's natural dignity came to his aid, stronger than foolish snobbery, and he spoke with cool authority.

"Lord Fitzmorris is mistaken," he said. "And I greatly resent the imputation."

Colonel Maitland was clearly impressed by Harry, standing there on the steps of his house, every inch the English gentleman.

"Of course, Mr. Clement," he said, "if you can positively assure me—"

Harry broke in. "I dismissed Rory O'Manion from my service because I found him to be disloyal," he said. "I give you my word of honor as a gentleman that he is not here."

The colonel's eyes met his, and there was a brief moment of suspense before the colonel nodded.

"Very good, sir. Thank you."

He nodded to his second in command. Orders were given, and the troop of soldiers wheeled and were trotting off down the drive. Rachel slowly mounted the steps and stood beside her father, watching them go. It was only as the last of them turned the bend in the drive that she swayed and almost fainted. Harry put his arm around her.

"Rachel? It's all right, my dear. There's no danger. He—"

A fearful suspicion rushed upon him. *"Rachel?* He's not *here?"*

. She slowly raised her eyes to his. "I'm sorry, Father."

He was stunned with horror. "Rachel, how *could* you?"

She moved from the protective support of his arm, holding onto the balustrade. He was still struggling to grasp what had happened.

"David—" he said. "How could you risk David's career in such a way?"

She turned to look at him. "David knew," she said. "He brought him here."

It was cruel, but she knew that it was the one way to ensure that Harry would in no circumstances inform the authorities that Rory was there. But still it was dreadful to see her father's stricken look.

"I gave my word of honor!" he said.

He turned and went slowly inside the house.

CHAPTER 13

"To *India?"* said Deirdre. "You are going to India?"

"The colonel has 'formed the opinion,' " mimicked David bitterly, "that I have 'too much sympathy with the local people.' I am being seconded to our battalion on the Northwest Frontier."

They were in the stone barn at some distance from the house, which was used for storing hay for the Ballyclam animals during the winter.

"How long," Deirdre faltered, "how long will you be gone?"

"I don't know."

They stared at each other. It was as though everything that mattered was being said between the words they spoke. He put his arms around her.

"Oh, my beloved Deirdre, you will write to me? I'll send you my address as soon as I arrive, and—"

He felt her go rigid, and she moved out of his embrace.

"What is it?" he said. "What's the matter?"

She spoke and turned away from him, her voice so low that he could hardly hear her. "I cannot read nor write."

"You—"

She suddenly turned to face him defiantly. " 'Tis not uneommon in Ireland. Here it is the boys who learn such things. Rory and—and Padraic—went to the hedge school, and Brian goes to the State School, bad cess to it! For *they* learned Greek and Latin and the beauties of the Irish language, and Brian is only taught what they think it right for him to know. But at least he can write his name, which is more than *I* can do."

"I'm surprised—" said David, hesitating, "that your father—"

"Ah, no!" Deirdre interrupted, "you must not blame my father! My mother could not read nor write, and I knew—I felt it would hurt her if I knew more than she did."

He was too moved for words, but she mistook his silence for rejection and lifted her chin defiantly.

"So now, you see, you can stop loving such an *omadaun!*"

"A what?"

"An ignoramus."

He came and took her very gently in his arms again.

"My little tender-hearted love," he said. "I shall never stop loving you, in this world or the next."

But then the thought of the coming separation was too much for him, and he brought her passionately to him. "But, oh God! Deirdre, how can I bear to be so far away, and never hear from you?"

"Oh, David! Oh, *mo ghra*! I am yours forever. Don't you know that? Oh, don't you know it?"

She put her arms around his neck, kissing him again and again, seeking to give that proof of love and giving it at last.

It was a wonderfully clear, golden evening, but Deirdre turned her face away from the westering sun making a nimbus around the little Catholic church which stood beside the road.

"It was a sin," she said. "It was a mortal sin."

"I can't believe that," said David. "I think of you as my wife. Think of me as your husband—"

"But we are not," said Deirdre with that simple, invincible logic of the Irish peasant girl which she was never to lose.

David suddenly grasped her hand more firmly. "Come on!" he said.

In the small, new, whitewashed church David and Deirdre knelt before the candlelit statue of the Virgin Mary.

"I, David," he said, "in the sight of God, take thee, Deirdre, to be my lawful wedded wife."

She hesitated. He nodded at her, pressed her hand and smiled to give her courage. She spoke very firmly, and forever.

"I, Deirdre, in the sight of God and of the blessed

Virgin, take thee, David, to be my lawful wedded husband."

She crossed herself and prayed and was going to rise.

"Wait!" he said.

He took the signet ring off his little finger and put it on the third finger of her left hand.

"My beloved wife!" he said and kissed her, kneeling there in the church's lengthening shadows.

They emerged from the church with that blessed illusory feeling of immunity which comes now and then to lovers.

"I'll send messages by Rachel," said David, "and she will send news of you."

Deirdre looked at him quickly, and he smiled.

"Oh yes," he said, "she knows about us. And she and Rory—"

"She and Rory—?"

David's face hardened. "I've promised her that I'll do my best to get him safely away to America. But that's all." He stopped and turned to her. "We're luckier than them, Deirdre. We have a future together. They have none."

"Hush!" said Deirdre.

They both heard at the same moment the troop of soldiers riding on the hard road past the O'Manion cabin.

"You mustn't come any further," she said. "And my father will be looking for me. He needs me now."

The moment of peace was over. They kissed in the anguish of parting, and then she turned to run home.

"Deirdre!" called David.

She stopped and turned. He saw her as he had first seen her, barefoot, with her hair about her shoulders.

"Wait for me, Deirdre!" he called. "Only wait for me!"

"Can you doubt it?" she called back, and turned again and was gone.

Much later that night Rory heard the same troop of soldiers returning from their unsuccessful search. He shrank back into the old cow byre and waited until the last sound of their passing had vanished from the quiet land, and then he crept down the hill and into the house.

He looked around the small, familiar room, lit only by the dim glow of the banked-down turf fire, and went quietly to look in at the tiny bedroom where Deirdre lay asleep, with the tumbled golden head of Maeve beside her on the pillow. He glanced toward the door which led to the other bedroom but did not dare open it for fear of waking his father. The guilt of Padraic's death was heavy upon him, and heavier still in this place. He had come to say good-bye to them in his heart, but he could not face his father's eyes.

Sean was in his cradle, and Rory knelt down beside him, torn by the defenseless look of the sleeping child.

"Oh, Mother," he said, "forgive me for breaking my promise! If I could give my life to keep him safe, I would!"

He took the holy medal from around his neck awkwardly because of his injured shoulder and gently put it around the baby's neck. Sean stirred in his sleep, and his little fist closed firmly on the chain.

"That's right," said Rory. "Hold it fast, and hold Ireland for me till I return, for return I surely will."

He heard a sound from the doorway, looked up and

saw his father standing there in shirt and trousers. Rory slowly rose to his feet but could not speak or move, weighed down by the dreadful burden of guilt. But Shane stepped forward and held out his arms, and Rory stumbled to him and was clasped to his heart.

"Forgive me, Father!" he said. "Oh, forgive me!"

He heard Shane's voice, full of love. "Forgive yourself, Rory, or it will kill you, too."

Deirdre heard them talking and came out in petticoat and shawl, and they roused Brian and Maeve for those last sleepy, half-understood embraces.

"I will send money from America as soon as I get there," said Rory. "But if things get much worse here, you may all have to leave."

"Leave Ireland?" cried Deirdre.

Shane moved to take the violin down from its place of honor by the fireplace. He caressed it and spoke as though he spoke to himself.

"But if this fiddle leaves Ireland," he said, "who will sing and dance until the good times come again?"

Rory felt a fearful premonition that he would never see his father again, but Shane looked up at him and smiled.

"Come, my boy," he said, "no more tears. Be off with you now. A new land awaits you, and I will play you away with a good Irish tune."

To the distant strain of fairy music that was his father's farewell to him—so brave, so cheerful and so full of sorrow—Rory climbed the hill beneath the stars and looked back and saw the tiny thatched house.

Next morning David and Rachel drove to Galway. David's baggage was strapped on behind, for he was to travel on by Bianconi car to Dublin, where he was to take ship for India. The Ballyclam carriage was driven by Michael O'Connor, Patrick O'Fee having been declared drunk and incapable, or rather, since he was Mrs. Docherty's first cousin on her mother's side, "not quite himself that morning."

"Poor Patrick!" said Rachel. "It was dreadful to get him drunk so early in the day."

A voice spoke, muffled, from beneath the traveling rug. "The day that Paddy O'Fee objects to being drunk, early or late, is the day the pope turns Protestant!"

Rachel chuckled, but David spoke repressively.

"It had to be done," he said. "We know we can trust O'Connor, but we would have been taking a chance with Patrick. And I'm taking no more chances than I have to."

He looked Rachel sternly in the eye. "I suppose you know," he said, "that if Rory is discovered, he won't be the only one to be hanged."

"Oh, David!"

He saw the alarm in her face and relented. "Don't worry," he said. "I have a healthy regard for my own skin. If I thought there'd be any real danger, I wouldn't have suggested it."

The coach jolted over a stone, and Rachel heard Rory groan. It was a feature of Michael O'Connor's driving to find every boulder in the road and take the wheels over it.

"Rory!" she said. "Are you all right?"

She drew the rug back and was reassured by his grin.

"I'm fine," he said. "I just wish I was a size smaller."

"You can stretch out a bit now," said David, "but keep down when we get near the quay."

But as they approached the quayside, they heard Michael O'Connor's voice from above.

"Look out, sir! There's trouble ahead."

David lowered the window and looked out. He saw the gates closed, guarded by soldiers, and saw a dog cart turned away. He sat back in his seat and drew the rug over Rory, crouched in the space intended for their feet.

"Keep down," he said.

"Very sorry, sir," said the sentry. "No vehicles allowed on the quay."

David looked at him, astonished. "Why on earth not?"

"Orders, sir," said the sentry uneasily. "A search for a wanted man."

David's amusement was immensely convincing. "Well, he's not in here. I am Lieutenant Clement, traveling with my sister."

He caught sight of a fellow officer and called out to him. "George! What the devil's going on?"

He opened the door and descended, strolling through the gate. Michael O'Connor let the horses move a few feet forward.

"David, my dear feller," said George. "What are you doing here?"

"My sister has a package for my aunt in Philadelphia," replied David, "lace, ribbon for a bonnet, or some such feminine gew gaws, and I promised to give it to the captain—make sure it arrives safely. But I don't particularly want to walk along the quay amid all the Irish unwashed!"

He laughed, and George laughed with him.

Rachel drew a small envelope out of her pocket and

passed it down to Rory beneath the rug. She spoke without looking down. "Here is a letter to my uncle," she said. "I'm sure he'll give you a job." And then, urgently, "Rory, you will write to me, won't you? Every week, every day! I won't breathe until I hear from you!"

He took the letter, but there was a long silence before he spoke. "I won't write," he said.

She caught her breath and looked down before she remembered that she must not and stared straight ahead. "What do you mean?"

"I won't write to you," said Rory. "I won't allow myself to think of you. I don't want you to think of me. The kindest thing I can do is to go away and never let you hear from me again."

Rachel sat motionless, one screaming, silent statue of anguish.

"How can you say such a thing?" she finally managed. "How can you *think* it?"

"I am going to America as a fugitive," said Rory, "and when I return it will be with guns. After all that has happened, I owe you the truth. There is no future for you and me."

"There is always a future," said Rachel, "for people who love each other. There must be!"

He did not reply. The cheery voices from outside the coach mocked their misery.

"When do you sail for India?" cried George.

"On Thursday, from Dublin," David called back. "I'm driving there as soon as we have delivered this package."

He was at the coach now, calling back, laughing. "Thanks, George. I'll send you a tiger skin!"

He got into the coach, saying, "Drive on, O'Connor."

Michael prepared to do so as the sentry opened the gate, but observed with alarm that George was approaching the carriage. He peered into the coach as Rachel hastily rearranged the rug after David's entrance.

"Miss Clement!" said George. "More charming than ever!"

Somehow Rachel forced the flattered, flirtatious smile. "Thank you," she said. "How kind of you to say so!"

The foolish young officer saluted, and Michael drove the coach onto the quay.

"You'll have to take your chance when you can," said David curtly to the motionless figure beneath the rug. "I'll try and make a bit of a stir."

He opened the door, and Rory lifted the rug to look at him.

"Thanks," he said. "I owe you for this."

Their eyes met, and David's face softened. "Good luck!" he said.

Rachel and Rory heard the bustle outside as David called to a sailor on the ship and Michael descended from the coach to assist him, with much explaining to passersby of the nature of his mission and the importance of the English officer. Rachel saw a moment when there was no one watching the near side of the carriage.

"Now!" she said and reached down to open the door.

Rory took hold of the canvas bag beside him on the floor and prepared to slip out.

"I love you forever," said Rachel.

He looked up at her, and in spite of all that he could do, his feelings were too strong for his resolve. "And I you!"

He said it fiercely, angrily, against his will, but he said it, and that was enough for Rachel. He was gone, and the door closed behind him. She sat with tears running down her cheeks, but they were partly tears of joy. He had never before said he loved her. Suddenly she heard a sharp voice from the quayside.

"Here! You!"

She saw Rory, halfway up the gangway of the ship, the canvas bag hiding his face, and a policeman standing below, shouting up at him.

"You! That sailor!"

Rachel saw David and Michael motionless with horror for a moment before they tried to seem busy themselves and unconcerned. Rory slowly turned. He was still in Irish waters. To flee was certain death. He slowly descended. To have been so near to freedom, and now—!

"Would you give this letter to me cousin in Philadelphia?" said the policeman.

Rory could hardly speak but managed it at last, and fortunately the policeman was fumbling in his pocket for the letter.

"Sure, I'll be glad to," said Rory.

"Jim O'Casey," said the policeman, consigning the rather grubby missive to Rory's care. "I've never met him, but he owns a saloon, the Black Horse, in Black Horse Alley. He tells me it runs straight up from the quayside, and a grand place it must be."

"If he sells good Irish whiskey, I'll be glad to go there!" said Rory.

"Well, good luck to you!" said the policeman.

Rory felt all the irony of this farewell from a peeler, but, after it, it was an Irish voice which spoke it.

"Thanks," he said, and jumped aboard the *Sylvania* bound for Philadelphia, leaving behind him all that he cared for on earth.

PART II:

AN ALIEN LAND

CHAPTER 14

"Right!" yelled the foreman at the tramway construction site. "Ten cents an hour, and I'll take twenty men."

Rory fought with the rest, using fists and elbows, but he knew too well that the months of near-starvation and desperate physical drudgery had robbed him of the strength he needed, and the twenty men were chosen before he could struggle to the gate. He was about to turn away when the foreman said, "I'll take one more man."

A dozen other men were ahead of him, but Rory shouted, "I'll do it for eight cents!"

The foreman looked at him contemptuously. "Irish!" he said disgustedly, but jerked his head. "All right. Get to work."

Rory was aware of the anger of the men about him, and he got shoved and punched as he pushed through them. There was a time when he would have been ashamed to undercut his fellow workers, but now all he cared about was earning a few dollars a week—enough to keep body and soul together while the rest was sent home to Ireland.

Rory swung his pickax vigorously whenever the foreman was near, but by the end of the day he was so exhausted that he could have flung himself down in the corner of the yard with the shovels and pickaxes. He collected his money—only ninety-six cents, but it was better than nothing—and turned and trudged away, buttoning up his threadbare coat against the bitter cold.

"Down with Ireland!" yelled a voice just behind him.

Rory turned with fists clenched, and saw with astonishment the grinning face of Eamon Fleming.

"Why—you—! Eamon!"

They fell upon each other, laughing and pummeling, though the joy of seeing a face from home after all the hardship and loneliness was almost too much for Rory. He knew that there were tears in his eyes and was grateful to Eamon for pretending not to notice.

"Well, you old rebel!" said Eamon. "How are you?"

"I'm still alive," said Rory, "and with things in Philadelphia the way they are, that means I'm ahead. How did you find me?"

"An Irishman in the Black Horse Saloon said that there was work going here and that you might be after it."

"Third time lucky," said Rory, and added bitterly, "You know the notice they put up here—No Irish or Catholics need apply!"

He saw Eamon's dismayed look and grinned. "You'll be all right, you damned heretic! Just use your English voice and say you hate the pope!"

He turned and led the way along the dirt road that led toward the city. "Why didn't you let me know you were coming?"

"Had to slip out the same way as you did. The peelers had a price on my head."

"Ah, great!" said Rory. "So the fight is still going on!"

Eamon glanced at him sadly. "Rory," he said, "the only fight in Ireland now is the fight to stay alive."

They turned off onto a paved road, passing an alley which led beside a church. At the entrance to the alley, they saw men with pickax handles and heard a voice yell, "There he is! There's the Mick! Get him, boys! The stinking Irish pig."

"Run, Eamon!" said Rory. "Run for your life!"

They both took to their heels, but Rory, weak and exhausted, fell behind. Rough hands seized him and dragged him into the alley, hitting and kicking him. Once he broke free but was dragged back again.

Then a policeman's whistle was heard nearby, and Eamon came running.

"It's the law! The law!"

The men dispersed quickly, and Eamon leaned over Rory, relieved to find him still alive.

Just then a young boy with a tin toy whistle came around the corner. "Well done, lad," said Eamon, and tossed him a penny.

The Black Horse Saloon was not the palatial establishment envisaged by Jim O'Casey's cousin, the policeman in Galway. It was, in fact, a stinking bar in a stinking narrow alley which ran up from the quayside into the stinking slums and rookeries where the Irish immigrants found a desperate, fever-ridden existence. But Eamon had discovered that Rory lodged near there, so it was to the Black Horse that he supported him, dazed and bleeding. Jim O'Casey, a tough, bald Irish-American, stood behind the bar.

"Whiskey!" said Eamon. "Quick!"

O'Casey polished a glass and eyed him coldly. "Can you pay?" he inquired.

Eamon, assisting Rory to a small table near the door, glanced around at O'Casey indignantly. "Yes, I can pay," he said. He felt in his pocket and took out half a sovereign. "Will you take that?"

O'Casey accepted the gold piece and bit it cautiously and nodded.

Eamon glanced anxiously at Rory. "You might have some feeling for a fellow Irishman!" he said.

"Fellow Irishman, is it?" demanded O'Casey. "My father fought in the War of Independence. He didn't come off no stinking immigrant ship!"

Eamon glared at him. "I should have thought—"

"What would you have thought?" broke in O'Casey. "Would you think those of us who've been here for a hundred years and won some respect in the community would be glad to see a beggarly rabble bringing disease and starvation and making the name of Irish stink throughout America!"

He banged two glasses up on the counter and prepared to fill them.

"Only one," said Eamon.

He could see that he was going to need every cent of the change from that half-sovereign.

Rory let out a yelp as the whiskey touched his cut lip but then tried a grin and began to recover.

"Come on, then," he said, "tell me the news from home. My father—Deirdre—all of them. How are they?"

"Wait till you feel better. Here, have some more whiskey."

Rory took the glass and put it down on the table, his eyes fixed on Eamon's face. "Eamon? Tell me!"

"Your father. He couldn't bear to see the little ones go hungry. He left a note saying he'd heard there was work in Limerick, and he set out to walk there in the middle of the night."

"Limerick!" exclaimed Rory. "He'd never be able to walk as far as—"

Eamon put a hand on his arm. "Rory. They found him in the snow, a hundred yards from the house."

"*Dead?* My father's dead?"

"I'm sorry, Rory."

Rorry tossed the whiskey off and, fighting back his grief, took refuge in anger. "And what was our fine landlord, Mr. Clement, doing all this time?"

"Dying," said Eamon.

"What?"

"The fever doesn't care whether you're rich or poor."

Rory sat silent for a moment, afraid to ask the next question.

"And—Rachel?"

"She worked to save the sick and starving as though —as though she were one of us."

Rory sat silent, his face haunted. Eamon hesitated.

"She said she wrote to you several times, care of the General Post Office. Didn't you get her letters?"

"I got them."

"But you never answered."

"What was the point?" said Rory with a violence that made him groan at the same time as he jarred his injured ribs. "Look at me. I couldn't even earn enough to save my own father's life!"

O'Casey came over with a bottle and filled Rory's glass. Eamon glanced up at him and began to feel in his pocket.

"This one's on the house," said O'Casey crossly, and he produced another glass from behind his back and filled that, too. "You'd better have one yourself," he said, scowling, and stamped back behind the bar before Eamon could thank him.

"I should stay clear of that tramway construction," said Eamon after a while.

"I will," replied Rory grimly, "if I can find work somewhere else. It's no good, Eamon. I've got to make enough money to bring the family over."

"Rachel said she gave you an introduction to her uncle."

"That's right," said Rory. "Mr. Kent. He owns the Kent Powder Manufactory."

Eamon saw that O'Casey, polishing glasses, glanced up at the name.

"I went to the house," said Rory, "and he wouldn't even see me."

"You should've gone to the mill yard," said O'Casey. "Since the last explosion they'll take on anyone. Especially Irishmen!"

The Kent Powder Manufactory stood beside a fast-flowing creek which was a tributary of the Schuylkill River. As Rory and Eamon walked along the path on the far side of the stream, they could see the cluster of stone buildings, resembling something between mills and oast houses, and above them the small stone houses where the workers lived. Above the yard a private road wound up to a graceful colonial house above.

"That's a lordly-looking house for a decent republic," remarked Eamon. "It reminds me of Ballyclam."

"Yes, it must be a family resemblance," said Rory, pulling a face. "That's the Kent House."

Approaching, they became aware of a commotion in the yard, with men running about and shouting and smoke rising from one of the buildings.

"Come on!" said Rory, and he plunged into the water.

"I can't swim!" said Eamon, plunging in after him

and was relieved to find that the creek was fordable at that point.

On the other side workmen were filling buckets and racing back toward the fire.

"What's going on?" inquired Rory.

"Fire in the charcoal-drying house. If we don't get it out, the powder mills will blow!"

"A sensible man would run like hell," said Eamon.

"So he would," Rory agreed.

They both seized buckets and headed for the fire.

A big man who struck Rory as being more brawn than brains appeared to be in charge. "Get that tar shifted out of the powder mill!" he yelled.

Rory went up a ladder and passed his bucket to a black-faced powderman who was tipping water under the burning roof. Taking the empty bucket back and passing up a full one, Rory grinned down at Eamon.

"Gunpowder, charcoal and tar," he said. "Sounds like a great recipe for conflagration!"

"So it is," said the powderman with a disgusted look over his shoulder at the big man, "and you don't see Ed Miller taking any chances trying to put it out!"

The powderman tipped the bucket of water on the roof, and an alarming blast of steam went up, nearly knocking Rory off the ladder.

"Rory, for God's sake, get away from there!" shouted Eamon.

Rory passed him the empty bucket and grinned at him. "Away with you and get some more water," he said. "I need this powder factory if nobody else does."

"All right! Back to work!" yelled Ed Miller. The powder mill was intact, but the charcoal-drying house was still smoking and being doused with water. One of the powdermen gazed at Miller, astonished.

"You think we're going back inside there, with the roof still warm?"

"There's an order to be filled."

"Then fill it yourself!" said the powderman and walked away.

Ed Miller, turning in a rage, came upon Rory and Eamon. "What do you two want?"

"We're looking for work," said Rory. "It looks as though you have a vacancy for a powderman."

"Maybe you could find work for two," suggested Eamon. "It seems to be a life full of incident."

Rory looked at him and began to laugh for the first time since he left Ireland.

CHAPTER 15

Standing on the deck of the ship as it sailed toward Philadelphia, Rachel could not help remembering that other voyage to Galway only two years before. She still wore black for the death of her father, but through her grief she was haunted, too, by the thought of the parting from Ballyclam. Rachel had tried to explain to the Irish servants the nature of bankruptcy but the old butler, Tobin, wandered about like a ghost, polishing with his sleeve the furniture which was so soon to be sold to pay her father's debts. And Mrs. Docherty, whose pleasure it had been for so long to abuse landlords, refused to believe that the departure of the last landlord could leave her and her relatives homeless.

"Banks, is it?" she exclaimed belligerently when Rachel assured her that a bank in London now held the mortgage on Ballyclam House. "Well, God break hard fortune! There's never a landlord could turn me out of me kitchen, and devil a bank there'll be can do the same!"

At least, thought Rachel, Mrs. Docherty represented that tragicomic element in the Irish character which refused to accept facts and accordingly tended to overcome them. It might be that she would defeat the bank as she had always defeated the landlords.

Much more heartbreaking had been the farewell to Deirdre. During the past hard months Rachel and Deirdre had become dear friends, living together in that interlocked tragedy which held them both and from which neither could escape. Shane died in the snow and Harry from the fever in the same week. And David was far away, fighting in India. Rachel, receiving the invitation from her aunt and uncle to come to America, wrote swiftly back, begging to be allowed to bring her Irish maid, Deirdre O'Manion, and fully intending to find some means of transporting Brian, Maeve and Sean with her. But she received in reply a cold letter from her Aunt Charlotte remarking that they had plenty of Irish servants in Philadelphia without bringing another one from Ireland at her uncle's expense.

That letter more than anything else made Rachel realize that she was a mere object of charity, dependent on the Kents even for her passage money, as helpless as any other emigrant from Ireland to America whose landlord had paid for his escape from destitution.

They were fast approaching Philadelphia now, and Rachel received an impression of a very neat, sturdy, red-bricked city with nothing slipshod or foolish about it. The ship was moored. Reluctantly she stepped ashore and was greeted by a smiling, elegantly dressed man.

"Rachel! Rachel, my dear!"

"Uncle James?"

He removed his hat and kissed her tenderly on the cheek.

"I wasn't sure that you would know me," said Rachel.

He put his hands on her shoulders and held her away from him, surveying her lovingly. "I would know you anywhere," he said. "You are so like your mother."

He folded her in his arms. "I am so sorry about your father," he said. "So sorry."

Tears came into her eyes. It seemed so long since she had been loved and cherished.

"Dear Uncle!" she said. "Thank you for all you have done."

He drew away and surveyed her again. "You look very beautiful—but too pale."

Suddenly Rachel felt it was good to be paid compliments again.

"Thank you, Uncle," she said, laughing through her tears. "But I have heard about you and your flattery!"

"Flattery?" exclaimed James Kent. "Nonsense!"

But a twinkle in his eyes showed that he did not resent the imputation.

"My mother told me," said Rachel, "that there was not a woman in London or Philadelphia who could resist your charms."

"Ah," said James Kent, "except for your mother! But now I have you."

He held both her hands in his. Rachel laughed at him.

"And now you have me, what do you mean to do with me?"

"Spoil you to death," said Kent.

"Oh!" cried Rachel, glad in that moment to fling behind her all the sorrow, the hardship, the death. "I think I shall like that!"

But still when she was sitting in the carriage and her uncle was seeing to her luggage, she looked eagerly about the quay for Rory. She had written to tell him the name of her ship and the date she was sailing. He had never answered any of her letters, but she knew from Deirdre that his father had written to the Post Office and received replies. Even if he didn't answer, surely he would have been there on the quayside! If he is not here, she thought, that means it is all over. I will never think of him again. But she could not forget the look in his eyes in that instant before they had parted, when she had said, "I love you forever!" and he had replied, "And I you!"

"Uncle," she said as he mounted into the carriage beside her, "there was a young man, Rory O'Manion, who came here from Ireland. Did he come to see you?"

"No, my dear," replied James Kent. "He never did."

Rachel was astonished by her first sight of the Kent House as they drove up the graceful drive. She knew that her uncle owned a powder mill, and somehow she had thought that he would live in a grimy house by the mill yard. It was true that the mill yard was below, with smoking chimneys and workmen, but even that was quite picturesque, with the big waterwheel and the tree-lined stream. As for the house—it was an elegant mansion, with a beautiful view across the wooded Pennsylvania countryside, which was so much like England. It occurred to Rachel that in America, where there were no dukes or lords, it was the manufacturers, like James Kent, who were the real aristocracy.

It occurred to her also that it was rather odd of her aunt not to come out into the hall to meet her after such a long time and such a long voyage. One would have thought that she might be glad to welcome her sister's child so far from home.

"Charlotte," said Mr. Kent, leading the way into the drawing room, "here is our little girl."

Charlotte Kent rose from her seat by the fire. She was fashionably dressed, and even at first glance Rachel could see what expensive jewelry she wore.

"Well, Rachel," she said, and did not advance but waited for Rachel to come and kiss her on the cheek. "You had no trouble finding each other?"

Rachel's uncle answered for her. "None at all," he said. "Isn't she the living image of your sister?"

Charlotte fixed her eyes upon Rachel's face. "Yes," she said, and Rachel realized that this was not precisely a recommendation to her aunt.

"Thank you for taking me in, Aunt Charlotte," she said.

"Well, good gracious!" said her aunt, "you are one of the family, after all!"

There was nothing wrong with the words, but there was, thought Rachel, something peculiarly chilling in the way she spoke them, as though they sprang from duty, not from love.

She looked Rachel up and down. "I can see we shall have to buy you some new clothes. You cannot go on wearing that dreadful black."

"Aunt Charlotte," cried Rachel, "I am in mourning for my father!"

"Of course you are, my dear, and I am so sorry, but all that happened in Ireland, and you must put it behind you. You are in Philadelphia now, and we have to introduce you to society."

"My dear," said James Kent, "it is much too soon for Rachel to want to socialize. We'll keep her to ourselves for a little while."

Charlotte laughed. "So like a man!" she said. "I'm sure Rachel enjoys parties and dances as much as any other young girl! We must make haste to introduce her to some eligible young men."

She moved to ring the bell by the fireplace. "Rachel, I expect you are tired after your voyage. I will have one of the maids show you to your room."

"Thank you, Aunt Charlotte," said Rachel.

But what she thought was, Oh, Aunt Charlotte, what I need is love and tenderness!

Her uncle seemed to understand, because he put his arm around her. "Welcome home, my dear," he said.

She looked gratefully up at him. "Thank you, Uncle," she said, and reached up to kiss him on the cheek.

After Rachel had left them, Charlotte Kent turned to her husband. "What did you tell her about the Irishman?"

"Exactly what we agreed," Kent replied.

To Rachel's surprise it was her uncle who took her shopping for new clothes, and Madame Lucette, the owner of the discreetly fashionable dress shop on Wal-

nut Street, seemed to know him well. He sat at his ease
in a velvet armchair, a glass of champagne in his hand,
as Rachel emerged from behind a screen in a low-cut
evening gown.

"Charming, my dear!" he said. "Charming!"

"But, Uncle," Rachel demurred, "don't you think it
is rather—?" She gestured toward the uncovered bosom.

"Ye-es," said James Kent. "Madame Lucette, I did
tell you that Miss Clement is my niece."

Madame Lucette's face showed a certain confusion.
"Ah, *oui*, Monsieur Kent, this *is* your niece!"

Clearly it was a new situation, but Madame Lucette
rose to it triumphantly. "I think, perhaps, a touch of
lace?"

"Excellent," said James Kent.

Madame Lucette clicked her fingers to a saleslady
and hastened to supervise the choice.

"Uncle," said Rachel, "I really do want to find Rory
O'Manion."

"Why, my dear?" He drank his champagne.

Madame Lucette was trying to drape the lace about
her bosom, but Rachel waved her away. "Rory
O'Manion, the son of one of our tenants. Please,
Uncle, will you help me find him?"

He looked up at her. "No, my dear, I won't."

Rachel stopped, stunned.

"Your father wrote to me about him," said James
Kent.

Rachel gazed at him, aghast. "My *father*?"

"He said that this O'Manion was a troublemaker.
He advised me against employing him."

"Oh no!" cried Rachel.

Her uncle put down his glass, stood up and put a

kindly arm about her. "My dear," he said, "your father told me that you had formed an unfortunate attachment to this young man. Is this true?"

"I—"

"My dear Rachel," said James Kent, "promise me that you won't try to find him. Promise me that you will never see him again."

"Voilà, mademoiselle," said Madame Lucette, returning, *"un petit manteau?"*

"Yes," said Rachel. "Thank you."

Her eyes met her uncle's. "I'm sorry, Uncle James," she said. "I can't give that promise."

She thought that his face hardened and for a moment she was afraid, but then, to her relief, he smiled and shook his head at her indulgently. She put the little silk cape around her shoulders and pirouetted.

"There, Uncle! What do you think?"

"Charming," he replied. His eyes rested on her admiringly. "Much too good for any Irishman," he said.

Rachel laughed and kissed him, but still that slight chill remained. She had no money and nowhere to go. She was, after all, in James Kent's power.

Looking down from her bedroom window that evening, Rachel watched the men in the mill yard. They were too far away to be individually identified in the dim light, but she guessed that they were lining up to receive their wages. She turned away from the window and looked around the pretty room with its dimity curtains and elegant Early American furniture, and she wearily began to dress for dinner in one of the new gowns chosen to please her uncle.

* * *

Down in the yard Rory, waiting to collect his wages, saw a familiar, sturdy figure and curly mop of hair ahead of him.

"Jim!" he yelled. "Jim O'Brien!"

O'Brien turned and gave him that sardonic look Rory remembered so well.

"Wait till I get my money," he said, "and then we'll go up to the house and see what Molly has to say to you."

"How long have you been working here?" asked Rory as they climbed up to the makeshift houses of wood and tar crowded together above the yard.

"Since almost as soon as I arrived," O'Brien answered. "I've been away for a week, driving a load of powder."

Rory whistled. "You're a driver?"

He had been there long enough to know that, while the powdermen were the noblemen in the business, the drivers of the Conestoga wagons, by reason of the danger of their task, were the kings.

"Lucky for me a powder wagon blew up just before I applied for the job," said O'Brien. "Mr. Kent doesn't much like the Irish, but he was glad to get anyone. I heard there were two mad Irishmen tried to put a fire out when anyone else would have run like hell, and I guessed one of them was you."

"Eamon was the other," said Rory, "but he takes off every night to work in the hospital. He wants to practice as a doctor here one day."

Sitting in the O'Brien shack, Rory could almost imagine himself back in Ireland. There was wood and coal in the stove instead of a turf fire, but Molly O'Brien had brought away, as Jim said, "everything she could carry on her back," inculding the old iron pot, the holy-water stoup and the picture of the Sacred Heart. And holding little Maureen on his knee, although it made him homesick for Maeve, was a comfort, too.

"Will you bring the family over, Rory?" asked Molly.

Rory sighed. "As soon as I can scrape the money together. At least I'm earning a decent wage now, but I have to make a place for them to live, apart from saving the passage money. It's a terror to my heart every day that when I send for them, it'll be too late."

Rory saw a look pass between Jim and Molly O'Brien.

"I believe we owe you the cost of three passages," said Jim.

Rory started to protest, but Molly put a hand on his shoulder. "Unless you think the life of Jim O'Brien is worth nothing," she said.

Jim fetched the money and put it into Rory's hands, and Rory looked at it and had trouble speaking.

"I'll—I'll write the letter and send for them tomorrow," he said. "God bless you both. I'll never forget this as long as I live."

And he buried his face in the curly red hair of the child on his knee.

"My dear Rachel!" cried Charlotte irritably next morning. "Will you *please* decide which bonnet you mean to wear."

"I was waiting for you to decide, Aunt, which one you thought the young man would like."

"He is *not* a 'young man,' " said Charlotte. "At least, he *is,* I suppose, but—Caleb Staunton is legal adviser to the largest bank in Philadelphia. And since the bank is one of the principal shareholders in your uncle's business, Mr. Staunton's influence is quite valuable. Everyone thinks he'll be an important man in politics one day."

"Oh dear!" said Rachel. "I'm sure he'll think all my bonnets are much too frivolous. I will wear the plainest I have."

It was just like her aunt, she thought, to endeavor to pair her off with some dreary middle-aged lawyer just because he could be useful to her uncle!

But when she came downstairs and was introduced by Charlotte to Caleb Staunton, she found that, on the contrary, he was tall, fair-haired and extremely handsome in a rugged, backwoods style, and that his eyes rested on her with obvious appreciation even of her plainest bonnet.

"Now I know what they mean," he said, "when they speak of an English rose."

"Why, Mr. Staunton!" Rachel exclaimed. "I thought that Americans were famed for their bluntness."

"I would say rather, for their honesty," he replied.

Rachel found it enjoyable to be flirting again, even if it *was* with a man her aunt had chosen for her.

"Of course," she said, "I can't take all your pretty speeches *quite* at face value. I have to remember that you are a lawyer and a politician."

"Which means that I am much too busy to pay idle compliments," said Caleb.

Rachel gasped. "Oh!" she exclaimed. "Now I don't know whether I should feel insulted or pleased."

"At least I have you guessing!" he said, and suddenly they were both laughing.

When Caleb Staunton took Rachel's hand to help her into the carriage beside her aunt, she felt the first stirring of interest in another man that she had known since she had watched the sails of Rory's ship sink below the horizon off Galway Bay. She liked Caleb's strong, square, workmanlike hand, his fair hair, the Scandinavian blue eyes—not dark blue, like Rory's, but calm and clear and yet, she felt, likely to become icy and threatening in a different way if he should be made angry. He was, thought Rachel, very American, her first American young man—for he *was* quite young, in spite of the black frock coat and tall hat.

"It was so kind of you, Mr. Staunton," said Charlotte Kent as they set off down the drive, "to offer to escort us today."

"Not at all," replied Caleb with a touch of dryness.

Rachel glanced at him and met his eyes. Clearly he had not volunteered. He had been commandeered for this sightseeing tour of Philadelphia. But—

"It is an unexpected pleasure," said Caleb, his eyes still on her face, and Rachel was amazed to find herself blushing.

As the carriage turned out of the drive onto the turnpike road to Philadelphia, passing the entrance to the mill, Rachel glanced ahead and saw a tall man in workman's clothes trudging up the road. She could not see his face. She could not even see his hair beneath the shabby cap. But she knew him instantly.

"Stop!" she shouted. "Stop the carriage!"

Startled, the young black coachman hauled on the reins.

"My dear Rachel!" exclaimed Charlotte. "Are you mad? Drive on, Tom."

Tom glanced over his shoulder, dismayed by the conflicting commands.

Rachel spoke with authority. "Stop the carriage," she said. She did not wait for him to obey but wrenched the door open and stumbled out before the horses had been brought to a halt.

"Rory!" she called, running up the road.

Rory turned. Rachel stood still. They stared at each other, she in that absurdly fashionable dress and bonnet her uncle had bought for her, and he in the clumsy, threadbare clothes of poverty. They could not speak. They felt too much.

Rachel heard the carriage approaching. "Rory! Where are you living?"

"Lodgings. You can't come there. It's not fit."

"Rory—"

"Really, Rachel," said her aunt in a voice of icy control, "Mr. Staunton is a busy man. We can't keep him waiting."

Rachel glanced over her shoulder and saw Charlotte's look of outrage. She remembered that moment in the shop when her uncle's face had hardened and did not dare to introduce Rory to her aunt.

"I'm coming, Aunt Charlotte," she said.

In answer to a gracious smile and nod from Charlotte Caleb hesitated and then opened the door and descended, waiting for Rachel. It was like a nightmare, seeing Rory after so long and being unable to speak to him, not even knowing if she would see him again. He actually began to turn away. It was unthinkable. She took a step after him.

"I must see you!" she said, low and urgent. "Tonight, at the Kent House!"

She was almost sure that he had heard her. She rather thought that Caleb Staunton had heard as well. Rory glanced back, and their eyes met. He touched his cap.

"Good day, Miss Clement," he said, and walked on.

The instinct for self-preservation was not strong in Rachel. English people did not need to practice such arts. But her instinct to defend Rory from any danger was more basic, as was her desire to have him at all cost.

"The son of one of my father's tenants," she said carelessly as Caleb helped her back into the carriage.

She saw her aunt's sharp look behind her unamused laugh.

"My dear! I hope you don't mean to leap out of the carriage for every Irish immigrant you see or we shall never get our sightseeing done! Drive on, Tom!"

They drove on, and Rory did not turn his head as they passed him on the road.

It was a continuation of the nightmare to endure the rest of the day not knowing if he would come—or rather, almost certain that he would not. She saw the fine, sturdy, red-brick city of Philadelphia: Chestnut Street, the United States Hotel, the Liberty Bell, as though it were all quite unreal. She nodded and smiled and moved like a mechanical doll, and she fancied that Caleb Staunton understood that she was in trouble and tried to help her through it.

At dinner that night James Kent had never been more charming, amusing and flattering, but Rachel was certain that her aunt had told him about that encounter on the road, and she found it more frightening that he did not mention it.

But the worst moment came when she went upstairs to her bedroom. She felt such an anguish of desire for Rory that she could not keep still, and yet with every step she took across the room, the wide walnut floorboards creaked like Puritan informers. At last she could bear it no longer. She saw the lamplight from her uncle's office shining out into the garden and knew that she should wait until he was asleep, but it was impossible. She put a cloak on over her dress and lifted the latch of her bedroom door and crept downstairs and out of the house.

From the darkness she heard a voice call, "Rachel!"

Rory was standing in a clump of trees, and she ran toward him, but pride overtook her and she stopped short.

"Why didn't you answer my letters?"

"You know why."

But you came tonight, thought Rachel. You came!

And suddenly nothing else mattered, and she was in his arms, and he was touching her, feeling her, kissing her. Rachel, responding, tried to draw him further into the shadow of the trees.

"My uncle—" she said.

"Nothing's changed, has it?" he said harshly. "You're still in the Great House, and I'll still lose my job if we're seen together!"

"You mean you're working at the mill?" She was overjoyed. "But that's wonderful!" she said. "It means we can see each other every night!"

He released her. "No!" he said fiercely.

"Rory—"

But she was more dismayed when he spoke quietly and without anger. "It's no use, Rachel. I've sent for my family, and every penny I earn will go toward keeping them alive. You and I have no more business to be together here than we had in Ireland."

"But this is America!" cried Rachel. "Things are different here!"

"Are they?" asked Rory. "Your uncle lives off the

desperation of his workmen, just as the landlords lived off the desperation of their tenants in Ireland."

"Rory!" she exclaimed, horrified. "You aren't going to—?"

"Fight your uncle?" he said. "Yes, if I have to."

"You don't care for me at all," she cried angrily.

"God help me, I care for you!" he said, "or I wouldn't be here!"

"But not enough!" she cried. "You never care for me enough! There's always something that matters to you more!"

They gazed at each other as they stood a little apart, illuminated in the distant lamplight from the window of the Kent House.

"You take me as I am," said Rory, "or not at all."

"Oh," cried Rachel, "I take you!"

The lamplight dimmed for a moment as Rachel, running into Rory's arms once again, silenced all argument with a passionate kiss.

CHAPTER 16

"So today's the great day?" said Eamon as he and Rory walked to work.

"Deirdre, Brian, little Maeve and Sean." Rory spoke the names like a litany. "To think of having them in my arms again!"

"Fleming!" yelled Ed Miller from outside the yard office. "I need you in the rolling mill today."

"Right you are," said Eamon cheerfully and set off.

Rory called after him. "Eamon, will you come down to the docks with me to meet my family after work?"

"Try and stop me!" said Eamon.

Rory, turning toward the charcoal-drying shed, paused. "Miller!" he shouted. "This vat is mighty dangerous here, isn't it?"

Miller eyed the vat outside the door of the rolling mill.

"It's empty."

"It may be empty, but it's coated with powder," said Rory. "One spark and it'll go up!"

"Mind your own business!" said Ed. "*I'm* foreman here!"

"Does that give you the right to risk men's lives—" began Rory angrily, but he felt his arm grasped and looked around to see O'Brien.

"Don't say it, Rory! You need this job, and he can fire you!"

Rory glared at him. Servitude! Always servitude! He wrenched himself free and walked off toward the charcoal-drying house.

James Kent, looking out the window of the yard office, was waiting for Ed Miller when he returned.

"That man there," he said. "Is his name O'Manion?"

"Yes, sir."

"Get rid of him immediately."

"Yes, Mr. Kent," said Ed Miller.

Eamon, starting work in the rolling mill, the dangerous trays of powder all around him, glanced toward the door and saw two workmen moving the empty, powder-caked vat under Ed Miller's supervision.

"Hurry up, there!" said Miller. "You know what Mr.

Kent says—time's money!" He walked on. "O'Manion! I want you!"

Rory, emerging from the charcoal-drying shed, saw the workmen moving the vat, leaving a trail of powder behind. They knocked the vat with its iron band against the door of the rolling mill, and a spark flew out.

"Look out!" yelled Rory, and he ran past Ed Miller to stamp out the trail of burning powder.

He realized that he was too late and saw Eamon and O'Brien, startled, inside the rolling mill. "Eamon! Jim!" he shouted. "Get down!"

A gigantic explosion roared through the powder mill.

Rachel, in her bedroom, was awakened by the blast and saw the curtains still blowing and a jagged edge where the windows had been. She found her slippers, flung her coat over her nightdress and ran out as her aunt emerged onto the landing in her wrapper.

"What was that?" cried Rachel. "What happened?"

"The powder mill," said Charlotte Kent. "An explosion. Your uncle is down at the yard."

Rachel stared at her. "Rory!" she said and ran down the stairs, through the front door and out.

The women were already running down from the workers' dwellings, shawls over their heads, and Rachel joined them. She saw James Kent staggering out of the yard office and Molly kneeling down beside Jim O'Brien, wiping blood from his face, with little Maureen pulling at her skirts. Eamon, dazed and bleeding, was already trying to help an injured man. She ran toward him.

"Eamon! Eamon, where's Rory?"

He looked up at her. "He was in the middle of it. I'm afraid—there's no hope."

* * *

It was less than an hour later that Caleb Staunton drove into the yard in his one-horse carriage. He jumped down and looked, aghast, at the scene around him. It was like a battlefield, with arms and legs and fearfully injured men. He was amazed to see Rachel in the midst of it, searching, helping bind up the bleeding wounds, and searching again.

"Miss Clement!" he exclaimed.

He was shocked by the ravaged face she turned toward him. They could have known each other twenty years and she would not have revealed so much of herself to him.

"I can't find him!" she said. "I can't find Rory!"

Eamon limped up to put his arm round her. "Rachel," he said, "Rory's dead. You have to accept it."

"I won't!" she cried. "I won't!"

Eamon looked helplessly at Caleb. Rachel's eyes went past them. "What's that?"

There was a piece of white cloth hanging from the branch of a tree across the creek. Rachel set off running.

"Stop her!" said Eamon.

She still wore her nightdress under her cloak, and she lost her slippers in the stream. She found him lying facedown on the far side of the stream, his shirt in rags. Caleb caught hold of her, and Eamon very gently turned him over. With that fearful whimsicality of blast, he looked almost uninjured but pale as death.

"Is he?" said Caleb.

"No," said Eamon. "God knows how, but he's still alive."

* * *

"Rachel, my dear," said James Kent, "everything possible is being done. Come home now."

Rachel looked around the makeshift infirmary. Injured men were being tended by their wives, and Eamon, white with exhaustion, was consulting with a stout, prosperous, elderly doctor who was glancing at his watch, his thoughts obviously on his dinner waiting for him back in Philadelphia. Beyond them in the corner lay Rory, unconscious, still deadly pale.

"I can't, Uncle," said Rachel.

He spoke with a surge of jealous rage. "You're just as headstrong as your mother!" he exclaimed.

"Really, Rachel," said Charlotte, "you are making an exhibition of yourself!"

Rachel turned and walked away. Charlotte glanced at her husband. "What shall we do?" she said.

"Hope her Irishman dies," said Kent.

He turned on his heel and was slightly dismayed to see that Caleb Staunton had heard his words. He hesitated for a moment, then walked firmly out.

Caleb followed Rachel into the infirmary.

"Miss Clement!"

She turned defensively.

"Please let me know if there is anything I can do."

"Thank you, Mr. Staunton," she said, touched, "but—"

Could he make the dead come alive? She sat down beside Rory's bed, her eyes fixed on his face.

Eamon moved quickly after Caleb as he went toward the door. "Mr. Staunton! We're very short of medical supplies. Mr. Kent says we must make do with what we have."

He had a list in his hand, which he did not quite offer. Caleb smiled and took it from him.

"I'll see to it."

He glanced toward Rachel, sitting motionless beside Rory's bed, as though she meant to will him back to life.

"Does O'Manion have any family?" asked Caleb.

Eamon looked at him, suddenly aghast. The horror of the explosion had pushed all else from his mind. "His family!" he said. "They were arriving here this evening!"

The cab was driven at a furious pace onto the quayside. Eamon, leaping out, found himself among a crowd of Irish people wandering, crying or just standing, stunned. He saw a girl with blond hair and ran toward her.

"Deirdre!"

She turned. It was not Deirdre. He searched on, but the O'Manions were not there. He saw a policeman, stolid and detached in his tall hat and silver buttons, and hurried toward him.

"I'm looking for a family," he said. "They landed from Ireland today—a young lady, a boy of about fifteen with red hair, a little girl with fair hair and a child in arms."

The policeman looked at him stolidly.

"They were expecting their brother to meet them," said Eamon. "Surely they would wait here for him."

"They would," said the policeman with an Irish accent that could have come from Galway, "if they were alive."

Eamon looked at him, aghast, and followed his gaze to the ship moored at the quay.

"A floating coffin, she was," said the policeman.

"The worst one yet. If his family aren't here, you can take my word for it, they're dead."

Rachel stood with Eamon and Caleb, gazing at Rory's still, white face.

"How shall we ever tell him?" she said.

All the inquiries they had made, with Caleb's help, had been in vain. There had been fever on the ship. with bodies, often unidentified, slid overboard every day. And onshore—a girl called Deirdre, a boy called Brian, two children? The O'Manion family? "Never heard of 'em." No record." Between Ireland and America, Rory's family had vanished, just as the famine had devoured his land.

"The curse of God," said Eamon.

Rachel looked at him quickly.

"Brian told me," said Eamon, "that those were Padraic's last words. Do you believe that a man can suffer from a dying curse?"

She looked in terror from him to Rory. "No!" she cried. "No!"

She knelt down by the bed and took Rory in her arms, trying to will life back into him.

Caleb glanced at Eamon. "Will he recover?" he asked.

"I don't know," said Eamon. "It's nearly a week now. There's nothing more I can do."

"Oh, by the way," said Caleb, "here's the authorization for the medical supplies."

Eamon took the list and couldn't resist a grin. "Thanks. I don't know how you persuaded Mr. Kent to sign that."

"Don't ask!" said Caleb.

He looked toward the door of the infirmary, and Eamon followed his gaze. A priest was hesitating in the corridor, with an amber-haired young woman beside him. Eamon went quickly out.

"Deirdre?" he said.

She looked so thin and worn that he hardly knew her. She said dazedly, "Eamon?"

"Thank God!" he said. "Where's Brian? And little Maeve, and—?"

He saw the young priest give a quick shake of the head and stopped, dismayed.

The young priest drew him aside. "Are you a doctor?" he asked.

"I'm all there is," said Eamon grimly.

"I am Father Brendan. I visited the fever hospital and found Miss O'Manion had been brought there from the ship. She had a letter from her brother saying that he was working at Kent's Powder Manufactory, but when I saw in the newspaper the report of the explosion—"

He glanced at Deirdre, who stood in that dazed, passive state which great shock or grief leaves behind.

"Do you have a man here called Rory O'Manion?" asked Father Brendan. "And is he—?"

"He's here, and he's alive," said Eamon. "But—"

Father Brendan crossed himself. "Thanks be to God!" he said and turned back to Deirdre. "My child, you are spared one grief at least. Your brother is here."

Deirdre's face lit up through its pallor. She turned eagerly toward Eamon. "Rory?"

"Yes," said Eamon hesitantly. "I'll take you to him—"

He looked toward the door of the infirmary, and in

a moment Deirdre had slipped past him and was inside, gazing eagerly around.

"Stop her!" called Eamon instinctively.

Caleb, standing just inside the door, caught Deirdre in his arms. But she had caught sight of Rory in the bed in the corner, and in an instant he might have been trying to hold a wild bird in his hands.

"Let me go! Let me go!" she cried.

Caleb released her, and she fled to Rory like an arrow to the heart. Rachel rose quickly, but Deirdre saw no one but her brother.

"Rory!" she cried. "Oh, Rory, I have lost him! I have lost Sean!" She knelt down beside him.

"Deirdre, he can't hear you," said Rachel, distressed. She saw Eamon approaching, followed by Caleb and Father Brendan.

"What's happened?" she asked. "Where's Brian, and —and the children?"

"Brian wouldn't come," said Deirdre. "He walked with us as far as Galway, but on the quayside he stopped and he said, 'While there's an O'Manion on our land, it still belongs to us.' And then he looked down at Father's violin, and he said, 'If I take this fiddle out of Ireland, who will sing and dance until the good times come again?' So we left him there alone."

Rachel was haunted by the thought of that young, redheaded boy trudging back alone to the empty, silent house in the wild Galway countryside.

"Deirdre," she said. "Dearest, let me take you home now. You need to rest, and Rory—"

"Ah, no, don't make me leave him!" cried Deirdre piteously. "There's only the two of us left now."

"Let her stay!" said Eamon suddenly.

Rachel looked at him, startled. Eamon's eyes were on Rory's face.

"I thought I saw—"

Rachel looked back at Rory's face in a wild hope. He was still deeply unconscious.

"Perhaps I imagined it," said Eamon, "but I have heard that sometimes a familiar voice—"

He put his hand on Deirdre's shoulder. "Tell him, Deirdre," he said. "Tell him what happened."

Deirdre took Rory's hand in hers. It was limp and bloodless, but she put it to her lips.

"We went on the ship, Rory," she said, "and I will never tell anyone what it was like—no, not even you! And then Maeve took the fever. Oh, Rory, I tried to save her, indeed I did, but she was such a little thing, and the fever was too strong for her!"

She had forgotten them all now. She spoke only to Rory.

"Then I caught the fever, and they took Sean from me. I tried to stop them, Rory, but they said 'twas best for him. And the next I knew, I was being carried off the ship, and Sean not with me. And I said, 'No, not without the child! Don't take me without the child!' But they thought it was the fever speaking. They thought I meant Maeve. I screamed and screamed, but they took no heed. They carried me off to hospital, and they left Sean behind."

She had been speaking in a low voice, but now she suddenly screamed in an anguish of grief. "And now he is lost, Rory! Sean is lost! We must find him. Oh, help me, Rory! Help me!"

The words—those very words his mother had spoken to him when Sean was born—reached down to Rory's deep unconsciousness. He stirred and opened his eyes.

"Deirdre?" he said.

James Kent stormed into Caleb's office next morning and slammed a newspaper down on the desk.

"That stinking ragpicker!" he said.

Caleb picked up the paper and looked at the banner headline: "SLAUGHTER AT KENT POWDER MILL."

Kent snatched the paper back. " 'Ignoring safety regulations,' " he read aloud, indignantly, " 'Mr. Kent exploits the ignorance of illiterate Irish immigrants. The death toll is mounting hourly, and one of these unfortunate fellows, Mr. R. Manion, was blown clear across the yard. No doubt it was the thickness of his skull which accounts for his survival, though he lies at this moment fatally injured.' "

"Fatally?" inquired Caleb, raising his eyebrows in amusement.

Kent threw the paper onto the desk again and flung himself down into a chair. "The whole thing is a tissue of lies," he said.

Caleb picked up the paper and read the final sentence. " 'We demand that Mr. Kent and his death-dealing enterprise be put out of business.' "

"Yes, that's what it's all about," said Kent. "The editor is in Treadwell's pocket, and as long as I'm not making powder, Treadwell can sell his at a better price. I'm relying on you, Caleb. I need that loan from the bank immediately. I'll rebuild as cheaply as possible, but—"

Caleb looked sharply up at him. *Cheaply?* he said. "I keep telling you, James, your safety record just isn't good enough. This latest accident—"

"It was caused by a careless Irish workman—this—O'Manion. I've already dismissed him."

"You've *what*?" said Caleb. "*Dismissed* him? His name has been specifically mentioned in the paper as having been injured in the explosion. He is the one man in your entire work force whom you can *never* dismiss!"

James Kent stared at him, aghast.

"If O'Manion told the editor of this paper the real cause of the accident," continued Caleb, "no one in Philadelphia or New York would lend you a red cent."

"Now, Rory," said Eamon in the infirmary, "will you show a bit if sense and stay in bed at least another day?"

"I will not," said Rory, pulling on his pants. "I am going to look for Sean."

"Caleb Staunton has promised to do everything he can to find him, and he is a lawyer and a councillor."

"But Sean is not his brother," said Rory, and he began to pull on his boots.

Eamon eyed him disgustedly. "I think that editor was right," he said.

"Editor?"

"About the thickness of your skull."

Eamon got the newspaper from his coat pocket and gave it to Rory and then was alarmed by the expression on his face as he read it.

"Rory?"

"Do you mind if I keep this?"

"Now, Rory, don't do anything crazy."

"Crazy?" said Rory. "Certainly not. But after I've seen O'Casey about Sean, I think I might just have a word or two with this editor."

* * *

It was the habit of the editor of the *Philadelphia News,* when time hung heavy on his hands in the course of the day, to read through his editorial now and then, especially if it happened to be, as he would put it, rather a lively one. The editorial on Kent's Powder Manufactory was, in his opinion, a particularly good one, and he was just savoring it again when he heard the sound of hubbub and alarm from outside his office. As he looked up the door was flung open; and he observed a tall young man with black hair and dark-blue eyes.

"I think," remarked the young man, "I'm that thick-headed Irishman you mentioned!"

It was the misfortune of the editor that his newspaper offices happened to be on the second floor. To his incredulous horror, the mad Irishman had hold of him by the tie and dragged him out of his office.

"Only I was 'fatally injured' at Kent's Powder Manufactory," he was saying, "so it can't be me that's doing this to you, can it?"

The editor, too much astonished to speak, found himself out on the landing.

"I ought to boot you down the stairs!" said the Irishman. "But I won't."

"My dear Manion——" began the editor, relieved, but his relief was premature.

The grip on his tie became firmer, "O'Manion is the name. I'm rather partial to that *O!*"

The editor found himself backed toward the iron banister and pushed over. The only thing that prevented him from falling was his tie—and it was a thin tie and not particularly new. He saw his editorial staff rushing out of the outer office.

"Stand back," said O'Manion, "or I'll let him go!"

"Stand back!" gasped the editor unhesitatingly. "Stand back!"

He was bent backward over the stairwell, with the sardonic face of the Irishman above him.

"*Illiterate* means I can't read or write, doesn't it?" he demanded. "Then how did I manage to understand all these lies in your filthy rag?"

"I don't know!" said the editor, and immediately realized that it had been the wrong reply as another inch of his tie was paid out over the stairwell. "I mean —you're not illiterate!"

"Right," said O'Manion. "I'm not, and neither are most Irishmen, even if our school was behind a hedge."

He hauled the shaken editor up and released him.

"As for Kent's Powder Manufactory . . ." he said.

The editor looked at him, astonished. The fiery, violent Irishman had been replaced by a cold, hard determined young man.

"I am advising Mr. Kent on the rebuilding, with improved safety precautions, so what you wrote about me was damaging to my professional reputation. Unless you print an apology tomorrow, both to myself and to Mr. Kent, I shall sue you for libel. Good day to you."

He drew the editor solicitously away from the stairwell, dusted him down, turned and walked briskly away down the stairs.

"Well," said James Kent, surveying next day's paper with considerable satisfaction, "that's more like it."

There was a knock at the door.

"Come in," he said, and glanced up to see Rory. "Ah yes, come in, O'Manion."

Rory saw Caleb sitting by the window and came to stand in front of the desk, quietly alert.

"I sent for you because Mr. Staunton tells me that you had something to do with this."

He tapped the paper with the large box and its heading "APOLOGY."

"Not that I approve of violence," said Caleb.

Rory glanced at him and caught the look of amusement.

"I am arranging," said Kent, "for you to have an extra ten dollars next payday."

"Thanks," said Rory, "but that's not quite enough."

"What?"

"I want quite a lot more," said Rory. "To begin with, when you rebuild, I want the charcoal-drying shed entirely apart from the tar and other inflammables."

"Are you giving me orders?" demanded Kent.

"I want an infirmary built near the mill—a proper infirmary—and a full-time doctor. Eamon Fleming."

"You want?" said Kent on a rising note of anger.

Caleb spoke unexpectedly. "Good medical care might get the men back to work faster."

"Now why didn't *I* think of that?" said Rory.

Caleb's lips twitched at the innocent note of admiration, but Rory was continuing relentlessly, still towering over James Kent as he sat at his desk almost speechless with astonished indignation.

"And you can build the workers decent houses while you're about it," he said.

That brought Kent to his feet in a rage.

"Decent?" he roared. "They didn't even have roofs over their heads in Ireland! They were living in bogs, like animals!"

That touched Rory's sorest nerve. He turned instantly away toward the door. "Right! I shall just tell the editor that I made a mistake and that the accident was caused by—"

"Do it!" Kent shouted after him. "If you think I can be blackmailed by a—!"

Caleb rose to his feet, speaking as he did so. "Gentlemen, I suggest we cut the cackle and get down to business."

Rory was stopped in his tracks. He was still in a rage, but that cool, Yankee voice was like a bucket of cold water.

Caleb eyed him for a moment, then turned to look at Kent. "O'Manion is right," he said. "Explosions not only cost lives, they cost money, too. I'd say it's good business to rebuild in a way which avoids them."

"It's easy to say that," replied Kent, but the note in his voice was more of desperation than anger. "If I don't get back into production immediately, I shan't even be able to pay the interest on my debts!"

"Give the job to me," said Rory, "and I'll get the building done in record time."

Kent gave a short laugh. "So now you want to be foreman?"

"Why not?" replied Rory. "You need someone to take Ed Miller's place."

Ed Miller had been blown to pieces in the explosion, and Kent's manner of running the business, at once autocratic and careless, had left no obvious successor.

"Maybe I do," he said, "but what do *you* know about running a powder mill?"

"Enough to do it better than Ed Miller did," said Rory promptly, "and you know it."

"I know no such thing!" Kent's temper was rising again. "A half-savage Irish immigrant, just off the boat, managing my business?"

Caleb intervened before Rory could speak again. "James," he said, "it's immigrants just off the boat who have enough fight in them never to give up."

"Yes, like vermin!" Kent broke in. "And that's just what they are, vermin, coming here, bringing dirt and disease—"

Rory felt another surge of anger, but Caleb cut in. "And an instinct for survival. That's what you need now."

"I don't need to have some crazy hothead in charge of my mill in order to survive," said Kent.

Caleb spoke very quietly. "I think you do," he said. "You inherited this mill from your father, and the day-to-day running of it bores you. There have been too many mistakes; there's been too much cutting of corners and there have been too many fatal accidents. Unless a great many changes are made, the business won't survive, becauses the bank won't lend you any more money."

Kent stared at Caleb in silence, and Rory glanced at both of them. So, he thought, it's the quiet man who has the big stick after all.

Kent turned and moved away to the window and stood looking down into the yard. When he turned back, his face was pleasant and amused.

"Very well," he said. "If you guarantee that the bank will lend me the money I need to rebuild, I will put the work in the hands of this man—since you seem to think he has such an instinct for survival and that I have not."

He looked directly at Rory. "I'll take you on as foreman for a trial period of three months. If at the end of that time the rebuilding is not completed and orders being filled, you're dismissed."

"Three months?" exclaimed Caleb, startled. "That's not long enough for—"

Kent's eyes never left Rory's face. "Ninety days," he said. "Is it a deal?"

Rory hesitated. He knew that Kent had used a wrestler's hold on him, seeming to yield and then throwing him to the ground. But Rory had done a bit of wrestling himself, and besides—Kent was right—the Irish had been made to live like rats, and rats fight hard when cornered.

"It's a deal," said Rory. "Mr. Staunton here is witness."

Kent glanced at Caleb and smiled. "So he is," he said.

CHAPTER 17

Rory set off for the mill next morning before it was light and was knocking on the O'Briens' door when the first smoke was rising from the sagging chimneys.

"Jim!" he yelled. "Jim O'Brien!"

O'Brien opened the door, his ribs still bandaged and his face scarred from the explosion. "What the devil—"

"Have your breakfast, Jim, and make haste about it, and then come down to the yard and bring the other fellows with you!"

"Come in for a cup of tea, can't you?"

"No time!" Rory called back, already sliding down the rough path. "I'm meeting Deirdre at the Foundling Hospital, and I want to set the men to work first!"

When the men descended in twos and threes, uneasy and confused, they found him examining the machinery and hauling timbers about to see which could be used again. He waited until they were all there—all who were not lying in the cemetery above the hill—and then set off for the yard office.

"Come on!" he said. "I've something to tell you!"

They followed him, but very doubtfully, especially the Americans among them. He pulled a chair out of the yard office and climbed up on it.

"Mr. Kent has made me foreman in place of Ed Miller."

His voice rose above the murmur of anger and incredulity. "Now I dare say you're thinking, what does an ignorant Irishman hardly off the boat know about running a powder mill, and I dare say you'd like to tell me to vanish up me arse, but before you do—"

He got the little laugh he was after, and now he held them silent for a moment.

"Mr. Kent has agreed that in the rebuilding of the mill, we'll have greatly improved safety. I've been up all night making a plan of what I propose. It's a bit rough, but I've stuck it up there on the outside of the yard office, and you can all have a look at it afterward."

The men glanced at each other and at the sheet of paper nailed to the sagging wooden wall: something solid they could look at—not just promises.

"He's also agreed to proper houses," Rory continued. "No more damned shacks of wood and tar. Those of us who came from Ireland said that never again would our families live like pigs, and one place it won't be happening is at the Kent Powder Manufactory. We'll have decent stone houses, with a proper hearth—and though there's not a deal of peat around here, still I hear there's plenty of coal in Pennsylvania!"

There was a bit of a cheer at that, but Rory knew

he had not won them yet and saw from O'Brien's quick glance around that he knew it, too.

"There'll be a proper infirmary," said Rory, "and Eamon Fleming, once he's got his license to practice, will be the official doctor, so there'll be no waiting for some fat quack from Philadelphia to finish his dinner before he comes to stop a man bleeding to death."

There was a big cheer at that from the Irish, but Rory saw the Americans scowling, not liking the slur on a Philadelphian professional man.

"But if we want these things," he said, "we've got to work. You know what they say of the Irishman—that he works one day and drinks the next."

That got a big laugh from the Americans, but the Irishmen were indignant. He was playing the crowd like a fish, but it was a fish with two heads, and he had to make it one.

"Well, there's no difference here between Irish and American. If we want to save the mill and have a good job and a steady wage, and a decent place to live, we've got to earn it. We've got to work not ten hours, but twelve—fourteen—all night if we have to—and don't worry, I'll have torches put up, so that you can go on working in the dark!"

They began to groan humorously, but he wouldn't give them time. He pointed a fierce finger at them.

"But if you ever find there's a single man in this yard working harder than me, I give you leave here and now to boot me out—and you might even manage to do it before Mr. Kent does!"

He let them laugh and then spoke very softly, so that they had to crane to hear.

"But isn't it worth it, for the sake of ourselves, our

wives and children, and for the sake of our future in this country?"

He prepared to jump down but instead turned back to them and shouted at the top of his voice. "Are you with me?"

The cheer they gave him reached up the hill to the Kent House. James Kent, sleeping beside his wife, for once, turned his back on her and lay staring angrily into the dawn light. Rachel jumped out of bed and ran to the window.

"I'm off to order some timber," said Rory. "I want all this rubble cleared away before I get back . . ." and the men laughed.

Rachel could not hear the words, but, looking down, she saw the men moving about, some to look at a big sheet of paper pinned to the yard office, and some beginning to shovel rubble and sort out bricks and timber. And she saw a tall figure with black hair running through the gates onto the turnpike road.

"Rory!" she said aloud. "Rory!"

He had his first foot on the ladder to success. She knew that her uncle would do his best to shake him off it, but it was a ladder, and Rory had his foot firmly on it. She smiled.

Rory managed to keep running until he was around the corner, and then found a tree by the roadside and leaned against it, gasping for breath. Eamon was right. The explosion had left him as weak as a cat, but he had no time for weakness. He was like a drowning man who sees a floating spar too far away. He must find the strength to swim toward it or else sink forever.

As his breath came back, his strength returned, and

with it a sense of exhilaration. He had won the first battle. The men were with him. He had his army. Now all he had to win was the war.

But at the Foundling Hospital all sense of triumph was lost. Caleb had arranged the visit and watched sympathetically as Deirdre and Rory searched among the children with that destructive mixture of hope and pity and resentment that each child was not the child they sought.

They had reached the last room and hope was almost ended when Rory saw a child crouching in a corner, hiding his face in his hands. He ran and caught him up in his arms and turned to Deirdre.

"This one?" he asked.

"Ah, no, Rory," she replied. "Isn't he at least two years too old for our Sean?"

"Oh, God!" cried Rory, anguished. "I don't even know what he would look like now!"

Deirdre took the child from him and held it close. "Sure, now, my little gossoon," she said, "you're somebody's fine young brother, but you're not ours."

She kissed him and put him down again, and Caleb's face showed that he was touched by the gentleness which could feel for the child's disappointment in the midst of her own.

But as they emerged from the Foundling Hospital, Deidre's grief overwhelmed her again.

"Oh, Rory!" she cried. "We have lost him forever!"

Rory put his arms around her and looked hopelessly at Caleb above her head.

"Don't give up hope yet," said Caleb.

He paused on the top step and took a piece of paper out of his pocket. "I have something to show you."

"An answer to the advertisement!" exclaimed Rory quickly.

He released Deirdre and they both turned toward Caleb in that hope which is born of desperation.

"But why didn't you tell us sooner?" cried Deirdre.

Caleb's eyes met Rory's. "I hoped—that the child might be here," he said.

He unfolded the grubby piece of paper and read aloud.

" 'I can tell what happened to the boy. Need ten dollars first.' And it's signed, 'Patrick Delaney.' And written on the other side, 'Send money to Post Office.' "

"Thanks be to God and the Blessed Virgin!" whispered Deirdre and crossed herself.

Rory's eyes met Caleb's again. "He may know nothing and just want the money," he said, and saw that Caleb thought as he did.

"Sure, no one would be so cruel!" cried Deirdre.

"You'd be surprised what a man will do for ten dollars!" replied Rory bitterly, and he began to walk down the steps.

The loss of Sean was like a stone in his heart, and he was tormented by the thought of how little they knew after all their inquiries. They had found out that a couple called Gavin, from County Mayo, had taken care of Sean on the ship when Deirdre was ill. Presumably the Gavins had carried him ashore, but even that was not certain. Neither Father Brendan, Caleb nor O'Casey could find any sign of them. They had vanished into the slums of Philadelphia. Sean might or might not be with them. He might be alive or he might be dead. All that was certain was that their little brother, who had always been used to so much love, might be alive somewhere, abandoned and cruelly treated, and they could not find him, or he might be dead, and they would never know it.

Rory heard Caleb and Deirdre descending the steps behind him and turned, trying for her sake to conceal the pain he felt.

Caleb untethered his horse and turned to Deirdre. "May I drive you somewhere?"

"Oh—I don't like to put you to the trouble."

"Where do you want to go?"

"To the Kent House," she said, and her eyes met Rory's with a touch of defiance.

Rachel had somehow persuaded her aunt—or more likely her uncle—to agree to employ Deirdre as her maid.

"Rachel needs me," she had said when Rory protested, and he, thinking of leaving her all alone in the miserable little shack he had rented for them in Kensington, still haunted by Maeve's death and the loss of Sean, could not persist in his disapproval, though he had not come to America for his sister to be a servant.

Caleb helped Deirdre into the carriage and turned to Rory.

"No, thanks," said Rory curtly. "I have to see a timber merchant, and besides—I need to walk."

He strode away, trying to outpace the longing and the dread.

"We will find your brother, I promise," said Caleb to Deirdre as he turned the horse into the tree-lined road that led toward the city.

"Please God we will!" she replied. "It's so hard on Rory. It near tore the heart out of him to be driven out of Ireland, and now to lose Sean as well!"

He glanced at her. "It was not his choice, then, to come to America?"

"Ah, no!" cried Deirdre. "His heart will always be in Ireland. He would never have left of his own free will—and never would he have left Sean!"

Caleb drove in silence for a while.

"You know," he said, "I envy you and Rory."

"*Envy* us?"

"To be part of such a warm and loving family."

"Sure," said Deirdre, "all families feel as we do."

Caleb smiled. "Not quite," he said. "I was an only child, and my parents weren't young when they married. A small farm on poor soil can grind the heart out of a man—and a woman, too."

"But your parents loved you!" Deirdre protested impulsively.

"Perhaps they did," said Caleb, "but they couldn't show it."

As he turned onto the turnpike road that led toward the Kent mill, he became aware of Deirdre's silence and turned to look at her.

"What are you thinking?"

"That your father was a farmer, like mine," said Deirdre. "I thought you had been a rich man all your life."

Caleb laughed aloud. "Far from it!" he said. "I worked on the farm all day, and taught myself to read and write, and studied by a tallow candle in my bedroom at night. I remember running to my mother when the letter arrived to say that I had gained a scholarship to law school. In my excitement when I told her, I caught hold of her arm, and she said, 'Careful, now, Caleb! You have made me spill the buttermilk.'

I believe in all my life there will never be another moment of such bitter disappointment."

They drove on in silence, but this time it was a silence of understanding and sympathy.

"But now you're a famous lawyer," said Deirdre, "and I—"

He looked at her inquiringly.

"I don't mind you knowing," she said. "I cannot read or write. I tried to teach myself, but I am not as clever as you. It was too hard for me."

"Would you like me to teach you?"

She turned to him eagerly. "Would you really?"

"It would be a pleasure."

"Ah," cried Deirdre, "if I could only write a letter!"

Caleb reined in the horse. "I could write it for you, if you would tell me what you want to say."

Deirdre was silent for a moment. "Thank you. You are very kind. But this letter I must write myself."

"It must be to someone very special." He forced a smile. "To some fortunate young man back in Ireland, perhaps?"

"Not Ireland," replied Deirdre shyly, "India."

"Indeed?" said Caleb, struck by the coincidence. "Miss Clement's brother is in India."

He glanced at her and saw her blush and smile.

"Yes. David."

"Well," inquired Charlotte Kent of her husband as they were finishing lunch, "how is that Irishman getting along at the mill?"

"Not very well, I am afraid," replied Kent. "It is almost time for production to begin, and he has not even managed to get a proper roof on any of the buildings."

"Dear me!" said Charlotte, glancing at Rachel. "So you will have to dismiss him."

"That was the bargain—at the end of three months," replied James Kent tranquilly, "and you know, my dear, I always keep my bargains, however distasteful they may be."

Rachel sat very still and forced herself to eat her pudding. One of the most uncomfortable features of living in the Kent household was finding herself constantly in the middle of this grim, concealed warfare. But she realized also that the fact that James and Charlotte were themselves locked in such a miserable marriage made them the more inclined to unite in making others unhappy, like savage animals striking together through the bars of a cage.

In the silence they heard a loud cheer from the mill yard below.

"Something's happening!" cried Rachel impulsively.

She met her uncle's amused gaze.

"I dare say O'Manion has given the men the rest of the day off. I hear he has been working them mighty hard, and the Irish have not a great deal of staying power."

They were about to move from the table when there was a loud knocking at the front door. Joseph, the black butler, came in.

"Excuse me, sir," he said with an apologetic note in his voice, "but Mr. O'Manion would like a word with you."

"What does he think he is doing," exclaimed Charlotte, "coming up to the house?"

Kent glanced at her and went out into the hall.

"Good day to you, Mr. Kent," said Rory. "I thought

you'd like to know we'll be starting production again tomorrow."

Kent stared at him. "What are you talking about?" he demanded. "You haven't even got a single roof on."

"Indeed we have," said Rory. "There'll be no more stone slabs on the new buildings. I took advice from an expert Mr. Staunton recommended at the university. With a light roof, if there's an explosion, the blast will go up and blow the roof off. There'll be less damage and fewer injuries."

Kent, finding himself on unknown territory (slab stone roofs had been good enough for his grandfather!), hastily shifted ground. "Are you telling me the rebuilding is completed?"

"No, it's not," answered Rory.

"And after all your fine talk you are prepared to endanger the men's lives by starting production while the work is still going on?"

Rachel, coming to the doorway of the dining room, saw Rory smile slowly.

"The men would not do it to make more money for you, Mr. Kent," he said, "and I would not ask it of them. But this is their powder factory as well as yours. They work here. If it prospers, they prosper, and if it fails, they starve. We have orders to fill and, starting tomorrow, we'll fill them."

He opened the door and was gone, and it slammed behind him. Kent, turning away, saw Rachel.

"Like most Irishmen," he said, "he is a gambler." He smiled. "Let's hope he doesn't take one chance too many!"

Rachel felt a chill at his words, but she refused to allow him to spoil her pleasure. She ran upstairs to enjoy Rory's triumph alone in the seclusion of her bedroom. She was surprised to see Deirdre there, rising and turning quickly from her desk by the window.

"Oh, Deirdre!" she cried. "He has won! Rory has won!"

She was puzzled to see that Deirdre seemed to be hiding something behind her on the desk. Impossible that Deirdre should be stealing, and yet—

"Oh, Miss Rachel!" cried Deirdre, "forgive me."

She moved aside, and Rachel came to see.

"Why, Deirdre! you've learned to write."

" 'Twas Mr. Staunton who taught me, and I've not mastered it yet. But—I had a mind to write a letter, and I knew they'd laugh at me in the kitchen. Sure, I've only borrowed a sheet of paper and a dip of your ink."

"Oh, Deirdre!" cried Rachel and put her arms about her. "How could you think I'd mind? You sit and write your letter here in peace and quiet, and—shall I address the envelope for you?"

"Ah, Miss Rachel!" said Deirdre, laughing, "if you would! Sure, I'm getting the hang of the printing, but that writing that runs itself together is beyond me, indeed it is!"

Rachel sat down in the rocking chair, smiling, and watched Deirdre struggling away with those intractable letters.

"Dear David," wrote Deirdre with that childish intentness which was so touching and so beautiful, "I write to you my very first words. I love you. Deirdre."

There was a knock at the door, and Rachel answered without thinking. "Come in."

"A letter for you, Miss Rachel," said Joseph.

"Thank you, Joseph," replied Rachel, and took it, but with her mind still lovingly and amusedly on

Deirdre. Joseph went out, and Rachel looked down at the envelope. Deirdre was anxiously reading her letter through and correcting a mistake.

"It's from the War Office!" Rachel exclaimed.

She tore the envelope open. Deirdre's attention was caught, and she put the pen down and turned. Rachel read the letter, and her face showed her alarm.

"Miss Rachel?" said Deirdre and stood up, trembling.

Rachel read aloud. " 'Dear Miss Clement, it is with great regret that I am commanded to inform you that your brother, Lieutenant David Clement, was killed in action on the Northwest Frontier, in the course of—' "

She could not continue.

"Oh—Deirdre! It cannot be true!"

They clung to each other and shared their tears as both their worlds seemed to come crashing down.

CHAPTER 18

"You *signed* it?" exclaimed Rachel, startled.

"Why not?" said Rory.

"Won't—Uncle—?"

"He's in New York."

She knew that very well or she would not have been in the yard office, perched on the stool, delighting in being close to Rory while he worked on the books.

"But do you have the right to sign contracts?" she asked.

Rory shrugged and then grinned at her. "Maybe not, but we need the business, and it'll pay good money. I never yet knew your uncle to turn down money."

She laughed. "He has a great many expenses."

"So I've heard," said Rory dryly, moving to put an account book on the shelf.

Rachel eyed him severely. "When we're married—" she said.

He turned sharply. "What?"

"When we're married," she continued, undaunted, "I shall make very sure that *you* never have that kind of expense!"

She stood up and put her arms around his neck and kissed him. He responded to her (when had they *not* responded to each other?) but tried to move her away from the window.

"For God's sake, woman!" he said.

Rachel laughed. "If the men don't know that I love you," she said, "they must be blind, and in that case they have no business to be working in a powder factory!"

She kissed him again and went out, still laughing. Rory followed her to the door.

"Just wait till you're asked!" he yelled.

She paused and looked back at him. "Are you asking me now?" she shouted.

"No! And don't be sure I ever will!"

"You'd better!" she shouted.

He opened his mouth but saw the men glancing at them and grinning, and he turned, scowling, and went into the office and slammed the door. But as soon as he was inside, he began to laugh.

Rachel, climbing the steep path from the mill yard, saw Caleb driving Deirdre up to the Kent House. Still wearing black in mourning for David, Rachel felt for a moment a pang of jealous sorrow for David, left for dead on some barren hill in Afghanistan and spared all the pain. But who was she, with happiness almost within her grasp, to deny Deirdre any fragments of happiness Caleb could persuade her to accept?

"Next week?" said Caleb as he helped Deirdre down from the carriage. He had kept hold of her hand.

Deirdre hesitated. "I—I think it would be best if we did not see each other anymore. I am very grateful for all you have done, but—"

"I don't want your gratitude," said Caleb. "I want your love."

Deirdre caught her breath at this. She knew that his honesty matched hers, but she had not expected him to speak so openly.

"You must know that," said Caleb.

"Yes," she said. "Yes, I do. And I wouldn't want to hurt you."

"Let me take that chance, if I'm willing to," he said, "and I am."

Their eyes met, and for a moment he let his feelings show, and she felt a mixture of flattery and alarm.

"I mean to make you love me, Deirdre," he said.

She drew her hand away. "No!" she said. "No. I shall always love David, and only David."

She turned and went inside the house.

Rachel, entering the drawing room, saw her aunt turning angrily away from the window.

"That Irish servant has no business to be using the front door," she said.

"You could hardly expect Caleb Staunton to drive around to the kitchen entrance," answered Rachel, amused.

"Exactly," said Charlotte. "He should be calling on

you, not your servant. You chose to reject Mr. Staunton for that—that penniless Irish adventurer—"

"Just as my mother chose the man *she* wanted!" Rachel broke in.

It was a dreadful thing to say, and Rachel regretted the words the moment she had spoken them. It had never been acknowledged between them that Rachel's mother had been James Kent's first choice, and while it was unacknowledged it was bearable. To show that she knew of it made Rachel a party to the insulting, never-forgotten crime.

"I won't forget that, Rachel," said Charlotte.

"Aunt—" began Rachel, willing to apologize, but Charlotte turned away and sat down with her embroidery.

"If you choose to neglect your best interests," Charlotte said, "that is your business. But I won't have you encouraging Caleb Staunton's attentions to an illiterate Irish servant. I shall give her notice."

"No!" cried Rachel. "I won't let you!"

Charlotte raised her eyebrows. "You seem to forget that you are living here on our charity. As for O'Manion—"

"As for Rory, I mean to marry him," Rachel said.

Charlotte stared incredulously. "But he is a Catholic."

"Then I shall become one," Rachel stated flatly.

Charlotte regained her composure and pulled the wool through the embroidery before glancing up.

"Sooner or later he will make a stupid mistake, and your uncle will get rid of him."

Charlotte's smile drove all caution out of Rachel's head.

"If he goes," cried Rachel, "I shall go with him!"

She saw the look of triumph in Charlotte's eyes and in that instant knew that she had put herself and Rory into her aunt's power.

It was late at night when James Kent returned from New York, and Charlotte and Rachel had eaten their silent dinner, sat silent in the drawing room and gone silently up to bed. Only at her bedroom door did Charlotte turn and say icily, "I shall give that Irish maid a week's notice from tomorrow."

Deirdre was waiting in Rachel's bedroom to help her undress and brush her hair. They hardly spoke. Since David's death, Deirdre had lost that fresh sparkle which had always seemed ready to light up from inside, no matter what troubles assailed her. Now she was silent and subdued, a little removed from life around her, as though she mourned, and would forever mourn, that missing spark of joy.

Rachel knew that she should warn Deirdre of her aunt's threat, but guilt kept her silent, and also she could always persuade her uncle to do what she wanted. She would appeal to him to let Deirdre stay. She would say that her aunt had provoked her into foolish words about Rory—and then, very carefully, very cleverly, she would begin to win him over to the notion of her marriage to Rory.

Nevertheless, her heart leaped with fear when she heard her uncle's footsteps on the stairs. She sat up in bed and for a moment was ready to run out and stop him before her aunt could pour the poison in his ears. She even got out of bed, but then paused, her wrapper in her hand. It was hardly a matter to be discussed on the landing, with her in her nightclothes and her uncle just returned, tired and probably cross, only wanting to go to bed. If she *did* try to talk to him then, it would only irritate him and seem to give too much importance to what she had said to Charlotte. She got back into bed and sat, clasping her knees, and heard her uncle go into his dressing room and close the door. Perhaps her aunt was already asleep, or perhaps he would sleep in his dressing room, as he sometimes did when he was late.

"I'll talk to him in the morning," said Rachel to herself.

But she lay awake for a long time, and then fell asleep at last and did not wake until Deirdre brought her breakfast.

"Is my uncle up?" she asked.

"Oh yes, Miss Rachel," said Deirdre. "He had his breakfast early and went straight down to the mill."

Rory was surprised to see Kent in the yard so early. He was strolling about, glancing into the different buildings, inspecting the work and occasionally speaking to the men. It occurred to Rory that he was looking to see if he could find something wrong.

"Let him look!" thought Rory and stayed where he was in the yard office.

He knew that the men worked far better for him than they had for Ed Miller, and Jim O'Brien was an excellent lieutenant to him, keeping a sharp eye on things when Rory was not there.

However when Kent turned toward the office, Rory came out to meet him.

"Good morning, Mr. Kent."

"Good morning. How have things gone while I've been away?"

"Very well," Rory replied as they turned together to walk back toward the office. "I've made a deal to sell a big load of powder to the Pacific Railroad."

Kent stopped short just outside the office. "You've done *what*?"

Rory felt a slight qualm but wouldn't admit it. The deal was a good one. Surely even Kent must see that.

"I signed the contract three days ago," he said.

"You signed a contract?" demanded Kent incredulously. "You had absolutely no authority to do any such thing!"

He had raised his voice, and although Rory had opened the office door for him, he made no effort to. go inside. Rory saw several men glance toward them.

"I had to," said Rory, "if I wanted to make the deal. You were in New York."

"You could have telegraphed me."

Rory knew that this was his weak point. The truth was that he had never thought of it. He raised his voice, too.

"There wasn't time," he said. "The chief engineer of the railroad was traveling West next day, and I had to sign the contract before he left or we'd lose the sale!"

He saw Jim O'Brien unlocking the storehouse and pausing to glance toward them, troubled.

"Before you start complaining about the deal," said Rory, "you'd better come inside and look at the contract!"

Kent looked at him and spoke very softly. "Oh, I mean to," he said, and followed Rory into the office.

Rory watched Kent in some anxiety as he glanced over the contract. It had seemed like a good proposition to him, but admittedly he was not an experienced businessman.

"You must be mad!" said Kent.

"What the devil's wrong with it?" demanded Rory. "I've sold five hundred kegs of powder at a time when it's damned hard to sell any."

"Yes, with a heavy penalty for late delivery!"

Once more Rory knew that was the awkward clause in the contract. He had fought against it and lost. But he spoke calmly. "That's not unusual," he said. "I had to guarantee that we would have the powder there in time for them to start blasting before the snow came."

"And how do you propose to deliver it? You know the railroads won't carry big loads of powder anymore."

"By wagon."

"Wagon?" repeated Kent. "All the way from here to—where is it?"

"Fort Wayne. I won't ask the drivers to do anything I wouldn't do myself. I'll drive the first wagon. I know it's risky, but it's a risk I'm prepared to take."

Kent banged the contract down on the desk. "You can blow yourself to hell for all I care, but not with my powder and not at my expense!"

Rory was determined to keep his temper. "Surely you must see," he said, "that if we want this company to survive, we have to take risks."

"*We* have to take risks?" said Kent. "This company is *mine*. The only thing which is yours is your name on this contract, which I fully intend to repudiate!"

Kent moved toward the door, and Rory looked after him, shaken.

"I agreed, against my will, to employ you as foreman. You have overstepped your authority, and that gives me every right to dismiss you."

He opened the door and turned. Rory was shocked by the controlled fury and hatred in his face.

"One more thing. I understand you hope to marry my niece. I'll see you damned first! Get out, and take that—scheming—sister of yours with you. If I see either of you on my property again, I'll have you thrown in the river!"

He went out and slammed the door. By the time Rory had wrenched it open again, Kent was walking fast toward the yard gates where the carriage was waiting.

O'Brien came up. "What's the trouble, Rory?" he asked.

"Go to hell!" said Rory, ready to hit anyone who came in his way, even Jim.

He turned on his heel, went into the office, dragged his coat down from its peg and, on an impulse, picked up the contract from the desk and took it out with him. Jim O'Brien was waiting outside, and Rory gave him a long look which was the nearest he could get to an apology. Then he saw Kent driving in his carriage away toward Philadelphia and rage possessed him again, a blind, frustrated fury, and he began to run and scramble up the steep path to the Kent House.

Rachel and Deirdre heard the hammering on the front door, and then Rory's voice in the hall, yelling at the top of his lungs.

"Deirdre! Where are you, girl? Deirdre!"

They came, startled, out to the landing, and saw old Joseph closing the door and glancing back at Rory, shocked.

"Right," said Rory, seeing Deirdre and ignoring Rachel. "Get your things and come with me."

"Rory," said Rachel, "what are you doing? What's happened?"

"Stay out of this, Rachel," he said. "You've done enough."

She was horrified. He had never spoken to her in such a way before, as though she had suddenly become quite inconsiderable.

"Deirdre—"

"I was just telling Miss Rachel, Rory—I've been dismissed."

"Have you, now?" said Rory. "So have I. Come on. We'll get out of here."

"No, Rory, no!" exclaimed Rachel, getting her courage back again. "Don't do anything in a hurry. I can manage my uncle, and—"

She was coming down the stairs toward him when he turned on her. "As you did when you said I wanted to marry you?"

Rachel caught her breath but answered defiantly. "I didn't say that. I said that *I* wanted to marry *you*."

"That was enough for your uncle," said Rory, grimly.

"At least let Deirdre stay until—my aunt gave her a week's notice—"

"Do you think I'd let Deirdre stay here a week—do you think I'd let her stay for a single day after she's been insulted?"

Rachel heard not only rage in his voice but also pain, because Deirdre was all the family he had left, and he did not have the power to protect her. Deirdre must have heard it, too.

"I'll get my things," she said and turned and went

upstairs toward the attic room she shared with the housemaid.

"I'll wait outside," said Rory.

"No, Rory!" cried Rachel. "Take Deirdre if you must, but don't go like this—not without—"

She ran down the last stairs, but he was already through the door, and it slammed behind him. She knew it was useless to go after him in his present mood, and she turned and went slowly back up the stairs and met Deirdre coming down with her bundle of possessions.

"Oh, Deirdre!" she said, and they clung to each other and kissed.

Rachel saw her aunt's bedroom door ajar and heard her sharp voice. "Use the back stairs, girl, if you please!"

Deirdre began to draw away, but Rachel held her fast. "I must know where you'll be!" she whispered urgently.

Deirdre looked at her and leaned forward to kiss her cheek again, and Rachel was afraid she was not going to tell her. But she heard the voice in her ear, no louder than a breath.

"Black Horse Alley, behind the corn chandler."

As Deirdre turned toward the back staircase, Charlotte spoke again without turning around from where she sat at her dressing table.

"I hope you don't expect a week's wages in lieu of notice."

Deirdre paused. "Indeed, I do not, ma'am," she said, "for I leave today of me own free will. I've only stayed here for the joy of being with Miss Rachel, for you yourself have neither heart nor breeding, and musharoon gentry I cannot bear and never could!"

Charlotte turned around at that all right and got up and came to the door in a rage, but Deirdre was already on her way.

"That girl!" cried Charlotte Kent when she could get her breath back. "At least I shall make sure that *she* never enters this house again!"

Rory got a ride into the city from a passing wagon and took Deirdre to the squalid little one-room shack which was all he had been able to afford when he was first preparing for his family's arrival.

"If I'd known you were going to be living here, I'd have tried to find something better," he said, "as soon as I was on foreman's pay."

"Maybe it's just as well you didn't," replied Deirdre with that little touch of astringency which keeps Irish dreams on the ground, "since your foreman's pay lasted about as long as a drunkard's repentance!"

She glanced around and smiled at him and fetched her apron out of her bundle. "All it needs," she said, "is a bit of spit and polish, and I'll be giving it that now!"

"Right," said Rory, relieved. "I'll leave you to it."

"Where are you going?"

"To Caleb Staunton's office on Chestnut Street. I have a little proposition which I think might interest him."

Caleb sat behind his desk, looking at Rory thoughtfully. "So you want to sell the powder yourself."

"I believe the railroad will buy it. After all, my name's on the contract and the terms are agreed."

"I doubt if Mr. Kent will sell it to you," said Caleb. "Do you have the money?"

Rory grinned. "I'm hoping that my partner will have it, or be able to borrow it, and that Kent won't have any objection to selling the powder to *him,* especially if he's on good terms with the bank."

"Hey!" said Caleb, grasping what he meant. "Now wait a minute!"

"Caleb, it's a good investment," said Rory. "If Kent is such a fool that he can't see it, others won't be. Treadwell, for example. Whoever gets this first contract will get the rest."

He saw that Caleb was inclined to agree with him.

"The railroad needs powder, and it'll pay almost any price for it," said Rory.

"But they have to have it in time to blast through the mountains before the snow."

"That's right," said Rory lightly. "That's why there's a penalty clause."

"No delivery, no sale," said Caleb. He shook his head and stood up. "It's nothing more or less than a gamble—and I'm no gambler."

"Ah, come away with you!" said Rory and grinned again. "You're as much of a gambler as I am. There's a deal of ambition in that Yankee hickory head of yours. You mean to be senator one day—or maybe even President."

Caleb looked at him sharply. Rory laughed.

"I hit it there, didn't I? But if you're to get ahead in politics, you need money, and you didn't inherit it any more than I did. Come on, Caleb, try your luck."

"With powder wagons on rough mountain roads, and the drivers in a hurry? I don't like the odds."

Rory stood up and shrugged. "All right," he said, "if that's your decision—"

He moved toward the door as though it was all

over, and perhaps Caleb felt, as he meant him to, a moment of doubt as to whether he had thrown away a fine chance.

"But I admit I'm surprised," said Rory, and he paused and looked back. "If you wouldn't take a chance for yourself, I would have thought you'd gamble on the future of this country. And that means the transcontinental railroad."

"I agree," said Caleb. "Until she is united from the Atlantic to the Pacific, America will always be two countries, not one. It means the true union of the States. I'd put my money down for that and borrow more."

Rory came back to confront him. "Then in God's name, Caleb, what are you waiting for? The railroads need this powder, and I can deliver it!"

Caleb hesitated. "Would you answer me one question honestly?"

"I'm not in the habit of lying," said Rory cheerfully, "except to the English."

He caught a sharp look from Caleb and frowned, puzzled. Caleb turned away to the window, looking down at the press of wagons, coaches and hackney carriages in the busy street below.

"This deal could be worth a lot of money," he said. "You know what I'd do with my share. What would you do with yours?"

"Buy food," replied Rory promptly, "to feed my starving people—and guns to set Ireland free."

"And for that you'd take any risk?"

"Of course," answered Rory, surprised that he should trouble to ask the question.

Caleb turned to face him. "That's what makes the odds too long," he said. "You want me to take all my savings, and borrow from the bank and gamble that, too, with a partner whose loyalties lie elsewhere, and who would take any risk to serve them? No. I'm sorry."

Rory looked back at him in silence for a moment.

"You mean, I have to stop being Irish before you'd be interested," he said. "I'm sorry, too," and he turned and walked out.

Caleb sat down again behind the desk, still wondering if he had been too cautious, still uneasy at Rory's last words.

Rory came out of Caleb's office building and stopped short. Rachel sat waiting outside in the carriage, with Tom on the box. Rory glanced around.

"Where's your uncle?"

"Back at the house. I told him I needed the carriage to come to the library."

"What else did you tell him?"

"Nothing," said Rachel. "I had to talk to you first. Please get in, Rory. I want to show you something."

He shrugged and glanced up at Caleb's window. "Why not? I've lost my job, and I've nothing else to do.

"How did you know I was here?" asked Rory as he got in.

"Tom drove me to your lodgings first and Deirdre told me."

"You shouldn't have gone there," said Rory, "and she shouldn't have told you."

Rachel glanced at him but didn't answer, and they drove in silence. Rory realized that they were traveling into the woods which bordered the Kent property.

"Where are we going?"

"To the Old Mill."

Tom stopped the carriage outside an old brick building with a small, eighteenth-century stone house beside it, set in a framework of trees above a valley with a stream running through it.

"Isn't it beautiful?" said Rachel as they got out of the carriage, and Rory looked about him. "Uncle's grandfather built it when he first came to America. This was the first Kent Powder Manufactory."

She led the way inside, and Rory reluctantly followed her. The front door opened straight into the sitting room. It was plainly furnished, with unvarnished wooden furniture and rag rugs on the wooden floor. There was a big stone fireplace and low, small windows.

"Who lives here now?" asked Rory.

"Nobody. We do." She put her arms around his neck. "I'm going to ask Uncle to give it to me as a wedding present."

He tried to free himself, but she held him tight.

"Oh, Rory, I'm sorry I said what I did to Aunt Charlotte. She made me lose my temper, and it was stupid of me. But I know I can bring Uncle James around, and once we're married—"

"No!" said Rory furiously, and this time he did break away. "I didn't leave Ireland to be a beggar, living on your charity, and that's what marriage to you would mean!"

"No, Rory, it wouldn't!"

"What else would it be? I've no money, and if I got my job back, it would be because you begged for it for me. I've never been free in my life, but free here I will be—and one day I'll go back and make Ireland free, too."

"You'll never be free," said Rachel, "until you put the past behind you. You'll never be free as long as you live with ghosts."

They weren't quarreling now. They stared at each

other, a few feet apart in the small, bare, friendly room, but the whole world might have lain between them.

"Those ghosts are part of my life," said Rory. "I'll win with them or not at all."

His temper began to rise again and he walked about the room, frustrated and angry. "And I *would* win," he said, "if I could just lay my hands on five hundred kegs of powder! Damn Caleb! And damn your uncle!"

He glared at her, and his temper finally boiled over. "And damn *you*," he said, "for meddling in my affairs!"

He slammed out of the Old Mill and saw Tom at the horses' heads quickly look around.

"It's all right," said Rory. "I'll walk."

CHAPTER 19

·

"Do you want anything from Levy's Dry Goods Store, Rachel?" asked Charlotte, putting her gloves on as she came downstairs next day.

Rachel had never heard her speak so pleasantly before. It must be, she thought, because her aunt knew that she had won. But if *she* was pleasant in return, Charlotte would know that Rachel hadn't given up yet, so she put down her book and frowned crossly.

"If you are going into the city, Aunt," she said, "I should like to come with you. I don't particularly want to sit *here* all day!"

"Just as you please, my dear," replied Charlotte. "I can quite see that the mill yard might not have quite so much appeal to you now."

Rachel gave her a scornful glance and stood up. "I'll get my jacket," she said.

But as soon as they were inside Levy's large, pillared establishment and Charlotte was seated by the counter, well engrossed in matching ribbons, Rachel, having bought a spool of thread at random, rose to her feet.

"I'm just going to walk to Evans' Bookstore," she said. "There's a book I want to buy Uncle James for his birthday."

"Rachel—wait—"

"I'll be back before you've finished, Aunt," said Rachel, "or if I'm not, you can wait for me in the carriage."

And, satisfied at having annoyed her aunt and escaped from her in the same instant, she walked briskly out. But she did not go to Evans' Bookstore. She went to Caleb Staunton's office.

It was fortunate that Caleb was free to see her, and when she gave her name to the friendly young clerk, Caleb came to the door of his office and greeted her cordially.

"I've never been in a lawyer's office before," she remarked, looking with interest at the shabby furniture and secondhand law books. "It all looks very business-like—but I am glad of that, because I have come to talk to you about business."

She saw a wary look in Caleb's eyes as he went behind his desk, but she settled herself in the rather hard client's chair, looking at him brightly.

Caleb sat down and smiled at her. "How can I help you? I don't think that a young lady as pretty as you should really talk business."

He was warning her off, and she knew it. She decided that it was no good trying to be ingenious with Caleb.

She had better meet him on his own ground of bluntness.

"Why won't you invest in Rory's powder deal?"

Caleb's smile hardened. "I'm afraid if you came here to ask me that, you have wasted your journey. I've already given my answer to Rory."

"And you think it's none of my business? But you know that anything which affects Rory affects me."

He was silent for a moment. "Yes," he said, "I know. I'm sorry I can't help." He stood up. "I have to go to the courthouse. Is there anywhere I may escort you on the way?"

He had come around the desk and was moving toward the door, expecting her to rise. Rachel remained where she was.

Caleb paused and looked at her. "I am not going to change my mind," he said.

"Not even for Deirdre's sake?" asked Rachel.

Caleb was absolutely motionless for an instant, like a granite statue.

"I know you want to marry her," said Rachel.

"She has made it very clear," said Caleb with a difficulty which showed how deeply he felt, "that she would not consider it."

"I could make her consider it," said Rachel, "if you help Rory with this powder deal."

He turned on her in a cold fury. "Are you trying to *bribe* me—and with *that*?"

She found Caleb's icy rage more frightening than Rory's hot temper, but she concealed her tremor of alarm.

"Oh, pooh! Nonsense!" she said. "I want what's best for all of us, and so do you. I know that Deirdre is very fond of you, because she told me so."

"Did she?" The quick question showed his vulnerability.

"She asked me if it was fair to continue to go out with you, and I said yes, because I knew that given time—But now, everything is different."

He didn't ask her what she meant in words, but he frowned and perched on the end of the horsehair sofa and waited.

She turned her chair around to face him. "You know where she and Rory are living? In an awful shack in Black Horse Alley. He's lost his job; he has no money. Do you think Deirdre would ever leave him while he's in trouble? He's all the family she has. And Rory will never marry me—"

She found she could not speak so calmly on that subject and got up and walked about the room.

"He'll never marry me until he's—until he can feel that he is independent."

"If it succeeded," said Caleb, "this powder deal would certainly give him some degree of financial independence. But he means to spend the money on guns for Ireland."

Rachel turned to look at him. "He might change his mind if he had a wife in America. And even more if he had a son." She smiled. "A little American O'Manion might turn even Rory into a good American businessman."

"It would certainly give him a stake in the country," said Caleb thoughtfully.

"Especially if Deirdre was married to an American."

Caleb got up quickly. "Now, wait a minute, Rachel!" he said. "I've no intention of allowing Deirdre to be persuaded to marry me against her will!"

"As if I *could*!" exclaimed Rachel. She hesitated. "You know that she was in love with David."

"Yes." He answered curtly, as if he didn't want to talk about it.

"Deirdre told me," said Rachel, "how kind and understanding you were when he was killed."

This time he didn't answer. It must be a very uneasy feeling, thought Rachel, to be jealous of a dead man. She looked down at her black dress.

"I'm still in mourning for David, and although she can't wear black for him, so is Deirdre. But the time comes when you have to put off your mourning and look to the future. I think she does love you already in her heart. All I would do would be to try to show her that there would be no disloyalty to David's memory if she admitted it—and that when I marry Rory, she will be free to marry you."

She saw Caleb's face, irresistibly tempted, but uneasy, too.

"Oh, Caleb!" she cried. "Deirdre is Rory's sister and my dear friend. We went through dreadful times together in Ireland. Do you really think that I would ever do anything to hurt her?"

His face cleared and warmth came back into it. "No," he said. "No, Rachel, I don't think you would."

Rachel held out her hand, and he took it.

"Even if I did help Rory find the money to buy the powder," he said, "I'm far from certain that your uncle would sell it to him."

"You can leave my uncle to me," said Rachel, smiling.

She shook his hand, released it and turned toward the door. "Don't tell Rory I've talked to you, will you?" she said over her shoulder as she went. "Just say you've changed your mind."

"Rachel—" began Caleb, taking a step after her, but she had gone and closed the door behind her.

Caleb turned away and found himself in a state of confusion very strange to a man who had always kept his thoughts clear and his emotions under control. Had he changed his mind? He supposed he had.

When Rachel returned to Levy's, having taken the precaution of making her purchase at Evans' Bookstore, she found Charlotte fuming with indignation.

"I have been sitting in this carriage," she said, "for nearly half an hour. It is simply outrageous of you to keep the horses waiting like this. Your uncle would be furious if he knew."

"I dare say you will feel it your duty to mention it to him, Aunt," suggested Rachel.

It was not exactly an ingratiating remark, and it wasn't meant to be. Rachel knew that if Charlotte was angry with her and showed it, her uncle was much more likely to be amenable.

When she went upstairs that evening to change for dinner, Rachel opened the closet and hesitated. There was no Deirdre now to lay her dress out lovingly on the bed. Rachel took out her black dinner gown, paused and put it back. Instead she took out one of the dresses bought at Madame Lucette's when she first came to Philadelphia. It was distinctly decolleté for an evening at home, but it was her uncle's favorite, and she knew why. There was a portrait of her mother in just such a dress. James Kent had gone to England as a young man, fallen in love with one sister and, being refused, had been obliged to settle for the other. But in Rachel he saw the reflection of his lost love—and she wanted him to see that reflection very clearly tonight.

"Good heavens, Rachel!" said Charlotte predictably as she entered the drawing room. "I thought you were in mourning!"

"I know, Aunt," said Rachel, "but I felt I had been such a trouble to you ever since the explosion. This is my way of showing that I mean to be more agreeable."

She spoke to her aunt but looked at her uncle as he stood by the fireplace and let his eyes rest on her with obvious pleasure.

"We certainly are not going to complain," he said, "at having our cheerful little girl back again."

"James, she is *not* a little girl!" said Charlotte sharply.

"No, and I am so thankful, Aunt, that I am not," agreed Rachel warmly, "for if I were, I am sure you would spank me and send me to my room with bread and water, and I am dreadfully hungry."

She caught her aunt's eye mischievously. "I'm sure you must be hungry, too, after all that fresh air. Aunt says you will never forgive me, Uncle, for keeping the horses waiting."

"She should know," said Kent, "that I can forgive you anything."

James Kent was an immensely pleasant and amusing dinner companion that evening. He told them about his trip to New York, described a visit to the theater and how an actress appeared wearing an extraordinary garment called a crinoline—a sort of hoop. She was not accustomed to it, and when she sat down—

"I know that gentlemen are not supposed to know that ladies have limbs," said Kent, "but for my part, I found that any doubts I had on the subject were totally banished."

"Shame on you, Uncle!" cried Rachel, laughing.

She glanced at her aunt, and suddenly, because she was so near to happiness herself, she wanted some little measure of that happiness to be passed on to Charlotte.

Laugh, Aunt! she thought. Don't scold him. Laugh!

But the pattern was too deeply ingrained. "Really, James! I thought you went to New York on business."

"So I did, my dear," replied Kent blandly. "But business and pleasure are like love and marriage—one should always combine them if it is humanly possible."

After dinner Kent went off to his library as usual. Rachel and Charlotte sat in their customary uncompanionable silence until Joseph had brought in the tea tray.

"Well," said Charlotte, putting her embroidery together, "I shall go to bed."

Rachel glanced up from her book. "I think I will just finish this chapter," she said.

When she had heard her aunt's footsteps go up the polished staircase, Rachel sat on, afraid to move. What if her uncle would not agree? What if there were truly no future together for her and Rory? She closed her book. Kent *must* agree, and she must make him.

The library door was ajar, and James Kent sat reading by the fire. Rachel pushed the door hesitantly open.

"Uncle—" she said.

He looked around and smiled.

"I must talk to you about Rory," said Rachel.

For a moment her uncle sat very still, and then he held his hand out to her. "Now, my dear, come and sit down and let us talk this over together."

She came gratefully to kneel beside him, and he put his arm around her.

"I love him so much, Uncle. We loved each other in Ireland, but there it was impossible."

"My dear girl," said Kent, "it is just as impossible here. He is an unscrupulous adventurer—"

"Oh, no!" cried Rachel, but he held her closer.

"You know he is. He will use anyone and anything to get ahead."

"No," said Rachel. "He's ambitious, but not for himself."

She saw Kent shake his head at her, but very kindly, and it gave her courage. She clasped his hand. "Uncle, this powder deal—"

"What do you know about that?"

"Only that Rory—"

"You've seen him!"

"I—saw him in the city today, by accident."

She had not prepared the lie, and she knew she had not said it well, so she hurried on.

"He wants to buy that powder from you and sell it to the railroad."

"Can he get the money?"

"Yes."

She hoped he would not ask her where, and he didn't.

"I see," he said.

He was silent for a moment.

"Very well," he said. "I am prepared to let him have the powder."

"Oh, thank you, Uncle! Thank you!"

"But on one condition," he said. "That you promise to give up all idea of marrying him."

"Uncle—I—can't!"

He smiled at her pleasantly, his face very smooth and handsome in the firelight.

"It's your choice, my dear," he said. "If he succeeds in this venture, it will mean that he can make his own way in the world—and I'm sure he will. But I want him away from here, and away from you."

Rachel stared at him, aghast at the choice he offered her, and all the more because she knew which choice, if she really loved Rory, she would take. She would give him his independence and set him free. But she couldn't—oh, she couldn't!

"Uncle!" she cried. "Please!"

She clung to him, trying to will him to give her what she wanted. He gently held her away from him, his hands on her bare shoulders.

"Now, my dear," he said, "you know I only want what is best for you. He isn't worthy of you. You deserve someone so much better—someone who would cherish and care for you, and build his life around you."

He bent down to kiss her affectionately, but the kiss was on her lips. There was disguised sexual passion in it, and in the instant that Rachel realized this, she felt Kent lose control. His lips clung to hers, and when at last she freed herself from the kiss, he still held her close, kissing her neck and shoulders.

"Rachel!" he whispered. "My darling! My darling girl!"

His lips were on hers again, one hand feeling for her breast and the other pulling at her dress. For a moment Rachel felt all the terror and outrage of impending rape. Then desperation gave her strength and she wrenched herself free.

"No!" she cried. "No!"

She stumbled to her feet, clutching her dress, which had been torn in the struggle. She saw his face as horrified as her own.

"Rachel," he said. "I—I didn't mean—"

He stood up. She backed away.

"Don't. Don't touch me! Don't ever touch me again!"

She turned away, trembling and sobbing for breath. When she turned back she saw him standing motionless.

"We'll—we'll pretend this never happened," she said, still trying to recover from the shock. "We must. You've always been so kind and good. I don't want to forget that. But I can't go on living in this house."

"Rachel—"

His eyes rested on her torn dress, and he was silent. Shaken as she was, Rachel began to understand that power now rested in her hands instead of his.

"If you let the powder deal go through," she said, "and take Rory back into the business, I can marry him at once."

"No! I won't allow it."

"I hope you will, Uncle," said Rachel, "and I hope you'll tell Aunt Charlotte that you have given permission for our marriage, because otherwise it will be very difficult for her to explain why I can't go on living here."

She turned and walked out, but before she went she saw Kent sag into his chair and put his face in his hands like a man whose world has just collapsed in ruins about him.

CHAPTER 20

"It looks beautiful, Deirdre!" cried Rachel.

Deirdre surveyed herself in the mirror in Rachel's bedroom. "Sure, it may *look* beautiful," she said, "but it feels like a suit of armor. I never wore corsets in me life!"

"You're going to wear corsets on your wedding day," said Rachel. "And you'll be the most beautiful bride in Philadelphia."

Deirdre smiled but then threw an anxious glance toward the door. "Are you sure Mrs. Kent would not mind if she knew that I was here?"

"Of course not," responded Rachel cheerfully. "After all, she's giving the wedding breakfast here."

She never knew what her uncle had said to Charlotte after that dreadful night. She only knew that her aunt never voluntarily addressed her again. Whenever Rachel asked for something, she replied, "Just as you like," or "Very well." Rachel should have felt some triumph, but she did not. It was as though poison came with each acquiescence, and it was terrible to live on in the Kent House, making awkward conversation with her uncle but avoiding his eyes, and aware all the time of her aunt's sick, impotent hatred.

Rachel hardly saw Rory now. Kent had sent a message to him by Caleb, offering him his job back and agreeing to sell the powder. Rory had told Deirdre that he only accepted in order to ensure that the blasting powder was made and the wagons prepared in time for the journey west, and he spent all his time hard at work. He never came to the Kent House, and Rachel, conscious of her uncle's brooding face at his library window, never went to the mill yard. She might as well, she thought, have made that bargain her uncle had suggested, to give Rory his freedom and let him go. But Caleb and Deirdre were to be married, and dearly as she hoped for their happiness, she knew that she clung even more tenaciously to the hope that this alliance and the partnership with Caleb would lead to her own marriage with Rory. At least now he would be free to choose. She knew he loved her, but did he love her enough to marry her? She saw Deirdre regarding herself doubtfully in the long mirror, and in a sudden rush of affection which had in it a grain of guilt, she put her arms around her and kissed her.

"Now let's try on the headdress," she said.

She turned away to pick it up but was stopped by Deirdre's voice.

"No! No, Miss Rachel. They say 'tis bad luck to try on the veil and all before the wedding day."

"Oh, Deirdre!" said Rachel, amused, but saw that Deirdre's eyes were resting on the miniature portrait of David which stood on the dressing table beside the veil.

"Are you sure I'm doing right?" she said.

"I know you are," replied Rachel. "You have such a capacity for loving. Isn't it better to make Caleb a happy man than to bury your heart in David's grave? And Caleb is such a fine man—"

"He's such a fine man," Deirdre broke in, "that he deserves better than second best."

As Rachel hesitated for a reply, they were both startled by a loud rat-a-tat on the front door and the sound of a slight commotion downstairs. They heard Joseph's dismayed voice.

"Mr. O'Manion! Mr. O'Manion!"

Deirdre and Rachel looked at each other.

"That Rory!" exclaimed Deirdre. "What's he doing now? Sure, if he died and went to hell, the devil would turn him out of doors to get a bit of peace!" She went to open the door.

Rory came briskly in, carrying an envelope. "There's a letter for Miss Clement," he said, "so I thought I might as well save Joseph the stairs."

He looked Deirdre critically up and down, and then looked across the room to Rachel.

"And if you can find another dress as pretty as that one, we might have a wedding of our own."

Rachel's heart leaped for joy, but she would not let him see it. "Oh, really?" she said.

"The bank's agreed to lend the money, and as soon as the shipment is ready, I'll be off, so you and I might as well be married before I go."

"Perhaps you'd like to ask me first," said Rachel.

"Well, if I must—" said Rory, and he was across the room and took her in his arms. "Will you marry me, me darlin'?"

She flung her arms around his neck. "I will! Oh, Rory, I will!"

He swung her off her feet, and they kissed.

"What kind of a proposal is that?" cried Deirdre, scandalized. "You're mad, the pair of you!"

"Don't you worry," said Rachel. "I'll get some pretty speeches out of him on our honeymoon."

"Well, I'm off," said Rory. "I've work to do." He headed for the door but turned back. "Oh, here's your letter."

He glanced at it as Rachel came to take it. "Who do you know in Marseilles?" he asked.

"Marseilles? No one," answered Rachel, and took the letter without looking at it and seized the chance to snatch another kiss. He kissed her back and went out.

"Oh, Miss Rachel, I'm so happy for you!" cried Deirdre.

"It's 'Rachel' now. We'll be sisters. And, oh, Deirdre, I know you'll be happy, too!"

Deirdre smiled but turned away.

"I think I will just try the veil on," she said. "I don't see what harm there can be."

Rachel looked down at the envelope in her hand, puzzled by the unfamiliar handwriting and the foreign postmark. She opened it, strolling toward the fireplace. There was a single sheet of paper inside, with a few words written on it.

> My dearest Rachel,
>   A friend is writing this for me. I am sorry for the pain which must have been caused by the report of my death. Tell my darling Deirdre not to worry. I am getting better now. All my love to you both.
>
>   David.

In an instinctive gesture Rachel crumpled letter and envelope and threw them in the fire. As the flame flared up, she flinched and would have taken them back if she could, but it was too late. She stood paralyzed for a moment. Then she heard Deirdre's voice behind her.

"Could you help me with this veil?"

"Yes," said Rachel, turning. "Yes, of course."

Rachel did not, after all, have to ask James Kent for the Old Mill as a wedding present. She found the deeds in an envelope beside her place at breakfast one morning. When she thanked her uncle, he merely said, "You will need somewhere to live. I had left it to you, anyway, in my will. Now that David is dead, you will get everything." She felt a chill at his words. She was trying to forget the letter she had received. It had not been addressed in David's handwriting. It had not even come from India. No one need ever know about it. In due course, when David had recovered, he would write himself, and then she would rejoice at the news that he was still alive, as everyone else would—even Deirdre. Or so she had convinced herself. Meanwhile, she was thankful that her uncle had always meant her to have the Old Mill and that the little house would always be filled with love and not hate.

"Will there be anything else, Mrs. O'Manion?" asked the little maid, Bridie, who just chanced to be O'Casey's niece.

Rachel caught her breath at the unfamiliar name and saw Rory smile.

"Nothing more, thank you, Bridie," she said. "You may go to bed now."

"Yes, ma'am," said Bridie.

Rachel and Rory lingered at the candlelit table beside the sweet-smelling wood fire. It was their wedding night—the wedding had been simple and quiet—and this was the first night in their own home. No more tormented, secret meetings; for the first time, they belonged together.

Rachel sipped her wine and watched Rory, who was peeling an apple very meticulously, keeping the peel in one long piece. There was something very sensuous in the way he did it and in his awareness of her watching him. As his knife freed the last piece of peel, she reached out and took it from between his fingers. She twirled it three times over her head and threw it behind her onto the wooden floor.

"That should give me the name of my true love," she said.

Rory suddenly stood up and pulled her to his feet. "Oh, no!" he said. "The name of our first son. Come on!"

He picked her up and carried her up the narrow staircase.

Rory was up early the next morning, woken by the piercingly sweet song of a bird. He had not heard birds sing like that since he left Ireland. They were different birds, but they made a devil of a racket. He reached his hand out across the embroidered sheet and found the other side of the bed empty.

Getting out of bed, he wandered outside where he found Rachel, in her nightgown, with a shawl about her shoulders, sitting with her knees clasped in the little wood behind the house.

"So 'tis here you are," said Rory with a tremendous Irish brogue. "And why isn't the woman of the house inside, fixing me breakfast?"

"Because Bridie will do it much better," said Rachel, and then dropped into a brogue of her own. "And because I'm out here listening to the birds, and finding them a great improvement on your snoring."

"Do I snore?" said Rory, startled into dropping his brogue.

"Certainly not," said Rachel, dropping hers. "And I must say, it's a great relief. We were never together long enough for me to find out."

"Woman, you're shameless!" said Rory.

"I know," she said, laughing. "I never was until I met you."

He sat down beside her and they were silent, listening to the birds and seeing the sunlight glinting off the delicate green leaves.

"I'm afraid," she said.

"Afraid?"

"Of being too happy."

He put his arm around her but didn't speak.

"I think perhaps," said Rachel, "all we can ask for is to be perfectly happy, just for a little while."

She looked up at him. "And you?"

His face was at peace for the first time since she had met him. "I feel like a man who's made a truce with the enemy," he said, "in the middle of a war."

"Am I the enemy?" she asked.

He turned to look at her. "Oh, no," he said. "Not anymore."

He kissed her, very gently at first, and then they made love, there in the grassy wood with the birds singing above them.

A few weeks later Deirdre was awakened by a knock at the door in the tall, unfashionable house Caleb had bought on Vine Street.

"No one who is anyone," Charlotte had always said, "lives north of Market Street!"

"Come in, Annie," she said, sleepily.

But it was not Annie but Caleb who was bringing her breakfast tray. She sat up in bed and laughed at him.

"Ah, Caleb, you're too good to me, indeed you are!"

He had been smiling, but suddenly his face was serious. "You've made me happy," he said, "for the first time in my life."

She was troubled, knowing that he loved her more than she loved him, and she saw in his face that he understood what she was thinking, as he always did. He put the tray on the table beside her and sat down on the bed.

"I'll make you happy, too, I promise."

She felt a great flood of tenderness toward him and put her arms around him and kissed him. "Oh, you have!" she cried. "You have!"

The undisguised joy in his face increased her tenderness toward him.

"I'll pour your tea," he said.

It was a characteristically practical demonstration of affection, but she was beginning to know him. Normally he would be anxious to be off to his office.

"Caleb?" she said. "What is it?"

He gave her the cup of tea as though it was designed to give her strength for what he had to tell her.

"My clerk brought a note around from the office. That man, Patrick Delaney—"

"The one with news about Sean," said Deirdre instantly.

"I asked O'Casey to look out for him," said Caleb, "and he's sent a message to say we can see him this morning."

He stood up. "I'm going to fetch Rory. Have your breakfast, and—"

He hesitated.

"I know," said Deirdre. "Don't get my hopes up."

Rory was into the Black Horse Saloon and yelling at O'Casey while Caleb was still paying off the cab.

"Patrick Delaney!" he yelled. "Where is he?"

"Where he always is," replied O'Casey, "when he's not in jail."

He nodded toward a corner table. Rory turned to Caleb, who arrived to join him.

"So that's why he never came!" said Rory. "God defend us, he was in jail!"

A small, ineffectual-looking Irishman replied from the corner of the saloon, "I was not," he said, mildly offended.

"Yes, you were," said O'Casey, polishing glasses, as usual.

Rory strode over to Delaney and towered over him, eyes blazing. "Where's the little boy?"

Patrick Delaney looked vaguely up at him. "What little boy?" he asked.

"Oh, God!" said Rory, and he turned away in despair.

Caleb quietly drew up a chair and sat down opposite Delaney. "You answered an advertisement some time ago," he said, "about a missing child."

The little Irishman looked blankly back at him with bleary blue eyes.

"Some people called Gavin brought him off a ship," said Rory.

"Gavin?" repeated Delaney.

Rory clasped his head. "Heaven give me patience! A

drink! I'll get him a drink. Maybe that'll stir his wits up." He set off for the bar.

"Gavin," said Patrick Delaney. "They died of cholera."

Rory stopped short, as though he had been shot, and turned. "The child! Did the child die?"

It was fearful to wait until the question penetrated the gray fuzz which was all that remained of Patrick Delaney's brain, touched some chord and wandered slowly back with the reply.

"No. Some people called Murphy took him."

"Murphy?" said Rory.

"How do you know?" asked Caleb, always cautious.

"They was loading up their wagon," said Delaney, "and I gave them a hand."

"He'll do anything," remarked O'Casey dispassionately, "for the price of a drink."

A tiny hint of animation appeared in Patrick Delaney's face. "Sure, there was no harm in it," he said. "They said he was an orphan, and they'd lost their own little one—died of fever on the ship—so they took him."

He looked brightly up at Rory. "Do I get my drink now?"

"When you've told us where they are," said Rory.

Caleb glanced at him uneasily and back to Delaney. "You said they were loading a wagon," he said.

Delaney pondered the matter. "They was going out West," he said.

"West?" Rory looked at Caleb, horrified. "Man, it's the whole damned country!"

He saw that tiny, beloved child with the silver medal around his neck, vanished like a drop of water in the ocean into the trackless wilderness which was called

America, and he was overcome by despair. Sean was gone. They would never see him again.

"I suppose," said Caleb to the vague, inebriated little Irishman, "that you wouldn't—I don't imagine you know where they were going?"

"Oh, sure," replied Patrick Delaney briskly, "they were joining a wagon train. Headed for Evan's Landing, Indiana."

He looked from Rory to Caleb. "Do I still get my drink?"

Since it was already afternoon Rory and Caleb decided to skip work and head back to tell the women the good news. They picked up Rachel. Then headed over to the Stauntons' with a bottle of champagne.

The champagne cork popped from the bottle, and Rachel, Deirdre and Rory laughed as Caleb filled their glasses.

"He'd forgotten the ten dollars," said Rory, "but we decided to give him twenty and the drink as well!"

Caleb raised his glass. "Here's to Sean," he said. "May you soon be reunited!"

As they drank Deirdre's eyes met his in love and gratitude.

They heard the knock at the door with surprise, but without foreboding.

"Who can that be?" said Rachel.

Deirdre was nearest. "I'll go," she said.

She put her glass down and went out into the hall and opened the front door. David stood there. The sunlight shone on his fair hair and smiling face, as though she was a vision of her dead lover. He stepped inside.

"Deirdre!" he said. "Deirdre, my darling!"

She fainted, and he caught her. Caleb, coming to the doorway of the living room, saw David kneeling with Deirdre in his arms, her head on his shoulder. She was already beginning to recover.

"David?" she said faintly.

She began to struggle up, and Caleb moved quickly to help her to her feet.

"Thank you," he said, and his eyes met David's. "I'll take care of my wife."

He half-led, half-carried Deirdre into the living room and helped her lie down on the sofa.

"Wife?" said David, and followed him to the doorway, limping slightly from his war wound.

Rachel moved quickly to fling her arms around him and kiss him.

"David! Oh, David, how wonderful! You're alive!"

"Yes," he said, his eyes still on Caleb and Deirdre.

Rory came to shake his hand. "Glad to see you," he said. "We were told—"

"I was wounded and left for dead," said David, "but as soon as I could—"

He turned to Rachel. "Didn't you get my letter?"

"No," said Rachel, and, prepared for the question, she spoke convincingly.

"I got a friend to write it for me," said David. "He was going to England, so I asked him to post it in Marseilles."

"I never got it!" said Rachel quickly.

She was aware of Rory's sharp turn of the head and of Deirdre's eyes turned toward her. David's eyes were on Caleb, and Caleb's on his. Rachel spoke at random.

"How did you know we were here?"

"I went to the Kent House," said David. "They were

out, but their butler sent me to the Old Mill. Your maid told me you were with the Stauntons."

"I am Caleb Staunton."

The words were a kind of challenge, and David looked quickly back at him. Deirdre began to sit up, and Caleb helped her. Rachel moved toward her.

"Lie still, Deirdre. I have some smelling salts in my—"

"No, thank you!"

Deirdre's tone stopped Rachel in her tracks. Caleb had kept his hands on Deirdre's shoulders and now bent over her solicitously.

"You've had a shock, my dear," he said. "I think you should go to bed."

He glanced up at David. "And I'm sure Lieutenant Clement will want to be alone with his family."

Rachel, anxious to be gone, began to move toward the door.

"Yes. David, you must come back to the Old Mill with us, and—"

"I'm not leaving," said David.

They were all startled by his tone. Although he wore civilian clothes, he seemed much more of a soldier now than when he left Ireland. He was burned brown by the Indian sun, and though he was very thin, his illness had matured him. He had suffered and survived, and now he had returned, single-minded, to claim his own.

"Deirdre is my wife," he said. "I'm not leaving her here with another man."

Rory and Rachel exchanged a startled look.

"Deirdre?" said Caleb, and was shocked by her expression. "You weren't—? You and he were never—?"

"We were married before I left Ireland," said David.

He looked at Deirdre as if they were alone in the room, and she looked helplessly back at him, the memory of that moment silencing all protest.

"You were *married*?" Caleb demanded. "By a *minister*? Before *witnesses*?"

"You sound like a lawyer!" said David contemptuously.

Caleb's slow temper began to burn dangerously, like a fire beneath the earth. He was proud of being a lawyer. He had worked hard to earn that title.

"None of that matters," said David. "We took hands. We made vows. I gave Deirdre a ring. We are man and wife in every way."

Caleb looked back at Deirdre and saw a flush creep into the pallor of her face. In that instant he knew with absolute certainty that she had not been a virgin on their wedding night. He looked back at David, and now it was like a hand-to-hand struggle between them. Rachel and Rory were both aware of it, and aware, too, of the danger, but both were held motionless, Rachel because of her guilt, and Rory because he hardly knew David, or, rather, because he only knew him as a rebellious slave knows his master. When he last saw David, he had been a helpless fugitive, saved by David's magnanimity.

"I owe you for that," he had said.

If David had been a friend, Rory would have known how to intervene, but David was not a friend nor quite an enemy. So Caleb and David were left to confront each other.

"I must ask you to leave my house," said Caleb.

"I absolutely refuse to leave," answered David, "without my wife."

Deirdre stood up. "David——" she said, pleadingly.

But her intervention did more harm than good. Caleb took hold of her and put her behind him, as a man defends what is his.

"Leave this to me, Deirdre," he said, and to David, "Mrs. Staunton——"

David's smile was contemptuous again. "Mrs. Staunton?" he said. "Our marriage was binding to both of us. It still is. As far as I am concerned, your marriage is null and void. Dierdre is my wife."

He said it once too often. Caleb hit David across the face with the back of his hand.

Deirdre gave a cry. David staggered slightly, caught off balance, and then recovered.

"You will meet me for that, sir," he said.

Rory came to his senses at last and caught Caleb by the arm. "For God's sake, man! Have you gone mad?"

Caleb threw him off and never took his eyes off David. "With the greatest of pleasure," he said.

"My second will wait on you tomorrow," said David. "A brother-officer traveled here with me. I am sure he will be happy to represent me."

Caleb gave him a formal nod. The whole thing was so totally unexpected that Rachel and Rory found themselves standing helpless in the face of disaster as David turned and went to the door.

"I shall take a room at the United States Hotel," he said, and went out.

Deirdre took a step after him. "David!" she called.

The front door slammed behind him. Caleb stood without moving, his face expressionless.

"Caleb!" cried Rachel, and then to Rory in a desperate appeal, "Rory, can't you——"

He turned on her. "Get Deirdre out of here, can't you?" he said fiercely.

"Yes," said Rachel. "Yes. Deirdre—"

She came to put her arm around Deirdre and led her toward the door.

"Come away, Deirdre. Leave the men alone. Rory will settle it."

The moment they were in the hall and the door was closed, Deirdre freed herself.

"Come upstairs," said Rachel. "I'll help you get to bed."

She was about to follow Deirdre up the stairs, but was stopped by Deirdre's face as she turned. Rachel saw on those gentle and loving features a look of implacable hatred.

"I will never forgive you," said Deirdre, "as long as I live."

"Will you be my second, Rory?" asked Caleb.

"Your *second*?" cried Rory, exasperated. "What do I know about duels and that kind of rubbish?"

He saw with dismay that Caleb was taking out of the desk drawer a flat case and that it contained two pistols.

"Ah, Caleb," he said, "show a bit of sense! You don't mean to go through with this?"

Caleb sat down at the desk and began, very meticulously, to examine the pistols and prepare the powder and shot.

"Come on, now," said Rory, "the whole thing took us all by surprise."

He stopped for a second, remembering Rachel and the letter, and then continued. "If you want to know, Clement and I have had a few differences in the past.

There've been times when I could have shot him myself, and been glad to do it. But—look at it from his point of view, walking in on this situation, quite unprepared. All right, so he behaved badly enough—"

Caleb glanced up at him. "Will he apologize?"

"How can he?" cried Rory, exasperated, "now you've hit him in the face? He's an officer in the British army!"

Caleb closed the case of pistols. "Maybe you'd let me know," he said, "if you are not prepared to be my second, so that I can find someone else."

"All right!" said Rory. "I'll be your second. But only to keep it in the family, and only because the one thing I know about a second's duty is that he's there to stop the two idiots from killing each other."

Caleb glanced up at him. "This duel could be stopped immediately," he said, "if Lieutenant Clement would declare that he renounces all claims to my wife."

Rory gazed at him, dismayed, remembering that day at Ballyclam when David had faced a loaded gun rather than declare that he would never see Deirdre again.

It was raining when Rory drove Rachel home in their one-horse carriage. They drove in silence until they turned off into the road through the woods, and then Rory said, "You knew that David was alive."

"No!" said Rachel quickly.

Rory glanced at her. "You can lie to the others, but don't you ever lie to me. That letter I brought up—that was the one, wasn't it?"

"I—"

He was right. She couldn't lie to him.

"You tricked Deirdre into that marriage," said Rory. "Treating her like an Irish slave!"

"Don't, Rory!" begged Rachel. "It wasn't like that." And she added desperately, "You never wanted her to marry David!"

"Was that why you didn't tell her he was alive?" he demanded contemptuously.

She could not answer.

"Or was it that you thought I wouldn't marry you if the powder deal fell through?"

Rachel's temper suddenly flared. "Well, *would* you have?" she cried.

They were outside the Old Mill, and Rory reined in the horse.

"I don't know," said Rory. "I just know I can't live with a woman who destroys other people's lives to get what she wants."

They sat and looked at each other. It was as though they had walked together into a mine field, both dreadfully injured, blaming each other for their injuries and unable to help each other. The rain ran down Rachel's face like tears. Rory reached across and unhooked the apron.

"Go inside," he said.

She got down, but then looked up at him, startled. "Aren't you coming?"

"No," he said. "And I won't be back tonight."

He turned the horse in the narrow road and drove away.

The maid brought Deirdre a drink of hot milk and said that Mr. Staunton had told her to put a few drops of laudanum in it. Deirdre drank it without resistance.

"Caleb," said Deirdre timidly when the maid had left the room, "about David—"

"My dear," Caleb interrupted, but with immense

courtesy, "that subject is closed between us. We will never mention it again."

She lay awake, thinking of David. It was as though her love had been quiescent like a dead tree in winter and now sprang fully into bloom again. She could not remember every single moment they had spent together, and yet she knew that each one was there, in her mind, in her heart, in her body, as a child will have flowing through it forever the blood which gave it life. Then the laudanum claimed her and she slept awhile.

As the dawn light edged around the blind, she was awakening and felt Caleb get out of bed. She lay and listened while he got dressed, and heard him open the door, and then she knew where he was going and that she must stop him. She started up.

"Caleb!"

He looked back at her but did not speak. He went out and shut the door. Deirdre stumbled out of bed and across the cold floor in her bare feet, wrenching the door open and screaming after him in the silent house.

"Caleb! No! No! Caleb, please!"

He ran down the stairs, picked up a flat case from the hall table and went out. Deirdre ran back to the bedroom and pulled at the cord of the blind. It flew up like a pistol shot, and she saw in the street below a closed cab. Caleb jumped into it, and it drove off. It was black, like a hearse.

"Oh, God" cried Deirdre. "Oh, God, help me!"

She dressed quickly and went downstairs. On an impulse she crept like a criminal along the passage and into Caleb's little office, where he worked when he brought papers back from Chestnut Street, and where he and Deirdre sat each week to go through the household accounts. It was very neat and tidy, as it always was, and the desk was almost bare. But right in the middle of it was an envelope with some words written on it in his firm, rounded hand. Deirdre could read them now. He had taught her. "To be opened in the event of my death." Deirdre turned and ran out of the house, pulling her shawl over her head.

The church was lit only by the candles burning before the statue of the Virgin Mary. Deirdre crossed herself with the holy water and went to kneel before the altar.

"Dear God," she said, "save him. Save my husband, and don't let him—don't let him—"

She could not go on. She looked despairingly up at the calm face of the Holy Mother and suddenly flung herself full-length on the floor.

"Oh, Blessed Mary, forgive me my sins! Save David's life. Oh, if you will only save him, I will never see him again! Never! I promise, faithfully!"

She stayed there for a long time. It was almost daylight when she came out of the church. At the foot of the steps, she saw Caleb. She could not prevent her look of horror at the sight of him.

"I thought I'd find you here," he said. He came up the steps and grasped her wrist. "Whose life did you pray for anyway," he said, harshly, "his or mine?"

CHAPTER 21

"You must have known what would happen," said Rory. "David's a gentleman. Of course he fired in the air."

"Well, I'm not a gentleman," replied Caleb, "and I didn't. Maybe that'll teach him not to run after my wife," replied Caleb.

He spoke with a cold, unemotional ruthlessness. Maybe, thought Rory, he *will* make President one day. But suddenly that hard American determination to get what you want at all costs and hang onto it grated on him.

"If this ever comes out," he said, "your political career is finished. As it is, we were only able to hush it up because David Clement is Kent's nephew. If you'd killed him—"

"I shot at his shoulder," said Caleb, "and that's where I hit him. But my political career means nothing to me compared to Deirdre."

Rory felt a qualm at his words. Would *he* sacrifice everything he wanted in life for the sake of Rachel? He knew that he would not, and he thought that Rachel knew it, too. He loved her passionately, but still there were limits to his love, and he knew that there were no limits to hers. She would destroy her friends and her family, even herself, for his sake. The knowledge of that disparity made him feel guilty, and yet, illogically, hardened his heart against her.

"Right," said Caleb, briskly putting David and the

duel behind him. "Here's our partnership agreement for your signature."

He passed the document and a pen across the desk. Rory read the paper through and dipped the pen in the ink, then paused and glanced up.

" 'Manion?' " he said.

He saw the wariness in Caleb's face, but Caleb replied in a matter-of-fact way. "That is the signature the bank would prefer."

"Something wrong with "O'Manion?" demanded Rory, firing up.

"No," answered Caleb calmly. "Something wrong with the bank. They think their shareholders will feel that 'O'Manion' sounds too Irish."

"Damn their shareholders!" said Rory furiously. "Are you telling me that if I sign my real name, we won't get the loan?"

"That's about the size of it," said Caleb, and added with a change of tone, "I'm sorry, Rory. Believe me, I fought it, but I couldn't budge them. If you decide you won't do it, I'll quite understand."

Rory sat for a moment, pen in hand. "Ah, what the hell!" he said. He dipped the pen in the ink and signed with a flourish. "There you are—" he said, "R. Manion."

He passed the document back and grinned unexpectedly. "If your fine bank only knew it, there are more Manions in Galway than there are O'Manions. Manion is a very Irish name!"

Caleb stared at him, open-mouthed, and then began to laugh.

"Well, I'm off to the mill," said Rory.

Caleb pulled his watch out and looked at it, startled. "It's a bit late, isn't it?"

"It's not worth going home," replied Rory carelessly. "I've a lot of work to do. Ours isn't the only shipment to be got ready. There's a rush order for the mines to go off tomorrow, and since I'm taking Jim O'Brien with me, I have to make sure everything runs smoothly while I'm away. I'll probably stay with the O'Briens till I leave. It won't be the first time I've slept on the floor."

He saw from Caleb's face that he was not being understood but it didn't matter. Rory knew that Deirdre would not have told Caleb about Rachel's duplicity, any more than he had told David. The reason he had left home was between him and Rachel and no one else. He and Eamon had driven David to the Old Mill after the duel, and Rory had stayed long enough to make sure that David was in no danger. They decided that the story to be put about would be that he was still suffering from the wounds he had received in India.

Rory had looked at Rachel. "Shall I tell the Kents, or will you?" he said.

"You'll be seeing him at the mill," answered Rachel. "Perhaps it would be best if you did."

He nodded and walked out. He had not seen her since.

"By the way," said Caleb as he opened the door of the office in Chestnut Street, "I take it you've had no reply from the Murphys?"

"No," said Rory. "I hear the country's pretty wild out there. A letter has to go by railroad and then stagecoach, and by the time the Indians have shot a few arrows at it, it's a wonder if it gets there at all. Once I've delivered the powder, I shall go there myself."

* * *

It was only a week later than he had intended that Rory was supervising the loading of the wagon train. He was conscious of James Kent standing outside the yard office with Caleb, watching impassively.

"Right, Jim," Rory said as the last Conestoga wagon was loaded, "I'll go and collect a good-luck message from His Lordship, and then we'll be off."

Benevolence was not the dominating feature of Kent's face as Rory walked toward the yard office.

"That's the last of them," said Rory.

"Perhaps you would be good enough to sign a receipt," said Kent.

He turned and led the way into the office, spread out the document, and Rory came to sign it. He hesitated and then signed, "R. Manion."

Kent glanced up at him, and Caleb spoke with a hint of haste. "And here's the bank draft for the full amount."

"Thank you," said Kent, and took it.

"We'll be moving out, then," said Rory. "May as well make the most of the daylight."

Kent nodded pleasantly enough.

"Good luck, Rory," said Caleb and shook him by the hand.

"Thanks," said Rory. "We'll need it."

As he went out, Caleb glanced at Kent. "I'm sorry you wouldn't come into the deal with us, James," he said.

Kent laughed. "Oh, no! I don't have quite the faith in your Irish brother-in-law which you seem to have!"

He might have observed on Caleb's face an uneasy awareness of the risk he was taking, but fortunately he was gazing out into the yard, and by the time he looked back, Caleb had concealed the thought.

"You've made your bet," said Kent. "I hope you don't have cause to regret it."

"At least this sale of powder to us means that you can pay off your loan to the bank," answered Caleb.

"Yes," said Kent. "In full."

Caleb was struck by his tone. Kent continued pleasantly.

"I doubt if I shall have occasion to do business with your bank anymore—or with you."

The pleasant tone deceived Caleb for a second, but only for a second. He looked back toward the train of Conestoga wagons in the yard. His future now depended entirely upon the success of Rory's venture. He was distracted by the sight of David, riding in at the yard gates, his arm in a sling.

Rory, turning away from a consultation with O'Brien, saw David and walked toward him.

"And what are *you* doing here, might I ask?" he said. "I thought you were supposed to be convalescing."

"My doctor recommends a change of air," said David. "And I thought you could use an extra man."

"Maybe I can," said Rory, "but this is no pleasure trip. We're transporting powder, and you know the dangers."

"Of course," replied David. "I've often escorted gunpowder to our hill forts in India. Besides, do you think I care about danger *now*?"

Rory looked at him in silence for a moment.

"All right," he said at last, "if Eamon says you're fit, I'll be glad to have you."

"You can ask him now," said David, and Rory saw Rachel driving into the yard with Eamon beside her.

O'Brien came up to Rory. "All ready, Rory."

"Right," said Rory. "Let's get moving before we think better of it!"

The yard was full of noise and bustle, the mules tossing their heads and rattling their harness and the drivers shouting jokes to each other and farewells to their wives. Eamon descended from the carriage and strolled toward Rory, and Rory went to meet him and jerked his head toward David.

"He wants to come. Is he fit?"

"His shoulder's still hurting like hell," said Eamon, "but it'd be doing that anyway. After what's happened he needs to get away from here."

Rory scowled. "I've got enough on my mind without acting as wet nurse to him!"

"Just as you like," replied Eamon calmly. "I doubt if he'll need much, but he's Rachel's brother, and if ever a man needed a helping hand . . ."

Rory scowled more than ever. "All right," he said. "I'll take him."

They both glanced at David, who was riding toward Rachel where she sat in the carriage, and Eamon began to walk in the same direction, expecting Rory to accompany him. But instead Rory turned away toward the wagons.

"I'll do my best to take care of him," said David, and Rachel nodded, trying to smile.

"With that shoulder," remarked Eamon, "you need to take care of yourself."

"Oh, I'm a survivor," said David bitterly. "Hadn't you noticed?"

Rory climbed up onto the leading wagon.

"Right, boys!" he yelled. "We've a long way to go, so don't get careless. And keep your distance. Don't let your mules get too friendly with the wagon in front of you. Remember, if you think you're about to take the short road to heaven, that's one trip no one wants to take with you!"

The men laughed. Rory settled himself on the seat, gathered the reins and cracked his long whip. "Let 'em roll!" he called.

"Good luck, Rory!" shouted Eamon as he passed.

"Thanks!" Rory shouted back. "Don't kill any patients while I'm gone!"

His eyes rested on Rachel's face, but the mules trod on, and he didn't rein them back.

"Rory!" called Rachel suddenly, "I hope you find Sean!"

The wheel of his wagon lurched over a stone as he took the awkward turn out of the yard gates, and she caught her breath and never knew if he heard her.

The Conestoga wagons rolled westward down the turnpike road, each one a lurching, jolting powder keg primed for disaster.

"I hope he gets through," said Caleb as the leading wagon turned the bend out of sight.

"Do you?" inquired Kent amiably. "Personally, I hope that Irishman will blow himself to hell and all your powder with him."

He carefully closed the door of the yard office and walked away toward the Kent House, but before he climbed the path, he paused and looked back toward Rachel, sitting very still in the carriage.

"Can I drive you to the hospital, Eamon?" she asked.

"No, thanks. I'd better have a look at Molly O'Brien

while I'm here. She was very poorly yesterday. I doubt if she'll live until Jim gets back."

He looked up at Rachel. It was a long time before she replied. She was listening to the receding rumble and rattle of the Conestoga wagons, dragging her heart along behind them.

"I'm sorry," she said, recalling her attention with a great effort. "Mrs. O'Brien is a kind woman."

"Yes."

Eamon prepared to turn away but paused. "Rachel," he said, "I thought you came here to tell him."

Rachel's anger suddenly blazed out at him instead of at Rory. "I *would* have told him, if he'd stopped to say good-bye!"

Her voice broke in spite of herself. Eamon put his hand on her arm.

She looked at him defiantly. "I won't use the baby to bring him back to me," she said.

The first part of the journey was as pleasant as driving mules can ever be. The leafy Pennsylvania roads were comparatively smooth, and the danger was no more than any driver of a powder wagon was accustomed to. Only David, riding hour after hour with his injured shoulder, was gray with pain and exhaustion. When they stopped to eat, he could hardly walk, and the first bite of food gagged in his throat, but he said nothing and got a cup of coffee down, laced with brandy from the flask he had brought with him.

As the wagon train prepared to go on its way, Rory strolled over to him. "Would you rather suffer the tortures of the damned on your horse," he inquired, "or will you risk going to hell on my wagon?"

David, hanging onto his horse's mane and wondering

if he could make it to the saddle, turned. For the first time in their acquaintanceship, Rory was in a position of strength and he of weakness. But vanity was not one of David's vices, and he answered Rory's grin.

"I think I'll take my chances with you!" he replied.

Rory was surprised to find what an enjoyable companion David was as they traveled together on the wagon. David's encounters with the Afghan tribesmen had just that blend of the heroic and the absurd which had always characterized the Irish struggle—then again, most of David's soldiers had been Irish. The army had always represented to Rory tyranny and stupidity, but now he began to see that men facing danger together must always have a comradeship stronger than those differences of nationality and class which seemed so important to the little, careful civilians living in safety back home.

After a while the mixture of grinding weariness and constant danger made the journey westward feel like a long war. Once they had traveled beyond their own familiar wagon trails, Rory was glad to make use of David's professional skill as a map reader, and the Irish and American drivers, who had been ready enough to grin at the Englishman's clipped voice and fancy duds, slowly became aware that his study of the maps and the terrain saved them many miles and many awkward mountain roads. They appreciated the courage, too, which made him refuse to give in to the pain of his wounded leg, and he would ride ahead for hours in the evenings, scouting the next day's route for hazards and returning to dismount and limp toward the campfire when the rest of them had finished eating. Such a journey made each campsite a renewal of comradeship, with shared jokes, teasing, good-natured abuse and even squabbles, and above all with the humorous mutual acceptance of the fact that a broken trace, an ornery mule, a misjudged gradient could any day mean the death of one or all of them.

Inevitably, after many narrow escapes, it happened. They were traversing a mountain pass. On one side the trail was bounded by sheer rock, and on the other an area of scrub led to a deep canyon. The leading wagons were already beginning the downward gradient when something—possibly a snake—startled O'Brien's lead mule. It bolted and took the others with it. O'Brien stood up in the seat, hauling on the reins in vain. As usual, they had left extra space between the wagons because of the rough terrain, but his mules, plunging downhill, threatened to crash into the whole powder train in a fearful accumulation of disaster. O'Brien could do nothing but wrench on the left-hand rein, managing to turn the mules though he could not stop them. They galloped, demented, toward the precipice. Rory, hearing the clatter, turned, aghast.

"Jump!" he yelled. "Jump!"

David, riding ahead to reconnoiter the descent into the plains, heard the explosion. He rode back in time to see Jim O'Brien picking himself up, bruised and shaken, and walked with him and Rory to the edge of the drop and saw the smoking ruin of wagon and mules below.

"Sorry, Rory," said O'Brien. "It was me or the powder."

"I'm not sure we got the best of the bargain," said Rory, and then grinned. "Lucky I brought an extra load," he said. "I can replace you anytime."

*   *   *

At the Old Mill, Eamon walked to the door with Rachel.

"You're fine," he said. "Now remember, you can take a little exercise, but only walking. No more riding from now on."

In human life, minds and bodies take a different course. Rachel, standing there in the stone-flagged living room of the Old Mill, did not see Eamon. She saw two horses galloping toward the stone wall which bounded the abbey at Ballyclam, saw Rory's face above her in the grass.

"No riding," she said, "I promise."

She opened the door, and they saw Caleb dismounting at the gate.

"Caleb!" she called.

He came quickly up the path, anxious to save her anxiety. "I've had a telegram from Rory. He's delivered the powder safely."

"Thank God!" said Eamon. He kissed Rachel on the cheek. "Take care of yourself," he said, "and of the baby."

She smiled and kissed him on the other cheek. "I will," she said. "I promise."

Caleb took the telegraph form out of his pocket as he came into the living room.

"What does he say?" asked Rachel eagerly.

" 'Jim O'Brien bringing wagons back. David and I riding to Evans Landing. Pray we find Sean. Rory.' "

Involuntarily Rachel said, "Is that all?"

He gave her the telegram to look at. "I'm sorry, Rachel," he said.

She read it through and gave it back to him, and tried to laugh. "He never was much good at writing letters."

They were both silent for a moment.

"How is Deirdre?" asked Rachel.

"She's—"

Caleb could not continue. He and Rachel looked at each other in silence.

"That bargain we made," said Caleb, "it wasn't such a good one, was it?"

They looked at each other, both desolate.

"You shouldn't be alone here," said Caleb. "Why don't you move into your uncle's house?"

"No!" said Rachel quickly. "This is my house, mine and Rory's, and if he comes back—"

"He will," said Caleb.

Rachel's courage broke down under his calm, kind glance. "Oh, Caleb," she cried, "even if he does—I'm so afraid—"

"Afraid that you love him more than he loves you?" he said. "Yes. That's not a good basis for a marriage."

He put his arm around her, and they held each other close for comfort.

Evans Landing appeared to consist of a ramshackle ferry and a one-story building that sported a false front which read EVANS LANDING GENERAL STORE. David had lost the bet that day which decided who should inherit the tiresome chore of hauling the pack-horse, so Rory had dismounted and was already inside while David was still at the hitching rail.

There were farmers in the store, examining plows they could not afford to buy, and trappers dressed in the skins of their trade, but Rory saw only the store-keeper, a pudding-faced man.

"Are you Evans?" he inquired.

"Nope," replied the storekeeper, a man of few words.

"I'm looking for a family," said Rory, "who came out here in a covered wagon. Murphy."

"Murphy," said the storekeeper.

The door banged as David came in, and Rory glanced around at him. "Murphy," Rory said again. "Mr. and Mrs. Murphy, and a little boy called Sean."

"Lots of wagons come through here," said the store-keeper. "Murphy."

He took time to think the whole thing over again. A faint glimmer of memory reached him.

"Murphy," he said. "Right. Them. They never made it."

David saw the anguish on Rory's face and moved quickly to the counter. "Quick, man!" he said. "What happened to them?"

"They decided to move on," said the storekeeper. "I warned 'em. Told 'em not to cross the river after the snows had melted. But they wouldn't be told. Irish!"

He spat in the sawdust and looked up again.

"Wagon was carried away," he said, "and they was both drowned."

Rory and David looked at each other, the same question in their minds. Rory managed to get it out. "But— the little boy!" he said. "What happened to him?"

The storekeeper, having dredged up the information from his memory, delivered it like a package of gro-ceries on the counter.

"Never even found his body," he said.

Rory turned away, receiving that dagger blow to the heart. David looked at the storekeeper with dislike. Here was a man who had seen emigrants come and go and only knew that he made money out of them.

"Whiskey," said David.

Sitting by the potbellied stove, Rory drank and began to recover. "Well, that's that," he said. "We may as well turn for home."

"I won't be coming, Rory," said David after a moment.

Rory looked at him, startled.

"I wrote to Deirdre, you know," said David, "before I left. She wouldn't see me. She even returned the ring I gave her."

"She's married to Caleb," said Rory. "You'll have to accept it, David."

"I'll never accept it," said David. "But I don't want to make her unhappy. I shall try my luck out here, probably in the cattle business."

Rory nodded. They drank in silence for a while.

They had sat beside enough campfires for David to know how long to keep silent and when to speak.

"Rory," he said, "Rachel loves you. Go home. Don't lose that as well."

They rode together to the railroad junction. Rory left the horses with David and promised to arrange to have David's army half-pay forwarded to a bank in Chicago. As the train pulled out and David raised his hand in farewell, Rory felt a great pang, not only because David was now a friend and he wondered if he would ever see him again, but also because in parting from him, he seemed to abandon all hope of finding Sean alive.

As the prairies rolled by with their little farming settlements clinging to the skirts of the railroad, Rory saw only the image of that little body with the silver medal around its neck tossed and tumbled in the floodwaters of the Wabash, and could only hear his mother's voice saying, "Rory, you're the strong one. Look after my Sean." He might have in his pocket the key to a fortune, but to the end of his life he would know that he had failed in the one thing that mattered.

From the railroad station Rory went straight to Caleb's office.

"Here's the contract," he said, "promising that the Pacific Railroad will give us all their orders from now on. When they finally blast through the Rockies to get to California, it will be our powder that'll do it."

"Well done, Rory!" said Caleb.

"A stake in the future, eh?"

"Yes," said Caleb, "a stake in the future. Rory—"

"Oh, and here's your share of the payment for the shipment of powder," said Rory, "that is, unless you want to invest half of it again."

"Invest it?" said Caleb, startled. "What in?"

"I've bought ten miles of land on each side of the proposed route of the Pacific Railroad," said Rory.

"But it may not take that route!" exclaimed Caleb.

"I think it will."

"My dear Rory," said Caleb, "it is a complete gamble!"

"That's right," Rory agreed cheerfully. "Do you want to come in on it with me?"

"I'll think about it," said Caleb, and saw Rory grin and knew that he would share that gamble, too, and that Rory knew it. But there was something Rory did not know.

"Have you been home yet?" he asked.

"No, I came straight here."

"I think you should go home," said Caleb. "Eamon is there."

"Eamon?" said Rory, puzzled, and then, "Rachel!"

"I'll drive you there," said Caleb.

At the Old Mill Bridie opened the door to Deirdre. "Oh, ma'am!" she cried. "Thank God you're here!"

Deirdre answered the words but not the tone. "Good day to you, Bridie," she said. "I got the message from Dr. Fleming. Is he here?"

"Yes, ma'am, he's upstairs with herself."

Deirdre, stepping inside, looked up and saw Eamon on the landing.

"Bridie," he said, "would you fetch a bowl of cool water to bathe your mistress's forehead? She is very hot and uncomfortable."

"Yes, Doctor."

When Bridie had gone, Eamon came down the stairs toward Deirdre. "Thank you for coming," he said. "She wants to see you."

"No," replied Deirdre. "I'm sorry. I cannot."

She turned toward the door but heard Eamon's voice, low and urgent.

"Please, Deirdre! I don't think I can save the baby. And I'm far from certain that I can save *her*."

Deirdre's face did not change but she turned back, and as Eamon stood aside, she went ahead of him up the stairs to Rachel's bedroom. She opened the door but did not approach the bed where Rachel lay with her eyes closed in silent suffering. Rachel opened her eyes, wearily turned her head and saw her.

"Deirdre!" she said, and tried to struggle up. "Oh, Deirdre!"

"Lie still, now," said Deirdre, but it was as though she spoke to a stranger.

"No!" Rachel whispered. "No. Forgive me. Please say you forgive me!"

Deirdre was touched in spite of herself and took a few steps toward the bed. "Don't be thinking of that now," she said.

"I must!" cried Rachel. "I must! It was such a dreadful thing I did. I can't die thinking that you still hate me!"

The words broke through Deirdre's wall of anger. "Ah, Rachel!" she cried. "How could I hate you after all we've been through together?" She came to kneel beside the bed.

"God will punish me," said Rachel, "I know he will. He'll take my baby away from me."

"Ah, now, Rachel, don't be saying such a thing! Sure, wasn't our Blessed Lady a mother, and doesn't she understand our faults?"

"It was because I loved him so much," said Rachel.

"I know," said Deirdre, "I know," and held her close.

Rachel, clutched with agony, still struggled to speak. "But say you forgive me!"

"Why, then, I forgive you, as God surely does. And now let's have no more talk of dying!"

When Rory burst in at the front door, he saw Eamon coming down the stairs, rolling down his shirtsleeves.

"Eamon?" Rory said, and then saw the expression on his face, and demanded, "Rachel?"

"No, no," replied Eamon, quickly. "She's all right. We nearly lost her, but—"

Caleb followed Rory in and saw Deirdre follow

Eamon out onto the landing. Their eyes met. Her face was full of sorrow and pity, and Rory saw it.

"The baby?" he asked.

"I'm sorry, Rory," said Eamon.

Rory struggled in silence with the awful blow, but at last managed to ask, "Was it——"

"It was a boy," said Eamon.

He came down and put his hand affectionately on Rory's shoulder. "Rory," he said, gently, "Rachel needs you now."

Rory went into the bedroom where Rachel lay, exhausted. He knelt beside her, afraid to wake her, but she was not asleep. He saw the tears run down her cheeks as he took her hand in his.

"Oh, Rory," she said, "I'm so sorry! Your son, Rory. Our son!"

"Hush, now!" he replied. "You're here. You're safe. And we're together."

"Oh yes!" she cried, and put her arms around his neck. "Thank God! Thank God!"

"Don't worry, we'll have more children," said Rory lovingly.

He held her close in his arms, but the empty cradle beside the bed was dazzled in his tears.

Caleb and Deirdre had instinctively drawn close together, glancing upstairs.

"Poor Rory!" said Caleb.

"Poor Rachel!" said Deirdre.

Caleb put his arm around her. He had never known what her quarrel was with Rachel, but he knew it had to do with David, and that, with its ending, some poison had gone out of their relationship, too.

"There's worse," said Eamon.

They both looked at him, startled.

"There's something I haven't told them. If they value Rachel's life, they must never have another child."

PART III:

HOME

CHAPTER 22

"See, Benjamin!" cried Deirdre. "See Uncle Rory with his soldiers!"

Rory looked up at the balcony of Caleb's office and gave a splendid salute and a smile which seemed to go straight to Rachel's heart.

"I must say," said Charlotte Kent, "it seems very odd to me that they should ride through the city with that— that green flag!"

Rachel's eyes met Deirdre's in amusement.

"It *is* the Irish Brigade, Aunt," she said, "and that is their flag. And, you see, they are carrying the American flag as well."

"Hmm!" said Charlotte.

Little Ben Staunton jumped up and down, ecstatic. "Here's Father! Here's Father!"

Rachel looked, smiling, down at Caleb, who in spite of his handsome colonel's uniform somehow managed to look like a Pennsylvania backwoodsman returning from a successful coon hunt. But while Ben jumped about and Deirdre smiled proudly, Rachel's eyes traveled on to catch a last glimpse of Rory riding through the streets of Philadelphia with the pride of the Irish unfurled above him. They had fought as Irishmen, and many of them had fought out of hatred for England, but they had fought for America, too, and that would never be forgotten.

As Rachel lost sight of Rory, riding at the head of his troops while she remained behind on the balcony, she thought about how their paths had diverged so widely that, in effect, they had lived two entirely different wars within the same one.

The Kent Powder Manufactory had worked around the clock, supplying powder and ammunition to the government, with the powder yards perilously lit by kerosene lamps. After Rory obtained his commission and left, taking half the Irishmen with him, James Kent had worked as hard as any of them. His hair had turned gray. He dressed carelessly, and he no longer, Rachel suspected, visited any of the pretty ladies in the town. One day a flare of oil from a swinging lamp lit a fire which threatened the press mill.

"Run!" ordered Kent with his usual brusque authoritarianism.

The workmen obediently took to their heels, but Kent moved to extinguish the fire as though careless of his life. The press mill exploded, and he was found amid the ruins. He lived through that night, blinded and with a broken back, and Charlotte sat beside him. In the morning Rachel heard what had happened and came to sit beside him and take his hand.

"Marianne!" he said, and died.

It was her mother's name.

Charlotte moved out of the Kent House into a fashionable house near Rittenhouse Square. She had always hated the powder mill, and, as she said, her nerves were quite destroyed by the latest explosion and by James Kent's death. It was ironic that she always called him now "My dear husband," as though, now he was dead, he became the husband she had always wanted him to be.

Rachel moved into the Kent House. With her uncle dead and Rory and David away fighting, there was no

one else to take charge. She was there through all the
accidents caused by day-and-night work, and helped
nurse the injured in the infirmary. There was always
another danger, too—the danger that the Confederate
Army would capture the mill. The worst time was in
1863, when Lee's army actually reached the Susque-
hanna River. But in the evening they heard that Lee
had been turned back at a place called Gettysburg.

Slowly, slowly, as the winter night turns to gray
dawn, Rachel realized that the war would soon be over.
She moved back to the Old Mill, leaving the Kent
House empty and half-ruined by wartime occupation,
with offices where the library and drawing room had
once been and with a little makeshift bedroom at the
back where the manager had slept in times of crisis.
The manager had been appointed by her aunt directly
after James Kent's death, but Rachel discovered that
he had his fingers in the till and got rid of him, much to
Charlotte's annoyance, and put O'Brien in his place.
She knew that Rory would approve, but she could not
ask David for his consent. She could not correspond
with him at all, and certainly not about a powder factory, because on the day that Mr. Lincoln agreed to
blockade British ships, David had volunteered to fight
for the South. Ironically enough, David was fighting
for the Rebels while Rory fought for the government.

And now it was all over, and Rory was safely home.
The helpless, despised, half-starved fugitive who had
crawled into America more dead than alive was now
riding through Philadelphia as a conquering hero. A
hero he *had* been, as witness the decoration he had received when he led his *Irish* troops to plug the breech
in the Union line at the second battle of Bull Run. But
Rachel had gained something far more valuable to her

than a husband who had become known as a distinguished soldier. She had gained a husband who had opened his heart to her in his letters.

Rory had never written to her before, but all the time he was away at the war, he wrote faithfully whenever he had a moment, whether crouched in a muddy ditch, shivering in a small wood waiting for supplies which never came or in his tent by the light of a shaded lantern. She learned more of his true thoughts and feelings from those letters than she had known in all the time they had spent together. It was as though the Irish, who love to talk, had yet become accustomed during all the years of living in an occupied country to give nothing away in their conversation. But in their writing they freely yielded the truth, and so it was with Rory. While he and Rachel were parted, they came closer than they had ever been.

The day before he came home, she put all the letters together and took them up to the attic of the Old Mill. She sat on the floor reading them before tying them up with pink tape. She had kept every scrap he had ever sent her, including one with a spot of blood on it when he had received a saber cut and wrote left-handed to reassure her. She had even kept, in her own handwriting, a copy of a letter he wrote to Brian and sent to her to be forwarded to Ballyclam with money enough to buy seed potatoes. She read it through now:

My dear Brian,

It was good, indeed, to receive your letter after long delays. As you say, the Irish Brigade has acquitted itself grandly. We seem to have been in the thick of things, and those of us who survive will return as hardened fighting men.

I hope you will never have to see the sights I have seen on the battlefield—men with arms and legs blown off, horses screaming in agony, young boys with no more than minutes to live crying for their mothers. I could not help thinking that any one of them could have been our Sean if he had lived. Believe me, Brian, I will never speak lightly of killing or war again. Please God this one will soon be over.

Well, now it *was* over, thought Rachel, putting the letter with the others in a tin box to protect them from mice, and Rory would never fight again—not even for Ireland.

There were certainly quite a few cries of "Up the Irish!" at Kent's Powder Manufactory that evening, but they were hardly warlike. Rory and Rachel drove in under a great banner which read, WELCOME HOME MAJOR MANION and another which read, WELCOME OUR BRAVE BOYS. They went inside the new Woolen Mill, which had been built under Rachel's direction to make Union uniforms during the war. They were greeted with cheers and applause, and the Mill Band played "When Johnny Comes Marching Home."

Jim O'Brien was waiting by the door.

"Welcome home, Rory!" he said. "We've held you in our hearts these four years though you've paid no rent —but may God forgive you for keeping me from fighting with the Irish Brigade!"

"Get away with you, Jim!" cried Rory. "You were far more use here, making ammunition that wouldn't blow up in our faces!"

Beside O'Brien stood a tall, slim and yet somehow

voluptuous girl with a mass of curly red hair and eyes as green as the hills of Galway.

"Heaven preserve us!" cried Rory. "Is this Maureen? Is this the little bit of a thing I used to catch up in my arms and hold above my head?"

"*I* don't mind if *you* don't, Major Manion!" said Maureen, invitingly demure, and they all laughed.

The band struck up the first dance.

"Major and Mrs. Manion, would you do the honors and take the floor?" said O'Brien.

The music of fiddle, pipe and drum was full of memories as they moved in each other's arms.

"It's like that night in the kitchen at Ballyclam," said Rachel.

"Except that you're more beautiful than ever," answered Rory.

Rachel laughed.

"At thirty-five years old, and in a dress I've had since before the war?" she demanded. "Where did *you* learn to pay such compliments? I've heard that some of those Southern ladies were not nearly as hostile to the enemy as they should have been!"

"There was not one of them could hold a candle to you," said Rory.

Rachel laughed again as he swung her in his arms. She noticed that he did not deny the Southern ladies, and she was glad of it. She was sure that he had had a great many encounters during the four years that he had been away. With such a hot-blooded man, it would have been very odd if he had not. It was enough for her that, as other dancers joined them on the floor, he had eyes only for her.

Caleb and Deirdre arrived with Benjamin as the first dance came to an end.

"Well, Colonel," said Rory, shaking Caleb by the hand, "the last time we wear these uniforms, eh?"

"For which I'm profoundly thankful!" replied Caleb.

"Ah, so you say!" cried Deirdre. "But I've yet to see the young man who doesn't fancy himself in a fine uniform!"

"It is an extraordinary thing," remarked Caleb, "that after four years in the field, the only person I have never managed to inspire with any respect whatever is my wife."

But he looked down at her lovingly as she clung to his arm. Their private war to struggle back to love and trust had been fought within the larger one which had torn the country apart.

"You should thank her for the 'young,' anyway!" remarked Rory, and they all laughed, glad to be home, glad to be safe, glad to be together.

Benjamin tugged at Caleb's coat, and he bent down and listened and then addressed them gravely.

"It seems that before I enjoy myself, I have to find my son a glass of lemonade," he said.

They made a delightfully incongruous couple as they went off together, Caleb tall and sturdy and Ben trotting along beside him, holding his hand, a diminutive version of him with his thatch of yellow hair. Deirdre looked lovingly after them, but Rachel watched her, troubled, afraid that the news she had received that morning might destroy their hard-won peace. The band struck up again, and she found Jim O'Brien beside her.

"Might I have the honor, Mrs. O'Manion?" he asked.

She laughed. They had been "Jim" and "Rachel" for a long time now. They had worked together very closely during the war and had learned to like and trust each other.

"It would be a pleasure, Mr. O'Brien!" she said.

Rachel was kept busy dancing with the workmen after that, and Rory with their wives, and it was not until late in the evening that he managed to escape.

"Don't I get another dance with my wife?" he inquired.

"I hope so," said Rachel, "but I really must warn Deirdre about David first. I want to give her time to get used to the idea."

He nodded. "You've no idea why he is coming?"

"His letter said for a special reason," said Rachel.

Rory's eyes turned toward Deirdre, who was straightening little Ben's tie and returning him to the festivities.

"I hope it's not the special reason he had last time!" he said.

Caleb was drinking whiskey with the men at the other end of the room, and Rachel moved to sit with Deirdre. Rory, turning away, came face to face with Maureen O'Brien.

"Will you dance with me, Major Manion?" she said.

"You don't want to dance with an old soldier like me," said Rory, and suddenly he wasn't joking.

To live through a war adds many years to one's age, quite disproportionate to those actually lived. They are years of experience which can never be shared, of self-knowledge which can never be forgotten and, above all, perhaps, years which contain in them forever the shadow of years which can never now be lived and are lost for all time. Looking at that glowing, fresh young girl, Rory felt suddenly very old.

"Where are all the young fellows?" he said. "I'm sure they want to dance with you."

"Maybe they do," answered Maureen with that irresistibly impudent smile, "but I've danced with them, and I've never danced with you!"

"Ah, well, if I must, I must!" said Rory, laughing, and took her in his arms.

He had known her for so long that she was like a sister, and he felt no sense of danger.

Rachel and Deirdre saw Benjamin dancing solemnly past with an equally solemn little girl in a white frilly dress, and Deirdre laughed.

"I'm thinking Ben is no lighter on his feet than his father," she said.

Rachel smiled, too, but her smile slowly faded. She seemed to see her son and Rory's—that child who had never even breathed in the world—moving among the dancers like a ghost. She became aware of Deirdre's anxious glance.

"Is there something wrong, Rachel?"

"No!" she said, quickly. And then, "No." She paused. "Deirdre, David is coming to Philadelphia."

Deirdre sat very still for a moment, but when she spoke her voice was calm. "You will be glad to see him."

"Yes, very glad," answered Rachel warmly. "But I didn't want you to be—to be taken unprepared."

"I know," said Deirdre, "and I thank you. I knew that we must meet again one day, if God spared him. But I cannot let that old, sad story hurt the innocent." Her eyes rested for a moment on her young son, and then she turned back to Rachel. "I'll be glad to see David again as a friend. And I hope that's how he'll see me."

"I'm so glad," said Rachel.

They sat in silence for a moment, and then Rachel

added, "We should warn Caleb, too. Will you tell him?"

Deirdre hesitated. "Maybe—maybe it would be best if Rory did," she said.

Rachel felt a slight uneasiness. Could love really be so subdued? But her attention was distracted by the sight of Rory dancing past with Maureen. The tune was an old Irish one, and he had a young girl in his arms. They danced lightly and sweetly together, and she gazed up at him with obvious admiration.

"Hmm," said Rachel, "I think it's about time Rory had another dance with his wife, and then I shall take him home."

She stood up, laughing, but Deirdre stood up, too, and caught her arm.

"Rachel! Don't take any chances!"

Rachel pretended not to know what she meant. "Chances?" she said.

"Ah, now, Rachel! With him back from the war, and you with the heart near torn out of you all this time, longing to have him home! Now you're together again —you will be careful?"

Rachel laughed back at her. "Careful?" she said. "When were Rory and I ever careful?"

And as the dance came to an end, she moved to detach him graciously but firmly from his beautiful young partner.

"Champagne?" said Rory, as he followed her into the bedroom. "What's all this about?"

"A welcome home to the conquering hero," said Rachel, and kissed him. "Now, hurry up and unhook my dress. I've sent Bridie to bed."

She turned and felt his fingers at her back, neat and quick for all the homemade whiskey he had drunk.

"Do you remember," she said, "the trouble you had getting my dress off in the stables at Ballyclam? You've had more practice since." She laughed at him over her shoulder.

"You were always shameless," he said.

"So I was," she agreed, "but you were the only one who knew it."

The dress fell to the floor, and she kicked it aside and turned into his arms to kiss him. He returned her kiss with equal passion, but then she felt him draw away.

"Woman," he said, "what are you trying to do to me?"

She tried to draw him close again. "You know, darling!" she said.

"No!" said Rory, and he used all his strength to hold her away from him. "It's not just Eamon. Your fine doctor from England said the same thing."

"If I'm prepared to risk it," said Rachel, "why won't you?"

She stroked his hair, caressed him, used all the tricks of love which she had learned from him. He found himself responding and jerked himself free.

"Will you stop tormenting me?" he shouted. "It's not a game!"

"No," said Rachel, "it's not a game."

And suddenly she was clinging to him in desperation.

"Rory, don't take this away from our life together. If you do, I'll die in a different way. You've always been my lover as well as my husband. Don't let us lose that."

"We have no choice!" cried Rory. "Do you think I don't want it as much as you do?"

"Then—just this once! Oh, Rory, when you went away, I thought I'd never see you again. And now you're home and safe. Let me hold you in my arms tonight."

She had him by the hand, the arm, her other hand around his neck as she drew him toward the bed. Rory violently broke free.

"Haven't I enough deaths on my conscience?" he demanded. "I'll not add yours!"

He went into the little adjoining room which they had once thought would be the nursery, and he stood and listened to Rachel, sobbing bitterly.

Rory rode into the mill yard next morning and was glad to see that the banners were being taken down and normal work was being resumed. He dismounted outside the yard office and went inside, and O'Brien got up to greet him.

"Good morning, Jim," said Rory.

As he turned from closing the door, he saw Maureen, a dark pinafore over her print dress.

"Maureen!" he said, startled.

"She helps me in the office now," said O'Brien. "She's a fine little writer and is a great hand with the sums, which I never was."

Rory glanced at her casually. "Good girl," he said.

He sat down at the table. "Well, you'd better bring me up to date. How's business?"

"I'm thinking," said O'Brien, "that you and Rachel did not choose the best time to inherit a powder mill."

"Oh?" replied Rory, surprised. "We must have done well during the war."

"So we would," said O'Brien, "except that the government doesn't pay its debts. Maureen, me darlin', bring the books for Mr. Manion to see."

Maureen brought the account book and the order book and leaned close to put them in front of Rory. He opened the account book.

"Very neat," he said, and did not mean the words to have a double meaning, but how could he help it with that trim, full bosom so close to him?

"Thank you, Mr. Manion," said Maureen demurely.

Then Rory took in the figures on the page and forgot hers entirely. Red ink confronted him everywhere.

"If the government doesn't pay soon," he said, "we shan't have enough money for the wages."

"We haven't now," said O'Brien. "I've been laying men off."

Rory looked at him, shocked. "Where's the order book?" he asked.

Once more he felt that warm body against his shoulder as Maureen leaned close to put the order book in front of him.

"A bit of powder for the coal mines," said O'Brien, "and a bit less for the railroads, and that's the sad tale of it."

"Colonel Staunton told me yesterday," said Rory, "that the government is dumping powder on the market and that Treadwell and his consortium—or gang of thieves, whichever you like to call them!—are buying it up and selling it cheap."

"Then we shall have to sell ours cheaper," said O'Brien.

"Father," said Maureen, "if we lower our prices any more, we shall go out of business!"

Rory glanced up at her and saw intelligence in those

green eyes. "If we don't get some more orders, we shall go out of business anyway!" he said.

There was a brief silence.

"Maureen," said O'Brien, "would you step over to the house and fetch my pipe? I must have left it on the fireplace."

Maureen hesitated for a second. "Yes, Father," she said, and went out.

Rory's eyes turned after her in spite of himself. "Jim," he said, "your mischievous little girl has turned into quite a beautiful young lady."

"Ah, she's a grand girl," said O'Brien. "I don't know what I would have done without her since my Molly was taken from me."

He took his pipe out of his pocket and chuckled as he saw Rory's glance of surprise.

"But I don't tell Maureen everything," he said. "I think I know where we can find a customer for our powder."

"What sort of customer?" asked Rory.

"The best," replied O'Brien.

He began to fill his pipe. Rory got up and strolled to the window. He saw Maureen climbing up the path to the small, neat stone houses where the workers now lived. Jim O'Brien's voice came from behind him.

"I've not been idle," he said, "while you left me drudging here and went gallivanting off to your honor and glory. We've a fine little bunch of Fenians here in Philadelphia, and there's one of Ireland's top men, Seamus Doherty, coming over to meet us. I want you and Eamon there."

Rory turned back into the office. "But is there any more to it than talk?" he said.

"They're planning a rising," said O'Brien, "and you're the man who can make sure it happens."

"Oh?" said Rory, suddenly full of suspicion.

"They need powder," said O'Brien.

Rory nodded slowly. "And can they pay for it?"

"*Pay for it?* Did you pay for Lord Fitzmorris's coach when you used it to bust me out of Galway Barracks? What's happened to Rory the fire-eater?"

"Even a turf fire smolders out at last," said Rory wearily, "if you kick it enough."

He saw O'Brien's expression and laughed. "All right, you old rebel, I'll come to your Fenian meeting. When is it?"

"Tonight," answered O'Brien. "I'll get in touch with Eamon."

Maureen opened the door, breathless, just as O'Brien was preparing to light his pipe. Her eyes moved quickly from the pipe to his face. He smiled amiably at her.

"Found it in me pocket after all," he said.

Maureen's face showed that she didn't believe a word of it, and Rory found himself grinning at her.

It was not a section of Philadelphia with which Rory was familiar, but Eamon's practice took him all over the city, especially among the poorer parts. He led the way toward a shabby house on a deserted street and knocked on the door. He and Rory both glanced around as they waited, but there was no one in sight.

Sam O'Shea admitted them to the house. Rory knew him by sight. He was a powderman at the Kent Powder Manufactory, though he had only been employed there for a year or two. The house was empty—nothing more than a meeting place, and when the meeting was over, deserted as before. In the back room at the end of a dark passage sat an Irish-American Fenian whom Rory knew of old. He nodded to him.

"Brennan," he said, and glanced around. "Your man isn't here yet?" He took out his watch and looked at it and frowned. "I don't know about this other fellow, but it's not like Jim to be late."

"Jim said the British agents had been on Doherty's heels ever since he left Dublin," said Eamon. "They were probably watching out for him when he landed."

"As long as they didn't pick Jim up when he met him—"

"Ah, Jim's an old hand at this sort of thing," said Eamon. "He'll be showing them the sights of Philadelphia before he gives them the slip!"

They all started at the knock on the door, which sounded very loud in the empty house. But it was the same knock as Eamon had given—two doubles and a single. Eamon grinned at Rory.

"Up the rebels!" he said and went to the door.

The Irishman who followed him in with O'Brien was a dour-looking man of about forty, dressed as a seaman.

"Rory," said O'Brien, "this is Seamus Doherty."

Rory moved to shake hands, but the man spoke first. "So you're O'Manion," he said. "Beg pardon—it's *Manion* now, isn't it?"

Rory took an angry breath, but O'Brien intervened.

"That's Eamon Fleming, and this is Harry Brennan and Sam O'Shea."

Seamus nodded and sat down at the table without any further amenities. Rory, O'Brien and Eamon exchanged glances before joining him, with Brennan. There were not enough chairs, so Sam O'Shea perched on a packing case. He was a fair-haired, cheerful-looking man whose father had come from Limerick before he was born. Rory glanced at O'Brien again, and then at Seamus.

"It's good to have you here," Rory said, but Seamus cut in.

"I'm glad you think so," he said, "because I've been sent to make it clear that orders come from Ireland, and we expect them to be obeyed."

He could not have caused more instant rage if he had insulted the pope on St. Patrick's Day.

"The devil with your orders!" said Brennan. "We just fought a war over here, and we won it. If you think that we are taking orders from *you*—"

"It was a different kind of war," said Seamus, "and don't be giving me that 'Battle of Gettysburg' stuff, because we're not interested."

"Now, see here," said O'Shea, "if you just came here to—"

"That's enough, Sam," said Rory. "There's nothing the British would like better than to divide the Fenians in America from the Fenians in Ireland."

"Then divided we'll be, *Mister* Manion," said Seamus, "unless we get what we want. If the rising is to be in Ireland, then we're the ones who will decide when and where it will be. Otherwise—" He stood up.

"Sit down, Seamus," said Rory quietly.

Seamus hesitated and then obeyed, but very suspiciously.

"Thank you," said Rory. "Now, let's get down to business. We know what's been happening at home during the famine, and since. Do you think there's one of us who doesn't know or care? Four million starved or fled, and those who are left too frightened or too weak to raise their heads. Now we're asked to believe that there's a chance of a rising. We want to believe it, but we need to know the truth or we're all dead men. A rising there'll be, sooner or later, but is this the time?"

The Irishman's eyes did not quite meet Rory's. "If you do *your* part," he said, "we'll *make* it the time!"

Rory had his answer. It was what Caleb would call a gamble. But it was not a good gamble. From the sound of it it was not even a good gamble for Ireland. He was no longer a foolish young fellow of twenty, ready to take any chance for Ireland's freedom, however crazy. He had fought a winning war and had learned that courage was not enough. If it had been, maybe the South would have won.

"I see," he said and was aware of Jim O'Brien glancing at him uneasily.

Seamus leaned his fists on the table and took charge of the meeting again.

"We need guns, and we need gunpowder," he said. "Do we get them?"

Brennan grinned. His family, like O'Casey's, had lived in America for many years. Ireland to him was a dream and an adventure, but not a reality. "I can lay my hands on two thousand guns," he said, and added, grinning, "and what's more, it's all quite legal. They're government surplus."

"But we need men to fire the guns," said Rory. "Are there fighting men in Ireland now?"

"They are there," said Seamus, "the length and breadth of the land, and they're ready. Will you give us the powder?"

"Can you pay for it?" asked Rory.

Seamus glanced at O'Brien and then back at Rory. "I hear America is a rich country," he said.

"We are patriots over here," said Rory coldly, "but we are not *idiots*! I am not bankrupting my mill to give you powder for nothing."

"Oh, I can see you're a fine patriot!" said Seamus with a sneer.

Jim O'Brien suddenly fired up, banging his fist on the table. "He is," he shouted, "and don't you ever say otherwise!"

"Ah, come on now, Jim—"

"No, Rory, I'll tell him, for he needs to know!" He put a hand on Rory's shoulder and glared at Seamus.

"Wouldn't this man be a rich man today but that as soon as he could lay his hand on some money, he filled a ship with food and sent it to Ireland!"

Seamus sat still and silent for a moment, looking down at the table, and then turned his skeptical face toward Rory. "I hear you have an English wife," he said. "What did she think of that?"

"She saw every sack and cask aboard," said Rory, "and when the ship sailed, she was so tired that she fell asleep on the quayside—so we'll just leave my wife out of this, if you please!"

His eyes met the eyes of Seamus. It was a trial of strength, and Seamus's eyes fell first.

Rory stood up. "I must go," he said. "I have an appointment. I'll let you know about the powder, but in any event, I shall want to see the color of your money."

He went out of the room and along the dark passage and straight out of the house. He had heard of these new Fenians, who would kill for nothing and who seemed to feel such hatred that they would bring Ireland tumbling down in the ruins of their struggle for freedom. He remembered the brave young comradeship of the Young Irelanders and could not bear to think that it had come to this. He came down the broken steps and walked away very fast, as though he could outwalk his thoughts, and he never saw the tall, elegant British agent standing watching in the opposite alleyway.

Rory fetched his horse from the livery stable and decided to call in at the mill on the way home. There was no night shift, so the yard was deserted, but he was puzzled to see a light in the yard office. It certainly could not be Jim O'Brien, who would be taking Seamus to a "safe" house in the city. Rory tethered his horse outside and opened the door and saw Maureen.

"Oh," he said.

He felt that he had about enough complications in his life just now, without a pretty girl in his office when he wanted to do some work quickly and get home. But she responded instantly to his mood.

"Good evening, Mr. Manion," she said in a businesslike way. "You said you wanted a list of all the stocks we had, so as Father was out, I thought I might as well get it ready for you."

"Thanks," said Rory, relieved. "Good girl."

He sat down at the table and studied the list she put in front of him before standing quietly back.

"Saltpeter, sulfur, graphite—is all this paid for?" inquired Rory.

"It is not," replied Maureen, "and we've enough dunning letters to paper a room. Did you get that order you went after?"

"I'm not sure," answered Rory. "They want the powder; I just want to be sure they can pay for it."

He pondered for a moment and then drew a piece of paper toward him and began to write, trying to weigh up in his mind the amount of powder that would be needed against what could be transported and hidden—and paid for. The great advantage of it would be that it would be rifle powder, which was hard to get rid of just now, whereas there was always a small—and soon would be a growing—market for blasting powder. On the other hand— He glanced up at Maureen.

"I suppose you couldn't do a costing on that for me?" he asked.

"Certainly," she said promptly, "I'll have it for you by tomorrow."

"Right." He stood up, slightly amused. "Tell me, do I pay you for all this work you do?"

"No," replied Maureen. "I do it for love."

Her mischievous smile tempted him.

"Then here's the first payment," he said.

He leaned forward, meaning to give her a light kiss, but she put her arms round his neck and returned the kiss with ardor.

"Hey!" said Rory, "that's no way for a respectable young lady to behave!"

"Who says I'm respectable?" said Maureen.

Her face was very close to his, her body pressed against him. Rory had to struggle with himself with a great effort of self-control before he made himself seize her hands and take them away from round his neck.

"I'll have you remember, Maureen," he said, "that I've known you since you were a child."

"I'm not a child now," replied Maureen.

It was a dangerous moment, but fortunately she continued, eyeing him defiantly.

"And you needn't think that's the first time I've been kissed!"

Rory laughed. Suddenly she wasn't a beautiful red-headed girl, warm and desirable, but little Maureen, whom he knew like a sister, seventeen years old and boasting of having been kissed.

"I dare say it isn't, you hussy! Now be off with you before your father has my liver for his breakfast!"

She turned toward the door, and he gave her a smack on the bottom to help her on her way, as though she were, indeed, his sister. But when she turned, her eyes were a challenge.

"I'll have those figures for you tomorrow," she said and left quietly.

Rory was smiling as he began to ride home, but he soon forgot Maureen and began to frown. It had been Rachel's idea to invite Caleb and Deirdre to dinner on David's first evening. She felt that the longer the meeting was delayed, the more awkward it would be, and that a family party would make everything easy and pleasant. Rory profoundly hoped that she was right, but he had his doubts and he more than suspected that Rachel had, too.

"Rory is late," said Deirdre.

Rachel replied with an amiability she did not feel. It was too bad of Rory to leave her to struggle with a social situation that was not in the least easy and pleasant. Caleb was propping up the mantelpiece in impenetrable silence, like a statue of George Washington, while she and Deirdre made desperate efforts at conversation.

"He said he might be kept late at the mill," she said.

Caleb spoke at last. "I'm glad Rory is putting in

some time there," he said. "Jim O'Brien was a good enough foreman, but he's no businessman."

"I know," Rachel agreed. "But we were glad to have him at the time. With Rory and David away at the war—"

"Your brother knows nothing about the powder business!"

The words were harmless enough, but the tone expressed Caleb's instinctive, naked jealousy. There was a horrified silence, while Rachel tried to think of an innocent reply.

Rory walked into the silence and glanced around. "David not here yet?" he said. "That's good. But I hope he won't be long. I'm starving."

He stopped short, and his eyes met Deirdre's. "God forgive me," he said, "that I should say those words and not mean them!"

He went to kiss her. "Caleb," he said, "how about a glass of Irish whiskey? That is, if you don't think it'll ruin your chances as senator to bend the law a trifle?"

"If it's anything like the whiskey at your welcome-home party," said Caleb, "I would break the Constitution for a drop of it!"

They all laughed, and Rachel's eyes met Deirdre's in relief. Now that Rory was here, everything was easy and pleasant, as she had hoped.

They heard the sound of horse's hooves and wheels, and a knock at the front door.

"There he is!" cried Rachel.

She was eager to see David after so long, and she ran to the door before Bridie could emerge from the kitchen. David came in, bronzed and handsome, in the clothes of a Western rancher.

"David!" cried Rachel, kissing him. "Oh, I'm so glad—"

She saw someone over his shoulder and stopped short and backed away. Rory, pouring whiskey, was struck by her sudden silence, and turned.

David was not alone. With him was a young man in the uniform of a Confederate soldier.

"Padraic!" said Rory.

But Deirdre was on her feet and running toward the stranger. "Sean!" she cried. "Sean!"

Her arms were around him, though he stood motionless in her embrace.

"Oh, my Sean!" she sobbed, and then turned to David. "Oh, David, thank you! Thank you!"

Her arms were around him, her head down on his shoulder in a wild impulse of love and gratitude. Rachel saw the look on Caleb's face before he moved and was afraid of murder.

"Deirdre!" he said, his voice like a pistol shot.

She had come to herself before he reached her and drew away from David, turning toward him, ready to share her joy with him. But Caleb was glaring at David.

"How could you be so crass," he said, "as to bring him here without warning?"

Deirdre suddenly turned upon Caleb with all her old, fiery Irish temper, so long kept under control. For all her fashionable dress and expensive jewels, she could have been standing barefoot in the stream at Ballyclam.

"Would you be blaming David," she demanded, "for bringing our Sean back to us?"

The young man's face was quite expressionless. It was as though he had learned, no matter what was going on around him, to give nothing away, and he gave nothing away now. David ignored Caleb.

"I'm sorry, Deirdre," he said, gently. "I didn't expect you to be here."

He put his hand on the young man's shoulder and smiled at him encouragingly before he looked across the room at Rory.

"This is John Carpenter," he said. "I found him in a prisoner-of-war camp in Richmond, and I thought I ought to bring him to you."

He paused. Rachel, glancing at Rory, saw that he was still trying to recover from the shock of seeing that face which was the face of his dead brother.

"Yes," she said. "Yes, of course."

David turned his eyes again toward the young man who was a leaner, harder Padraic, wearing the shabby remnants of a Confederate uniform, and then looked back at Rory.

"I couldn't warn you," he said. "I thought if I did, you might see what you *wanted* to see. I had to know if you would see the likeness I did."

"Likeness?" Rory repeated. "He's Padraic's living image."

And suddenly he was laughing, as though a tremendous load of grief had rolled away.

"What does he call himself—'John'?"

He crossed the room in three strides and caught the young man in a great bear hug of joy.

"I'm Rory," he said. "I'm your brother, Rory. And your name is Sean! That's John in the Irish language."

CHAPTER 23

Rachel showed the young man into the neat little attic bedroom, all white frills and china ornaments. She caught a sardonic look in his eye as he glanced around, as though he felt the incongruity of his tattered uniform, worn boots and the army bedroll Joseph had carried up but, with the unspoken comment of ancient servants, had left unopened by the dimity bed.

"I hope you'll be comfortable," said Rachel.

"It looks too pretty to sleep in," he remarked. "I'm afraid if I snore too loud, I might break something."

His voice had a pleasant Western drawl, with no hint of Irish in it. Rachel laughed. "Snore as much as you like," she said.

He glanced around again as though he felt slightly imprisoned, and she was aware of it.

"It's rather close in here," she said. "Would you like a window open?"

As she struggled to open it, she sensed him behind her, putting his strong hand to the casement. She glanced up at him and became aware that he was very attractive, and that he found her attractive, too, and didn't mind her knowing it. She quickly withdrew and let him open the window himself.

"Mr. Carpenter," she said.

"John."

He turned to look at her. She smiled.

"John. My husband's dream for many years has been to find his missing brother. Don't be surprised if—if—"

"If he is so insistent?"

She smiled again and nodded. He was silent for a moment and seemed to be considering the matter.

"If I was him—" he said, and paused.

She looked at him inquiringly.

"I guess I'd be harder to convince," he said.

The reply took her by surprise.

"I would think that if you wanted something very much," he said, "you'd be afraid of fooling yourself."

It was such a perceptive remark that it took her by surprise. In that reflective mood his face lost its hard edge.

"Oh," she cried, "you look so like Padraic!"

He glanced at her. "Who is this Padraic, anyway?"

It was strange to hear him mispronounce the name! "He was Rory's twin brother," she explained.

"And what happened to him?"

She should have been prepared for the question, but she was not. She could almost hear herself saying, Rory killed him!

"He—he died in an accident," she said.

"I'd better be careful, then," drawled John.

It occurred to Rachel that Padraic's response would have been more sensitive, less self-centered.

When she had left him, Rachel listened for a moment to David and Rory talking quietly together, but she didn't go downstairs again. It had been an exhausting evening. Somehow they had gotten through dinner, with David and Rory exchanging wartime experiences. They discovered that they had both fought at Fredericksburg. The young man ate with hearty determination, as though he had learned to make the most of every meal that came his way. Caleb and Deirdre did their best to achieve normal social behavior, but she could not keep her eyes off John Carpenter's face, and Caleb could not conceal the fearful jealousy he felt every time he looked at David. They had left early, and Rachel noticed that in the bustle of fetching a forgotten glove, Caleb contrived to avoid shaking David's hand.

Rachel went into her bedroom and sat down. She thought of that look of joy on Rory's face, and she was glad for him. But there was one moment she could not forget. Caleb had asked the young man if he remembered anything about Ireland.

"Not a thing!" he had replied cheerfully, spearing a potato with his fork and putting it whole into his mouth.

"Never you mind, Sean!" exclaimed Rory. "You and I will go to Ireland together—and while we're about it, maybe we'll set the country free!"

The next day when O'Brien saw John Carpenter riding into the mill yard with Rory and dismounting outside the yard office, he gasped and crossed himself.

"Padraic!" he whispered. "But it can't be!"

Rory laughed. "It's Sean," he said. "Lost all these years, and now restored to us, thanks be to God. Sean, this is my old friend, Jim O'Brien, and he's manager here, so you'd best be civil to him. Jim, my brother, Sean Manion."

O'Brien held out his hand, but John hesitated, and Rory and O'Brien glanced at each other, surprised.

"Er—guess I'd rather use my own name," said John, "that is—the one I'm used to. John Carpenter, sir."

O'Brien took his hand, and Rory did his best to conceal the disappointment he felt.

"Sure," he said. "There might be times when it was useful if you weren't known as an Irishman."

O'Brien looked at him quickly, and Rory grinned at him.

"Can you find a place for him here, Jim?" he asked. "I want him to learn the business, and he may as well start from the bottom. How about powderman?"

"*Powderman?*" said O'Brien, startled.

"That's where you and I began," said Rory. "Besides, he might as well learn how the stuff works, in case he ever has need of it."

O'Brien suddenly gave a great laugh. "I knew it!" he cried. "We're going to make that powder!"

"I always said I'd talk about it," Rory replied.

"Ah, but then you were talking with your head. Now you're talking with your heart."

John glanced around the yard. Rory had already noticed that he had a way of detaching himself from his surroundings when not directly concerned with them.

"Now see here, Jim," said Rory, lowering his voice, "they're going to have to pay for that powder. The government's selling at five cents a pound. I'm not taking less than that, and I need more to cover the cost of transport."

"Rory—"

"I don't own this powder mill," said Rory. "David inherited Kent's interest, and Rachel and Caleb both own shares in it. Maybe I'd bankrupt myself for Ireland, but I won't rob my wife and family."

"All right," said O'Brien. "I understand. I'll talk to Seamus Doherty."

"Thanks," said Rory, relieved. "Meanwhile, can you

find somewhere for my brother to lodge? Rachel wants him to stay at the Old Mill, but I want him to make his own way."

"Quite right!" said O'Brien heartily. "He can stay at our house—and I'll charge him only a token fee."

Rory, glancing toward John, saw that his eyes were fixed on Maureen, hanging out washing outside the O'Brien house. He felt an irrational—quite irrational—disquiet.

"Jim," he said, "I didn't mean—that is—wouldn't that be too much for Maureen?"

"Ah, there's no more work in looking after two men than one," said O'Brien cheerfully.

Rory, looking at John Carpenter, saw in him all Padraic's charm and sweetness, but with toughness added to it.

"I'm not sure Maureen would agree with you," he said, and instantly knew that he had made a stupid mistake.

O'Brien drew himself up, the Irish father of the family to whom women must be subservient.

"Maureen will do as *I* say!" he said. "If I want to take your brother into my house, I'll do it and I'll hear no objections from her!"

"Thanks," said Rory.

But he didn't feel as grateful as he should have.

A week later John picked up a keg of powder from beside the glazing mill as it churned noisily around. It was heavier than he had expected, and he staggered slightly as he carried it out the doorway. In staggering, he knocked it against the side of the door. Two workmen were walking by.

"Watch what you're doing, Reb!" said one of them. "You'll blow us all across the river."

"Maybe that's too heavy for him," said the other. "We ought to give him a hand. Don't want the boss's pet to hurt himself."

John carefully put the keg down on the ground. "What did you call me?" he inquired in his slow Western drawl.

"You heard."

John, moving with deceptive swiftness, punched him in the guts and then, as the man doubled over, brought his knee up under the other man's chin. He was just turning away when his opponent gripped his arm and swung him around, flinging him with sickening force against the water trough.

Rory, watching from outside the yard office, saw the workmen gathering to cheer the fight. O'Brien ran outside to join him.

"They're crazy!" he said. "They'll blow us all to Kingdom Come!"

He was just setting off to stop them, but Rory caught hold of him.

"No," he said. "Wait. Let's see how he does."

Jim O'Brien looked at him, astonished. It did not at first sight look like a fair fight. The other man was Sam O'Shea and John was much slighter in build. But it soon emerged that he had that little extra edge of courage, together with the unexpectedly fierce art of the street fighter. Flat on his back, John flung Sam off so that he stumbled over the keg of powder. The other workman ducked.

"For God's sake, Rory!" exclaimed O'Brien.

"All right," said Rory and smiled. "He fights like a Manion, anyway."

Caleb rode into the yard as O'Brien ran to separate the combatants, and he paused to watch.

"Sam," said O'Brien, "you know better than to fight in the powder yard. You're fired."

"You can't fire a man for fighting," said John.

O'Brien looked him up and down. "You haven't worked around gunpowder," he said.

He looked back at Sam O'Shea. "Get your money and go," he said. "Right, lads. Back to work."

"If he goes, I go," said John.

O'Brien, turning away, paused and glanced up at Rory, and turned back.

"All right," he said. "But that's the last chance for either of you. Get cleaned up and back to work."

The workmen began to disperse. John, breathless and bleeding, eyed his opponent suspiciously. Sam Kennedy grinned painfully and stuck out his hand.

"Now I know why the Rebs nearly won the war!" he said, and they both laughed, and groaned, and laughed again.

Caleb, dismounting beside Rory outside the yard office, found him still watching John as John parted from Sam O'Shea and began to climb up to the O'Brien house.

"Rory," Caleb said, "I want a word with you about John Carpenter."

Rory looked at him quickly. "Sean."

"That's what I want to talk to you about," said Caleb.

Rory turned and led the way toward the Kent House. "Well?" he said over his shoulder, a defensive note in his voice.

"I think we should have him investigated," said Caleb.

Rory turned on him angrily. *"Investigated? My brother?"*

"Is he?" asked Caleb.

Rory didn't answer but walked on into his office in the Kent House and then turned and confronted Caleb with a touch of defiance.

"I know," said Caleb, "that he looks like your brother Padraic. And he's about the right age?"

Rory laughed. "He says he's lied about his age so often that now he doesn't know how old he is. Yes, I suppose he's about twenty. Ah, why do we bother with all this? Didn't you see him fight just now? I tell you, he's a real Manion!"

Caleb shook his head. "There's no evidence that would stand up in a court of law. He's called Carpenter. The people who took your brother were called Murphy."

"They were drowned!" said Rory quickly.

"But there's nothing to link this boy with them, or with you. If you want my opinion"—his voice hardened —"Clement showed a great lack of judgment in bringing him here before he'd checked him out properly."

"Caleb—" Rory protested.

"It's not like you to deceive yourself, Rory," said Caleb, and Rory was silenced.

Caleb spoke more gently. "And I don't want Deirdre to be deceived."

"He isn't trying to—he's never pretended to be anyone but—"

"I'm not blaming him. I'm just saying what if Deirdre gives him the affection she's been saving all these years, and he isn't Sean? Wouldn't it be better for all of you to know the truth now?"

"I know the truth," answered Rory obstinately. "He's Sean."

But he turned away toward the window. "I asked him if he had the holy medal I put around Sean's neck before I left Ireland," he said.

"And?"

Rory turned to look at him. "He'd never heard of it," he said, and Caleb knew the battle was won.

"I'll make inquiries, then," he said.

Rory nodded his reluctant agreement and looked, frowning, toward the O'Brien house.

Meanwhile, inside, Maureen eyed John severely as she bathed the cut on his cheek.

"Ouch!" he said.

"Hold still now," she said. "If you're going to start fighting almost the moment you arrive—"

"It was worth it," said John, and put his hand around her waist.

"Just keep your hand to yourself," she said and slapped it hard.

"It was the pain," he said apologetically. "I had to grab something."

"Well, you're not grabbing me, John Carpenter!" she said.

She stood back and surveyed her handiwork. "I'd better put some witch hazel on that eye of yours."

She went to fetch the bottle, and John looked about him with pleasure, enjoying the neatness and homeliness of the small, oblong room with the fire burning in the hearth and the black pot hung over it.

"Is this like a house in Ireland?" he asked.

She shrugged. "I've no idea," she replied. "I was only a child when my parents brought me here. I dare say it might be, though. My mother was so homesick for Ireland, I sometimes thought that's what killed her."

She returned with the witch hazel, looking at him curiously. "You don't remember it, either?"

"I don't even know if I was ever there," said John.

"You told Father you were adopted by some people called Carpenter."

"That's right. They kept telling me I was an orphan, and what a favor they was doing me. Then one day I caught onto the fact that to them I was just cheap labor, so I lit out."

"Where did you go?"

She sprinkled witch hazel on a piece of rag and put the pad on his eye. As she stood behind him, he leaned his head against her bosom.

"I saw an advertisement for the Pony Express," he said. "They said they wanted skinny young fellows who were orphans. The Carpenters didn't feed me so good, and I was an orphan, so I reckoned I fitted the bill."

"You were a Pony Express rider?" said Maureen, impressed in spite of herself.

He looked up at her and grinned. "That's right. Then I had a few close calls, and I reckoned the Injuns would get my scalp next time, so I moved on. Worked when I could get a job, and starved when I couldn't. The war came, and a lot of darned fools were joining up, so I had to be a darned fool and do the same. Ended up in a prison camp, and that's where Mr. Clement found me."

Maureen was silent for a moment.

"You've had a hard life, Mr. Carpenter," she said, "for a young man."

"Just at the moment, Miss O'Brien," he said, "I'm not complaining."

She took the pad of witch hazel away from his eye and moved quickly away, finding herself blushing.

"Well, that's the best I can do," she said, resuming her severity. "You'd better get back to work."

He was still smiling at her mischievously as he stood up, but when he reached the door and turned, he wasn't.

"Thanks," he said. "No one ever took care of me before. I guess I kind of like it."

It was something of a shock to Rory to discover that David had not only returned to Philadelphia in order to bring John Carpenter. He had every intention of staying.

"I'm tired of being a wanderer," he said. "My foreman can run the cattle ranch better than I can, and besides—half the mill is mine now. I mean to claim my inheritance and settle down."

He glanced between Rachel and Rory and smiled.

"Don't worry," he said, "I won't impose myself on your household. I've taken a suite at the United States Hotel until I can find a house that suits me."

A few days later Rory rode into the yard and was met by Maureen.

"I'm glad you're here, Mr. Manion," she said. "Mr. Clement is going through the books."

"He's *what*?"

She nodded toward the Kent House. "He's in your office now."

"Murder-in-Irish!" said Rory and set off, followed by Maureen.

Rory found David sitting at his desk, studying ledgers.

"Well, well," he said with a cheerfulness he was far

from feeling, "and to what do I owe this honor? Are you inspecting the premises or raiding the petty cash?"

"I thought it was about time I put in an appearance," said David. "I am your partner, after all—or Rachel's."

This observation did not particularly gratify Rory, since he had only inherited his share of the powder mill through his marriage to Rachel, but he did his best to conceal his annoyance.

"Ah, now," he said, "why so serious? Everything is fine."

"I'm glad to hear it," said David. "But when every other mill is searching for customers, why are we manufacturing powder?"

"Because that's our business," answered Rory easily. "Or hadn't you noticed?"

"But who exactly is buying?" inquired David.

Rory, hanging his hat on the hat stand, saw Maureen seating herself at the desk in the smaller office across the passage and met her eyes for a moment before he turned back.

"The Vulcan Coal Company," he said.

"Oh?" said David. "A coal-mining company, is it? Miss O'Brien didn't seem to know much about it. And I can't seem to find it in the books."

Rory's temper began to build up in him. "My dear David," he said, "I've been running this mill perfectly satisfactorily since before your uncle died, and I've never had any complaints, so don't start now. You're not a businessman. You're a soldier."

"And I've handled regimental accounts often enough. I know an invoice when I see one."

He stood up. "Rory, I am your partner, even if I've been a sleeping one."

Rory was suddenly unnaturally jovial. "And now you've woken up, eh?"

He came to put his arm around David's shoulder and began to move him toward the door.

"All right, partner. First thing tomorrow I'll have every letter, ledger and invoice all neatly laid out on the desk here for your inspection!"

David turned to look at him and spoke without a smile.

"Thank you, Rory," he said. "I'll depend on that." He went out.

Rory let his breath go. He returned to the desk and looked down at the books and files.

"Mr. Manion."

Rory looked up and saw Maureen in the doorway.

"I think maybe we'd better provide the files with a few letters and invoices from the Vulcan Coal Company."

Rory threw back his head and laughed. "Maureen O'Brien," he said, "you're a queen—a queen of Ireland! We'll do it, and we'll do it this night!"

Maureen, sitting in the golden lamplight, writing a letter in her beautiful copperplate hand, heard a footstep and looked up and saw John, dressed in his best black suit, with a white shirt and a black string tie.

"And what might you be doing here," he inquired, "instead of prettying yourself up for the dance?"

Her face showed her dismay. "Oh—John!"

"Don't tell me you'd forgotten!"

"No, of course not—yes. I had."

She got up and came to him, full of contrition. "Oh, John, I'm truly sorry. But I have this work to do, and it has to be done tonight. It's important."

"More important than going to a dance with me?" he said lightly. "And me dressed to kill in my best bib and tucker!"

"And very handsome you look, too," she said, straightening his tie. "I'm sure you'll have no trouble finding another girl to go to the dance with you."

"That's true," he agreed, and saw her indignant glance and smiled. "But I'll never find one who can kiss like you."

Maureen gasped. "How do you know how I kiss?"

"That's right, I don't!" he said, and took her unexpectedly in his arms and kissed her.

"John!" she exclaimed, half-laughing and half-stirred. "John—you cheat!"

He laughed, but he was still holding her in his arms, and she wasn't making any effort to free herself. John looked down at her, and his face was suddenly quite serious.

"Maybe I *will* take another girl to the dance," he said, "but it won't be the girl I mean to marry, and *you* are."

Rory, coming to the doorway from his office across the passage, was in time to hear this, and paused, disconcerted. But John, holding Maureen lightly in his arms, looked back at him unconcerned.

"Since you're here, Sean," said Rory, "would you do me a favor? Go to Rachel and tell her I won't be home for dinner. Tell her I have some business to finish first."

John relinquished Maureen with reluctance. "I don't know why I should do *you* a favor," he said. "Your *business* is ruining my love life!"

Before Maureen knew what he was doing, he kissed

her again and went out. Maureen laughed, but then she saw Rory's grave look.

"Is he serious? He said—"

"Of course he isn't!" said Maureen. "You know what a joker he is! I'm sure he's said the same sweet things to half the girls in the West."

She turned to look out the window, and saw John running across the yard in pursuit of Sam O'Shea.

"Sam! Wait for me!"

Sam O'Shea turned at the gate. "I thought you were taking Maureen to the dance."

"I'll take her next time," said John. "I have a message to deliver first—and then let's go and get drunk!"

It gratified Rory's mischievous sense of humor to make the Vulcan Coal Company's transactions immensely convincing, and Maureen entered into the conspiracy with zest. When the job was nearly done he glanced through the books and files with satisfaction.

"That should be good enough for David's regimental accounts," he thought.

And then suddenly he tore the pages out and crushed them between his hands.

"Maureen!" he shouted.

She came, alarmed, to the doorway.

"It was a fine notion," he said, "but I can't do it. David Clement saved my life once, and he's a friend of mine. And Caleb trusted me and gave me a chance when no one else would. I can't lie to them, not even—"

"Not even for Ireland?" said Maureen.

He looked at her quickly. "You guessed!"

She nodded. "Would it help if I did the rest of it, and you knew nothing about it?"

He shook his head. "Thanks for the good heart of you," he said, "but, no. Get your things and I'll walk you home."

When she had gone out, he put his head in his hands. Ireland was like a lover whom he could not forget. He knew that if he went to her now, she would break his heart and the hearts of those he loved. Dearly as he loved her, he was older now, no longer so single-mindedly committed. Had the time come to abandon the dream?

From far away he heard Maureen's voice.

"Mr. Manion!"

He raised his head and looked, puzzled, at the dark hall. Standing up, he took the lamp out with him and stopped, catching his breath. Maureen stood outside the bedroom in her petticoat, with her mass of red hair about her shoulders.

"Maureen!" he said. "You look—you look like all the laughing, barefoot young girls of Ireland whom the famine turned into ghosts."

She came and took the lamp from him and put it down on the table and put her arms round his neck.

"I'm no ghost!" she said.

CHAPTER 24

When Rory got back to the Old Mill, unsaddled his horse in the stable and came through the kitchen to the living room, he was not surprised to see the lamp which was always left on turned low until his return. But as he moved to turn it out, he was startled to see

Rachel sitting in her nightdress and wrapper, a book in her lap.

"You're late up, my dear," said Rory.

She stood up and the book fell to the ground with a disregarded thud.

" *'My dear'?*" she said in a voice of suppressed fury. "You've never called me that before. It's a name you call your wife."

"I thought you were my wife," said Rory.

"So did I!" she replied fiercely.

Rory recognized the state of mind, familiar to any husband, in which whatever he said to his wife, he could not win.

"I'm glad we're agreed on one thing," he said peaceably.

"Are you?" said Rachel. She looked at him in silence.

Rory began to turn toward the staircase. "Well, I think I'll—"

Her voice stopped him. "What's going on, Rory? Home at all hours, making powder for an order you can't account for—"

He turned. "Who told you that?"

"David."

Thanks, David, thought Rory, and the sense of guilt with which he had entered the house began to be overtaken by anger.

Rachel spoke more calmly. "Where's the powder going, Rory? I think I have a right to know."

"Sure you have," said Rory. "It's going to Ireland, and I'm going with it."

It was the old spit-in-your-eye Rory, and Rachel gasped and then was furious.

"Why didn't you tell me?"

"I'm telling you now."

She sat down again, stunned. Rory walked slowly back to lean against the fireplace. His eyes rested for a moment on the painting which hung there. It was a water color of the O'Manion cabin, which Rachel had given him as a wedding present. It was not a good painting; she had no real talent. But it was wonderfully accurate, even though she had done it from memory, and because of that, and because she had taken so much trouble to give him pleasure, it was very dear to him.

He looked down at her. Sitting there in her night-clothes with her hair in braids and those troubled eyes, she looked like a child, and he felt a great tenderness for her—even if it was partly the tenderness a husband feels for the wife he has betrayed.

"You knew it must come, sooner or later," he said. "I never lied to you. I always told you I'd go back."

"And you're going to start a rising?"

"Yes, of course."

She was silent. He felt an urgent need to justify the venture, if only to himself.

"The time is right," he said. "We've proved—the Irish Brigade has proved—that we can fight in a disciplined way outside the British army. We can be a match for them. We have the Fenian organization in Ireland and in America, so we're not going into it blind. And I won't be going alone. I have Sean now to go with me."

Rachel started up. "Oh, no, Rory, don't! Don't involve him!"

"He's involved already," said Rory. "He's a Manion. He has the right to go and see his own land and fight for it."

She seized his arm and spoke with a new urgency. "You don't know he's a Manion. All that anger and hatred and bitterness which came from the famine—don't force it on him!"

"That anger and hatred and bitterness is his birthright."

"If he's Irish," said Rachel, "he has another birthright, too, a birthright of love and tolerance and gaiety, and a great gift of laughter. But he may not even *be* Irish! Caleb hasn't found any connection yet between the Carpenters and the people who took Sean away. He hasn't found any proof that he is Sean."

It was as though she had struck a spark in a powder keg as Rory threw her off and exploded. "I don't *need* proof that he's Sean! I *know* he's Sean! I know it in my heart, just as I would know my own son!"

The words were out. There was no way to recall them, any more than he could have recalled a bullet fired into her heart.

Rachel went quietly up the stairs and into her bedroom and quietly closed the door. Rory stayed where he was, quite motionless. He knew now why it was so important to him that John Carpenter should be Sean. Sean was not just his missing brother; he was the son Rory would never have. But even as he stood there and suffered with Rachel, he became more determined to go, as though the more Ireland's freedom cost, the dearer it became to him.

David was prompt next morning, and so was Rory. He was prompt, too, with what he had to say.

"I lied to you. The powder is going to Ireland."

"I knew it!" cried David. "Rory, you damned fool!"

"And I'm going with it," said Rory.

David made an indignant noise and limped about the

room. "I can't let you do it, Rory. You belong here now. To go off now on some crazy venture which hasn't a chance of success—I can't let you throw your life away!"

"If you stop me, that's what you'll be doing," said Rory.

He stood looking out of the window, but he did not see the busy mill yard below, the wagons or the charcoal-burning chimneys. "Ever since I was a young boy," he said, "and heard my father tell the stories of the old fights and the old chieftains . . . Ever since I sailed away from Galway Bay and left behind me everything I cared for in this world . . . In everything I have done since, somewhere there has been the thought that one day I would go back."

He turned. "You were in Ireland, David. You saw how things were."

"I saw a lot of violence, and all it produced was hatred. Won't you ever learn that?"

Rory didn't answer. Padraic used to say that, but Padraic was dead, and his violent death had to be justified.

"What about Rachel?" said David.

Rory looked at him and smiled. "If it was Rachel who stopped me going, then we would lose each other forever."

There was a long silence, and Rory knew that he had won. He spoke with a sudden change of tone and slapped David cheerfully on the shoulder.

"Come on, me lad!" he said. "Wasn't it yourself was so keen to be a working partner? Now's your chance! The government can't go on dumping cheap powder forever, and if you'll just go to Washington and give them hell until they pay us what they owe us, we'll weather the storm."

"*I* go to Washington? I fought on the other side!"

"I'm not suggesting you go in your Confederate uniform! But you've been a regular officer. You know how these muttonheads think."

"Much obliged," said David, but he began to be convinced in spite of himself.

Army bureaucracy worked the same way all the world over, and it would be good to be useful to the business by doing something he really understood.

"As for that other little matter," said Rory, "all you need to know is that it's a load of blasting powder which I've promised to export to Dublin, and that I'm going on a short business trip afterward."

David found himself nodding, and then stopped short.

"*Blasting* powder? It's rifle powder!"

"That's not what it says on the manifest," said Rory, laughing, and headed for the door. "Excuse me, I must just have a word with that young brother of mine!"

Rory was glad that he had to run to catch John. As he went leaping down the path from the Kent House, it was like the old days when he raced across the Galway Hills after a meeting of the Young Irelanders, with that thought that filled not only his head but his whole body until he had a giant's strength and the courage of Brian Boru and the crazy gaiety of a leprechaun. One day soon Ireland would be free, and he would have a hand in it.

"Sean!" he called. "Sean! I want a word with you!"

John turned and seemed about to say something, but

said something else instead. "Jim O'Brien wants me in the rolling mill."

"Fine," said Rory. "I'm not suggesting you take the day off."

His enthusiasm was slightly damped, but he wasn't going to admit it. "I'll meet you by the bridge at the end of the day's work."

"Right," said John.

Rory watched him walk away and felt that unreasonable exasperation Padraic used to arouse in him.

"The sooner I get him to Ireland," he thought, "the better!"

Rory spent a busy day in the city and returned late to the mill. He was glad to see that tall, lazy figure waiting for him on the bridge and went to put his arm around his shoulder.

"Come on," he said, "I've a few things to say to you. I've kept you all busy making powder when there's no great demand for it. I dare say you'd like to know where it's going."

"Ireland, I should guess," said John matter-of-factly, "from all Sam O'Shea says."

"Sam O'Shea told you that?" asked Rory sharply.

"No, but what with him and Jim O'Brien talking about the great Rory O'Manion and how he's going to set Ireland free, it wasn't hard to figure out."

"Hmm," said Rory. "Well, it's one thing to make the powder, and quite another to get it out of the country without having half a dozen British agents on our heels."

"So you have to keep the whole thing quiet?" inquired John.

"No," Rory replied, with a grin, "we move out the day after tomorrow, and we make sure that everyone knows it."

John paused and looked at him. "I reckon you lost me somewhere along the trail," he drawled.

"We'll drive the powder kegs to the docks here," said Rory, "and we'll load them aboard a ship bound for Ireland, and we'll make sure everyone knows it. Most likely the British will intercept the ship at sea or else wait and search it in Dublin."

"Then why send it?"

"We won't," answered Rory. "Those kegs have sawdust in them. The real ones are in a false bottom in the wagons—or will be by tomorrow. We'll circle around from the docks and drive them cross-country to New York, and ship it from there. What do you think?"

"Sounds all right to me," answered John, amused. "What do you want me to do?"

"Drive one of the wagons."

"I've never driven powder before, but I've driven mules. I don't mind having a shot at it."

"Good," said Rory.

He put his arm around John's shoulders again. "And then, my lad, it's you and me for Ireland!"

Those blue-gray eyes had an amused look in them. "And what do we do there? Start a revolution?"

"Of course," said Rory.

"You're asking me to go and get mixed up in a war in someone else's country?"

"It's not someone else's country, it's yours!"

John moved away so that Rory's arm was no longer around his shoulders. "I'm an American," he said.

"Don't you believe it, boy!" cried Rory. "Wait until

you see that green land. Wait till you see your brother, Brian. He's a wild little redheaded fellow with the courage of a mountain lion. Wait till you set foot on that Galway shore, and then you'll know you're Irish!"

A little edge of annoyance came into John's voice. "Now see here," he said, "being your brother doesn't make me Irish. I may have been born there, but I've lived here all my life, and this is my country."

"Sean—"

It was a shock when John suddenly turned on him with an unexpected blaze of anger which must have been building up in him for weeks. Don't call me that!"

Rory looked at him, startled.

"Sure I'd like to know who my family is," said John, "but I'm not that desperate I'll tag after anybody. Maybe I *am* your brother. I don't know. But I've been looking out for myself for the best part of the past twenty years, and I never gave you the right to tell me what to do. And when it comes to fighting wars, I'd just as soon pick 'em myself!"

There was something in John that had the power to provoke Rory's temper, just as Padraic used to.

"Fine!" he said. "Why not? But I'll tell you this— if you don't want to fight to set Ireland free, then you're no brother of mine!"

They stood and stared at each other in silence, and then John turned and strode away toward the city.

Walking with a quick, impatient step, John did not know that as he turned onto the paved road, the carriage that passed him contained Caleb and Deirdre. Caleb was standing for senator at the next election, and they had spent a long day campaigning—all the longer because behind their smiles was a miserably uneasy relationship.

Deirdre, holding little Benjamin asleep on her lap, glanced toward the dirt road that led to the Kent Powder Manufactory.

"You haven't been to the mill lately," she said.

Caleb glanced at her and away. "I understand Mr. Clement has decided to take a hand in the management."

"He has the right," said Deirdre. "The business is partly his."

"So no doubt you persuaded him to stay," said Caleb.

"Oh, Caleb!" cried Deirdre, aghast. "How can you say such a thing? I haven't even seen him since he brought Sean home to us!"

"If he is Sean."

Caleb turned the horse up Callow Hill and they jogged on in silence. It was a silence, Deirdre knew all too well, which could last for days while Caleb withdrew into himself, perfectly courteous if she spoke to him, but never voluntarily speaking to her.

But the sight of Caleb carrying Benjamin, still sleeping, up the stairs gave Deirdre courage to try to break through this cold barrier so alien to her warm Irish temper.

"Caleb, listen!" she cried. "Only listen to me. All those months when I thought that David was dead, your kindness and understanding meant everything to me—"

"That was soon forgotten, wasn't it?" said Caleb.

The words chilled her, but she struggled on. "I've been a faithful wife to you for fifteen years—"

Caleb paused outside the bedroom and looked at her above the sleeping child.

"Faithful? In your heart?"

. Deirdre could not quite answer that. Caleb pushed the bedroom door open and put his son down on the bed. Deirdre followed him, trying desperately to find the words which might break through that grim self-imprisonment.

"We've had such happy times together," she said, "and Ben is so dear to both of us."

"Is that all that keeps us together?" asked Caleb, but it was not really a question but a statement.

Deirdre looked at him despairingly as he began to unbutton Ben's jacket—so carefully and gently, too.

"Oh, Caleb, don't!" she begged. "You know how dearly I have loved you. You know I still do."

"Have you?" he asked, without looking at her. "Do you?"

He gently lifted Ben up to pull his arms out of his sleeves.

"I beg you, Caleb!" cried Deirdre. "Don't destroy our love. Don't destroy our marriage!"

He laid the child down again and straightened up and looked at Deirdre for the first time.

"Just what does our marriage mean to you?" he said.

Deirdre's Irish spirit rose up in her and she looked him fiercely in the eye. "It means more to me than it does to you," she cried, "since you are ready to tear it to pieces through your stupid jealousy!"

Caleb gave a quick frown.

"I thought I married a man who loved me," said Deirdre, "but I see you just think of me as one of your possessions, and *that* I will never be!"

She forgot to keep her voice down, and Benjamin woke up, looking confused between them. As they stared at each other in that emotional impasse, there was a knock at the door.

"It's probably for you," said Deirdre. "You go. I'll put Ben to bed."

As soon as she came out of Ben's bedroom, Deirdre knew that it was not a client or a constituent who had come to call on Caleb. She heard voices from the living room and recognized one as Sean's.

It seemed almost inconceivable that he had never before been to their house. Deirdre knew beyond all shadow of doubt that he was Sean. She alone had been with him every day from the first moment he was born until he was three years old. Rory knew him because of his likeness to Padraic, but she knew him because he was Sean. She recognized the *Sean-ness* of that child she remembered so well, the battling quality and the quiet instinct for survival which Padraic had never had. But what could she do? It was like being with a man who had lost his memory. She could not go to him and beat his chest with her fists and say, "I'm Deirdre! Remember me! I'm Deirdre!" She thought of that moment at the Old Mill when she had clung to him and he was stiff and embarrassed in her arms, and how, during the dreadful dinner which followed, he had avoided her eyes as though he was afraid that she might do it again. She was certain that she must not pursue him but let him come to her. And now at last he had come.

When Deirdre went into the room, Caleb and John were sitting quietly enjoying a glass of whiskey. It was so delightful to see him there that Deirdre smiled and instinctively cried, "Sean!"

He stood up, and she saw again in his face that look

which said, Don't rush me. Don't smother me. Don't offer me love because I don't want it.

"My dear," said Caleb, "this young man wants to ask you a few questions."

"Yes," said Deirdre. "Yes, of course."

She took care to sit down at a little distance. He sat down, too, and was silent for a moment. When he spoke he seemed to be choosing his words carefully.

"I was just telling—Mr. Staunton—that I can't go on staying here not knowing who I am. Mr. Staunton's detective hasn't found out anything—"

"He hasn't had time yet!" Deirdre broke in, and saw that wary look in his eyes again.

"Maybe," he said.

She clasped her hands tightly in her lap. She must control her feelings.

"I know," he said, speaking carefully again, "that your brother was real small when—when you lost him, but—is there anything he might remember? Anything you can think of—in Ireland, maybe?"

Deirdre had a desperate feeling that she must say the right thing, and that if she didn't she might lose him forever.

"Lying in the hearth by a turf fire, with a black pot swung over it—"

She saw a change in his face, and hers lit up. "You remember that!"

He smiled and shook his head. "It's like the O'Brien's house, that's all. Maureen—" (Even at that moment Deirdre noticed the warmth in his voice when he spoke the name.) "Maureen says her mother brought it from Ireland."

"You might remember Father—a tall, thin-faced

man, with gray hair—or little Maeve. She had golden, curly hair. She loved to play with you."

She saw his blank face and rushed on. "Or the ship. That was later. You might remember the ship. It was dark, and crowded, and people dying and crying out. 'Twould be like a nightmare to a child."

His blank face was like an enemy she had to conquer. She had one weapon left and knew she must use it.

"There's one thing I'm sure you'd remember," she said, "though I always hoped you wouldn't. It was on the ship. Maeve was sick, and I tried to get her to eat a little piece of bread, but she couldn't take it, and it fell from her hand. You were hungry—we were all so hungry!—and you picked it up and put it in your mouth. And I said, 'Would you take the bread from your dying sister?' and I hit you. God forgive me, I hit you! Then Maeve died and you were taken from me. It's haunted my mind ever since to think that might be the last thing you remembered—that moment when I hit you!"

Her voice broke, but she looked at him with desperate eagerness.

He shook his head. "I don't remember," he said. "Maybe I got hit too many times after that—or maybe I'm not Sean at all."

"You are!" cried Deirdre. "I know you're Sean! I know it!"

He finished his drink and put the glass down and stood up. She saw that he was going to leave, and she jumped up and caught his arm as he moved toward the door.

He looked down at her. "I'm sorry," he said. "Thanks for trying, anyway."

He was moving again, and she had to let him go.

"Sean!" she cried. "Sean! No!"

It was like that terrible day on the ship when he was inexorably taken from her, and though she screamed and screamed she could not stop it. She heard the front door slam and turned away with a cry of anguish and found Caleb's arms around her.

"My dear, my dear, don't cry. He doesn't mean to go immediately—and if he *does* leave, we won't lose touch with him."

"I know he's Sean, Caleb," she said. "I remember him. I *know* him."

"I believe you, my dear," he said with all his old tenderness. "We won't give up. Trust me."

"Oh, I do!" cried Deirdre. "And, please, Caleb, trust me, too!"

He didn't answer, but he held her close. Perhaps his jealousy would always lie between them, and perhaps it should. She had given her first, best love to David. What she had given to Caleb was second best, and they both knew it. But in the acceptance of second best could exist great honor and generosity, and that, at least, they had.

O'Brien, working on a wagon behind the mill, heard an innocent voice immediately behind him.

"Excuse me, Mr. O'Brien, but what are you doing with that wagon?"

He grabbed an iron bar and shone the lantern, and saw the grinning face of Rory and swore.

"One day I'll kill you, Rory," he said, "so help me God, I will!"

Rory laughed. "How's it going?"

"It'd go faster," said Jim O'Brien, "if there was someone else I could trust to help me with it."

"How about Sam O'Shea?"

O'Brien didn't reply at once. Their eyes met.

"How long have you known him?" asked Rory.

O'Brien shrugged. "He came to us during the war, when men were hard to get. I think he's all right, but—"

"I agree," said Rory. "Let's keep it in the family."

"So the drivers," said O'Brien, "are you, me, Sean—?"

"Of course, Sean!" said Rory.

"And Seamus—"

"I know he can drive a donkey cart," said Rory. "I just hope to God he knows how to drive a Conestoga wagon!"

O'Brien looked at him in silence for a moment. "Rory," he said, "since when was it a crime to be an Irishman and drive a donkey?"

"Oh, God, Jim!" said Rory. "I think when we go back to Ireland we'll have a lot to learn, and a lot to forget!"

"Please, Rory, let me come with you!"

"No," said Rory. "I doubt if I could get the load to New York without you, but after that I need you to bring the wagons back here and cover up for us."

O'Brien slammed the false bottom down on the wagon. "Right," he said. "That's done. I'll get on to the next one."

"And I'll get the paperwork in order," said Rory. "If Sean gets back, I'll send him along to give you a hand."

Maureen, hearing drunken voices and a loud thump, went to the door of the O'Brien house and found John, supported by Sam O'Shea. He beamed when he saw her.

"Up the Irish!" he said.

"Erin gebrah!" echoed Sam, and, waving his arm in the air, lost his grip on John, who nearly collapsed on the doorstep.

Maureen caught hold of him, and he smiled at her affectionately. "I'm drunk," he said.

"I can see that," replied Maureen. "If you bottled your breath, you could start a distillery!"

"He's just a drop or two over the edge," said Sam in a conciliatory manner.

Maureen was not conciliated. Since her mother died, her father had been drunk more often than before. She had never liked Sam, and she hated drunks.

"As for you, Sam O'Shea," she said, "you had better get yourself home while you can still stand on your two feet!" She hauled John inside and slammed the door.

"You're beautiful," he said.

"I know I am," she said.

Viewing him with the eye of experience, she kept him moving and propelled him into his bedroom, where he sank onto his bed.

"That's right," she said dryly. "You lie down. I'll get your boots off, and that'll have to do you for tonight."

He gazed at her fondly as she untied his bootlaces. "I love you," he said.

"Much obliged," she said. "Say it again when you're sober."

She got his boots off and pulled the cover over him.

"Don't go," he said.

"Go to sleep. You'll have a thick head in the morning, and no one can say you don't deserve it."

As she went to the door, he got up on his elbow.

"Where's your father?" he said with owlish solemnity. "I want to ask him if I can marry you."

Maureen laughed. "You'd better ask *me* first!" she said. "Anyway, he said he wouldn't be home until late." And she closed the door behind her.

Meanwhile, after a long hard day O'Brien, finally satisfied with his handiwork, padlocked the wagon yard, put out the lantern and set out, yawning, for his house. He noticed with mild surprise that the light was still on in the office in the Kent House and wondered if Rory could have gone home and forgotten to put the lamp out. As he paused he thought he saw a white figure flitting through the trees behind the house, but at that moment the wind stirred, and the moon traveled behind fitful clouds. It was a trick of the moonlight, he thought. And he saw a movement across the lamp in the office, so Rory was still there.

"Damned fool!" he thought. "A man who's starting a war tomorrow should take himself off home early tonight and get some sleep."

He was half-minded to go and tell him so, but Rory never would be told—and besides, he was tired himself.

The O'Brien house was in darkness except for the quiet glow of the fire banked down in the hearth. Maureen had left the kettle on the hob in case he wanted a cup of tea, and he smiled and at the same time sighed because he missed his wife, as he always did when he came home, even after all these years. He went to open the door to Maureen's bedroom for a last, silent good night, as he always had ever since she was a child. He stood in the doorway for a moment, looking at the sleeping figure in the bed. When she was a little girl, he used to go in and kiss her and tuck the bedclothes about her, but now that she was grown up, he felt a certain delicacy about entering her bedroom. He said a little silent prayer for her safety while he was away and crossed himself and was about to withdraw, when the moon came out from behind the clouds and shone through the window directly onto the pillow. It should have shown him that mass of red, curly hair, but it did not. O'Brien strode to the bed and pulled the covers back. The sleeping figure was nothing but a bolster. O'Brien stood dumbfounded for a moment, and then a suspicion sprang into his mind and he turned and banged open the door of the little lean-to bedroom.

John lay flat on his back, snoring. O'Brien shook him furiously.

"Maureen! Where is she? Maureen!" John looked at him dazedly. "Maureen? She—she—"

It was obvious that he had been raised from drunken sleep. In that instant O'Brien knew the truth, turned and rushed straight out of the house while John sat up, trying to get his wits about him.

O'Brien ran as he had not run for years up the path which led to the Kent House. As he reached the front door, he could see inside the lighted window of the office Maureen and Rory clasped in each other's arms, kissing, she in her nightdress with the shawl just slipped to the floor. He went through the door and into the room like a mad bull and charged straight at Rory.

"You lousy, stinking, treacherous—"

As Rory and Maureen, shocked, turned and fell apart, he was upon Rory, battering him with his fists.

Maureen screamed. "No, Father! No!"

She tried to pull him off, but O'Brien turned upon her.

"You whore!" he said and hit her with the back of his hand and sent her flying across the room.

Rory made a quick movement toward Maureen, but O'Brien caught his arm and swung him around. Rory crashed across the desk and saw O'Brien coming after him. He picked up the chair to protect himself, but O'Brien wrenched it from his hand and flung it through the window.

John, from outside the O'Brien house, heard the sharp noise of breaking glass and heard Maureen scream again. He set off running for the Kent House, where Rory, knowing O'Brien's strength, had now realized that he was fighting for his life, and turned from defense to attack. A fight between friends has a special deadliness about it, since they know each other's strengths and weaknesses. As John reached the doorway, he was in time to see Rory land a punch which sent O'Brien thudding back sickeningly against the wall. He sank down to the floor, almost finished. But behind the door propped against the wall was the shotgun Rory had put ready to take with him on tomorrow's journey. O'Brien seized it and staggered to his feet.

John was staring at Maureen as she stood there in her nightdress, and she met his eyes for a moment, before she saw her father on his feet pointing the shotgun at Rory.

"No!" she screamed. "Father! John, stop him!"

John hesitated for a second, and Rory saw anger and revenge in his eyes, but as O'Brien took aim, John moved quickly to take hold of the gun and force it upward. He wrestled with O'Brien for its possession, but O'Brien held fast, and Rory came to help.

"Let go, Jim!" he said. "It isn't loaded."

"You're lying," said O'Brien, and he was.

O'Brien, his face like a madman's, was still trying to bring the gun to bear on Rory, and his grip was like iron, defying the combined efforts of John and Rory to break it. Rory edged his hand down to the trigger, meaning to discharge the gun harmlessly into the ceiling. But just as he succeeded, his weakened grasp on the barrel enabled O'Brien to force it down until it was pointing at his head.

"Rory! Look out!" said John.

He wrenched the barrel aside, and Rory's finger was with O'Brien's on the trigger as the weapon exploded into John's body.

It was with superstition added to horror that Rory saw John stagger back and fall, his shirt covered with blood.

"Sean!" cried Rory. Then there flashed before his eyes a green where life was ebbing from another body. "Padraic," Rory sobbed.

CHAPTER 25

It was not until the early hours of the morning that Rory was able to go home, but he knew that Rachel would be waiting up for him. He had told her—God forgive him!—that he would be working late, but she had said that they would have a little supper together and a glass of champagne to wish him good luck for his journey.

"Are you still going?" Eamon had asked.

"Of course," said Rory.

It was as though John's injury, like Padraic's death, had made him all the more determined—perhaps to prove that violence need not always be wasteful and meaningless.

He had waited until he knew that John was out of danger, for the moment at least, though he had lost a lot of blood. Eamon had promised to spend the night with him at the infirmary, and Rory, remembering that look in John's eyes, did not delude himself that he would be welcome at the bedside when John recovered consciousness. If this was, indeed, his brother Sean, then in the moment that he saw Maureen with Rory in the Kent House, Rory had truly lost him forever.

When at last Rory mounted his horse and rode through the dark, leafy lanes toward the Old Mill, he felt exhausted and heartsick, in no mood to embark upon a daring and desperate adventure. He wasn't even sure if he could manage to transport the powder to New York without O'Brien's help. He supposed he would have to confide in Sam O'Shea and he felt the same kind of indefinite uneasiness which long ago he had felt about Joe Kerrigan. In every venture in which a man's life depends upon the faithful courage of his comrades, he develops the kind of instinct for the unreliable ones which enables a doctor to diagnose disease.

"Well," thought Rory, dismounting behind the Old Mill, "if I must trust him, I must."

In the living room the special supper was uneaten;

the bottle of champagne stood in melted ice. Rory went softly upstairs and found Rachel on her bed in night-dress and wrapper. Evidently she had meant to read until he came, but had fallen asleep. She looked calm and beautiful, and for a moment he almost let her sleep, but he knew that he must not. He could not let her hear what had happened from anyone else. He must tell her himself—and he must tell her everything.

"Rory, how *could* you?" cried Rachel. "Jim O'Brien's daughter?"

Rory looked at her in silence.

It took courage for her to say what she did, but she said it. "If you had to have someone, why couldn't you go to—to a brothel?"

"That wasn't what I wanted," said Rory.

She turned on him furiously. "So you wanted *her*? *Her*, not me? How dare you say that?"

"Rachel—"

She flew at him. "Don't you think it's enough that I have to live without *you*—without your body? Do you think that I can live without your love as well?"

All the long frustration and anguish broke into anger as she struck him on the chest and face and arms. He tried to defend himself without hurting her, but in hold-ing her off, he found that their struggle began to turn to passion.

"No!" he said. "No, Rachel! I won't risk your life!"

"Why not?"

She challenged him, as she always had. "You're risk-ing *your* life! You're going to Ireland tomorrow, and you may never come back. But now you belong to me. It's my right." She held him, and her eyes, her heart, her body challenged him. "If you love me, it's my right."

"God knows I love you!" said Rory, and he picked her up and carried her to the bed.

Her arms were around his neck, and she drew him down to her.

It was wonderful to wake next morning in the same bed. Rory made no effort to depart without waking her. Instead, he leaned over and kissed her, and she lazily responded.

"It's time for me to go," he said.

"I know," she said. "I told Bridie to make some of Mrs. Docherty's potato cakes for your breakfast."

She sat and watched him eat his breakfast. "They're not as good as Mrs. Docherty's!" he said.

When Tom brought his horse around and he went out to mount, Rachel called, "Give my love to Ireland, and then come back to me!"

He stopped and came and took her in his arms and kissed her. But he did not say he would return.

In the infirmary Rory looked down at John. In repose he looked more like Padraic than ever, but it was the dead Padraic he resembled now.

"Oh, God!" said Rory suddenly.

Eamon smiled at him. "He'll live," he said, "if he takes care of himself, though there's not much chance of that if he's a Manion."

Rory could not answer his smile. He looked down on the white face which had haunted his dreams.

"My brother Padraic died with a curse on his lips," he said. "Maybe Sean will live to forgive me."

He turned and walked out, and Eamon followed him.

In the yard the mules were being put to the wagons.

"I'm a man short, Eamon," said Rory, "even if Jim O'Brien comes, which I doubt. It's a long time since you drove a mule wagon. How about it? Why don't you come all the way with me to Galway?" His heart rose at the thought. It would be the young Irelanders again!

"I can't," Eamon answered. "I have my patients to think of, and even if I hadn't—"

"Ah, come on, Eamon, they'd survive. You're not the only doctor in Philadelphia."

Eamon turned to look at him. "It's over, Rory, for me."

"What's over?" Rory demanded fiercely. "Ireland?"

"No. Not Ireland. Just the fighting and the killing. I took an oath to save lives, not destroy them."

Rory felt a sudden surge of envy for Eamon. Dr. Fleming, for all his snobberies and failures, had worked and died for the people of Ireland, keeling over from the fever in Father O'Dowd's arms among the starving poor he was attending. And Eamon had found a cause in the slums of Philadelphia that drew on all the compassion that had once driven him to war. No divided heart for him now. The sick were his nation, wherever they might be.

"Rory—" began Eamon anxiously, but Rory laughed and punched him.

"Ah, do you think I didn't know that we just borrowed you for a while?" he said. "I knew we'd have to give you back in the end."

He glanced back at the infirmary. "At least you can make yourself useful and look after Sean. It's time I was off!"

He went down to the yard office and put the papers together—one set for Philadelphia and the other set to be carefully concealed until he needed them in New York. The doorway was darkened. He instinctively covered the papers, but it was Jim O'Brien. He was dressed for the journey.

Rory scowled to conceal his relief. "You're coming, then," he said.

"I'll come," said O'Brien. "Not for you, but for Ireland. I'll drive the powder to New York—and I'll hate you every mile."

Rory nodded without comment. What was there to be said?

"We shall need a driver in Sean's place," he said. "Will you tell Sam O'Shea to come?"

"Right."

O'Brien turned to leave.

"Jim!"

O'Brien turned with a face of thunder. "Yes, *Mister* Manion?"

Rory ignored this. "Just tell Sam he's driving the powder to the Philadelphia docks. We'll let the New York trip come as a surprise to him later."

When O'Brien had gone, Rory, putting the papers in their pouches, found that his hands were trembling. He was angry with himself. Such a thing had never happened to him before. Facing O'Brien's shotgun had not been so bad as facing Jim himself in the cold light of day, knowing he had betrayed him.

Rory took a deep breath and finished his task, but just as he was stowing the papers away, he heard a commotion out in the yard. Men were running about and shouting, and a team of mules was shifting about and having to be quieted. He went out quickly.

"What's happening?"

"Sam O'Shea's hurt his hand. He was just fixing the shoe on the wheel, and the mules shifted."

Rory saw O'Shea clutching his hand and Eamon hurrying down from the infirmary.

"I'm all right, Rory," said Sam. "I can drive! Honest!"

"Let's see," said Rory.

Sam groaned as Rory jerked the hand out to examine it, and then glared at him. It was already swollen and turning blue.

"Drive?" said Rory. "You can't even hold the reins! Eamon, take this fool away and bandage him up."

"I'm sorry, Rory," said Sam earnestly.

Rory recollected that this was supposed to be an ordinary shipment.

"Never mind, Sam," he said. "You couldn't help it."

He turned away and found O'Brien beside him.

"Have to leave that load here," said O'Brien.

"With sawdust in the kegs and powder underneath?" Rory demanded. "There's not time to unload it before we go, and if we did we'd give the whole show away. And there's no one we can trust to do it after we've gone."

"Can't be helped," said O'Brien. "We'll have to leave it here. There's no one to drive it."

Rory's eyes went past him and a little light of devilment came into his eyes as he saw David ride into the yard.

"Oh, I don't know," he said. "There just might be!"

And as the wagons moved out, David was still incredulous to find himself driving one of them.

"Rachel told me what happened," he had said as he

dismounted beside the yard office. "I'm very sorry. Is there anything I can do to help?"

"Sure," Rory had replied cheerfully. "You can drive one of the wagons."

Rory had from the beginning given the explanation that he and O'Brien were driving the powder themselves because it was of a new and particularly volatile kind. Now he somehow contrived to involve David by making it half-joke, half-challenge, with all the men laughing and cheering at the notion of the boss proving that he could still drive a mule wagon. And although David managed to tell Rory severely that he was still totally opposed to the venture and was only coming to keep him out of trouble for all their sakes—still, here he was, for God's sake, driving an illicit load of powder destined to start a revolution in Ireland!

Rory, driving the leading wagon, glanced up and saw Eamon outside the infirmary, looking, after all, rather desolate at being left behind, and with him Sam O'Shea with his bandaged hand. Rory felt again that uneasy qualm. Had it really been an accident, and if not, why not? Then he saw Maureen and forgot everything else. She stood motionless outside the O'Brien house, and there was a touch of defiance in the fact that she was not lurking inside but did stand there, clearly visible to everyone, watching them go. Rory loved Rachel forever, but Maureen was Ireland. She was youth. Against his will he carried her with him on this desperate venture.

When the last of the wagons had rolled out of the yard, Eamon turned to Sam O'Shea. "You'd better take care of that hand," he said.

"Yeah, I guess so," said Sam. "Maybe I'll take the rest of the day off."

Eamon, climbing into the one-horse carriage which was so like the one his father used to drive in Galway, glanced up and saw Sam O'Shea climbing the hill behind the Kent House and was mildly puzzled. But he had patients to see and drove on.

Sam was greeted by the tall man who had been waiting outside the meeting house in Philadelphia.

"Well?" he said.

"Manion's game is to make us think he's loading a ship in Philadelphia," said Sam. "But then he'll be taking the turnpike and getting the real powder to New York. I got it out of the boy when he was drunk."

The man with the English voice glanced up at Sam, who had the expression of a dog who has brought a rather smelly bone and hopes to be rewarded for it.

"Where can we stop him?"

"I've driven that road," said Sam. "Brasher's Bluff would be the place."

"Right," said the man. "We'll be waiting for him."

He turned away toward the horse, which was tethered to a nearby tree. Sam took an eager step after him.

"When do I get paid?" he asked.

"Now," said the British agent. "We always like to pay our debts as soon as possible."

He felt in his inside pocket. Sam waited confidently, but what came out was not a wad of dollars but a gun. Sam O'Shea fell, shot at point-blank range. The British agent mounted his horse and rode out. Sam lay motionless, but after a moment his fingers began to scrabble in the dust.

* * *

John Carpenter, lying in the infirmary, slowly returning to thought and memory, saw again Maureen in her nightdress in Rory's office and felt again that surge of jealous hatred. In that state of deathly weariness that follows serious injury, he neither knew nor cared whether he was Sean Manion. He just wanted to be quit of the whole damned business.

He heard a commotion and saw Sam O'Shea being carried into the infirmary by two men. They put him on the bed next to John. He had been roughly bandaged, and John thought that he was dead until he groaned. The two men looked at him and at each other.

"Best fetch the doc," they said.

When they had gone, Sam groaned again and opened his eyes.

"What happened, Sam?" asked John.

"Looks like I trusted the wrong fellow," said Sam, "same as you." His white lips moved in a grimace which tried to be a grin. "You sure were drunk last night!"

That morning Rachel had sent a note around to Deirdre to tell her that John had had an accident at the mill, and Caleb was just preparing to drive her to the infirmary when they heard a horse outside the house.

"There's Sean!" Deirdre exclaimed.

"And he certainly doesn't look fit to ride—"

Caleb saw John slide off the horse and hurried to help him into the house. "Deirdre, send for the doctor," he said, half-leading, half-carrying him to the sofa.

"No, never mind me," gasped John. "It's Rory. He's

driving powder to New York, and there's going to be an ambush."

"*Ambush?* Who would want to—"

"The powder's for Ireland."

"The damned fool!" exclaimed Caleb, and since he seldom swore, and certainly never in front of his wife, it was a sign of the anger he felt.

"Mr. Clement's gone with him instead of me," said John. "The British will be waiting for them with guns."

"Guns!" cried Deirdre, horrified, "and them driving wagons of gunpowder!"

"Do you know where?" asked Caleb brusquely.

"A place called Brasher's Bluff."

"I know it."

Caleb was still frowning angrily. He went to his desk and got out one of the maps he had used during the war.

"Rory will keep to the turnpike with a load like that, and mules don't move that fast—" He traced the route with his forefinger. "It should be possible to intercept them by riding across country."

"If you show me the way, I'll go," said John, and tried to get up from the chair but couldn't.

"No, no, Sean, lie down!" said Deirdre.

She saw blood seeping through the front of John's shirt and looked, horrified, at Caleb.

"You're not fit, my boy," said Caleb. "Deirdre, get him to bed and send for Eamon. I'll go."

Deirdre, torn between fear for Rory and anxiety for John, saw with alarm that Caleb had returned to the desk and was taking out his army revolver.

"Oh, no, Caleb!" she cried, realizing at last what it all meant. "Don't go yourself. Can't you tell the police—have the men arrested?"

"There isn't time," said Caleb curtly, "and besides"—he looked at John—"the shipment is illegal, I take it?"

He saw the answer in John's face.

"If it's illegal," said Deirdre, "and you're involved—Caleb, your campaign! If it comes out that you've been mixed up in—in—"

"I know," said Caleb. "Trust Rory! A candidate for the United States Senate involved in smuggling, violating treaties, inciting revolution—"

He was buckling on his cartridge belt as he spoke, but he looked up and saw Deirdre's troubled face and smiled, but without much amusement.

"I'll just have to hope that I can get there in time to warn them and clear out before anyone knows."

He began to move toward the door. "The sooner I get off, the better."

Deirdre quickly got up from her knees beside John and came after him. "Caleb—"

He smiled at her, and this time it was a real smile. "Don't worry. I'll save that brother of yours—mad Irishman that he is!" He hesitated, and the smile became rueful. "And—David, too."

She ran to fling her arms around his neck. "But *you*, Caleb! Take care! Oh, please take care!"

She clung to him and kissed him. If he had doubted whether she truly cared for him, he could not doubt it now, with David in danger and her thoughts only for him. He kissed her back with unstinted passion, as though in that moment the ice which had been in his heart since childhood had melted at last.

The warmth stayed with Caleb as he set out, and a great exhilaration. But this was gradually replaced by anxiety. There had been rain overnight, and the small roads were very muddy. More than once the route he had planned was flooded and he had to go around, and once he lost his way and valuable time with it. He was not, in fact, all that accustomed to reading maps. During the war he had not seen a great deal of active service. Against his will he had mostly been involved in staff work. So now it was borne in on him that he had lightly undertaken a task for which he was not equipped. David Clement, damn him! No, not damn him! But—David Clement, no doubt, would have managed better. Caleb's horse was not powerful or swift but a good workhorse for getting around Philadelphia and its environs. It soon wearied on heavy ground, and Caleb, increasingly anxious, forced the pace.

The journey which had begun as an annoyance and then turned into an adventure now became a desperate slog against all odds to save the lives of Rory and David and the rest, with failure closing in upon him at every thudding stride. He had by now given up all hope of intercepting the wagon train before Brasher's Bluff. His only chance was to arrive there in time to warn them of danger.

Rory, driving the lead wagon, saw a fallen tree across the road just beyond the huge, overhanging crag. He began to rein back the mules, raising his hand in warning to those behind.

Caleb, riding up the hill, could see the Turnpike Road with the wagons on it, and could see, too, men crouching among the rocks. He was too far away to shout a warning, and the wagons were still moving forward. He dismounted and began to climb as fast as he could, revolver in hand. He thought there were two men, but he could not be sure. He saw a man stand up and take aim with a rifle at the driver of the leading wagon. There was no time for thought. Caleb fired and the man fell, his shot going wild.

Rory, on the road below, heard the two shots, and brought his mules to a halt.

"Jump, boys!" he yelled. "Jump! Get away from the wagons!"

He grabbed his shotgun and jumped down and took cover behind the rocks on the far side. He found O'Brien beside him and Seamus nearby. David was crouched under the bluff on the other side of the road. They were all armed. Rory had given David his own army revolver, "in case of trouble," as he had carelessly remarked.

"Can you see them?" asked O'Brien.

"No," said Rory. "Keep your head down, for God's sake."

"They don't need to be marksmen," said O'Brien. "One shot in the powder will do the trick."

David called in a low voice from across the road. "I'll try to get behind them. Give me some covering fire."

He began to climb the bluff, protected by its overhanging crags, and Rory, O'Brien and Seamus did their best to discourage the unseen enemy with random fire.

Caleb heard a voice call out, a British voice. "Never mind the men! Fire at the wagons!"

From his cover behind a rock, Caleb looked quickly toward the voice and saw a second man moving forward. As he knelt to fire at the wagons below Caleb stepped out of cover and shot him.

David, scrambling up the last rocky slope, was in time to see Caleb shoot and the man fall. He saw, too, another man who stepped out from behind a clump of trees, his rifle leveled at Caleb's back.

"Caleb! Look out!" yelled David, taking aim, but he was too late.

Caleb turned as the man fired. David's shot was almost instantaneous—almost, but not quite. The third man fell dead, but not before he had shot Caleb in the chest.

"I can't stand this!" said Rory, hearing the shots. "Cover me."

Reckless of safety, he ran across the open road and began to scramble up the nearest way. O'Brien and Seamus saw a small man dart out from behind the rocks and begin to run away.

"Don't let him get away!" yelled Seamus.

He and O'Brien stood up and loosed off wildly, but the man was too far away. Rory, hearing the shouts and the shots, turned and saw the tall, thin man, took aim and fired. He thought he hit him, but the man had reached a tethered horse, mounted and was away.

"Rory!" David called.

Rory turned and saw Caleb lying in David's arms. He ran to kneel beside him and was horrified by what he saw.

"You old Yankee!" he said. "What the devil are you doing here? I thought you never took chances!"

Caleb tried to smile. He spoke with his lungs full of blood, but the smile was real. "We've taken a few together in our time. I don't regret any of them."

Rory glanced at David and saw the truth in his face. Caleb was mortally wounded. Rory was consumed by guilt, and, suddenly, so was David. Caleb closed his eyes. He didn't seem to be in any pain. He was just drifting quietly away.

"Oh, God!" said David, "they shot the wrong man!"

Caleb opened his eyes, and looked directly at David. "No," he said. "I don't think so."

He smiled again, and died.

CHAPTER 26

It should have been a great moment when Rory saw once more the coast of Galway, but truth to tell, it was too dark, and there wasn't time. The captain of the French ship which had dropped anchor in the secluded cove was anxious to be off.

"*Dépêchez-vous!*" he said to his seamen, and to Rory, "It will be daylight soon."

He nodded to his first officer, who swung a signal lamp, and saw an answering flash from the shore. The longboats had already been lowered, and now crates and kegs were off-loaded with a haste which Rory hoped would not get them all blown up.

Then, when it was all off-loaded, it was, "*Bonne chance, Monsieur!*" and "*Merci!*" and Rory and Seamus were going down the rope ladder into the last of the boats.

Onshore all was haste and bustle as the sailors unloaded the crates and kegs, and dark figures came hurrying down from a small wood nearby to grab them and stumble away with them. There was no talk or laughter, and no sense of gaiety as, Rory thought, there would have been fifteen years earlier. He and Seamus lugged and lifted and stumbled with the rest, and in a remarkably short time the arms were safely in the shelter of the trees, and the longboats were streaming silently back to the ship, where the anchor was already being prepared for raising. Rory had time to look about him and try to single out individual faces as his eyes became accustomed to the last starlight before the dawn.

He had not dared to tell Brian that he was coming, in case the letter should be intercepted, but he had asked Seamus to pass the news on by word of mouth through the many Irish sailors who acted as messengers, and he had hoped against hope that Brian would be there to greet him. He saw one thin young man who seemed to be giving directions, and Rory touched him on the arm.

"Is Brian O'Manion here?" he asked.

The young man had his cap pulled low over his eyes, but glanced at him from underneath it. "Brian O'Manion?" he repeated with an odd note in his voice.

Oh, God! thought Rory. Don't say he's dead! Not Brian, too!

"Don't you know me, Rory?"

Rory stared at him for a moment. "Brian?"

The slight, redheaded boy had turned into a thin, shabby, thirty-year-old man, but the smile was the same.

"Brian!" said Rory. "Oh, Brian!"

And suddenly they were hugging each other, laughing and crying, and Rory knew that he was home. He knew at last that he held Ireland in his arms.

"Hey!" said Rory. "What happened to that wild little redheaded fellow with the courage of a mountain lion?"

"You're still bigger than I am," replied Brian.

"We won't fight about it," said Rory, laughing. "We've another fight on our hands now."

"Yes."

Brian's cap had come off in their embrace, and he put it on again, covering that red hair, which was thinner than it used to be and not so bright.

"We'd better get out of here," he said.

Rory saw the sharp sideways glance.

"They know you've landed."

"What?"

"Someone got word ahead of you. They didn't know what ship or where you'd be landing, but if they don't find you at Dublin, they might guess you'd come here. The sooner we get the stuff away from the coast, the better. Come on, boys! Hurry it up!"

It was so strange to hear Brian giving orders instead of scurrying around like a scared young rabbit that Rory stood still for a moment before he, too, began to lend a hand. He felt as though he had died and gone away, and returned to find that while *he* was the same age, everyone else was older. They were loading the kegs and crates into an extraordinary assortment of wagons and donkey carts and even a jaunting-car. A *jaunting-car*? Rachel would have recognized the bootlace.

"Michael!" cried Rory. "Michael O'Connor! How does that old jaunty-car of yours hold together?"

"With a string and a prayer, Rory," said Michael, "with a string and a prayer, like meself."

He at least looked the same, only a little more battered and disreputable.

"Sure 'tis like the bright beams of the sun, Rory, to have you here again. Now climb aboard. You see I had to part with me dear old Lightning, but now I have this young fellow instead—Speedy by name and speedy by nature."

The new horse looked even older than Lightning but had his awkward habit of stumbling over stones where they existed and pecking when they didn't.

"Jasus, Michael!" cried Rory. "I know you want to give this powder a fine pleasure trip, but if you don't take it easy, we'll all be taking the short trip to heaven!"

Brian laughed. " 'Tis the powder will be going to heaven," he said, "before it's through!"

Late next morning a splendid funeral cortege formed up in Ballyclam. Michael O'Connor was driving the hearse, all nodding plumes and black tassels, and surveyed the whole thing with proprietorial pride.

"Did you ever see such a funeral in all your life?" he demanded. "Sure, Lord Fitzmorris himself never had a finer."

"Is he dead?" said Rory, startled.

Somehow it had seemed as though that stupid, obstinate, bigoted old man would live forever.

"He is that," said Michael and amiably crossed himself. "But never be asking me where he is now, for if the devil wouldn't have him, I don't know who would!"

"Soldiers!" said Brian. "Come on, Rory, we'd better be off. We don't want them to wonder why we're taking an interest."

Rory and Brian retreated up to the ruined cow byre above the Manion house, from which they could see the funeral proceeding slowly toward the cemetery. The troop of soldiers whom Brian's sharp ears had heard before they came into sight were now trotting briskly along the road below. The young lieutenant spotted the funeral, stood up in the stirrups and then gave an order. Brian glanced at Rory and pulled a little face.

"I think it's time we went and said our prayers," he said.

In the cemetery Father O'Dowd was taking the service. He was older, and his experiences during the famine had aged him more than his years. There were plenty of mourners, but an astute observer might have noticed that for all the handkerchiefs and bowed heads, there were no tears.

The troop of soldiers rode through the sagging wooden gate and straight across the windswept burial ground, to the open grave. Father O'Dowd looked up, astonished.

"What do you want here?"

The young officer saluted. He had the air of a young man who operated strictly according to military law and whose brain, by long confinement within those bounds, did not possess that capacity for independent thought it might or might not have had when he was born.

"I'm sorry," he said, but did not sound particularly sorry, because being sorry was not enjoined in military law. "I'm afraid I must search that coffin."

Father O'Dowd gazed at him, astonished, and then at the coffin. "Have you no respect for the dead?"

"I have my duty."

He nodded to the troopers, and they dismounted and forced open the lid of the coffin. They looked, shaken, up at the lieutenant.

"Joseph Kerrigan," said Father O'Dowd. "A well-known and well-respected local man. I hope you are satisfied."

The lieutenant gazed at the dismayingly yellow, shrunken face of death. Bracing himself, he stepped to the coffin and peered in to ensure that there was no room for a false bottom. He nodded toward the open grave.

"Make sure there's nothing buried there," he said.

The troopers glanced at each other with increasing distaste for their task, but, like good soldiers, two of them jumped down into the open grave and poked about.

"Nothing there, sir."

"Right," said the lieutenant. "Mount up!"

The troop mounted and prepared to depart.

"You won't be disturbed again," said the lieutenant, and mounted and rode away.

The three men who knelt at prayer in the little Catholic church heard the door open but did not move until they heard Father O'Dowd's voice.

"It's good to see you at your devotions for a change," he said.

Rory, Brian and Seamus turned and rose, relieved. Brian and Seamus crossed themselves, and Rory, seeing them, hastily did the same.

"I'm sure Joe Kerrigan would be glad to know he's been useful to the cause at last!" he said.

"Now, Rory," said Father O'Dowd, with unexpected severity, "Joe Kerrigan suffered long and patiently and died at last a repentant sinner, forgiven by God, as I hope we all shall be."

Rory was shaken, remembering his father's words about Padraic's death: "Forgive yourself, Rory, or it will destroy you, too." It was as though Father O'Dowd knew what he was thinking, for he patted him kindly on the shoulder and moved to peer at the funeral table, which stood over a newly cemented floor. He eyed them in a speaking silence, and then tapped the wooden pulpit. It gave off a dull thud.

"I hope," said Father O'Dowd, "that you'll be getting this—stuff—out of here as soon as may be. If the bishop knew what I was doing, he'd send me to England."

He tapped the pulpit again. "And besides," he said, "I've no wish to be going to heaven in the midst of one of my best sermons."

"We'll get it out as soon as God wills, Father," said Rory.

Father O'Dowd eyed him coldly. Rory had quite forgotten the cold eye of realism of the native Irish priest.

"Sooner than that, I hope!" he said. "Now be off, the three of you, while I pray to our Blessed Lady to ask God to forgive me—for I know the bishop never would!"

"I'm off to Dublin," said Seamus as they cautiously emerged from the church. "There's a meeting of the Grand Council tomorrow, and then we'll get word out to the boys in Limerick and Tipperary and Kerry."

"And to us, I hope," said Rory, irritated.

Seamus looked at him coldly. "Of course," he said. "Everyone has to make the move at once, or it's no good."

He turned and walked away without a farewell.

"I hope he knows what he's doing," said Rory. "United we stand, divided we fall, eh? Well, I can tell you this—he set the American Fenians by the ears in one minute flat!"

When Brian didn't answer, he glanced at him and saw that thin, prematurely matured face. Brian was aware of his glance and smiled at him with a piercing sweetness which reminded Rory of Padraic.

"I have a notion," said Brian, "that if we are ever to be free, we must do it ourselves."

The words struck a chill to Rory's heart. Was he still one of them? But he refused to admit the question. Of course he was!

"Can we go to the house now?" he asked.

Brian shook his head. "If they know you're here, that's where they'll look."

Brian was right. From the woods above they looked down and saw the troops ransacking the O'Manion cabin.

"I should have been there," said Brian. "But I thought they might take me in and I didn't fancy it."

It was a great sign of maturity in him that he could admit that fear they all felt of that "questioning," in which their faces were turned to pulp and their guts ruptured. Rory felt like a child beside him. The troopers came out, mounted up and rode away.

"They'll be back," said Brian.

They both stood up, but it was Rory who looked to Brian for guidance.

"We thought you might be safe at Ballyclam House."

At first Rory thought it was a joke, but then he saw that it was not. "Who owns it now?" he asked.

"No one. Some English bank, I suppose. It's been empty since Mr. Clement died—and Rachel left."

Rory did not want to think of Rachel. He spoke with deliberate flippancy. "Sounds like a great military headquarters!"

Brian answered seriously. "Yes, but the soldiers might think of that, too. I'll go and check it out. Will you stay here?"

It was a question, but it was an order, too, and Rory had the grace to accept it. The days when he was leader of the Young Irelanders were long gone.

"Right," he said.

He sat clasping his knees, looking around the beloved landscape with the small, deserted house below. He looked cautiously around, but there was not a soul in sight. It might be his last chance, and he knew he had to take it. Slowly and silently he crept down the hillside. He had the strangest feeling that he had done this once before, and then he remembered that evening when he had refused to be Harry Clement's agent, and before he knew that Padraic had accepted. That was the last evening they had all been together, and yet he had approached the house like a ghost, as he now did.

He pushed open the cabin door and looked about him. It had the bare, hard look of an Irish bachelor, just managing to support life and hold the land. His heart ached for the long years Brian had spent there alone, too poor to marry, too religious to take a whore. But did he perhaps feel in the house, as Rory did, the warmth and sweetness that had been, the laughter, the stories, the music and the love—oh, the love! Rory moved to the fireplace and took down the fiddle from its place of honor and held it tenderly in his hands.

His mother's door banged open. He jumped so violently that he actually grunted. A trooper stood there. Rory turned quickly as Deirdre's door banged open to reveal another trooper. Rory turned toward the door and saw General Maitland, that thick-skulled dunderhead who had been David's commanding officer and engineered his posting to India but had himself remained in Ireland, stolidly working his way up through promotion to be Rory's nemesis.

"Well, well, O'Manion," he said. "We thought you would come back here in time."

CHAPTER 27

Rachel was planting bulbs in the flower bed beside the front door of the Old Mill. She hardly seemed to have heard what David said. Deirdre had risen from her knees beside her and glanced from David to Rachel as he continued.

"We just know that Rory has been captured and is being held in Galway. It is sure to be reported in the newspapers here. Rory is quite a hero in America."

"Then that will help!" cried Deirdre, instantly hopeful. "Surely the American government will help get him away!"

David hesitated. "Yes," he said. "I shall go back to Washington immediately. I've made a few contacts over this business of paying for the powder. I shall remind them of Rory's service during the war, and if I can convince them that he is an American citizen, then they might bring pressure to bear on the British government."

He went to put his hand on Rachel's shoulder and bent to kiss her cheek. "Keep your courage up," he said.

She finished pressing the earth around the bulb, then rose, rather clumsily, and turned to face him.

"Rory will come back," she said. "He must, to see his son."

She walked into the house. Deirdre made a move to follow her, but then paused and looked up at him. "Is there any hope, David?"

He didn't answer at once. "There's always hope," he said.

"But not as much as you gave Rachel to believe."

"The trouble is," he burst out, "that he's wanted in Ireland for murder!"

"Murder?"

"My father's agent, during that raid on the wheat. Ironic, isn't it, that after all he's done since, he could be hanged for the murder of Houlihan?"

He saw her stricken face. "I'm sorry," he said, "I shouldn't have—"

"No," replied Deirdre, "I'd rather know the truth. I think Rachel knows it already."

She walked with him to the gate. He stopped and turned to her. "Will you do something for me?"

"Of course."

He felt in his pocket and brought out the ring. "This belongs to you. It always has."

She turned away. She wore black in mourning for Caleb, and now David knew what it was to be jealous of a dead man.

"That day you fought the duel," she said, "I made a vow to God. I said that if only He would spare your life, I would never see you again."

"You did *what*?" He seized her furiously and turned her to him. "Didn't you know that I would rather have *died*?" he said.

She put her fingers on his lips to stop him. "Before

he left, Caleb forgave me for loving you, and if he could, I believe that God does, too."

He looked at her in silence, remembering Caleb's smile, and his simple, dying, "I don't think so." He took her tenderly in his arms and was not too proud to take her as the gift of a man who had loved her better than himself. He put the ring on her finger, beside Caleb's ring, and kissed her hand and then, very gently, her lips.

"I'll write from Washington," he said.

The door of Rory's cell banged open, and he flinched. He wasn't particularly proud of flinching, but it was difficult not to flinch when every opening of the door could mean more pain, or the threat of pain, which was almost as bad. He wasn't particularly proud, either, of not having told them where the powder was hidden. He knew that he might tell them one day, and the only promise he made to himself each day was to put that day off one more.

General Maitland stood there in the doorway. He was silent for the moment, and the silence was a threat Rory felt in the wall of his stomach.

"You're a very obstinate man, Mr. O'Manion," said the general. "Or should I say, Mr. *Manion*? I gather that is the name by which you are known in *America*."

His tone showed that he didn't think much of the place. He leaned against the doorway. He had a whip in his hand, and tapped his boot very slowly with it— tap, tap, tap.

"You seem to have some important friends there, and they have convinced our *politicians*"—he didn't seem to think much of politicians, either—"that it would be better if you were put on trial in Dublin. So you are going on a little journey."

It cost Rory some effort to speak casually. "A change of scene would be quite welcome."

"Ye-es," said General Maitland, and smiled.

There had been times during the past months when Rory had been made uneasily aware that he was not such a dunderhead as he appeared. It was, perhaps, part of the tragedy of Ireland that the English and the Irish, because of their contrasting temperaments, always underestimated each other's intelligence. Rory was not inclined to underestimate General Maitland at this moment.

"I think you should have a guard of honor," said Maitland, "befitting your new station in life."

"Much obliged," said Rory.

"Ye-es," said General Maitland, again. "I do hope the responsibility won't be too much for them. It's quite a long way to Dublin, and those new rifles—quite light on the trigger."

"I'll try not to make them nervous," said Rory.

General Maitland stopped tapping his boot with his crop and took a step inside the cell, lowering his voice so that the sentry could not hear his words.

"Save yourself the journey," he said. "You know as well as I do there's only one way it can end. Tell us where the guns and powder are hidden, and we'll put you on a ship for America tomorrow."

"Thanks," said Rory. "I think I'd rather take my chances in Dublin."

General Maitland stepped back and smiled. "Oh, I do hope," he said, "that you will arrive there safely."

* * *

At least it was something to wear clean clothes again, and to have his cuts and bruises patched up, and to have a good meal inside him, even if he was sitting manacled in the train with a guard consisting of Lieutenant Grant with a revolver in his belt and three troopers, all with rifles at the ready. He had not heard a word from the Fenians since that evening when he had been ridden from Ballyclam in the midst of the troop of soldiers with his hands bound behind his back, and had seen Brian's face, shocked and frightened, as he stumbled back out of sight into the ditch. Rory knew now that it was as he had suspected, and that Seamus had lied to him. The Fenians in Ireland were no more than a remnant, and those half-beaten before they began by the famine and the fever, and by banishment and by that more insidious enemy—the deep human desire to live in peace, to have a family and feed them and to support a society which would give them that simple, loving right. As for Brian—

"All I have done," thought Rory, "is to leave him alone, without wife or children, with a dream of Ireland's freedom which he has neither the strength nor courage to achieve."

Tre-dum. Tre-dum! Tre-dum! went the train over the tracks, and each beat was a *mea culpa!* to Rory.

The train passed under a low bridge, and Rory thought he heard a curious thud on the roof of the train and then, almost immediately another, as though someone had jumped from the bridge onto the train, or perhaps more than one. Lieutenant Grant seemed not to have noticed nothing. He seemed to have something else on his mind. Rory thought that General Maitland was a bit of a dunderhead after all to have given such a clear indication that he was to be shot while trying to escape. The question was, he thought, if he was given the chance to escape, could he manage to do so without being shot?

The train came to a screeching halt. One of the troopers stood up and fell over on top of one of his fellows.

"Not yet, you fool!" said Lieutenant Grant, and then added hastily, "I mean—see what's happened."

The trooper put his head out the window. "Seems to be an old cart across the line, sir," he said.

They heard a furious shout from the Irish engine driver. "Would you get that load of junk off the line?"

A voice replied in unfeigned indignation. "*Junk?* Me old jaunty-car that has carried the lords and ladies of England the length and breadth of this country, and proud to do it?"

Michael O'Connor's voice carried such conviction that if Lieutenant Grant had any suspicions, they were allayed. He knew, after all, that Irishmen were chronically incompetent and absurd and that it was quite characteristic of one of them to lose a wheel from his cart while endeavoring to cross the railway line. He descended with an irritable sense that it was up to him to sort the matter out.

"You two," he said to the escort, "come outside with me. Bates, stay with the prisoner. If he tries anything, shoot him."

Michael O'Connor was still insisting that his car could not be moved without the wheel being put on again and that his horse was a very spirited animal that should not be taken out of the shafts or who knew what might happen? Lieutenant Grant dispatched his two troopers to deal with the matter while he watched, exasperated, outside the open carriage door. Rory sat very still, having no desire to be shot by a trigger-happy twenty-year-old in uniform. Then two things happened simultaneously. Seamus dropped on the lieutenant from the roof of the train and put a pistol to his ear, and Brian opened the carriage door on the other hand, pistol in hand. Bates, gazing from side to side, was not sure what he ought to be doing, so Rory set his mind at rest by knocking his rifle up with his manacled hands, and Brian grabbed it.

"One word," said Brian to the trooper, "or the least particle of a sign, and you're a dead man. There's ten desperate Fenians with their guns trained on you at this very moment!"

The young soldier sat with his mouth open while Seamus hauled the lieutenant into the carriage.

"The key!" said Seamus.

The lieutenant made an involuntary move toward his pocket. He had the key handy, having meant to free Rory's hands before setting him loose to shoot him, and no doubt now intended to defend it with his life, but Brian saved him the bother by taking it from him, freeing Rory and chaining Lieutenant Grant's hands behind his back instead, stuffing his own handkerchief in his mouth for good measure. Seamus and Brian both had their faces covered, and Brian had that old cap pulled down over his eyes—to cover his red hair, thought Rory, with a twinge of memory. He and Seamus jumped out of the carriage, while Brian still held a pistol on the young soldier whose mouth was still open.

"Remember!" said Brian fiercely. "Twenty desperate Fenians!"

He landed on the track beside Rory and Seamus and slammed the door.

"Twenty Fenians?" said Rory. "They seem to have pupped!"

Brian pulled off the scarf and grinned. "Let's clear out," he said, "before Michael persuades them to put the wheel on his car."

The three of them took to their heels up the hill to the small wood, where Tom Noonan had two horses waiting. He looked just the same, except that his hair was sandy now. Brian mounted, but Rory paused, looking back at the train.

"Will you come on, Rory!" squeaked Tom Noonan, his courage always at its lowest ebb when the danger was nearly over. "I have to get in by the back window before me mother knows I'm out!"

"How about Michael?" said Rory. "Supposing they—"

They all peered down through the bushes. The wheel was on again, with the help of the soldiers. Lieutenant Grant staggered out of the carriage and fell over just as Michael gave them all a flourish of his whip.

"Much obliged to you, boys," he said. "Thanks for your help."

"Here! You!" shouted Lieutenant Grant, staggering to his feet and managing to get the handkerchief out of his mouth. "Stop! A prisoner has escaped."

"Ah, never you trouble yourself, sir," said Michael. "If I catch up with him, I'll send him straight back to you, so I will!"

And he whipped up his old horse and drove away as fast as he could, leaving Lieutenant Grant still not sure what to believe. There was absolutely nothing in any

military manual which covered an encounter with
Michael O'Connor and his jaunting-car.

Rory was still laughing when he drew rein with
Brian and found himself on the hill above Galway
where once he had plotted the escape of Jim O'Brien
from Galway Barracks.

"So Tom Noonan's mother is still alive?" he inquired.

"They say she means to outlive him," replied Brian,
"and follow him to heaven and give him hell for the rest
of eternity."

They dismounted.

"I'd better get these horses back where they belong,"
said Brian.

"Where did you get 'em?"

"A couple of soldiers had a drop taken in Geraghty's
bar," said Brian, "so Tom borrowed their horses. I'll
turn them loose somewhere near and no harm done."

He took Rory's reins. "There's a passage booked
for you on the *Arcadia*," he said, "sailing this evening
for New York."

"A passage?" said Rory, startled.

Brian spoke in a businesslike way which was oddly
disconcerting. "You're not shipped as a seaman this
time. You're an American called Masters. Go to the
ship's chandler on the quay. There's a man there called
Finegan. He's second mate on the *Arcadia*. He has your
ticket and some money. You should be safely aboard
and sailed before that lieutenant gets word through."

He saw the incredulous look on Rory's face. "What's
the matter?"

"You don't really think I'm leaving Ireland," said
Rory, "just when the fight is beginning?"

"There'll be no fighting for a while after this," said

Brian. "Seamus is going back to Dublin, and we'll all have to lie low."

"Yes, but I—I can—"

He saw Brian's face harden. "You'd just be a liability to us, Rory," he said. "We'd be spending half our time trying to keep you out of prison."

There was no sign of the gentle fifteen-year-old boy he had left behind, half the time frightened out of his wits and the other half fired with tales of Brian Boru. This was a new Irishman, hardened by years of lonely hardship. Rory knew what it was to feel the innermost core of his life threatened by one of those he loved best in the world.

"I have to go now," he said. "I can see that. But I'll be back."

"No," said Brian. "You can fight for us best in America now. If you love Ireland, never come back until we're free."

Rory stared at him, aghast. It was asking too much of him. To feel fear and be hungry and suffer pain, that he was prepared for. But surely that dark-haired beauty who had haunted his dreams since his earliest childhood could not ask of him this one worst thing of all—never, never to see her again? He turned away, chilled to the heart, and felt Brian's hand, and saw his face, no longer stern but full of love and sorrow.

"Oh, Rory!"

They were in each other's arms, and as they drew apart, it was Brian who was weeping.

"Ah, come on, now!" said Rory. "Do you think I would have let Jim O'Brien stay, to be a danger to us all?"

But with the words a great surge of sorrow overtook him and he was weeping, too.

"Ireland!" he said. "Oh, my Ireland!"

He and Brian clung together for the last time.

"It will come, Brian," said Rory as they drew apart. "Your children will live free, or if not them, your grandchildren. As for me—"

"You'll live free in America," said Brian.

"Yes," answered Rory, and smiled ruefully. "But remember one thing—it's not so easy to be free. If you're free there's no one to blame but yourself."

He saw his father's face in Brian's shrewd look. "I'll remember."

They looked at each other in silence for a moment.

"Give my love to Deirdre," said Brian, "and to Rachel—and to Sean."

"If he is Sean," said Rory.

Brian mounted the horse but spoke again urgently. "Rory! Don't forget us!"

"Can I forget myself?" said Rory.

Brian reached down, and they clasped hands, but the horse he rode and the horse he led were already on the move, and he and Rory were inexorably parted. Rory watched his brother out of sight and then turned and walked for the last time down to Galway and the waiting ship.

CHAPTER 28

John Carpenter, walking toward the Kent Powder Manufactory, overtook Maureen walking in the same direction, carrying a heavy basket. Evidently she bought her goods in Philadelphia now and not in the company store.

"Let me take that," said John.

She resisted for a moment but then shrugged. "Just as you like."

They walked into the yard and began to climb up the path toward the O'Brien house. A group of women stood gossiping. One of them raised her voice.

"Here comes the whore!" she said.

John paused, but Maureen's hand gripped his arm so fiercely that it hurt. "Don't say anything!" she commanded in a low voice.

They walked past the women who turned their backs but still looked at them over their shoulders.

At the door of the O'Brien house, Maureen turned to take the basket.

"May I come in?" he asked.

She shrugged again and opened the door and went inside, and he followed her. He put the basket down on the table and glanced around. Since he had recovered his health sufficiently, he had been working at the mill, helping David and Maureen's father with the paperwork, but he had not returned to his lodging in the O'Brien house. There was a cheerless look about it now, though it was hard to say exactly where the difference lay. Perhaps it was just that Maureen herself had lost that warm, laughing quality which had been so much a part of her.

"Those damned women!" said John.

She glanced at him. "I'm used to them." She began to unpack the goods.

"Maureen," said John, "Rory's coming home."

She was very still for a moment.

"Deirdre told me that Rachel's had a telegram. He's

landed in New York, and he's arriving here by train tomorrow."

She took a sack of sugar and reached up to put it on the shelf while he stood pulling at a loose piece of rush on the handle of the basket. Words never came easily to him.

"I haven't been around," he said, "since—since it happened, because—"

"Because you were angry."

"Yes. But with him, not with you."

She turned. "You should have been angry with both of us," she said.

"Maybe I should," he said, "but I wasn't. I kept away to let the—to let the talk die down."

He glanced toward the door and the voices of the gossiping women. Maureen laughed bitterly.

"It never will," she said.

He pulled the loose piece of rush right off and looked up at her and smiled. "I guess before I wreck your basket, I'd better come right out and say it. Maureen, will you marry me?"

She looked at him, astonished.

"You know how I feel about you," he said.

"I know how you used to."

"I still do," he said. "We'll get married and go away somewhere—"

"Somewhere where you won't have to be ashamed of me!" she flashed back at him.

"No! I was going anyway—"

"Then go!" she said angrily. "But not for *my* sake! I'm not embarrassed, and I'm not ashamed. I love Rory. I've loved him since I was a child, and I'll love him till I die. I hope one day I'll give him a son. So don't come here offering me your favors!"

She caught a glimpse of his face before he turned toward the door, and she ran after him, contrite.

"Oh, no, John, no! Don't go like that!"

She put her arms around him and turned him to her. "I'm grateful," she said, "indeed I am, and honored that you feel as you do. I'll never forget that you asked me. Maybe—maybe if I'd met you first—"

"Yes," he said. "Maybe."

His voice was hard, but his hands were very gentle as he took her arms from around his neck and turned.

"John!" cried Maureen. "Where are you going?"

"Away," he said, and walked out.

As John came into the Staunton house, Deirdre called to him from the living room.

"John!"

Still raw from the scene with Maureen, he did not want to see her at that moment. In the months since he had been shot, he had lived in her house, quiet and detached, like a lodger. Now he had to tell her that he was leaving, and he dreaded it. He remembered that first day when she had run to cling to him, and he had stood, stiff and embarrassed, not knowing what to do. He had spent so many years raising an arm to ward off a blow that he was an expert at it. But how did you ward off affection? And what was the value of affection which was given to you merely because people thought you were their kin?

She called again. "John?"

It struck him as odd that she should use that name. She had always called him Sean. He went into the room, and Deirdre got up from beside the fireplace. He thought she had been crying, and she held a letter in her hand.

"Is something wrong?" he asked quickly, and was surprised to find how much he cared.

"She shook her head. "No. But—Caleb's detective came here this morning. He has only just left."

His heart leaped in spite of himself. "And—?"

"He had a letter from Mrs. Carpenter. She said that Mr. Carpenter had just died, and—she sent him this."

Deirdre opened her hand and showed him the silver medal on its chain.

"It was around your neck when they took you from the river. Mr. Carpenter was ashamed to say that he stole it from a baby."

He looked at it, frowning.

She continued very calmly. "It is the holy medal that our mother gave to Rory before she died, and that he put around your neck before he left Ireland. You are Sean. But you don't have to be if you don't want to."

He looked up at her quickly.

"All those years," she said, "you were alone, and we couldn't help you. You couldn't know that we thought of you and prayed for you every hour of every day. You had to make a person of yourself, and you did a fine job of it, John Carpenter. That baby who was taken from us, he'll never come back. Too much has happened to him in between. Wasn't it a strange thing? I realized when I finally saw the medal that we had lost him forever."

She held the medal out to him. He hesitated and then opened his hand, and she put it into it.

"It belongs to you now," she said, "but you're free. We should never have tried to hold you. It's just that

—the family means so much to Irish people. Maybe it's because for so long they have had nothing else."

He looked down at the medal in silence for a moment, and then he suddenly closed his hand on it and put his arms around her.

"Oh, Deirdre!" he said. "I did so want a family, I was afraid to believe it was true!"

They held each other close.

"My Sean!" she said. "My little Sean!"

She had to reach up to kiss him, and he lifted her up, and they both laughed. But when he put her down on her feet again, he looked at her gravely.

"I have to go away," he said.

"Oh, no! Oh, Sean, not now! Rory arrives tomorrow."

"That's why I have to go," he said.

When Rory stepped off the train in Philadelphia, he felt defeated, depleted, the husk of a man. The fine thread which had bound him for so long to Ireland had been snapped when he landed in New York, and now there was nothing left.

It was good to be greeted by Deirdre and David.

"Welcome home, Rory," said David.

Rory checked for a moment, but then he smiled. "Yes," he said. "It's good to be home."

He looked around. "Where's Rachel?"

He saw David and Deirdre glance at each other.

"What's wrong?"

"Nothing!" cried Deirdre. "Nothing. Rory—she is expecting a baby."

"She wouldn't let us tell you," said David. "I wanted to write the news to Brian and hope he could somehow get word to you, but she wouldn't let me."

"Holy Mother of God, a baby!" said Rory, delighted, but then a shadow crept over his joy. "How is she?"

"She's fine, Rory," said Deirdre. "Eamon has been keeping her in bed most of the time, and she's been in such good spirits. God will be good to you this time, I know it."

"I'll find your luggage," said David.

"I've no luggage," said Rory. "Let's get home!"

It was not until they were in the carriage that Rory remembered to ask the question which had been so much in his mind.

"How is Sean?"

"He's quite recovered, Rory," said David heartily. "Eamon says he may always have a little weakness in the lung, but . . ."

David's good-news voice seemed to run out of steam.

"There's something else," said Rory, and saw that glance between them again.

"He's gone away," said Deirdre.

"Gone away? Where? When?"

"Yesterday," said Deirdre reluctantly. "When he knew that I was coming."

He saw from her face that it was true. It was a fearful blow.

Deirdre took out an envelope. "He left this for you."

It was a plain envelope with the one word "Rory" written on it in pencil. He took it and felt something hard and round in it. He tore the envelope open, and the medal fell out into his hand. He looked up at Deirdre.

"It was around his neck when they took him from the river," she said. "He *is* Sean."

"But where's he gone?" Rory demanded. "Where

can we reach him? Did he leave an address? David?"

David shook his head. "I'm sorry, Rory. He—just—"

"He just left *this* for me!" said Rory, and crumpled the envelope up and threw it on the floor of the carriage, and turned his head to look blindly out the window, clutching the medal tightly in his hand.

John Carpenter could not have devised a more terrible revenge than to vanish once more into the wilderness where they had searched for him so desperately and so long. His name *was* Sean, the name they had forced upon him, and he had thrown it back into their faces. Rory remembered Padraic's ashen face as he said, dying, "The curse of God—" Now Sean pressed his mother's holy medal into his hand, as though he said, "May the curse of God go with it, Rory O'Manion!"

David and Deirdre looked at each other, troubled. David glanced down at the crumpled envelope.

"You're sure he didn't leave a note with it?" he said.

He bent and picked it up and found a single sheet of paper inside and gave it to Rory. There were a few lines, written in a round, illiterate hand:

"Dear Rory, keep this for me. Maybe I'll come back for it one day. Your brother, Sean Manion."

Rory read it and looked up at them, his face transfigured with joy.

"It was not a curse!" he said. "It was a token."

He put the medal around his neck, and suddenly it was as though from having nothing, he had everything. He wanted to jump out of the carriage and run and leap along the leafy lane which led to the Old Mill as though it traveled through the Galway Hills. Sean was theirs again, and one day he would return to claim their love, and Brian or his children or his grandchildren would live in a free Ireland, and—now he began to realize it—Rory would have what he had always wanted most, next to Ireland's freedom—a child of his own.

They were nearly there now, and Rory's hand was already opening the carriage door while the horses were still in motion.

"There's Eamon's carriage outside," said David. "Were you expecting him to be there, Deirdre?"

"Oh, he visits Rachel every day now," she answered. "And I expect he wanted to see Rory."

But as Rory opened the front door, the first sound he heard was the cry of a newborn baby. He set off for the staircase, and saw Eamon on the landing.

"Eamon?"

"It's a boy, Rory," said Eamon, "but—but he was early—"

Rory was already dashing up the stairs three at a time. "Well, what would you expect?" he demanded. "The Manions have always been impatient!"

He was in the bedroom, and saw Rachel's face, gray and ravaged from the pain. But it became radiant with joy as she turned her head toward him.

"Oh, Rory, I was so afraid they'd kill you!"

"Not they!"

He fell on his knees beside the bed. "But I can never go back to Ireland, so now you have me for good."

He kissed her. It was as though he had never known until that moment how much he loved her.

"You haven't looked at your son yet," she said.

He really had forgotten in the delight of seeing her again, but now he looked toward the cradle and saw the tiny creature he and Rachel had made out of their love. He put his hand to the covers, and then hesitated. He recalled hearing Eamon say—what was it?—"but he was early."

"Is he—" he asked.

Rachel smiled. "He's perfect," she said. "The most perfect baby ever born. Look at him. He's yours. The first Manion of America."

Rory turned the covers back. For such a newborn child he was wonderfully sturdy. Rory touched the small, curled toes and felt them push against his hand, strong for all their minuteness. He covered him up again and let one of the little hands fasten on his finger.

"God save and defend us!" he cried. "I think he means to take hold of the world and never let it go!"

Rachel laughed, but very faintly, and when he looked at her, he saw that, after the first flush of joy at seeing him, she was deathly pale. He saw Eamon come in, with Deirdre and David behind him, and the first sense of danger crept over him. He clasped her hand again.

"Ah, Rachel, me darling," he cried, "how could you do such a thing? How could you make me risk your life?" She laughed again, more strongly this time. "Don't you think I'd risk my life a hundred times to give you what you want?"

Reassured, he followed her gaze toward the cradle, but when he looked back, there seemed to be a sort of shadow on her face, though the sun still shone brightly outside.

"Rachel?" he said.

With her last strength she smiled at him, but then

her eyes began to close. The hand he held was very cold.

"Eamon?"

He saw the answer in Eamon's face.

"No, Rachel!" he cried. "No!"

He caught her up in his arms, and as he held her, he felt her life slowly ebbing away. He saw Michael O'Connor's jaunting-car stuck in the river, and the foolish, beautiful, ignorant young English girl gazing defiantly down at him. He took with her that wild ride to the abbey walls, and smelled the sweet scent of the grass. He saw her, hesitant but daring, in the stables at Ballyclam, and confident and glowing in the firelight on their wedding night. He saw her fiercely claiming her rights of love before he left for Ireland, and he knew, too late, that she loved him more than life itself.

Then it was all gone. He held her, dead, in his arms, while the baby began to cry lustily in its cradle.

Once you've tasted joy and passion, do you dare dream of

LOVING

Danielle Steel

bestselling author of
The Promise and *To Love Again*

Bettina Daniels lived in a gilded world—pampered, adored, ador-ing. She had youth, beauty and a glamorous life that circled the globe—everything her father's love, fame and money could buy. Suddenly, Justin Daniels was gone. Bettina stood alone before a mountain of debts and a world of strangers—men who promised her many things, who tempted her with words of love. But Bettina had to live her own life, seize her own dreams and take her own chances. But could she pay the bittersweet price?

A Dell Book =========================== $3.50 (14684-4)

Dell Bestsellers

At your local bookstore or use this handy coupon for ordering: